About the Author

John S. Daniels is a pseudonym for noted Western author Wayne D. Overholser. Mr. Overholser has written many popular Western novels under his own name and, for Signet, as John S. Daniels. Several of his novels have been turned into motion pictures. He has also won three Spur Awards of the Western Writers of America, of which he was a charter member.

Mr. Overholser resides in Boulder, Colorado.

The Man from Yesterday *and* The Gunfighters

by *John S. Daniels*

A SIGNET BOOK
NEW AMERICAN LIBRARY
TIMES MIRROR

The Man from Yesterday was originally published in
Ranch Romances Magazine, in a slightly different form.

 Originally appeared in paperback
as individual volumes published by
The New American Library, Inc.

SIGNET TRADEMARK REG. U.S. PAT. OFF. AND FOREIGN COUNTRIES
REGISTERED TRADEMARK—MARCA REGISTRADA
HECHO EN CHICAGO, U.S.A.

SIGNET, SIGNET CLASSICS, MENTOR, PLUME, MERIDIAN AND NAL
BOOKS are published by The New American Library, Inc.,
1633 Broadway, New York, New York 10019

First Printing (Double Western Edition), November, 1979

3 4 5 6 7 8 9 10 11

PRINTED IN THE UNITED STATES OF AMERICA

The Man from Yesterday

Prologue

Neal Clark rode in to Cascade City shortly before noon, his Winchester in the boot. He would have gone directly to Olly Earl's hardware store if his father hadn't apppeared on the porch of Quinn's Mercantile and motioned to him.

Sam Clark created a multitude of conflicting emotions in the hearts of everyone who knew him, including his son. He was a big-chested, square-headed man, a driver, the kind of person who dominated everyone around him. In the twelve years he had lived on the Deschutes, he had built the Circle C into the biggest outfit on the upper river. That was typical of everything he did.

But there was the other side of his father that Neal knew well. He was a dreamer—some said a visionary. From the first day he had come to the upper Deschutes he had prophesied great things for the country: a railroad, saw mills, irrigation projects, and everything that went into these developments. If anyone else had talked that way, folks would have said he was crazy, but no one had the temerity to venture such an opinion of Sam Clark.

As Neal reined his horse toward the Mercantile, he wondered what was in his father's mind now. It would be something big. He was sure of that. Maybe something wild as well as big. Neal, nineteen and a little short of patience, often wished his father would be satisfied to stay at home and run the Circle C, but he knew that was like wishing for the moon.

"What fetches you to town?" Sam asked.

He stood with his big legs spread, hands shoved under his waistband, his elegant white Stetson tipped back on his forehead. The question irritated Neal because if his father didn't stay home where he belonged, he had no right to question his son's going and coming. At least that was the way it struck Neal, but he didn't let his irritation show. No one did with Sam Clark.

Neal patted the stock of his Winchester. "I want Olly to take a look at my rifle." He jerked his head in the direction of Olly Earl's hardware store. "I missed an easy shot at a buck this morning. Must be something wrong with the sights."

Sam nodded as if he considered that a pretty piddling excuse for riding into town when he should be working. "I'm glad I saw you. Save me a ride to the ranch. I'm going to Prineville this afternoon and I don't know when I'll be home." He stepped off the porch and walked to the hitch rail. "Neal, I'm going to run for the legislature this fall. I've been thinking about it for quite a while. You can manage, can't you?"

Neal nodded, refusing to let his feelings show in his face. This was typical of his father, always seeking something he didn't have when he already had more than enough to make most men satisfied. Actually this new activity wouldn't make much difference regardless of what it entailed because Neal had been rodding the Circle C for more than a year.

"Good luck," Neal said. "I guess you know what you're doing."

"I won't have any trouble being elected," Sam said, his tone briskly confident. "I'll see you in a few days."

He turned and walked back into the Mercantile. Neal rode on down the street to the hardware store. Funny thing about his father who was always working on some project of community betterment, always trying to help someone, yet there was a question in Neal's mind whether his father honestly wanted to give help as much as he wanted to advance his own career. Neal was ashamed of the thought, but he had grounds for thinking it. One thing was sure. Sam Clark was the best-known man on the upper river, and he probably would be elected.

Neal dismounted and tied, then pulled the Winchester from the boot and went into the store. Olly Earl wasn't in sight, so Neal laid the rifle on the counter. Three men rode past the hardware store. Neal glanced at them casually, saw they were strangers, and paid no more attention to them.

He rolled a cigarette and smoked it, wondering if the time would ever come when he was entirely free. Sometimes he doubted his strength, not sure he had a will of his own. Well, that was the price he paid for being his father's son. Apparently it never entered Sam Clark's mind that Neal wanted to do anything except rod the Circle C. It actually was the only thing he wanted to do, but the point was he never had an opportunity to make a choice.

He finished the cigarette and, going to the door, flipped the stub into the street. The three strangers had stopped in front of the bank. Two had gone inside, one remained in front with the horses. Neal stared at the horses, wondering why strangers would go directly to the bank. But maybe they weren't strangers. He didn't know everybody along the Deschutes.

He swung back into the store, his mind turning to Jane Carver. He'd been in love with her for a long time, or so it seemed. She was two years younger than he was, too young, maybe, to get married. Or was she? Was he too young? How did a man know about things like that?

He shook his head, his thoughts going sour. Their ages were no problem, but there was a problem and he might as well face it. What would it do to Jane to move to the Circle C and live exactly the way Sam Clark told her to live?

That was the nub of it, all right. Neal would do the work of running the ranch, but the decisions would be his father's, even down to moving a piece of furniture inside the house. That was the way Sam Clark was made. If Neal took Jane out there, they'd have to accept it as long as Sam was alive.

Suddenly impatient, Neal walked into the back room, calling, "Olly."

Earl came in from the loading platform. He said, "I didn't know you were here, Neal. I was helping unload some barbed wire."

Earl took off his gloves, laid them on a nail keg, and threaded his way through the crated machinery and barrels to where Neal stood. He asked, "What'll you have, son?"

Neal stepped back into the store. "I want you to take a look at my Winchester. The sights aren't right. I had a good chance at a buck and missed him clean."

"Hell, you just had a dose of buck fever," Earl said. He walked behind the counter and picking up the rifle, put it to his shoulder and sighted down the barrel. "Loaded?"

"Sure it's loaded."

"Well, can't tell nothing without shooting it," Earl said. "Let's sashay down the river. Isn't this the gun I sold you last spring?"

Neal nodded. "I haven't used it much. I was used to Dad's old . . ."

A shot sounded from the street. A .45, Neal thought, and remembered the strangers who had been in front of the bank. He jerked the Winchester from Earl's hands and ran into the street as a second shot shattered the noon silence. Two men raced out of the bank carrying partly filled gunny sacks. Someone across the street yelled, "Holdup! Holdup!"

The one with the horses, so slender that he must have been a kid younger than Neal, threw a shot at the man who had yelled. Neal didn't have time to think about what should be done, no time to make a decision or consider that these men were human beings. They weren't as far as Neal was concerned. They were wolves who had probably murdered the banker, Tom Rollinson, and his cashier, young Henry Abel.

Neal threw the Winchester to his shoulder and cut loose. The first man had reached his horse and was lifting a foot to the stirrup when Neal's bullet hit him. He went down in a rolling fall, his horse bucking along the street.

The second man didn't reach his horse. Neal's next shot cut him down as cleanly as if he'd been yanked off his feet by a rope. The third one, the kid, didn't wait to see what happened. He was in the saddle and hightailing out of town by the time Neal had squeezed off his second shot.

Olly Earl appeared beside Neal, a rifle in his hand. Both of them fired at the fleeing bandit, but he got away. He was riding hard, leaning low on his horse's neck, and as far as Neal could tell, he hadn't been hit.

Earl threw down his gun in disgust. "We missed him clean," he said bitterly, "but hell, that rifle of yours is shooting all right. We don't need to try it out."

They ran up the street toward the bank as men rushed out of stores and saloons and the livery stable, with Sam Clark in the lead. Doc Santee left his office on the run, his black bag in his hand. Neal and Olly Earl were the first to reach the fallen men. Neal was still carrying his gun. Doc Santee rushed past them into the bank, Sam Clark a step behind.

Earl knelt beside the outlaws. "Dead." He looked up at Neal. "Son, that was shooting. You got this big bastard through the guts and the other one through the heart." Earl rose. "Where's the sheriff?"

"He's at the M Bar," the liveryman said. "Went out first thing this morning. Said he'd be back by noon."

"Drag 'em over there against the wall and set 'em up," Earl said. "I'm going to take their pictures."

Doc Santee and Sam Clark came out of the bank carrying Henry Abel. Sam said, "Tom's dead. Henry's got a slug in the side. Give us a hand, somebody. Pick up that money and take it inside."

Through all of this Neal stood motionless, struggling for each breath. *He had killed two men.* His mind gripped that fact but could go no farther. He stared at the dead men as they were carried to the front wall of the bank and placed against it in a sitting position. Olly Earl returned with his camera and took their pictures, hats off, mouths sagging open, blood oozing from the corners of their lips.

Suddenly Neal was sick. He whirled and ran into a vacant lot next to the bank. There he retched until he was so weak he couldn't stand. Later, he didn't know how much later, Olly

Earl came to him and said, "You got no cause to feel bad about what you did. They murdered Tom Rollinson in cold blood and intended to kill Henry. Just bad shooting or they would have."

Neal leaned against the wall, wiping his face with a bandanna. He looked at Earl. "Maybe I got no cause to, Olly, but I never killed a man before. Did you?"

"No," Earl admitted. "Chances are I'd feel just like you if I had. Come on, let's go get a drink."

Neal went with him to O'Hara's saloon and had a drink. The bodies had been taken to Santee's back room. Several men, Quinn and O'Hara and others, came to Neal and shook his hand and told him that all three of the outlaws would have got away if he hadn't done some mighty good shooting, but their words didn't make Neal feel any better, even with the whisky in him.

"Who were they?" Neal asked.

Nobody knew, but Olly Earl said, "The big one's a middle-aged gent, the other one's young. Maybe in his early twenties. Father and son, I'd guess. The one that got away is porbably another son."

The sheriff, Joe Rolfe, rode into town a few minutes later and took a look at the bodies, but he didn't know them. He picked a small posse and started into the high desert after the boy who had escaped. They returned two days later, tired, dirty, and hungry, with Rolfe shaking his head.

"He must have crawled under a juniper and died," Rolfe said. "We didn't find his horse or nothing. We did pick up his trail a time or two on the other side of Horse Ridge, then lost it. The high desert just swallowed him."

But Neal didn't think the boy was dead. He rode to town every day for two weeks, asking Rolfe if he'd learned anything. Finally Rolfe was able to identify the outlaws Neal had killed by sending the pictures to other sheriffs in the state.

"It was the Shelly gang," Rolfe said. "They've been in a lot of trouble in Lane and Douglas counties. Came from the hills around Yoncalla. The sheriff in Eugene says the old one was Buck Shelly and the young one his oldest boy named Luke. The kid holding the horses was probably a younger son named Ed."

"If Ed isn't dead," Neal said, "he'll be back."

The old sheriff gave Neal a sharp look. "Son, don't fret yourself about it. I don't think he is alive. You or Olly probably plugged him, and he died of his wounds. But hell, even if he did make it, he won't be back."

Neal rode home, finding no comfort in Joe Rolfe's words. The sheriff was like Olly Earl, coming around the corner of the bank right after the shooting and telling Neal not to feel bad, then admitting he'd never killed a man. Joe Rolfe could talk until he wore his tongue off at the roots, but the fact was he hadn't killed Ed Shelly's father and brother.

That night Sam Clark showed up at the Circle C. He hadn't been home since the holdup. The first thing he said was, "I'm taking the bank over, Neal. Somebody's got to run it because this community needs a bank, and I'm the only one who can. I've been a stockholder for quite a while, and I know something about the business. Henry Abel's going to make it. He's a smart banker. We won't have any trouble."

Politics and now the bank. Neal turned away, nervous and irritable. He didn't trust himself to speak. He walked to a window and stared at the bare dirt yard. No grass. No flowers. No foofaraw of any kind because Sam wouldn't stand for it. A strange combination, his father. Standing there, he guessed what was coming before Sam got the words said.

"I've been giving a lot of thought to our affairs." Sam Clark crossed the big living room of the ranch house and placed a hand on Neal's shoulder. "You're going to learn the banking business. Henry Abel will teach you. Oh, not right now. I've got to learn it first. You'll be getting married one of these days and bringing Jane out here to live, but ranch life isn't good for a woman. I'll buy a house in town and you can take over the bank. No hurry, mind you. It'll take a little time to find the right man here."

Neal didn't say anything. He'd always done what his father wanted him to. He had no power to resist. No one did. Sam Clark was like a steam roller. If you argued or resisted, he simply overpowered you and flattened you out and went right on. Now Sam walked away, the idea never occurring to him that Neal might object to having his life managed for him, or that he might prefer running a ranch instead of a bank.

But his father was wrong on one thing, Neal thought. There would be no marriage for a while, not until he knew for sure what had happened to Ed Shelly. The days passed and no word of any kind came, and when Neal kept asking the sheriff, the old man lost his temper.

"Damn it, can't you forget that ornery devil?" Rolfe said. "I tell you he's dead."

So Neal rode home, his troubled mind finding no comfort. A week later he received a letter postmarked Salt Lake City. The address and letter were printed in pencil and so was the letter. "Some day I'll be back and settle up with you for killing my father and brother. Ed Shelly."

Neal stared at the sheet of paper for a long time, not really surprised, for it was about what he had expected. He had never believed young Shelly was dead. He took the note to Joe Rolfe who shook his head in disgust.

"Some crank," said the sheriff. "Hell, boy, people all over the country read about the holdup and the killing. For God's sake, Neal, forget it. You'll never see or hear of Ed Shelly again."

Neal rode home, jumpy and nervous and wondering if Ed Shelly was hiding behind each pine or lava outcropping that he passed. Maybe Rolfe was right, but that didn't help. Nothing would help, Neal thought, until he knew for sure that Ed Shelly was dead.

Chapter One

Neal woke at dawn on a chill April morning, trembling and weak and wet with sweat. He'd had the nightmare again. He wondered how many times he'd had it since he'd shot Buck Shelly and his son Luke eight years ago. But the nightmares hadn't started right after the killings. He remembered now. That warning note he'd received from Ed Shelly. The first nightmare. The night after he'd had the note. Yes, that was it. He couldn't forget.

Slowly the trembling passed. He turned his head to look at his wife Jane. She was beautiful. Even in the thin gray light she was beautiful, although he could not see her features distinctly. She was beautiful because he loved her, he guessed. It was equally true with his five-year-old daughter Laurie.

He could not imagine living without Jane and Laurie. That was why the nightmare lingered in his mind with frightening sharpness. It was never quite the same, yet there was always one element that did not vary. Sometimes he arrived home to find that Jane had been murdered. Or that Laurie had been kidnapped. Or he was shot in the back as he walked into the house.

But there was always this faceless man who had done these things. Neal was never able to catch him. He couldn't even describe him because he was invariably a shadowy figure Neal had not seen distinctly, but the knowledge was always in Neal that the man was Ed Shelly. He never discovered how he knew, but he never doubted that he did know.

Now, as always, a restlessness followed the nightmare. Neal couldn't stay in bed, so he eased out from under the covers carefully, hoping he wouldn't waken Jane. He picked up his clothes and slipped out of the room into the hall. He dressed quickly, then glanced into Laurie's room just to be sure she was all right, and, closing the door, went downstairs.

He built a fire in the kitchen range, put the coffee pot on the front, and stepped outside to cut the day's supply of wood. The sun was beginning to show over the juniper-covered ridge to the east, but the air was sharp and he had to work fast to keep warm. That was the only way to retain his sanity. If he was active, he was able to put the nightmare out of his mind.

When he returned to the house, the coffee was ready. He poured a cup, thinking of his father as he stood by the stove waiting for the coffee to cool. Sam Clark had been dead for four years, but he continued to dominate Neal's life. His father had built this house for him and Jane here in Cascade City, and Neal had gone to work in the bank. He often thanked the Lord for Henry Abel. Without him, it was hard to tell what would have happened to the bank.

The hard truth was that Neal's first love was the Circle C. He had often thought of turning the bank over to Abel and taking Jane and Laurie back to the ranch. He wasn't entirely sure why he hadn't unless it was that his father had wanted him to be a banker. But that was only part of the answer. Perhaps it wasn't even a part.

Neal had never been able to talk to anyone about it. Not Jane. Or Joe Rolfe who was still sheriff. Or Doc Santee. He found it hard even to bring it out into the open in his own thinking, but he knew vaguely that it had to do with Ed Shelly, who would someday return to Cascade City. The outlaw would strike at the bank just as his father and brother had done eight years ago. When he did, Neal had to be there.

Jane came in from the dining room just as Neal finished his coffee. She asked anxiously, "Neal, what's the matter this time?"

"Nothing," he said. "I just couldn't sleep."

She came to him and put her arms around him. "You're worried about Ben Darley and Tuck Shelton, aren't you? You've done all you could, darling. You can't go on carrying everybody's troubles on your back."

"I know." He never told her about his nightmares. He always said, as he had just now, that he couldn't sleep. It was crazy, and it would sound even crazier if he told her about it so he kept it locked up inside him. "Jane, you know how I used to get sore at Dad because he had to run my life like he did everybody else's, but he was a smart man. Now that he's gone, I keep remembering things he told me."

She smiled briefly. "He was a smart man, all right, but I'm not sure he had a heart."

"I think he did," Neal said thoughtfully. "I just remembered this morning how often he said that most folks didn't have any sense about money. They'd save and then turn around and blow it on some fool deal because they were promised big returns. That's exactly what happened here."

She turned away from him, shaking her head, and started getting breakfast. He knew how she felt. Let everybody go ahead and invest their money in Darley's and Shelton's phony irrigation project. It was their business. But Neal couldn't let them do it if he could keep them from it. This was something his father had taught him. It was proof that Sam Clark, for all his arrogant and domineering ways, did have a heart.

"They'll hate you," Sam used to say, "but you're smarter than they are or you wouldn't be where you are. They'll cuss you, sure, but if you let them throw their money down a rat hole, they'll cuss you for that, too."

Neither Neal nor Jane felt like talking during breakfast. But when he was ready to go, Jane kissed him, and whispered, "Don't let them upset you today, Neal. Please! Laurie and I should come first in your life."

"You do, honey," he said, "but that isn't the point. A man has to do what he has to do, even when he'd rather do something else."

"That's more of what your father taught you," she said with a hint of bitterness. "Many times I've wished he'd been just an ordinary little man like everybody else."

"But he wasn't," Neal asid, "and I'm his son. Maybe his shoes don't fit me, but I've got to try to wear them."

He kissed her again and putting on his hat, left the house. Laurie was still asleep, as she usually was when he left. He walked briskly along the street to the river. There he stopped for a moment, eyes on the water that moved slowly here, very clear and cold. A short distance north of town, it began its swift, tumbling descent to the Columbia. Fog lifted above the water like smoke. It would be gone when the sun rose a little higher. Life was like that, he thought, shifting and vague and transient.

Turning, he strode rapidly up the slope through the pines toward Main Street, his feet silent on the thick bed of long needles. When he reached the corner and turned toward the bank, the thought struck him that there had been little change in the town since his father had died. The railroad, the saw mills, the irrigation projects: still dreams, but Neal had no doubt that in time they would become reality.

For an active, ambitious man, Sam Clark had possessed a great store of patience. Even as a member of the legislature, he had been unable to bring progress to the upper Deschutes as he had hoped, but he had never become discouraged. "Destiny moves in her own way and at her own speed, and there isn't much any man can do except get things ready," Sam used to say. In that regard Neal knew he lacked a great deal. He was not a patient man as his father had been.

He reached the bank, unlocked the front door, and went in. Henry Abel was already there. He had built a fire and was sitting on his high stool near the window working on a ledger. He liked his job, and he would have been lost without it, but Neal was never quite sure whether he worked long hours because he loved the work, or because the bank was a refuge from his nagging, gossipy wife.

"Good morning, Henry," Neal said as he walked past the teller's cage to his private office. "You're here early."

"Morning, Neal," Abel said. "You're early too."

"I couldn't sleep last night, so I got up." Neal took off his hat and opened the door to his office, then he glanced at Abel, wondering if he ever had nightmares, or if he ever thought about Ed Shelly's return. Abel was under thirty-five, but he looked older, his face pale and pinched. He had not been well since he'd been wounded by the Shellys. He suffered a good deal, especially in cold weather, but Doc Santee said there wasn't anything he could do.

Abel looked up from his ledger. He said, "You're worried, Neal. It won't do any good. It'll take more than worry to stop Ben Darley."

"I aim to use something besides worry," Neal said. "Maybe I'll kill the bastard."

"And hang," Abel said.

Neal went into his office, put his hat on a nail in the wall, and shut the door. That was the trouble, he thought. For the first time in his life, he hated a man enough to kill him, but he didn't hate him enough to hang for it. Beyond any doubt Ben Darley was a crooked promoter, but he had a way of making people trust him. That was simply beyond Neal's understanding. Except for Henry Abel, Joe Rolfe and Doc Santee were the only men in the country who saw through Darley's scheming.

Neal had several letters to write, but he couldn't get started. He uncorked a bottle of ink, dipped his pen, and wrote "Cascade City, Oregon. April 28 . . ." Then he stopped and leaned back in his swivel chair, his thoughts returning to Ben Darley. The hell of it was Darley had turned old friends against Neal, men like Olly Earl and Mike O'Hara and Harvey Quinn that Neal had known since he'd been a boy.

Neal was still sitting there thinking about it when Abel opened the bank at nine o'clock. A moment later he slipped into Neal's office, as silent as a cat in the kangaroo-leather shoes he wore because they were soft and easy on his feet.

"We've got another one," Abel said. "Wants to borrow money to invest with Ben Darley."

"Who is it this time?"

"Jud Manion."

Neal groaned. Of all the men in the country who had asked to borrow money, Manion was the last one he wanted to turn down. During his growing-up years when Sam Clark had been too busy to work at being a father, Jud Manion, riding for the Circle C at the time, took on the job that should have been Sam's.

Manion taught Neal everything he knew about cows and horses and guns and ropes. With infinite patience he had shown Neal how to catch the big ones out of the Deschutes. He had taken the boy hunting. They had even explored the lava caves east of the ranch. Then Manion had fallen in love, and knowing he couldn't support a family on his thirty dollars a month, he'd taken a homestead. Now this man to whom Neal owed a great debt wanted to borrow money to pour down Ben Darley's crooked rat hole.

As Neal rose and walked to the window, Abel said in his precise way. "Don't let sentiment blind you, Neal. Not even for Jud."

"How much does he want?"

"One thousand."

"How many have we had this week?"

"Seven."

But Jud Manion was different from the others. At least he was to Neal. He had four children. Six mouths to feed. Six bodies to clothe and keep warm in that tar-paper shack in the junipers. They had existed and that was about all, but now, like almost everyone else in Cascade County, Jud was determined to throw away his means of existence.

"Send him in," Neal said.

Abel hesitated, then he said, "We can't loan him a nickel. His farm's mortgaged now for more than it's worth."

"Send him in."

"He's drunk and he's mean. I can get rid of him. . . ."

"Damn it, send him in."

Abel slipped out of the office, his thin face showing his disapproval. This wouldn't be easy, Neal knew. Manion seldom got drunk, but when he did, he was a ring-tailed roarer.

When he came in a moment later and kicked the door shut behind him, Neal saw that Abel was right. Manion was carrying a gun, the first time since he'd left the Circle C as far as Neal knew.

"Glad to see you, Jud." Neal motioned to a chair and, returning to his desk, sat down. "Haven't seen you since I was at your place last month."

Manion didn't sit down. He leaned against the door, scowling at Neal. He was a short, broad-bodied man who worked hard, but he was a poor manager and his farm showed it. He was the only cowboy Neal knew who was trying his hand at farming, and it had gone against his grain from the start.

"I didn't ride in just to pass a few windies," Manion said. "I want to borrow a thousand dollars. Abel says you ain't making no loans these days, but I allowed that didn't mean me."

"It does as far as the bank's concerned," Neal said, "but if you're up against it, I'll give you my personal check for as much as you need."

"I ain't asking for no handout," Manion said. "I've got some security. I own a team, a couple o' milk cows. . . ." He stopped and wiped a hand across his face, anger growing in him. "Damn it, Neal, you know what I've got. You likewise know your bank ain't gonna lose nothing on me."

"What do you want the money for?"

"That ain't none of your business. What does the bank care how I spend money I borrow?"

"It cares a hell of a lot, Jud. Ben Darley and Tuck Shelton are a pair of thieving liars and their irrigation scheme is a swindle from the word go."

Manion stared at Neal with loathing. "You're turning out worse'n Sam. All the time I was trying to teach you something . . ."

"I know what I owe you, Jud." Neal rose. "I'll do anything I can for you. I said for you, Jud, not Ben Darley and Tuck Shelton."

Manion walked to the desk, so furious he was trembling. "Sam or you have run this bank for years. What have either one of you done for this country? Nothing! Just nothing! Now Darley gives us a chance to make some money and develop the country to boot, but you're so damned ornery you won't let any of us take it."

"I'm trying to keep you from losing what you have got," Neal said patiently. "Maybe you can't see it now—"

Manion interrupted with an oath. "It's like Darley says. You wanted a controlling interest in the deal, but he figured it was smarter to let all of us in on it than to help make a banker fatter'n he is already."

"Darley's a liar," Neal said. "I never offered to put a nickel into his scheme."

"You're the liar," Manion shot back. "Darley's got a letter of your'n saying you wanted to buy fifty thousand dollars worth of stock."

"Ever see the letter?"

"Alec Tuttle and Vince Sailor have." Manion clenched his big fists. "I never thought you'd go like this, but I was dead wrong. Put a man behind a banker's desk and something happens to him every time."

"I'm sorry you feel that way," Neal said.

Manion didn't leave. He stood there, the corners of his mouth working like a child struggling to hold back the tears. He put a hand on the butt of his gun. "Neal, I've got to have that money. You don't know how it is to have a wife and four kids who never get enough to eat. I work sixteen hours a day, but I can't make enough to feed 'em. Darley says he'll still let me in if I can get the money. He says every share of stock will double in value in six months."

"It won't, Jud." Neal laid a gold eagle on the desk. "Take it. Buy the grub you need. I'll give you more when that's gone. Or you can get your old job on the Circle C."

"A thousand dollars, Neal." Manion drew his gun. "Give it to me or I'll kill you. I've been shoved a long ways since we used to ride together, downhill all the time, but you ain't gonna make me lose this chance."

"Put that gun away, you fool."

"I ain't a fool." Manion raised the gun, the hammer back. "You never heard a baby cry all night because he's hungry. I have. My babies, Neal. All I'm asking for is a chance to take care of 'em. Write me a check. Or call Abel in here and have him give me the cash. I don't care how you do it. Just see that I get it."

Hard work and privation and a little whisky had turned Jud Manion's head. Looking at him now, a big trembling misfit of a farmer, Neal knew he would do exactly what he said. He'd be sorry about it later, but by then Neal Clark would be a dead man.

"I'll give you ten seconds," Manion whispered. "I can't wait no longer."

"They'll hang you."

"I don't care. Gimme the money so I can take it to Darley before it's too late."

The office door slammed open. Startled, Manion whirled and fired, but Abel had lunged sideways out of range. The instant Manion started to turn, Neal dived head first over the desk. Manion threw a shot at him, a wild shot that missed by five feet, then he was going back, and down, Neal on top of him.

Manion hit the floor hard, the wind jarred out of him. He struck at Neal, but there was no real power in the blow. Neal twisted the gun out of his hand and rose, breathing hard.

"You've gone crazy, Jud," Neal said. "I ought to turn you over to Joe Rolfe."

"You're crazy if you don't," Abel said. "He'll try it again."

"No, I can't do it, but I'll keep his gun." Neal turned to the desk and picking up the twenty dollar gold piece, dropped it into Manion's shirt pocket. "Go get that grub for your kids."

Jud rose, looking at Neal with no repentance or regret in his eyes whatever. "Abel's right. Taking my gun won't stop me."

He walked out, reeling a little. Abel said, "You're soft, Neal. Too soft."

Neal shut the door leaving Abel outside. Maybe he was soft, softer than Sam Clark would have been under the circumstances, but he wasn't his father and he was glad of it. He walked to the window, still breathing hard. He'd been scared, and he had a right to be, with Jud Manion half crazy as he had been.

A wind had come up in the sudden, gusty way that was typical of April, blowing so much dust that he couldn't see the Signal Blue Inn on the other side of the street. Staring moodily into the gray fog, Neal thought that being a banker hadn't been so bad until Ben Darley came to town with his wife Fay and his partner, Tuck Shelton.

They had rented the office rooms over Quinn's Mercantile and started promoting an irrigation project on the high desert east of town. Darley was a smooth operator, the smoothest Neal had ever seen. He'd made big promises of quick profit, so it was natural enough, Neal thought, for the farmers and townspeople to swallow the man's lies.

Neal walked back to his desk, the smoldering hatred he felt for Ben Darley suddenly fanned into flame. He couldn't blame Jud Manion for trying to kill him, but it would never have happened if Darley hadn't come to Cascade City.

One solution was to kill Darley. Neal opened the top drawer of his desk and took out a loaded .38. He remembered his father saying, "A bank occupies a special position in a small community like this. Sometimes it has to protect people from themselves."

That was exactly what he had tried to do when he'd turned down requests for loans to invest with Darley. But why should he make enemies out of friends who wanted to go broke? It was a good question. Still, he couldn't rid himself of other people's burdens. Jane had told him he couldn't carry all of them on his back, but they were there just the same.

Then, staring at the gun, he made his decision. He'd see Darley. A lot of problems would be solved if he were forced to kill Ben Darley.

He slipped the gun into his pocket, buttoned his coat, and taking his hat off the nail, left the bank.

Chapter Two

Ben Darley and Tuck Shelton's office was over Harvey Quinn's Mercantile, across the street and at the other end of the block from the bank. Neal paused on the boardwalk, looking at the men who sat on the weathered benches in front of the Signal Butte Inn. Alec Tuttle and Vince Sailor were among them, two farmers who were more vocal than the others in condemning the bank for its attitude toward the Darley-Shelton project. Jud Manion was not with them, and Neal was thankful for that.

Still he hesitated, wondering if this was the day the smoldering trouble would break into flame. He shrugged his shoulders and crossed the street, hoping there would be no trouble with these men who were his neighbors and had been his friends. But friendship was too often a transient thing, and lately he'd had a feeling that trouble with these men was inevitable.

The wind was still blowing, although it was not gusty and dust-laden as it had been a few minutes before. Neal tugged at his hat brim, setting it more firmly on his head so the wind wouldn't send it rolling down the street. The last thing he wanted to do was to run after his hat in front of the men who were sitting on the bench of the Signal Butte Inn.

As it was, he felt their eyes on him before he reached the boardwalk. If they jumped him, he'd have a hell of a fight on his hands. Ben Darley was the man he wanted, not Tuttle or Sailor or any of the other farmers who were eyeing him with cold malevolence.

Neal felt the weight of the gun in his pocket, but he couldn't use it on these men even in self-defense. They hated him, but it was a kind of childish hatred, as if he had deprived them of candy that had been dangled in front of them for weeks.

Neal was directly in front of Tuttle when the man said, "Clark."

Stopping, Neal looked down at the man. He said, "Well?"

He had made a mistake crossing the street here. It had been an act of bravado. He hadn't wanted Tuttle or any of them to think he was afraid. Now he realized he should have kept his mind on Ben Darley and let Tuttle and his friends think what they wanted to.

Tuttle let the seconds ribbon out, then he said, "I hear Jud Manion has joined our club, and him claiming it would be different because he was your friend. I wish to hell he'd have drilled you. We heard the shooting and figured he had."

The time when Neal could have reasoned with them was long past, so he didn't try. He said, "I guess that's the way you would have liked it."

He would have gone on if Vince Sailor hadn't jumped up and grabbed his arm. He was a tall, jaundiced-looking man, so thin that the old saw about having to stand up twice to cast a shadow was used repeatedly to describe him.

Neal jerked free from the clawlike hands as Sailor said, "Maybe we could get a loan from the bank if we wore boots and a ten-gallon hat like you do, but we're farmers, Clark. Is that why your bank won't loan us any money?"

"No, Vince," Neal said. "You know it isn't."

"I ain't so sure, money bags," Sailor said contemptuously. "It's too bad for us that the only bank in the county is run by a son of a bitch who thinks nothing is important but cows. Ninety-five per cent of the people in this county are farmers. Are you too bullheaded to admit that?"

"No, I'll admit it," Neal said.

This accusation that he was a cowman and was prejudiced against farmers was a fiction that Ben Darley had built up in the minds of all the farmers and most of the townsmen. Sam Clark had been a rancher before he was a banker, and Neal had run the Circle C for years before he had taken the bank over, so he habitually dressed like a rancher because he was more comfortable than he would have been in a sedate business suit such as Henry Abel wore. These were the facts that Darley, skilled operator that he was, had played upon successfully.

Neal knew there wasn't the slightest use to deny anything or explain his position. He had attempted too many times and had not been believed, so he tried to go on, but Tuttle grabbed his arm just as Sailor had a moment before. He was set for trouble and nothing else would satisfy him.

"Listen to me, you bastard," Tuttle said. "You wouldn't lose a nickel loaning us money, but you're so damned afraid that one of us will amount to something in this county you won't—"

Neal jerked free. "You're pushing, Alec. You're pushing too hard."

Tuttle laughed. "I'm just starting to push, mister," and swung.

Sensing this was coming. Neal ducked Tuttle's wild blow and drove a straight right squarely to the point of the big farmer's chin, knocking him off the walk into the street. Neal jumped back and whirled, expecting the men on the bench to rush him. They would have, he thought, if they hadn't seen Joe Rolfe coming along the walk. So they sat there, sullenly silent except for Sailor who called, "Kill him, Alec. Kill the son of a bitch."

Tuttle got to his feet and shook himself, cursing. He came at Neal with both fists swinging, a powerful man, but an awkward one. Neal knew how to handle himself, for he had done his share of fighting when he was younger, even taking boxing lessons from a drifter who was riding the grub line but had been a professional in his younger days. Neal cut Tuttle down as efficiently as if he were using an ax on a pine tree, a right and then a left, and Tuttle was on his back again.

"Get up, Alec," Sailor begged. "Get up, damn it. You can't let a man who sits on his rump in a bank all day lick you like that."

Tuttle tried. He struggeld to his hands and knees, looking up at Neal, blood running into his mouth from his nose. He licked his upper lip, spit out a mouthful of blood, and lunged forward, big arms spread. The very weight of his charge carried him into Neal. A right to the side of the head didn't stop him. Neal stumbled back, Tuttle's arms around his middle, hugging him as he tried to squeeze breath out of him.

Still retreating, Neal stayed on his feet as he supported almost the entire weight of the big man. For a moment he was afraid he was going down. If Tuttle got him into the dust of the street, it would be a different fight, Tuttle's kind of fight. Neal had seen him whip too many men to want any part of it. He hit Tuttle on one side of the head and then the other, but still the heavy arms hugged him, Tuttle's head shoving hard against his stomach.

The man was like a grizzly. Now the pressure was beginning to take its toll. Neal couldn't breathe. Red devils danced in front of his eyes. In desperation, he brought his right fist down squarely on the back of Tuttle's thick neck, a blow that might have killed a lesser man.

Tuttle's grip went slack. Neal stepped back and let the man fall face down into the dust. He lay motionless. Neal looked at the men on the bench; he heard Vince Sailor's bitter cursing, then he turned to Joe Rolfe. He said, "I hope he broke his damned neck. You holding me, Joe?"

Rolfe knelt beside Tuttle and turned him over. He stood up, his face gray as he shook his head at Neal. "Not this time," he said. "Go on before somebody else tries to whip you."

Neal swung around and strode on to the Mrcantile, more thoroughly convinced than ever that only Ben Darley's death could bring peace back to the Deschutes.

Chapter Three

Neal's face showed no marks, but his ribs hurt from the pressure Tuttle had applied to his sides. The thought occurred to him that Darley might have put Tuttle and Sailor up to starting the fight. Darley claimed he needed only a few more thousand dollars to start work and he blamed Neal because the money had not been raised. If Neal were killed in a street brawl, Darley would be free of his principal opponent without raising a hand.

At the foot of the stairs that led to the office rooms over the Mercantile Neal met Tuck Shelton. He paused, not sure whether this was trouble or not. After Jud Manion had pulled a gun on him and Tuttle had started a fight, he could expect anything.

Shelton stopped, his pale blue eyes on Neal. He was a strange man, silent and withdrawn. He was average-looking, average-sized, the kind of man who never seemed to warrant a second glance. He was younger than Darley by a good ten years. When he did speak, which was seldom, his voice was soft and inoffensive. From the first Neal had wondered how Shelton fitted into the irrigation scheme, for Darley had done all the work.

"Looking for me?" Shelton asked, smiling as if he had some secret knowledge that was not known to Neal.

"No," Neal answered. "I want to see Darley."

"He's in the office," Shelton said, and went on.

Neal stared after him, thinking that Darley claimed his partner was the real brains of the company, but Joe Rolfe, who was a good judge of men, had another idea. "Watch out for Shelton," Rolfe had said. "He's hiding behind that easy way of his. He's got the eyes of a killer. I'm guessing that's what he's here for, if Darley needs any killing done."

Neal had been surprised at that, then suddenly it struck him that he had never actually noticed the man's eyes. After that he had. They were strange eyes, with too much white like the eyes of an outlaw horse. At times Neal had surprised him staring at him, his face turned bitter.

But now as Neal climbed the stairs, he realized he had never learned anything from Shelton's expression. Usually they held as little feeling as if they were made of glass. He put the man out of his mind. Darley, not Shelton, was responsible for what had been happening in Cascade County.

Neal's quarrel was not with Jud Manion or Tuttle or Sailor. They had simply been carried away by Darley's glowing promises. If he could show them what the man was, their attitude would change. But how could you prove anything to people whose minds were closed?

At this moment Neal did not have the slightest idea how to answer that question, and he doubted his own good sense in coming here. Darley was too slick to attempt to use a gun. No matter how much Neal wanted to kill him, he knew he was incapable of killing any man who refused to fight.

Well, he'd come too far to back out. He paused in the hall, staring at the black letters on the glass half of the door: DARLEY AND SHELTON DEVELOPMENT COMPANY. It looked solid and dependable, just as the brochures did that had been spread all over Central Oregon with pictures of Darley and the lakes he intended to tap for irrigation. The writing was dignified, never flamboyant. The final perfect touch was the blackface type at the bottom of each page: WE ARE HERE TO STAY.

Smart! Plenty smart. You had to say that for them. Shelton might be the brains, or he might be the gunslinger, but there was no doubt about Darley. He was the front, the contact man, the one who did the talking and made all the public appearances and shook hands; he was the substance, Shelton the shadow.

Not once as far as Neal knew had Darley ever made a definite, get-rich-quick promise that could be pinned down as to time and place or percentage of profit. Still, he had consistently inferred that those who invested in his company would soon double their money. Therein lay the man's skill.

Darley had the appearance of an honest, humble man, the kind people instinctively trusted. He talked glibly about what his project would do for the county and the town, bringing life to a parched desert, creating homes for hundreds of families, making possible the raising of more food for a rapidly expanding nation that was wearing out its best soil. Then he would recite figures about the profits earned by other irrigation projects, invariably picking the most successful ones and overlooking those that had failed.

When he made a speech, Darley always finished with the statement that he and Tuck Shelton were bringing fifty thousand dollars of their own money to the project. If the people of the community had faith in Central Oregon, they'd raise another fifty thousand. Work would start on the project the day the company had one hundred thousand dollars in the treasury, for that was the amount it would take to complete the ditch. He would not, he said, turn a shovelful of dirt until he could assure both the investors and prospective settlers that the project could be successfully completed.

Neal did not believe Darley and Shelton had fifty thousand dollars of their own, and he was convinced that more than fifty thousand dollars worth of stock had been sold.

He opened the door and went in, feeling the weight of the gun in his pocket. Now that he was here, having been prompted by a cold-blooded desire to kill a man, he wished he had left the gun in the bank. If Darley did force a fight and Neal killed him, the men outside would never believe it was anything but murder.

He closed the door glancing around the room. This was the reception room, furnished with several rawhide-bottom chairs, a hat rack, and a desk where Mrs. Darley worked. She served as receptionist and bookkeeper, working for nothing, Darley told the stockholders, because she believed in what the company was doing and wanted to do her part.

Neal would have turned around and left, thinking to hell with it, if Mrs. Darley had not glanced up from a ledger, and rose, a smiling, handsome woman in her early thirties.

Now pride would not let Neal go. He stood there while Mrs. Darley moved toward him, her hips swaying a little but not too much, just enough to touch a torch to a man's imagination without promising anything. Neal had talked to her a few times, and on each occasion she had bothered him because he sensed she was an eager, vibrant woman with keen animal desire.

As he watched her, he was possessed again by the haunting hunger he felt every time he was with her. He was instantly ashamed, for he was completely in love with Jane, who was everything a man could want in a wife.

She held out her hand, and when he took it, she let it remain longer than necessary in his, asking, "What brings the enemy here?"

"I want to see your husband," he said.

She stood looking at him, her face quite close to his, her full, red lips slightly parted at the centers. Her eyes were dark brown, her hair so black that it seemed to hold a blue tone. She was wearing a brown skirt and white shirtwaist that was buttoned sedately under the chin, a manner of dress that marked her as a very moral and respectable person.

Just as Ben Darley managed to convey the impression he was honest and idealistic, so his wife kept within the bounds of propriety in both her manner of dressing and her behavior. Still, she contrived to let Neal know the respectable-appearing woman was not the real Fay Darley.

"I have a great admiration for you, Mr. Clark," she said. "Everybody in town says you're wrong about us, but that doesn't change you. You're the kind who would go after anything you wanted, wouldn't you?"

"I guess I would," he said.

"I'll tell Ben you're here." She started toward the door of Darley's private office, then stopped and turned her head to look at Neal. "If you went after something you really wanted, I believe you'd get it."

He liked the way she held her shoulders; he watched the sweep of her firm, perfectly pointed breasts. With an effort he turned to look at the big map on the wall of the proposed project, his throat suddenly dry. He heard her laugh as she went on into Darley's office, as if she sensed the effect she had upon him and was pleased.

She was gone for several minutes. Neal could hear the hum of talk, but he could not make out the words. He stood there, studying the wall map that showed the Deschutes River, Cascade City, and the Barney Mountain area with the two lakes near the summit. The lakes, he saw, were drawn far larger in proportion to the country around them than they actually were. From the eastern edge of Big Lake a dotted line representing the proposed ditch curled down the slope in a northerly direction.

Beyond the end of the line was the high desert with its tens of thousands of acres of public domain waiting to be taken by land-hungry settlers. Water was the only thing that was needed, Darley had said repeatedly. Like many lies that are spoken often enough, it had finally been accepted.

For years Neal had run cattle on the high desert. He knew there were two other factors Darley ignored which would whip the project regardless of the water supply. One was the short growing season. It was short enough here on the Deschutes, but not nearly as short as it was on the high desert.

The second, and this was the one which proved to Neal that Darley was a liar and a crook, was the fact that the ditch had to be built across miles of lava rock, not through dirt which would be comparatively inexpensive to move. The water would have to be carried by wooden or steel flumes because blasting the lava would open up seams through which the water would trickle away.

One hundred thousand dollars would not begin to pay for the miles of flume that would be necessary, a point Darley generally managed to evade. Once when he had been pinned down in a public meeting he had answered that he had the right business connections. He could buy metal fluming, he said, for a fraction of what it had cost the companies that had developed the projects along the river, a statement Neal knew was a lie.

Fay Darley opened the door and walked toward Neal. "I'm sorry I kept you waiting, Mr. Clark, but I'm leaving now and there were a few things I had to talk to Ben about." She put her hands on his arms and pulled him toward her. He felt the pressure of her breasts, he smelled her perfume, and he heard her whisper—her lips were close to his ear—"Be careful. Be awfully careful." Then she hurried out of the office.

Neal stood rooted there, thoroughly disturbed by what she had just done. He brushed a hand across his face and looked at the sweat on his finger tips, then wiped his hands on his coat, convinced she was a wanton and startled because, knowing what she was, she still affected him the way she did.

He walked into Darley's private office and stopped, flat-footed. The promoter was standing behind his desk, a cocked gun lined on Neal's chest. He said, "I can think of only one reason for you to come here, Clark. It won't work. I propose to kill you before you have a chance to kill me."

Chapter Four

For a long moment Neal stood just inside the door of Ben Darley's private office, the sound of his labored breathing a rasping noise in his ears. He was completely dumbfounded, not even suspecting that Darley owned a gun. Tuck Shelton, yes, but not Darley.

Neal had known Darley as a homely, awkward-appearing man, slightly stooped and plagued by a speech impediment that gave the impression he was pausing often to select the right word for the particular occasion. He appeared to be the exact opposite of the sleek, attractive animal who was his wife, possessing qualities which would have been fatal for many tasks, but were exactly the characteristics he needed to convince people he was humble, honest, and unselfish.

Now, staring across the room at him, Neal saw a different Ben Darley than the stockholders saw when they talked to him about the project. He was homely enough, for nothing could change his rough, irregular features. In every other way he was changed. He was not stooped. He spoke without the slightest difficulty. And there was nothing awkward about the way he held his gun.

For a moment panic gripped Neal. Darley could murder him with reasonable safety. He could claim self defense and people would believe him, for everyone knew how Neal felt. All Darley needed to do was shoot him, fire the gun in Neal's pocket, drop the gun on the floor, and get Joe Rolfe.

The panic passed as quickly as it had come. Darley, a careful man, wasn't one to take chances. Neal said, "You can't pull it off, Darley. You'll have a little trouble proving it was self-defense to Joe Rolfe."

Darley's indecision held him motionless for a time. He chewed on his upper lip, then he said, "Why did you come here, Clark?"

"I'd like to kill you, Darley," Neal said. "Don't make any mistake about that, but I'll never get you into the street for a fair fight."

"Shelton will oblige you," Darley said.

"It's got to be you," Neal said. "Shelton may be the brains of your outfit, but you're the man people believe in."

It was a left-handed kind of compliment, and Darley seemed amused. "I'll ask you again. Why are you here?"

"I wanted to talk," Neal said, aware that there was nothing he could do but play for time and hope to leave here alive.

"Talk," the promoter said hotly. "Well mister, I've had too damned much of your talk already. You've done everything you could to block us from the day we moved in here."

"And I've just heard too much of your talk," Neal shot back. "The secondhand kind. Jud Manion told me Tuttle and Sailor claim they've seen a letter from me asking to buy fifty thousand dollars worth of your stock. Somebody's lying and I figure it's you."

To Neal's surprise Darley laid the gun on his desk and sat down. He motioned to a chair. "Sit down, Clark. We'll talk, but I don't know what good it'll do you. Sure I lied. I forged your name to a letter for Tuttle and Sailor to see. They gave you a cussing, mister, a hell of a good cussing."

Neal dropped into the chair across the desk from Darley. He said, "I'll say one thing for you, Darley, you're a good actor. You'd have to be to convince people you're a saint when actually you're a liar and a thief."

Darley's thick lips thinned in a grin. "Now I'll tell you what I think of you. You're stupid, Clark, too stupid to run a bank. If you made the loans folks want, and if you're right about me, you could take over every farm in the county."

"Maybe a stupid man sleeps better than a crook." Neal leaned forward. "How much would it take to get you and Shelton to return the money you've taken in and leave the county?"

"More than you've got." Darley laughed. "You're wasting your time. You don't have an ace in your hand. People don't like you, and before this is over, they'll hang you."

"They'll hang you first," Neal said, "because you're wrong about me not having an ace. The figures you've been quoting for construction of a ditch are phony. I've got a survey crew working out there now. They'll be finished in a day or two and then I'll have the information I need to prove you're a crook."

For a moment Darley's surprise shattered his composure, then the mask was in place again. "You're bluffing. News like that gets around and I haven't heard it." He rose and moved to the end of the desk, his gun still within easy reach. "I'm busy."

Neal glanced at the big safe in the corner, remembering what a job it had been to pull it up the stairs and get it into place here. At the time he'd wondered why Darley and Shelton needed such a heavy safe, but now he thought he knew. The money that had been collected was right there, not in a Portland bank as Darley claimed.

"What happens if someone cracks that safe and cleans you out?"

"They won't. Shelton sleeps here every night. Don't try it, Clark. It's all the boys would need to string you up."

"When are you starting work on the ditch?"

"When do you think?"

"Never."

Darley's patience suddenly snapped like a frayed rope. "You seem able to answer your own questions. Now get to hell out of here and let me alone."

Still Neal didn't move. He stood with his feet spread, eyes on Darley. He had been afraid when he'd come in and faced a gun in Darley's hand. Darley had been scared and was therefore dangerous, but he'd ceased to be dangerous the moment he'd laid his gun down. Now, thinking about what had been said, fury suddenly boiled up in Neal. With no one to hear, Darley had tacitly admitted that everything Neal suspected was true.

"I've lost almost every friend I had in the county on your account," Neal said, "and that includes Jud Manion. He was in the bank today talking about hearing his baby cry because he was hungry. If you get away with this, there'll be babies crying all over the county."

"You trying to make me cry like the babies?" Darley motioned toward the door. "Damn it, get out of here before I throw you out."

"Try it," Neal challenged. "You're a bastard, Darley, a stinking, lying, stealing son of a bitch."

One moment Darley was standing there, his hands at his sides. The next he had exploded into action, a fist catching Neal on the chin and sending him reeling. If Darley had followed up, he might have whipped Neal, but the blow seemed to be an expression of his anger and he was satisfied to let it go at that. Neal wasn't. He rushed the promoter, smashing Darley's defensive fists aside and driving home a roundhouse right that knocked Darley flat on his back.

Darley got up and charged back. They stood there for a time exchanging blows, both willing to take one to give one. That was another mistake on Darley's part because he lacked the hatred that had grown in Neal for months. He was a madman, not feeling Darley's fists as he hammered wicked punches to the promoter's face, then his stomach, then the face again. A better man than Darley could not have stood up under than kind of punishment. He backed up, got his feet tangled in a wastebasket, and fell headlong, shaking the floor and rattling the pictures on the wall.

Darley rolled and got to his feet, whimpering like a hurt pup. He lunged toward the desk, shoved the chair back, and crawling under the desk, rolled up into a ball, his head buried in his arms.

Neal got him by the coat collar and hauled him to his feet, Darley grabbed for the gun on the desk, but didn't quite reach it. Neal hit him again, spinning him back toward a file cabinet. It went over with a tremendous clatter, papers spilling all over the floor, Darley falling across it.

Darley got up and charged Neal again, swinging both fists wildly, but he had been hurt too much for his blows to be effective. Neal ducked and drove at Darley, pumping a right and left into the promoter's middle, then catching him squarely on the jaw with an upswinging right. This time Darley went down and stayed down.

Neal would have hauled Darley to his feet and hit him

again if Shelton had not called from the door, "That's enough, Clark." Neal straightened, wiping a coat sleeve across his face. Blood was pounding in his head with pulsating throbs. He squeezed his eyes shut and opened them. He could see Shelton clearly then, standing in the doorway, a gun in his hand.

"Don't make a fast move, Clark." Shelton glanced at Darley's battered face and shook his head. "You did quite a job, but don't try it with me or I'll kill you."

Shelton backed into the front office, motioning for Neal to follow, the gun not wavering from Neal's chest. He seemed completely impersonal about this, but there was no doubt in Neal's mind that Joe Rolfe's estimate of the man was right. Under ordinary circumstances he was the most colorless man in town, the kind who could be in a crowd and afterward everyone would swear he hadn't been there at all. But right now he was a killing machine.

Shelton moved behind Fay Darley's desk, motioning toward the door that opened into the hall. Neal walked past the big map on the wall to the hat rack near the door, his gaze fixed on Shelton's face. There seemed to be more white in his eyes than ever; he was nervous and jumpy as if fighting a compulsion to kill Neal where he stood.

When Neal reached for his Stetson, Shelton said, "Keep going, friend. Right on out of town. Ben won't forget this. Neither will I."

His face was not ordinary now. It was contorted by a feral bitterness such as Neal had never seen on the face of any man before in his life. He left the office quickly, closing the door behind him, and went down the stairs. He knew he was lucky to be alive, that it would have taken only the slightest wrong move on his part to have made Shelton pull the trigger.

Neal dropped a hand into his coat pocket and felt of the gun. He considered going back and shooting it out with Shelton, but gave up the thought at once, remembering that Shelton's death would change nothing.

His fingers closed over a folded piece of paper. His pocket had been empty when he'd put the gun there earlier in the morning. He drew the paper out and unfolded it. A note had been printed with a dull pencil: "A man never escapes from what he did yesterday. When the times comes, I'll get square with you for what you done to my father and brother. Ed Shelly."

Neal leaned against the wall, staring at the note. For a moment he wondered if he were asleep, if this were part of the nightmare that was so terribly familiar. Then he began to tremble and shoved the note back into his pocket. No, this wasn't a nightmare. He was very much awake, and he had the weird feeling that he had lived through this moment before, a moment he had been sure for eight years would come sooner or later. But coming just now, on top of everything else . . . !

Very slowly he went down the steps, one hand clutching the rail.

Chapter Five

When Neal reached the boardwalk at the foot of the stairs, he saw that the crowd of men that had been in front of the Signal Butte Inn was gone. No one was in sight except Joe Rolfe, who stood at one end of the horse trough, his hands in his pockets, the afternoon sun reflected in the star he wore on his shirt.

This was the same star Rolfe had worn as long as Neal could remember, and it was as shiny now as it had been years ago when Neal had stared admiringly at it as a child. Rolfe's long term as sheriff was as shiny bright as the star. In Neal's mind he was the only man in Cascade County with the exception of Doc Santee whose honesty and integrity were above suspicion.

"What have you been into now?" Rolfe asked.

"Had a fight with Darley."

Neal handed the sheriff the paper he had found in his pocket and walked on past him to the horse trough. "You're having a right busy day," Rolfe said, not looking at the paper. "A ruckus with Tuttle and now one with Darley."

"And Jud Manion trying to hold me up for a thousand dollars," Neal said, "and Tuck Shelton throwing his gun on me and running me out of their office. Now that."

Neal sloshed water over his face, and dried with his bandanna. When he looked at Rolfe, the sheriff was staring at the note, as motionless as if he were paralyzed. Two townsmen walked by, both nodding at Rolfe and ignoring Neal. One was Dick Bishop, the jeweler, the other Olly Earl, who owned the hardware store. Neal had known them as long as they'd been in town, but now they passed him as if he were an unwelcome stranger in Cascade City.

Neal watched the two men until they disappeared into O'Hara's bar, but the old smoldering anger that had been in him for weeks since he had been ostracized by both farmers and townsmen did not break into flame as it had so many times. A man had to do what he had to do regardless of petty opposition, and this was hardly even petty after what Neal had been through today.

Still Rolfe stood staring at the note as if he were hypnotized by it. He was nearly seventy, his back as straight as a plumb line, and slender without the slightest hint of a paunch. When it came to trailing a fugitive, he could outride a man twenty years younger. His face, as withered and brown as an apple that had hung on the tree after a hard winter, betrayed no emotion when he folded the paper and slipped it into his coat pocket. He pinned his dark eyes on Neal, right hand coming up to curl a tip of his sweeping white mustache.

"Where'd you get it?" Rolfe asked.

"It was in my coat pocket. I didn't know it was there until after I left Darley's office just now."

"You trying to say somebody shoved it into your pocket without you knowing it?"

"That's exactly what I'm saying."

"Who had a chance to do it?"

"It wasn't there when I left home this morning," Neal said. "Must have happened today. Could have been any of a dozen people. Jud Manion. Henry Abel. Sailor or Tuttle. Mrs. Darley. Maybe Shelton." He frowned, thinking of Mrs. Darley. She'd had the best opportunity of anyone. She could have dropped a rock into his pocket without him knowing it when she'd stood close to him in her husband's office. "Mrs. Darley," he said thoughtfully. "Joe, I think she was the one."

Rolfe got his pipe out of his pocket and began to fill it. "Any stranger who comes to this burg is going to hear about that Shelly business," he said thoughtfully. "Folks still like to talk about it. Now if Darley or Shelton could get you to thinking about that and worrying enough, you'd quit fighting them. It makes sense, Neal. It's almost cleanup time for them two bastards, and you've been a burr under their tails right from the first."

"Could be, all right," Neal admitted. "I suppose I might as well forget it. Joe, a while ago Darley practically admitted they have no intention of digging a ditch."

"That ain't news," Rolfe said irritably, "but you didn't

prove nothing by going up there and scrapping with Darley."

"I know it. I aimed to kill the son of a bitch if I could get him to go for his gun, but it didn't work that way."

"Lucky for you it didn't," Rolfe said. "If you're figuring to smoke it out with Darley, you'd better have a crowd of witnesses." He held a match to his pipe, looking at Neal through the smoke. Then he added, "You think you've got trouble. Well, I've got some, too. I can't do nothing but sit here and wait for them two buzzards to clean out their safe and run. Just knowing what they're gonna do ain't enough to arrest 'em for."

"Let's go get a drink," Neal said.

"I need one, all right," Rolfe said, "but I've got some advice to give you before I forget it. Stay out of trouble. You'll get yourself killed the way you're going. It's my guess Darley and Shelton will fly the coop before long. When they do, I'll need you. Nobody else I can count on."

Neal was silent until they went into O'Hara's bar. Bishop and Earl glanced at Neal, finished their drinks, and walked out. Neal said, "I must smell pretty bad."

"I've got the same stink on me," Rolfe said. "Same with Doc. He was telling me the other day that for the last three months he's had about half the calls he had a year ago. Anybody who can travel goes to Prineville." He motioned toward O'Hara. "Whisky."

"The same," Neal said.

O'Hara waddled toward them, set a bottle and two glasses in front of them, then leaned forward, fat hands palm down on the bar. "You two and Doc Santee have bucked Darley from the first. Nobody can figure out why. It ain't as if they was taking water out of the river and maybe coming up short. Or spending money to build a reservoir. It's a surefire proposition, with Darley giving us a chance to make a profit on our investment. All he's trying to do is to develop the community and give homes to a hundred families."

O'Hara straightened, wiped his hands on his apron, and pointed a finger at Neal. "You're the one that's stopping it. Darley was saying just this morning that they don't need more'n another ten thousand to start work. Your bank could loan that much without hurting nobody. I've tried to borrow a little—"

"Sure, I know, O'Hara," Neal broke in. "I'm the dog in the manger."

For a time they glared at each other across the bar, Neal fighting an impulse to grab the saloonman by his fat neck and shake some sense into him. But he hadn't knocked any sense into Alec Tuttle. He wouldn't do any better with O'Hara.

"You're a hell of a lot worse'n a dog in a manger," O'Hara muttered, and walking to the other end of the bar, began polishing glasses.

For a moment Neal stared at his drink. He wondered, as he had so many times, how much a man could take before he went crazy or killed somebody or ran away.

"I've known O'Hara for years," he said, "but he'd rather believe a crook who came here six months ago than me."

"You can savvy why they feel that way, O'Hara and Manion and all of 'em," Rolfe said. "They know the irrigation companies along the river have made money. Darley's promised 'em bigger profits with his deal because he's fixing to tap the lakes. Won't have the expense of building reservoirs. Just human nature to want something for nothing."

Neal nodded and took his drink. The sheriff's explanation didn't make it any easier. A solvent bank was as essential to the prosperity of a community as a fire department or a supply of drinking water. If he backed Darley and Shelton and the bank went broke, he'd be criticized more bitterly than he was now. On the other hand, if he made the loans that were being demanded and then had to go to law to collect what was owed, it would be worse.

Rolfe put his hand on Neal's shoulder. "I know how you feel, son. I've been in the same boat more'n once. So was your dad. You just can't please everybody. Take Sam now. He was proud and pushy and bossy as hell, but he had some damned fine dreams. He used to say we'd have a town of fifteen thousand people here on the Deschutes with a railroad coming up the river and sawmills slicing up the pines." He dropped his hand and turned to the bar again, adding, "You inherited them dreams along with the bank, boy. Don't lose 'em."

Neal threw a silver dollar on the bar. "My money good, O'Hara?"

"It's good," the saloonman said sullenly. "Any you let go of, I mean."

As Neal turned away, Rolfe said, "Hang and rattle. This'll break in a day or so. That's why you got that note, the way I figure."

Neal walked out. He wouldn't go back to the bank today. Henry Abel could handle anything that came up. He'd go home, saddle his horse Redman, and take a ride to the Circle C. He had to get out of town, had to think, and somehow find a little peace of mind.

His fears and hatreds were all knotted up inside him so he

couldn't even eat a meal without having it lie in his stomach like a rock. Maybe he ought to go to Doc Santee. No, it wouldn't do any good. What ailed him was too much for any pill roller to cure, even a good one like Santee.

He walked with his head down, crossing the street and angling through the trees to the river. For a moment he paused, his gaze on the clear, swift moving stream. Maybe he ought to get Jane and Laurie out of town. If Joe Rolfe was right, it wouldn't be for more than a week at most. But then he'd have to tell Jane everything that had happened. And Laurie would be upset. No, it was better to just let it rock along.

He went on, leaving the river and walking rapidly along the dusty street to his house. He went in and closed the door softly, hoping that Jane and Laurie were gone, or that Laurie was at least asleep. He listened for a moment, hearing Jane's humming from the kitchen. Laurie must be out playing or taking a nap, or he'd hear her, for she was perpetually in motion when she was awake.

Crossing the parlor as quietly as he could, he climbed the stairs to his and Jane's bedroom, and taking off his clothes that had been badly soiled, he put on another pair of pants and a flannel shirt, then buckled his gun belt around him, his bone-handled .44 in the holster.

He went into the bathroom, the only one in Cascade City. This was something else people talked about. They said he had plenty of money to spend on a zinc tub and hot water tank, but when it came to helping his neighbors out, he didn't have a nickel.

He stared at the mirror, thinking he had been lucky not to have his face cut up more than it was. He had bruises on his chin and under his left eye, but maybe Jane wouldn't notice.

The instant he stepped into the kitchen, Jane asked, "What are you doing home this time of day?" She looked at him and frowned. "Who'd you have a fight with?" Then she saw the gun on his hip, and cried out, "Neal, what are you doing with that six-shooter?"

She stood at the table, a paring knife in her hands. She had been peeling potatoes, but now she just stood looking at him, frightened and worried. He walked to her, thinking how much he loved her and how beautiful she was even wearing an everyday house dress with a red-and-white checked apron and a dab of flour on one cheek.

He put his arms around her and kissed her. She dropped the paring knife and hugged him, returning his kiss with sweet, lingering warmth, telling him as she did every day when he came home that she loved him just as much as she had when they were married. Then she drew her head back, saying sternly, "Answer my questions, both of them."

"You're as pretty as a spotted heifer and I love you," he said, "and the world is full of trouble. We're going to let Henry Abel run the bank and we're moving back to the Circle C. Henry can decide who to make loans to and who not to."

He said it as if he were joking, but he was serious. The temptation had been a growing one for months. He was sure Jane would not object, but now, seeing how grave her face was, he wondered if he was wrong about her.

"I know the world is full of trouble," she said, "but I also know you never ran away from any of it. You're not going to now. I know you too well. You'll stay in that bank until your trouble with Darley and Shelton is settled. And you still haven't answered my questions."

"I had a ruckus with Darley." There was no reason to tell her about the note from Ed Shelly, he thought. "I'm going to take a ride out to the ranch. Redman needs some exercise. So do I."

"But the gun—"

"Just a precaution," he interrupted.

She sighed as if knowing he would not tell her more until he had to. But she wasn't ready to let him go. Her arms were still around him, her face close to his, and now he sensed that something was worrying her. She said, "Neal," and stopped.

"I'll be back in time for supper," he said, "but if you want to buy that new hat in Lizzie Arms' millinery shop, I guess our credit's good."

"Neal, stop it. I don't have to have a new hat every week like that Fay Darley." She bit her lower lip, then plunged on, "Neal, I can't help hearing gossip. About how folks feel because the bank isn't loaning money to invest with Darley. They hate you and they're saying terrible things. I'm afraid of what they'll do."

I can take care of myself," he said, "but I'm worried about you and Laurie. You'd better be careful and keep a close watch on her."

He kissed her and walked to the back door. "Neal, you don't think they'd hurt Laurie because of this?"

He still didn't want to tell her about Ed Shelly's note, and he wasn't sure whether Joe Rolfe was right. The note could well have been a clumsy effort on Darley's and Shelton's part to make him so worried he'd stop fighting them, but there was a chance Ed Shelly was actually here, that he'd hired someone to slip that note into Neal's pocket.

Suddenly the terror of the nightmare was in him again,

and he remembered how often he had dreamed that Ed Shelly was taking his revenge on Laurie or Jane. He said, "I don't know what they'll do. Just keep an eye on Laurie. Don't take any chances yourself, either."

He wheeled and left the house. He saddled his bay gelding and mounted, and when he reached the edge of town, he put the horse into a run. But it didn't help. Nothing helped. He just couldn't shake the eight-year-old fear that Ed Shelly would somehow take a terrible revenge, a fear that now was brought into sharp focus because Ed Shelly was back. He must be. Now that he'd had time to think about it, Neal didn't believe that note was Ben Darley's trick.

Chapter Six

A mile from town Neal noticed the remains of a camp fire between the road and river. He dismounted and examined the ashes carefully, irritated and concerned. This was Circle C range, and both Neal and Curly Taylor who was ramrodding the ranch now, discouraged saddle bums from camping here. This man was undoubtedly a saddle bum or he would have ridden on into town.

From the signs, Neal judged the fellow had been here two or three days. Neal walked back to his horse, wondering if there could be a connection between this man and the note from Ed Shelly. Or some connection with Darley and Shelton. Shrugging, he mounted and put his gelding up the slope east of the river, deciding he was jittery and imagining dangers that did not exist.

He took a switchback course to the top of the ridge, swinging back and forth between the barren outcroppings of lava. The horse's hoofs stirred the dust and pine cones and dry needles that had been here undisturbed for centuries. Once atop the ridge, he turned south, not stopping until he could look down upon the Circle C buildings.

Dismounting, he rolled and lighted a cigarette, hunkering down at the base of a pine. He often came here when the petty problems that stemmed from town living became so burdensome he could not stand it.

From this point Neal could see miles of the river, a band

of silver shadowed by the pines that crowded both banks. On the other side were the snow-capped peaks of the Cascades, and to the east the pines gave way to junipers and sagebrush. Mountains, river and high desert: these, to Neal Clark, were all a man needed to make his world complete.

Today the problems were far from petty, and Neal was unable to shake off the depressing feeling that trouble had only started for him. As he smoked, looking down at the Circle C, he thought how completely the stone ranch house symbolized his father. Huge and terribly permanent, it was the only kind of house Sam Clark would ever have thought of building.

Neal's father had lived in the big house very little, but apparently he had been happy for the short time he had been there, dreaming the big dreams Joe Rolfe had talked about in O'Hara's bar. Probably the thought never occurred to him that it was not the kind of house his son or his son's wife wanted.

At a time like this, in the silence broken only by the wind sounds as it rushed across the ridge, Neal could think of himself and his future, and Jane and Laurie, and of the many months Jane had lived in the stone house, forbidden to change anything, never allowed to feel it was really her home, and yet somehow managing to change it simply by being there. But if Sam Clark had felt the change, he certainly had never indicated it.

Now the old question that had plagued him long before his father died crowded back into Neal's mind. How far could a son go on letting his father dictate to him, either dead or alive? If Neal had had his choice, he'd have stayed right there on the Circle C, but no, Sam Clark had decided Curly Taylor could run the outfit, and Neal and Jane must move to town.

Perhaps he had no reason to regret what he had done, for certainly Jane's life was easier in town than it had been on the ranch. But he didn't think that was important, for Jane was not a woman to choose an easy life. He knew that she would accept his choice without question. He had done pretty well with the bank, he thought, largely because Henry Abel had taught him what he had to know. The bank was in good shape, again largely because of Abel's conservative influence. Neal, according to Abel, was inclined to be soft.

This reminded Neal of what people thought about him. It was that, he knew, which had brought his feelings to a head and made him want to leave the bank. He took criticism far too hard, Abel told him. So had Joe Rolfe and Doc Santee.

But there was one vital point that never occurred to them. If Sam Clark were alive and running the bank, the men who hated Neal today would not have hated his father. Chances were the older Clark would have succeeded in chasing Darley and Shelton out of the country.

Neal could not fill Sam Clark's shoes. That was the rub. On the other hand, he didn't really want to. He had to be his own man. He had resisted his father on occasion and sometimes he had won his point, but he invariably had the feeling these were only temporary victories. In the long run, Sam Clark's will overpowered everything else. It was small comfort to realize he was not alone in this, that Joe Rolfe or Doc Santee or Henry Abel would have said the same thing.

Then, because his restlessness would not permit him to return to the confines of the town, he mounted and put Redman down the slope toward the ranch. He often felt this way, even before the Darley-Shelton business had come into sharp focus, and it convinced him that sooner or later he had to return to the ranch, that he could not and would not spend a lifetime in town. In that regard he had much of his father in him. Perhaps it was this very restlessness which had kept Sam Clark on the move and prevented him from being satisfied with anything he attained.

It was noon when he reached the ranch buildings, set in a clearing in the pines on the east side of the road. A log barn, outbuildings, innumerable corrals, all shadowed by the sprawling stone house that was now empty. Actually it was an ugly structure, for Sam Clark had built with an idea of permanence rather than beauty.

Neal put his horse into the corral and stood for a time looking at the house. He remembered Jane saying that it sort of fitted the lava rock and the pines and the river across the road. If they returned there were things she could do that would entirely change the appearance of the place. Curtains at the windows. Grass in front of the house. A few flowers that would grow in this climate. Lilacs, for instance, and some decorative trees such as weeping willows. It would be entirely different than when Sam Clark was alive.

Neal went into the cook shack and talked to the cook. Later, he had dinner with him and asked him to tell Curly Taylor about the saddle bum who had camped on the river above town. After that he went into the house. It was cold, for it had been shut up for weeks. Occasionally he brought Jane and Laurie out here for Sunday, but it had been quite a while since he had even done that.

For a time Neal stood in front of the fireplace that made up most of one wall. Pictures of his father and mother in gaudy, gilt frames hung above the mantel. His mother had been young and pretty. She'd died when he was small, and he could barely remember her. She'd had a hard life, he thought, and that may have been the reason she'd died when she had. Sam Clark had been a poor man then, and that, Neal knew, might have been the cause of his father's driving ambition and restlessness.

He glanced around the big room at the massive black leather couch and chair, the enormous oak table in the middle of the room, the walnut bookcase, the floor bare of rugs. If they did come back, he thought, Jane could furnish the room as she saw fit. Certainly everything that was here now would go.

He walked into the small room that had served as his father's office. Now it was Curly Taylor's. Neal smiled at the tally books, the box of .45 shells, and a bridle that lay on the spur-scarred desk. He glanced around at the saddle and guns and odds and ends of leather and the rest of the stuff Taylor had succeeded in gathering. The room was a boar's nest, totally different from the orderly office Sam Clark had kept, but now it seemed a friendly room. Neal was shocked by the implications of that thought, and swinging around, walked out of the room and the house.

He saddled his horse, but he didn't mount for a time. He stood beside his gelding, a hand on the horn, his eyes on the house. The restlessness had died in him. He was ready to go back to town, to face whatever must be faced. He couldn't run away from either the ranch or the bank, or the problems that faced him.

It wasn't important what his father would have done or how people would have responded to his father. It wasn't even important whether he filled his father's shoes; it was important that he fill his own. He had charted his course and he could not change, even if it meant danger to Jane or Laurie.

He mounted and rode away, relieved and still vaguely uneasy when his thoughts fastened again upon Ed Shelly and the note he'd found in his pocket. He was so lost in his thoughts that he did not see Fay Darley standing between the road and the river until she called, "Good afternoon, Mr. Clark."

He reined up, startled. She stood holding the reins of a livery-stable mare, smiling in the provocative way she had. She was wearing a black riding skirt and a leather jacket and a flattopped Stetson which was tilted rakishly on one side of her head. She stood with her legs spread so that Neal could see her ankles, the skirt molded against her thighs, and again that titillating sense of excitement flooded him as it had every time he had seen her.

He touched his hat. "Good afternoon, Mrs. Darley."

He would have ridden on if she had not said, "Will you get down for a moment, Mr. Clark? I realize this seems bold, and I suppose it is, but the truth is I've been waiting for you. I knew you had left town and that you'd come along the road sooner or later, so I waited."

She must have been waiting for a long time, he thought. Nothing but trouble could come from having anything to do with this woman, but he stepped down, rationalizing that any other man would have done the same.

"I'm glad you waited," he said. "I've got a question to ask you."

She looked at him warily, then said, "I'll be happy if the question is what I hope it is. A man is supposed to do the pursuing, but I learned long ago that there are times when a woman must let her heart speak or she will always regret it."

She was a beautiful and experienced woman, and he was both attracted and repelled by her. He didn't understand the latter unless he was afraid of her. He glanced at her, then looked down, scraping a toe through the dust of the road.

"You're wrong, ma'am," he said. "About the question."

"Am I?" she asked softly, paused, and then said, "Did you have trouble with Ben?" She dropped the reins and walking to Neal, gently touched the bruise on the side of his face. "I warned you. He'd kill me if he knew I had spoken to you."

"I reckon he wouldn't go that far." He glanced at her and lowered his gaze again. "Anyhow, he got the worst of it."

"I'm glad," she said spitefully. "I hope you busted him good. He's bad. So's Shelton. I wish you'd leave for a while. They're arousing people against you. If you stay they'll hang you."

So that was the game! He should have known. Darley had sent her out here to wait for him in the hopes he could be scared out of town, then they'd be free of the man who had partially blocked them. He met her gaze, thinking that now he knew her for exactly what she was.

"I'd say you were trying to get me out of town for some reason you haven't told me," he said.

"That's right. It's the reason your life is in danger and why you've got to leave tonight. A man named Stacey is coming in on the stage from Portland in the morning. That's why Ben has stayed here as long as he has. He believes he can persuade Stacey to invest ten thousand dollars in the project. He realizes he's gambling against time, but with you out of town, he's convinced he's got a sure thing."

"It's safer to get me to leave town than to kill me," Neal said. "That it?"

"That's right," she said with honesty he didn't expect, "but what you don't know is that I'll be saving your life. I'm leaving Ben no matter what happens to you." She licked her lips with the tip of her tongue, her eyes not leaving his face, then she added, "A woman has to dream, Neal, or she'd go crazy. I've done my share of dreaming since I came to Cascade City. About you."

She stood with her hands at her sides, her breasts rising and falling with her breathing. The calm cloak of efficiency which she wore in Ben Darley's office was not on her now. To him she seemed a young, wistful girl, hoping for something from life which she did not actually believe she would ever have. That made him a fool for even thinking it, he told himself, for she was anything but young and wistful.

Then he remembered the note he had found in his pocket. It was the question he had meant to ask when he'd first dismounted, and had been sidetracked. Now he said roughly, "Maybe you'd like to tell me how that note got into my pocket this afternoon."

Wide-eyed, she asked, "What note?"

"From Ed Shelly. It said he hadn't forgotten what happened to his brother and father."

"Neal." She put her hands on his shoulders. "You don't think I had anything to do with putting it in your coat pocket? You . . . you can't."

"Who did?"

"I don't know," she said as if troubled by the question. "I didn't know there was a note, but Ben might have done it. Or Shelton. They know about your trouble with the Shelly gang. I heard them talking about trying to scare you out of town by using Ed Shelly's name, but I thought they gave up the idea." She shivered. "Neal, it might be true. Maybe someone around town really is Ed Shelly."

"Well by God," a man said behind Neal. "If this ain't a purty sight. I thought you was a married man, Clark."

Neal whirled to face the man who had come up behind him. As he turned, Fay Darley cried, "Ruggles," as if the name were squeezed out of her. She ran to her mare and mounting, rode toward town in a gallop.

Neal did not look at her, but stood staring at the stranger. He had never seen the man before. He was in his thirties, tall and very thin, with a sneering expression on his brown lips that told Neal how much filth there was in his mind.

"Your name Ruggles?" Neal asked.

"That's my handle." He walked toward Neal. "I've got a letter for you that a—"

"You've been camping here?" Neal interrupted.

"Yeah."

"You're on Circle C range. Get to hell off of it. We don't allow saddle bums to hang around. Too many things can happen. A fire. Or you might get a notion to eat some Circle C beef." Neal motioned toward town. "There's a hotel. . . ."

"To hell with you and hotels," Ruggles said angrily. "You've got gall, telling me where I can camp and where I can't. But it's all right for you to meet Mrs. Darley out here in the brush. If I'd have waited, I'd have seen something purty damned—"

Neal hit him, sending him spinning half around. Ruggles tried for his gun, but Neal let him have it again, a hard right to the side of his head that knocked him flat on his back. Neal bent over him and pulled his gun out of leather, then stepped back and shoved it under his waistband.

Ruggles lay on the ground, rubbing his face where Neal had hit him. He said, "I never forget a man who hits me. When I see you next time, I'll be heeled and don't forget it." He pulled an envelope out of his pocket and held it out for Neal to take. "I'm broke, and a fellow in town hired me to give you this. I was gonna take it to your house, but I won't need to."

Neal took the letter and jammed it into his coat pocket. He said, "If you start any talk about me and Mrs. Darley, I'll kill you. Understand?"

"Yeah, I savvy," Ruggles said. "But you don't look like no hero to me. You got it turned around. Soon as I get me a gun, I'll start hunting you."

Neal mounted and rode toward town. He looked back once to see that Ruggles was on his feet leaning against a pine tree. Suppose the man did start some talk in town? What would he accomplish, and what would Mrs. Darley do? Maybe make the story bigger and worse, Neal thought bitterly.

This probably was a put up job from the first, with Ruggles working for Darley, and Mrs. Darley knowing he was here. It added up to more trouble, dirty trouble he didn't want to bring upon Jane. Now that it was too late, he wished he had gone on and not stopped to talk to Mrs. Darley.

Then another thought came to him, hitting him hard. Could this Ruggles be Ed Shelly?

Chapter Seven

Neal did not tear the envelope open until he was out of Ruggles' sight. He was not at all surprised when he read, "Yesterday has become today, Clark. You'll pay for the murder of my father and brother, and so will your wife and girl. Ed Shelly."

No, Neal wasn't surprised. It was making a pattern in his mind and he didn't like the looks of the pattern. Mrs. Darley begging him to leave town and giving him that hogwash about having done her share of dreaming about him since she'd been in Cascade City. She knew the stranger Ruggles by name. The hours she must have spent there on the road south of town waiting for him to come home. Ruggles, too. Now he could spread a story about the respectable banker with a wife and child who had met Mrs. Darley out there along the river.

It was a pattern, all right, the dirty pattern set by men who didn't care how they pulled him down as long as they did it. Neal wasn't as concerned about this note as he had been earlier in the day when he received the first one. Ed Shelly was dead. He must be. Joe Rolfe had said so repeatedly and Neal had to believe it was true. Mrs. Darley had said that her husband and Shelton knew about his trouble with the Shelly gang and had thought about using Ed Shelly's name to scare him out of town.

That was the whole thing in a nutshell. Mrs. Darley had been honest with him to a point. She had mentioned a man named Stacey who was coming to town and had $10,000 to invest. Any sane man coming to Cascade City under those conditions would first of all go to the local banker for an opinion, so Darley and Shelton would do everything they could to get him out of town before Stacey arrived. They weren't done, either, and they wouldn't be done until he was gone or they were in jail, or they were dead.

He rode back to town slowly, arriving at his barn at supper time. He pulled gear from Redman and watered and fed him, then stepping into the runway, he was reminded of the gun under his waistband that he had taken from Ruggles. He didn't want Jane to see it, or to know about what had happened, so he took a look at it, a walnut-handled .45, a good gun with a fine balance that might indicate Ruggles was a professional gunslinger brought here to kill him.

In a sudden flurry of anger, he tossed the gun into the manger of a vacant stall and walking behind Jane's mare, left the barn. He stopped, remembering that both Mrs. Darley and Ruggles had been waiting for him beside the road, so they had known he was out of town and would probably return on the road. That meant, then, that they'd had him under observation all day, and undoubtedly many days before this because they knew his habits. He rode to the Circle C often, invariably following the same route that he had today.

Suddenly he realized that it didn't make any difference whether it was actually Ed Shelly signing these notes or not. The last one made a threat against Jane and Laurie. Darley and Shelton could be just as dangerous and ruthless as Ed Shelly had ever been.

He stood motionless, breathing hard, and fought for composure. He didn't want to go into the house and let Jane see him as thoroughly unnerved as he was now. He felt a sharp pain in the left part of his chest. It had been there before, but it was worse now. Nervous tension, Doc Santee had called it.

"It's not your heart," Doc had said a little testily, "so quit worrying about it."

Well, he wasn't worried about his heart. He wasn't even worried about himself. Jane's and Laurie's safety was enough to worry anyone. He could not understand how two men could be evil enough to work through a woman and child to control another man's actions, but now he was convinced that was exactly what was happening.

It could be only a bluff. Possibly it would be enough if he left town only for one day, just long enough to let Darley and Shelton fleece the new victim who would be here in the morning, but he couldn't do it. He was Sam Clark's son, and for all of Sam Clark's ambition, he had been a man who put duty first, and he had taught Neal to do the same.

Neal waited until he had regained his composure. Sooner or later he would have to tell Jane what had happened and what he feared, but he would put it off as long as he could. When he stepped into the kitchen, Jane was pouring gravy into a bowl. The room was filled with the tangy odor of supper. He took a long, sniffing breath of appreciation.

"That's enough to make a man's mouth water until he's likely to drown," he said.

Jane looked at him, a question in her eyes. She knew him well, sometimes sensing his moods and troubles before he said a word about them. Now she was wondering why he had stayed away so long, he thought, but she didn't ask him.

"Go upstairs and wash, dear," she said, smiling. "It'll just be a minute."

He walked through the dining room past the table with its white linen cloth and napkins, the lighted candles and the good silver and the Ironwood plates. She was putting on a show for him tonight, he thought, something she seldom did, but she sensed how deeply his worry had cut into him the last few days, and this was her effort to take his mind off his troubles.

He went on through the parlor and up the stairs to the bathroom where he washed. When he came back downstairs, Laurie had come in from the yard. She squealed, "Daddy," and ran to him. He picked her up and held her high while she kicked and kept on squealing, "Daddy, Daddy, you've been gone all day."

He brought her to him and hugged her, and she kissed him and put her arms around his neck. Jane came in from the dining room and stood smiling at them. She said, "Supper's ready." He put Laurie down and she ran to her chair at the table. Neal swallowed, fighting the lump in his throat. Nothing could happen to them, he told himself. Nothing! He wouldn't let it.

Laurie chattered while they ate, with Jane nodding and answering her questions. Neal didn't say anything. He didn't feel like it. He only knew he could not go on this way, torn by these fears for Jane and Laurie, and all the other worries that had come to him through these last months. He had let it go too long. He'd see Darley after supper and get the truth out of him if he had to beat him to death. If Shelton interfered, he'd kill him.

After they finished eating, Laurie said in a commanding voice, "I want a story, Daddy."

"She's been playing outside all day," Jane said. "Why don't you put her to bed, Neal?"

He nodded, and rose. "I want a ride," Laurie said in that same commanding tone. "Piggy back."

Jane laughed. "You'd think she was the crown princess, the way she gives orders."

"What's a crown princess, Daddy?" Laurie demanded.

Neal looked down at her, fighting again for composure. He had always known how much he loved her, but now it was hammered home to him with terrible, devastating force. She was a strange child in many ways; delicate features, small for her age, and very shy with strangers, but she was strong and healthy and got along unusually well with the other children in the neighborhood. She was curious about everything; her question about a crown princess typical of her.

"Well," Neal said, "I guess a crown princess is a princess with a crown on her head."

Laurie considered the answer for a moment, then she said, "I'd like to see one, a big crown with lots of diamonds."

Jane laughed. "So would I, honey. Run along, both of you."

Neal gave her a piggy back ride to her bedroom, undressed her and put her to bed, then he sat down on the side of the bed and told her the story of Cinderella, which was her favorite. Then he tucked the covers around her shoulders, kissed her good night, and blew out the lamp.

"Go to sleep now," he said.

She yawned. "I will, Daddy."

He walked to the door; the lamp in the hall shone into the room. He stood there a moment, looking back at her. She yawned again. She said, "Good night, Daddy." He said, "Good night, Princess," and closed the door.

He had reached the parlor when he heard the doorbell. He hesitated, then he heard Jane coming from the kitchen. "I'll get it," he called, and hurried across the room and into the hall. Then he paused again, uneasiness making a prickle along his spine. It could be Ruggles. Maybe the man had got a gun from Darley or Shelton.

Neal drew his pistol, hoping that it was Ruggles and he could get it over with. Holding the gun in his right hand, Neal flung the front door open. No one was in sight. Then he saw the envelope on the threshold. Stooping, he picked it up, not doubting at all what he would find.

He stepped inside, closed the door, and slipped his gun back into leather. He tore open the end of the envelope, took out the sheet of paper and, unfolding it, held it up to the bracket lamp on the wall. The note was printed with a dull pencil the same as the others: "After waiting eight years, Clark, I won't forget you. I'll make you suffer like you made me suffer. I'm going to get Laurie. Ed Shelly."

He crushed the envelope and note into a wad and shoved it into his pocket. He leaned against the wall, his eyes closed. Three times within a matter of hours. He had been so sure this was Darley's and Shelton's way of getting him out of town. Now he wasn't certain. A terrifying thought crept into his mind again.

Suppose this crazy man Ruggles was really Ed Shelly who had come back for revenge? Instead of Darley hiring Ruggles, maybe Ruggles had hired Mrs. Darley or Shelton or someone else to drop the first note into his pocket. If he followed this line of reasoning, he could reach only one conclusion. These notes had nothing to do with Darley and Shelton's irrigation scheme and their plan to trim Stacey when he reached town tomorrow.

He had to find out, someway. He didn't know whom to fight until he did. It was the uncertainty more than anything else that was bothering him. But how was he going to find out? He thought of Jane and Laurie again. Fear took possession of him, in his belly, in the crawling tingle that worked down his spine, in a desperate rump-tingling feeling he had never experienced before.

The door bell rang again, giving him a start and setting his heart to pounding again. He yanked his gun from the holster and jerked the door open, fully expecting to see Ruggles. Or Darley or Shelton. He was frantic enough to expect anything, but it was Henry Abel standing there, looking more tired and worried than Neal had ever seen him.

"Come in, Henry." Neal holstered his gun. "Come on in. Jane's probably got some coffee left from supper."

"I'd like to, Neal, but I can't," Abel said. "I haven't been home yet, and Lena will raise hell. What was the gun for?"

"I'm just jumpy, I guess. You can come in for a minute."

"I'd like to, but I can't," Abel said. "I stopped at O'Hara's for a drink and kind of ran into something. A lot of men were there. Quinn, Olly Earl, Jud Manion, Tuttle. All that bunch. They pushed me around a little, trying to make me promise I'd talk to you about changing the bank's policy."

Neal stepped outside and put a hand on Abel's shoulder. He was not a strong man physically and Neal had never thought of him as being a brave one, but he suddenly realized that no one could judge courage in anyone else.

"What did you tell them, Henry?"

Abel grimaced. "Nothing. How could I? I don't own the bank. I don't determine its policies."

Neal dropped his hand. He could have expected this. What Abel said was true, but what he hadn't said was that his judgment went a long way with Neal. If he had not been so convinced right along that the wise thing was for the bank to refuse all loans at this time, Neal might not have been as firm in his policy as he had been.

"That what you came to tell me?" Neal asked.

"No," Abel said. "I'm scared. You see, they're doing some talking about you. You don't realize how they hate you. They blame everything on you because Darley says he needs just a little more money to start work. It's the same old talk with just one difference. Now they're threatening to lynch you. They mean it, Neal. They're just crazy enough to mean it."

"With me out of the way, you'd be running the bank," Neal said. "They figure they can manage you. That it?"

Abel's face turned red. "I guess a man who's as scared of his wife as I am hasn't much right to claim he'll stand on his convictions, but I will." He shrugged. "Hell, Neal, that's not the point. You've got me, the sheirff, and Doc Santee on your side. That's all. You know how a mob starts. Some drinking and some talk and then it's out of hand. What are you going to do?"

"Nothing right now," Neal said, feeling a great flood of relief. "To tell you the truth, Henry, I hope they come after me. I need to fight somebody, somebody I can get my teeth into, not somebody that's like a handful of fog."

Abel looked at him and shook his head. "You're crazy, Neal. Clear, clean crazy."

He whirled and disappeared into the darkness. Neal stepped into the house and shut the door. Abel was right. His talk had been crazy. The situation couldn't be changed by fighting his neighbors. He returned to the parlor, wondering if there was anything to this lynch talk. He was afraid there was.

Chapter Eight

Neal pulled the couch closer to the fireplace and sat down, his long legs stretched out toward the fire. He heard Jane putting things away in the kitchen, and then her steps as she crossed the dining room and came into the parlor.

"Neal," she said, "I want to know what you're keeping from me."

He looked up and tried to smile, but it wouldn't quite come off. "Nothing," he said. "I mean, nothing you don't already know."

She knelt beside him and put her head against his leg. "Who was at the door? I heard it ring twice."

"Henry," he said. "I'd been gone most of the day and there were some things he had to know about."

She was silent for a time. He didn't want to tell her anything else, not until he had to, anyway. This was something he had to fight out himself, or with Joe Rolfe's and Doc

Santee's help. Not Jane's. His job was to protect her. There was nothing she could do but have faith in him and love him, but he didn't say that, for sweet words came hard for him.

"What about the second time," she said. "You might just as well tell me. I'm going to keep after you till you do."

"Henry was the second time."

"The first time, then?"

"Some prank, I guess. Nobody was there when I opened the door."

She looked up at him, her jaw set stubbornly. "Neal, we've got to talk. You don't make it easy. You've got a little of the flint that was in your dad, enough to make you pretty hard-headed sometimes."

He was irritated by that, but he was too tired to argue. He said, "I didn't get a chance to pick my father."

"Of course not. I'm just trying to say that you always keep me in one part of your heart, the nice, easy part. You let me share your triumphs and jokes and the good things that happen to you, but I never get a chance to share your troubles. I want to, Neal. This way you make me feel like I'm only half a wife to you."

He stared at her, hurt by what she'd said and wanting to strike back. He had enough trouble now without her adding to it by having her tell him he made her feel like half a wife. Then he saw the tenderness that was so plain to read in her face and the resentment left him.

"I don't mean to," he said, "but it's my job to take care of you."

She got up, and sitting down beside him, took one of his hands. "And it's my job to take care of you, too, as much as I can. Now you've got to tell me what happened today that's worrying you."

He hesitated, still not wanting to tell her and yet finding some justice in what she said. Maybe he did make her feel like half a wife, maybe there was more of Sam Clark in him than he realized. There had been times when he had felt like half a son, times when his father hadn't taken him into his confidence and he'd resented it just as Jane was resenting it now. Besides, and this was what decided him, he had to tell Jane about the notes so she would be careful with Laurie.

So he told her, beginning with Jud Manion's visit, told her everything except how he felt when he saw Fay Darley in the company office, and again on the road beside the river, and the real reason for Henry Abel's visit.

"Well, it looks to me like Joe could do something," Jane said when he finished. "They must have a criminal record."

"They probably have," he agreed, "but chances are they've changed their names."

She was silent for a moment, her leg pressed against his, her hand squeezing his. He had never been a sentimental man, not in the way Jane would have liked for him to be. That again was proof there was a great deal of Sam Clark in him.

He could never remember his father showing any overt sign of affection for him. Right now was the time for sentiment, the time to tell her how much he loved her. There were a lot of things he should tell her, but he didn't say any of them.

"I guess the part I don't understand is why men like Jud don't trust your judgment," she said. "They would have believed your father."

"That's what hurts," he said. "I'm young, and haven't been proved, I suppose. Darley's smart in putting it on a community basis. He's promised that the men who bought stock will have a chance to work in the ditch, so they'll have money to spend in O'Hara's bar and Quinn's store. The company will buy horses from the livery stable and equipment from Olly Earl. I can't say anything except that I'm saving them money when I won't make the loans they want. Darley twists that around by making it look as if I'm sore because I can't hog the profit."

"Neal, don't worry about those notes," she said. "They're probably just bluff, but I'll stay in the house tomorrow and keep Laurie in, just in case."

"My .38 is in the bureau," Neal said. "Better keep it handy tomorrow."

She nodded agreement, and putting a hand under his chin, tipped his head back and kissed him, her lips hungry for his and holding them for a long moment. Then she rose. "I'm going to bed. Are you going to sit up?"

He nodded. "Don't stay awake for me. I couldn't go to sleep now if I went to bed."

"You're tired, Neal." She hesitated, then murmured, "Good night, darling."

"Good night," he said. He watched until she was halfway up the stairs, then he called, "Jane."

She stopped and looked back over her shoulder. "What is it, Neal?"

"I was just thinking," he said. "I may go out and take a walk. I feel like a clock that's been wound too tight. I'll lock both doors, but maybe you'd better put that .38 under your pillow."

"All right, Neal," she said, and went on up to their room.

He heard the bedroom door close, then the silence was tight and oppressive. He smoked one cigarette after another, impatience goading him, but he couldn't think of anything to do. He felt like a duck sitting on a lake, his enemies in position to shoot at him, but he wasn't in position to shoot back because he didn't know whom to shoot at.

He thought of the lynch talk Henry Abel had brought to him, and suddenly a crazy fury took hold of him. He'd call every one of those money-hungry bastards into the bank tomorrow and loan them all they wanted. Let them give their money to a couple of thieving con men, and when the time came, he'd close them out to the last man. By God, there had to be an end to what you did for other people, trying to save them from themselves.

The fury lasted only for a moment. He thought again of his father as he had so many times these last days as the pressure had mounted. Tough, domineering, hard-headed, Sam Clark was a strange mixture, but he'd had some good traits. If he were alive today, he would have said the same thing to Jud Manion that Neal had. No matter how much he would have been threatened or hated, or how much a man like Ed Shelly, appearing from an eight-year-old yesterday, worried him, Sam Clark would have stuck to his guns.

Some of the flint that had been in his father had come down to him, Jane had said. Not all of it, Neal thought, but enough. That thought closed the door to any easy avenue of escape. He'd see it through; the bank would hold to the policy that he and Henry Abel had decided upon.

The clock on the mantel struck midnight. Neal rose and threw more wood on the fire. He had a strange feeling of detachment about all of this, as if he were a sponge that had been completely saturated and could hold no more.

Then, because he had to do something, he decided to get Joe Rolfe out of bed and talk to him. The old sheriff was pretty cantankerous at times and he wouldn't like it, but Neal had to talk to someone and the only choice he had was between Rolfe and Doc Santee. He didn't want to bother Doc, who often had too little chance to sleep at best.

He locked the kitchen door, thinking that he and Jane would not attempt to control Laurie's life as his had been controlled. Laurie! If anything did happen to her . . . ! He went upstairs, driven by compulsion he could not control.

Jane had left a lamp burning in the bracket on the hall wall. Laurie's door was ajar. Gently he pushed it open and stepped into the room. There was no possible way for anyone to get into her room except by coming up the stairs and along the hall just as he had done. No one had gone past him. He had been in the parlor from the time Laurie had gone to bed, or in the hall or back in the kitchen.

She was all right. She had to be. Nothing could have happened to her. But he could not see her in the thin light that fell through the door from the hall. Suddenly panicky, he ran across the room to the bed, the horrible fear that she was gone taking breath out of his lungs as sharply as if he'd been hit in the stomach.

He stopped at the side of her bed, breathing hard. She lay next to the wall on the far edge, almost hidden under the covers. For a time he stood motionless, shocked by what this moment of crazy panic had shown him.

He could barely make out her face and blonde hair against the pillow in the near darkness. Needing reassurance, he struck a match and leaned over her bed. She was all right, her small face sweetened by a half smile. Jane often said that Laurie talked to the angels when she was asleep. Shaking the match out, Neal told himself that she was not only talking to them; she was one of them.

No one else was as important to him as Laurie. Not even Jane. Certainly not his own life. He had known that all the time, but it took this moment of terror to make him fully realize it. He crumpled the charred remainder of the match between thumb and forefinger, fighting an impulse to reach down and take her into his arms.

If he woke her, she would sense the fear that was in him, and he would only alarm her, doing no good at all. Jane had done a fine job with Laurie, particularly in regard to fear. The child never fussed about going to bed or being left in the dark. Whatever happened, Laurie must not know about this threat against her.

He should go, he knew. Still, he lingered beside the bed, thinking how much Jane wanted other children, but afer Laurie's birth, Doc Santee had said the chances were slim that she would ever have another. For that reason Laurie meant more to both of them than she would under other circumstances. This was the most important thing in life, he thought, having a part of you perpetuated, gaining in that way the immortality that childless people could not have.

Reluctantly he turned and left the room, leaving her door open so Jane could hear her if she cried out. He felt a weakness in himself he had never felt before, a weakness that stemmed from the fact his most important possession was at stake, but the threat came from an enemy that was unknown except by these mysterious notes, an unknown that was vague and shapeless and terrifying.

He crossed the parlor to the hall, feeling a greater need

than ever to see Joe Rolfe. The sheriff had an ageless quality, a capacity for giving confidence to those around him. Right now that was what Neal needed.

He put on his hat and sheepskin and went outside, leaving the hall lamp lighted. The thought occurred to him that for a moment he would be silhouetted against the light and he would make a perfect target. Still, the possiblity of danger seemed remote until he heard the shot and saw the flash of flame from the far corner of the yard, the bullet slapping into the wall just above his head.

Chapter Nine

Neal dived headlong across the porch and stumbled and fell into the yard as another shot slammed out from that far corner, this one missing by a good five feet. He yanked his gun from holster and fired three times and rolled to a new position. He had nothing to shoot at except the spot where the ambusher had stood. The fellow wouldn't remain there, of course. A moment later he heard retreating footsteps as the man ran up the street.

For a time Neal did not move, aware there might be other men waiting. He heard someone inside the house, then Jane's voice, "Neal! You all right, Neal?"

"I'm all right. Blow out the hall lamp."

The hall went black, and Neal rose and slipped the gun into leather. No one else in the block had been aroused by the shooting. At least he saw no indication of it. Gunfire was not an uncommon thing this time of night, for O'Hara's bar stayed open until midnight or later, and cowboys often expressed themselves by emptying their guns as they rode out of town.

Neal went back to the house and closed the door. The lamp in the parlor was still lighted. He saw Jane standing in the hall wearing nothing but her nightgown; the .38 he had left on the bureau in their bedroom was in her hand.

Laurie was crying. Neal said, "Tell her it was just some crazy cowboys riding home."

Jane nodded and ran up the stairs. A minute or two later

Jane returned. "She's all right. She said she wished those cowboys would go home."

Jane tried to smile, but she couldn't control her lips and they began to tremble. Neal went to her and put his arms around her. "It's all right. I just got a scare. That's all. Funny thing. Just as I went outside, I thought it would be a good time for someone to take a pot shot at me, and then it happened."

Jane had buried her face against his chest. "Do you suppose it was that man Ruggles you had trouble with today?"

"Could have been. Or it might have been Darley or Shelton." Neal started to say Jud Manion or Tuttle or some of the townsmen, but didn't. It would only alarm her more if she knew how they felt, that lynch talk had been going around. Besides, they weren't the kind to bushwhack a man, so he said, "You go on back to bed. That fellow's gone for good."

Jane drew back, a muscle in her cheek twitching with the regularity of a pulse beat. She whispered, "I'm scared, Neal."

"I've got to see Joe," Neal said. "You'll be all right. Keep the doors locked. I'll lock the front one when I leave. Blow out the lamp in the parlor. I don't want any light showing when I go out this time."

He waited with his hand on the knob of the front door until the hall was dark, his hand on the butt of his gun. He had told Jane the bushwhacker wouldn't be back, but he wasn't as sure as he'd sounded. The man who had shot at him might have returned, or there might be another one waiting.

He eased outside, shut the door and locked it. Then he stood motionless for several minutes, listening for sounds that were not natural for this late hour, eyes probing the night for any hint of movement. There was none, just the darkness relieved slightly by the starshine. He couldn't stay here all night, he thought, and left the porch. Walking fast, he went down the path to the street and turned toward the east corner of the block. From there he started climbing the hill to Joe Rolfe's house.

The sheriff lived alone on the crest above the river. This part of the town had never been planned. The houses were scattered haphazardly among the pines and lava outcroppings, and the street, following the lines of least resistance, twisted and squirmed to avoid those same trees and upthrusts of lava.

All of the houses in this part of town were dark, there were no street lamps, and more than once Neal came close to bumping into a clothesline or stumbling over a ledge of lava. He walked more cautiously, taking a good ten minutes to reach Rolfe's house. It seemed to him, with his sense of time completely distorted, that another ten minutes passed before his pounding brought Rolfe's sleepy yell, "I'm a-coming. Leave the damned door on its hinges, will you?"

A moment later Rolfe opened the door, a lamp in one hand. He was barefooted, his pants hastily pulled over his drawers, and held up by one suspender, the other dangling below his waist. He squinted at Neal, hair disheveled, his mind not entirely freed of the cobwebs of sleep.

"Hell, I might of knowed it'd be you," he grumbled. "If there's another man in the county who can get into trouble up to his neck like you, I don't know who it is. Come on in."

As Neal stepped through the door, Rolfe said, "Trouble is you woke me out of the best dream I've had in twenty year. Purty girls swarming all over the place, and me reaching for 'em and never quite getting hold of one of 'em." Suddenly he sensed from the grim expression on Neal's face that something serious had happened. "Let's have it, son. Getting so I rattle on like a buggy that ain't been greased since Noah set the ark down on Mount Ararat."

"Somebody took a couple of shots at me when I left the house a while ago," Neal said.

"The hell." Rolfe sat down and stared at Neal. "I didn't think it would go that far. I sure didn't."

"That's not even a beginning." Neal handed him the note Ruggles had give him, told him what had happened, then gave him the last note that had been shoved under the door. Rolfe read it, shook his head as if he didn't believe it, and began to curse.

"What kind of damn fool proposition is this?" Rolfe shouted. "No sane man would lay a hand on a child . . ." He stopped and gestured as if to thrust those words into oblivion. "I know what you're fixing to say. We ain't dealing with a sane man, and by God, I think you're right."

"That makes it worse," Neal said. "I'm beginning to think Ed Shelly isn't dead like you've been claiming."

Rolfe pulled at his mustache thoughtfully, then he asked, "How old a man was this Ruggles?"

"Thirty-five maybe."

"If Ed Shelly was alive, he'd be just about your age. Not more'n twenty-seven at the most. Shelton and Darley are both older'n that. Besides, Ed was small. You'll remember you thought he was a half-grown kid. Well, he was about nineteen and a boy ain't gonna grow much after he's that old. Darley and Shelton are too tall, and you claim this Ruggles gent is likewise tall."

Neal nodded. "A regular splinter."

"There you are. It ain't none of them three, and the chances of another stranger hanging around and nobody seeing him is mighty slim."

"You heard of Ruggles?"

"Yep. I seen him in O'Hara's bar. Reckon it was him, the way you describe him, but I didn't know he was camped on your range. I figured he was just a drifter riding through."

"What are you going to do?"

"Do! Maybe you can tell me." Rolfe looked at the note that threatened Laurie. "Your girl's safe enough tonight, I reckon. Jane's got a gun?" Neal nodded, and Rolfe went on, "It'll be different tomorrow when she's out playing. If this bastard that calls himself Ed Shelly is half-cracked, there's no way to tell what he'll do."

"Darley wants me out of town on account of the man they've got coming in on the stage from Portland," Neal said. "I've got my doubts that anybody's half-cracked. I think it's all hooked together. They're smart, Joe, sneaky smart."

"Could be the shooting was done to scare you," Rolfe said. "A real good shot, and I figure Shelton is, could lay that first bullet in close, aiming to miss. He was just waiting for you, chances are, knowing that when you got the last note, you'd come after me sooner or later."

"Ruggles," Neal said thoughtfully, the name jogging his memory. "You know, Mrs. Darley knew him. What does that prove?"

"Nothing that I know of," Rolfe said blankly. "What are you getting at?"

"That there's some kind of a tie up between him and Darley and Shelton. Of course we know that, but suppose we can prove it? Prove that one of them hired Ruggles to get that note to me?"

"Sure, it'd look bad," Rolfe conceded, "but I don't know how we can prove anything of the sort."

"Maybe Ruggles came to town after dark," Neal said, "and told Shelton what had happened. He might be bunking with Shelton tonight. He wouldn't go to Darley because Darley and his wife are at Tucker's boarding house, but Shelton sleeps alone in their office."

"You're just grabbing at a handful of straws," Rolfe said, "but I wouldn't mind putting the screws on that bastard. We've been too easy on him and Darley both. Let's go wake him up and listen to him squirm. Wait'll I get my shirt and boots on."

Chapter Ten

Neal walked beside Joe Rolfe down the twisting street toward the business block, the pines giant spears pointing at the dark sky, the lava rock low mounds among the earth-bound shadows. They moved cautiously, but still stumbled over the lava outcroppings that edged sharply into the street. They would have fallen if they had not been walking slowly.

"Should have fetched a lantern," Rolfe muttered when they reached Main Street. "I damn near break my neck every time I come down that street after dark."

Neal said nothing. He had thought about a lantern, but decided against suggesting they bring one. On a night as dark as this a moving lantern would be as noticeable as a bright star in the black sky. Neal had a hunch Shelton expected him to do the very thing he was doing. If Shelton was watching from a window, a lantern would warn him, perhaps show him there were two instead of one.

Now, in the ebb-tide hours of early morning, no light showed along Main Street, not even in O'Hara's bar or the hotel lobby. Neal had the weird impression the town was deserted. It seemed to him that the sharp sound of boot heels on the boards of the walk echoed and re-echoed, the staccato beat inordinately slow to die in the otherwise silent night.

When they reached the foot of the stairs that led to Darley and Shelton's office over the Mercantile, Neal said, "Let me do the talking, Joe."

"Why?" Rolfe demanded.

"If he hears my voice and thinks I'm alone," Neal answered, "he'll tip his hand, but he'll play it close to his chest if he knows you're here."

Rolfe considered this for a moment, then he said, "All right, Neal, we'll play it your way."

Neal climbed the stairs, making no effort to be silent. Rolfe followed two steps behind him. Neal wondered if Shelton was asleep. Or was he sitting up expecting this visit? And did Darley know about the notes, or was it just Shelton's idea? Or was it either one of them? A lot of questions and no answers, but maybe they'd have some soon.

Standing beside the door, he pounded on it. One short moment of silence, then gunfire broke out from inside the company office, bullets slicing through the door and slapping into the wall across the hall. No warning, no demand for the visitor to identify himself. Nothing but the sudden burst of gunfire.

If Neal had been standing directly in front of the door, he'd have been hit. He drew his gun and fired, checking himself after the third shot as he realized he wasn't accomplishing anything. Shelton would not be foolish enough to remain in an exposed position on the other side of the door.

Then, after the last echo of the shots had faded, Neal was aware that Rolfe was not standing on the stairs behind him. He backed up, calling, "Joe?"

"Here," Rolfe said. "I got tagged."

The sheriff was halfway down the stairs when Neal reached him. Neal asked. "Where'd you get it?"

"In the arm. Just took off a hunk of hide."

"We'll get Doc up."

"No such thing . . ."

"Come on, come on," Neal said impatiently.

He was thoroughly angry, now that he'd had time to think about it. Not a word had been spoken. Whoever was in the office—and it must be Shelton—had cut loose the instant he'd heard Neal's knock.

By the time Neal and Rolfe reached the street, lights had bloomed in the hotel lobby, Doc Santee's office, and O'Hara's bar. Before they reached the doctor's office, doors were flung open and men ran into the street, some in their underclothes, others hastily pulling on their pants, fingers fumbling with buttons.

Someone yelled, "What happened?" And another man, "Who got shot?"

The last was O'Hara's voice. Neal called, "Shelton tried to shoot me and the sheriff." They were in front of Santee's office then. The doctor stood in the doorway, his bulky body almost filling it, with the lamp behind him throwing a long shadow across the boardwalk. Neal said, "Joe's hit, Doc."

"Fetch him in," Santee said, and swung around, content to ask questions later.

But the others had to know. O'Hara crowded into the office, Harvey Quinn shoving him forward. Olly Earl was a step behind them. O'Hara asked, "What happened, Clark?"

Santee had taken Rolfe into his back room. Neal did not follow, but stood looking at the men who formed a solid wedge in the doorway. Others had joined them. Six altogether. Now seven. No, eight as the Sorrenson kid who worked nights in the livery stable appeared in the rear.

Neal saw no trace of friendliness in their faces, only hostility. That was exactly what he expected. He remembered what Darley had said that afternoon: "People don't like you. Before this is over, they'll hang you." It would take very little, he thought, to turn these eight men into a lynch mob. Henry Abel had been right.

Damn it, you gonna answer me or not?" O'Hara shouted. "I asked you what happened."

"I went to Darley and Shelton's office with Joe Rolfe," Neal said. "We wanted to ask him some questions, so I knocked on the door. Whoever was inside didn't say a word. Just started shooting. Must have been Shelton. Joe got nicked."

Still they stood there, staring at him truculently as if not believing he was telling it straight. Finally Quinn asked, "Why would he do that?"

"Ask him."

"We will," O'Hara said, and wheeling, motioned the others out of the doorway.

They were gone, O'Hara leading, the sound of their passage reminding Neal of the sullen departure of a storm. He stood in the doorway watching them, thinking how quickly the town had come to life. Only a few minutes before he'd had the impression it was deserted. Now it seethed with the strongest of human emotions: fear and greed and hate, violent emotions that could easily lead to death.

These men might be back with a rope for him. Was that what Shelton and Darley wanted? There was no way to know. How could you fathom a human mind that was as near the animal level as Shelton's? Or Darley's? Or both?

Turning, he walked across Santee's outer office to the back room, a little sick with fear. He would have no hesitation whatever if he had to shoot and kill Darley or Shelton. But he could not kill O'Hara or Olly Earl or the Sorrenson kid. Still, he would not be dragged out into the street with a rope on his neck.

Santee was putting a bandage on Rolfe's arm. He glanced up when Neal came in. He was a big, bald man with huge hands that were miraculously nimble for their size, and like most doctors who served a vast area with a thin population, he was always tired and sleepy, for he spent more hours in the saddle than he did in bed.

"Joe'll have a sore arm for a while," Santee said. "He's staying here for the night. I'll give him something to make him sleep."

"The hell you will," Rolfe said angrily. "I'm going up there and drag Shelton out by his ear."

"You'll have a riot on your hands if you do," Neal said. "The bunch that was here went to see him. You know what he'll tell them."

"No I don't. Nothing he can say. Hell, he started throwing lead before . . ."

"You'll wait till morning. They'll be cooled off by then." Santee picked up a bottle from a shelf, poured a drink, and handed it to Rolfe. "I'll tell you what he'll say if you don't know. He didn't hear your voice before you knocked on the door. That right, Joe?"

"Yeah, but—"

"That's it in a nutshell. Shelton will claim he fired because he didn't know who was in the hall, but he had to protect the company money that was in the safe. He figured nobody would be pounding on the door this time of night unless it was a holdup."

"That's the size of it," Neal said. "Doc, did Joe tell you about this Ruggles gent? And the notes I've been getting?"

"He told me," Santee said, "and I don't have any idea what it means, either, if that's what you want to know. But it doesn't seem reasonable for a man like Ruggles to be hanging around for the fun of it. And I don't think the notes are just a bluff."

"I'm scared," Neal said. "I'm so damned scared I don't know up from down. If Laurie's really in danger . . ."

"Go home, Neal." Santee laid a hand on his shoulder. "Stay with Laurie. Keep her in the house."

"All right." Neal started to turn, then stopped. "Doc, would anybody but a crazy man think of using a child to get revenge?"

"You're thinking Ed Shelly is really around here?"

"It's possible."

"I don't think so," Santee said thoughtfully. "I'm convinced that Darley and Shelton will play every dirty, stinking trick they can to get you out of the country."

"But we don't know how far they'll go," Neal said, "so my question hasn't been answered. Would anyone but a crazy man hurt a child? It doesn't make any difference whether he's getting revenge or filling his pockets. A sane man just wouldn't use a child."

Santee reached for his pipe and filled it, scowling as he tamped the tobacco into the bowl. "Neal, I'm a doctor. I'm good at jobs like this." He nodded at Rolfe. "Or helping babies into the world." He tapped his forehead. "When it comes to saying whether a man is sane or crazy, well, I just don't know. All I know is that there's times when a crazy man acts sane, and vice versa."

"But if a man lives with his hate long enough—"

"He can go crazy," Santee interrupted. "I'll agree to that, but our trouble is we're shooting in the dark. We don't know our man. If he is crazy, then Laurie's really in danger. All you can do is be damned sure she's never left alone."

"If you leave the house in the morning," Rolfe said, "be sure Jane keeps Laurie inside."

"She will," Neal said and, turning, trudged wearily out of the office and along the boardwalk toward his home.

Neal walked through the pines, thinking that imaginary trouble can become real trouble within a matter of seconds. For eight years he had been plagued by his fear of Ed Shelly, his certainty the man would someday return. If he had not stepped into the street that day and shot Buck and Luke Shelly . . . But it was foolish to think about the might-have-beens. Not knowing even now whether Laurie and Jane were in real trouble or not, the only thing he could do was to take every precaution that was possible.

When he reached his house, he crossed the yard rapidly, his hand on gun butt, realizing that if Ruggles was the one who had shot at him before, the man might have returned. He unlocked the front door, opened it, and slipped inside. He closed and locked it, relieved. He leaned against the wall, breathing hard, and asking himself it he was being jumpy over nothing. He was a little ashamed, then thought he shouldn't be. The notes he'd received might be only bluffs, but the bullets that had been fired at him tonight were real indeed.

He lighted the lamp on the table in the parlor and went upstairs. He waited a moment outside his bedroom door, listening to Jane's even breathing, then went on to Laurie's room. The bracket lamp in the hall was lighted. He glanced in, saw that she was all right, and went back downstairs.

Drawing a chair in front of the fireplace, he threw on more wood, and then sat down to wait, his gun across his lap.

Chapter Eleven

Jane slept later than usual this morning. Ordinarily Neal got up half an hour before she did. It was his habit to build the fire, set the coffee pot on the front of the stove, then go to the woodshed and split the day's supply of wood. Jane would remain in bed, torn between the knowledge that she should get up and start breakfast, and the desire to linger in the comfortable warmth of the bed, enjoying a luxury she had never been able to afford when she and Neal had lived on the Circle C.

This morning she woke suddenly, the sharp April sunlight falling across her face from the east window. She had not slept well during the night, waking often and reaching to the other side of the bed to see if Neal was there. But he hadn't come. He wasn't there now, and suddenly she was afraid. Something must have happened to him or he would have come to bed hours ago.

The fear passed. If Neal had been hurt, she would have heard. Joe Rolfe or Doc Santee would have come to the house before this. Besides, she had faith in Neal's ability to handle any situation. He had always seemed indestructible to her. He still did, even though she realized he was more worried than he had ever been before in his life. He wasn't worried about himself, she knew. Being shot at last night had not bothered him as much as the warning notes that threatened her and Laurie.

Her thoughts went back to the early years of their marriage when Neal's father dominated everything they did. Sam Clark was the only man she had ever hated and she had been relieved when he died. Neal must have felt the same way, and instantly she knew she was wrong. In spite of all the things that were wrong with Sam Clark, Neal had never hated him.

She thought how helpless she had been on the ranch, just living and working and never having the slightest opportunity to do what she wanted to with the house. She had been tested as few wives were ever tested. Even moving to town had not been a free choice on Neal's part.

She got up and dressed, thinking that this trouble would be settled soon, today or maybe tomorrow. One good thing would come out of it, she was sure. Sam Clark's hold upon Neal would be shattered. They would go back to the Circle C, and Neal would be happier. She would be, too. She had never fitted socially in town, not with women like Mrs. Quinn and Mrs. Earl and the rest.

Pinning up her hair in front of the mirror, she wondered why Neal, in many ways a tough and unyielding man, had yielded to his father as much as he had. Habit, maybe. On occasion he had stood up to his father, but on the big things, like taking the bank, he had submitted. Neal had a right to live his own life, she told herself defiantly. If it meant selling the bank, they'd do it.

She went down the stairs, determined to push Neal into the decision she knew he wanted to make. When she reached the parlor she forgot all about it. Neal was dozing in a rocking chair, his pistol on his lap.

For a moment Jane stood motionless, vaguely alarmed. Neal should have been upstairs in bed. She walked across the room and shook him awake. He grunted and rubbed his eyes, then rose, and slipped the gun into his holster. He left the parlor and crossing the dining room to the kitchen, closed the door after Jane who had followed him.

He grinned ruefully. "I sure turned out to be a good guard, going to sleep like that. I'd get shot if I was in the army."

She gripped his arms. "Neal, what happened? You've been up all night, sitting there with that gun on your lap. . . ."

"Wait'll I build a fire," he said. "I need some coffee."

She waited beside the stove until he had the fire going, the pine snapping with staccato cracks, then she set the coffeepot on the stove, and dropped into the chair Neal had placed there for her. He pulled up another chair and sat down, his angular face hard set, the muscles at the hinges of his jaws bulging like half marbles.

"What happened after you left the house last night?" Jane asked.

He hesitated, then told her about getting Joe Rolfe out of bed and going to Shelton's office and being shot at. "We still don't know whether those notes are bluffs, or whether Ed Shelly is alive and hiding around here."

"It's a trick," Jane said. "It's got to be. Joe has always told you Ed Shelley was dead."

"Sure, he's told me." Neal got up and walked to the window. "It's this thing about Laurie, Jane. If anything happens to her . . ."

"It won't," Jane said. "We won't let it." She stared at his

back, feeling the tension that was almost a physical sickness in him. "Neal, did you think they might be sending you those notes to keep you in the house? Darley and Shelton, I mean."

He turned sharply to face her. "And while I'm staying here watching out for Laurie, they get out of town with the money. No, I hadn't thought of it." He frowned, and added thoughtfully, "And this is the day they have a man coming from Portland, a fat goose they aim to pick. It would work just as well for them if I stayed in the house as if I got out of town."

He would be safer here, she thought, but he would never forgive himself if he stayed at home, falling into the trap they were setting. No, he couldn't stay, built the way he was. She said, "You go on to the bank. I'll take care of Laurie. I promise."

He looked at her doubtfully. "I don't know. This is Joe Rolfe's business. . . ."

"You've made it yours, darling. You can't hand it to Joe now." She rose, and going to him, put her hands on his shoulders. "Ed Shelly's been on your mind eight years, hasn't he?"

"How did you know?"

"You've talked in your sleep," she said. "You were dreaming about it, I guess. Sometimes it seemed as if you were having nightmares."

"I've had nightmares, all right," he said. "It was always the same whether it was you or Laurie or me who was being hurt. Ed Shelly had come back to Cascade City."

He whirled away from her, and going to the stove, poured himself a cup of coffee. "If Ed Shelly wanted to get square by worrying the hell out of me," he said, "he's getting it. Maybe I've worried so much about it I brought it to pass." He tried to grin at her over the top of the coffee cup. "Fool notion, isn't it? I think I knew all the time I'd have to face something like this, but it's worse because of Laurie."

"Neal, maybe we're excited over nothing. They won't hurt Laurie if it is just a bluff. And even if Ed Shelly is hiding around town or out in the timber, he wouldn't take it out on Laurie. No man would."

"You're wrong," he said. "I've seen too many men do cruel things that were unreasonable. When I was a boy a man who lived north of us beat his wife to death. And I knew a kid who skinned a cat while the cat was alive." He threw out his hands. "Don't ask me why men do things like that. Just something in them that makes them enjoy watching another person or an animal suffer."

"We'll be careful, Neal," she said. "That's all we can do, I'll get breakfast. . . ."

"No, this coffee's all I want." He turned toward the dining room door, then paused as he said, "I've got to see Laurie before I go."

Jane nodded, understanding, and followed him across the dining room and up the stairs to Laurie's room. She was awake, and when she saw Neal, she jumped out of bed and ran to him, squealing, "I had the nicest dream, Daddy. I thought you were bringing a pony from the ranch for me to ride."

"I will, honey. I promise."

He caught her in his arms and held her high while she kicked and squealed, then he hugged her and her arms came around his neck and squeezed him hard. "Dress me, Daddy," she said.

Jane stood in the doorway watching while Neal sat down on the edge of the bed and dressed her, his big fingers awkward with the little buttons on her dress. There was a lump in Jane's throat so big that it made her throat ache. This might be the last time Neal would ever dress Laurie. No, it couldn't be. She found herself thinking a prayer. "Don't let it happen, God. Don't let any harm come to either one of them."

She turned her back to them and wiped her eyes. She heard Neal say, "I'll let Mamma put your shoes and stockings on. I've got to go to the bank. Laurie, your dream is going to come true. Not today, maybe, but real soon."

Jane turned around. She said, "Isn't that fine, Laurie?"

Laurie was staring at Neal, her eyes wide. "That little bay with the white stockings?"

"That's the one," Neal said.

He picked her up and kissed her, then he whirled away and walked out of the room. Jane said, "Let's get your shoes and stockings on. Then we'll go down and get breakfast."

"What's the matter with Daddy's eyes?" Laurie asked. "He was blinking all the time?"

"I guess he had something in his eyes, honey. I've got a speck in mine, too."

Jane finished buttoning the child's shoes and set her on the floor. Laurie asked, "Can I go now?"

"Yes, you can go, but you'll have to stay in the house today."

"Why?"

"It isn't very warm outside and it's awfully windy. I don't want you to get a cold. Remember now."

"I'll remember," Laurie promised.

Jane left the room, walking fast and keeping her back to Laurie so the child wouldn't see the tears that were in her eyes again. There was so much that was good in their lives, she thought, Neal's and hers and Laurie's. Why did it all have to be threatened now? Would they have to live with Ed Shelly's ghost the rest of their lives?

Chapter Twelve

Neal stepped out of the house into the morning sunlight that still held little warmth. He looked around, half expecting to see Shelton or Darley, or Ruggles, but no one was in sight. He glanced at the threshold. No note this time. He closed the door and crossing the yard, walked rapidly up the street toward the business block. Everything would come into focus today, he thought. It had to. He'd go crazy with the waiting if it didn't.

When he reached Main Street, he saw no one except the hardware man, Olly Earl, who passed without speaking. The irony of it struck him. He had been in Earl's store the day he'd shot the Shelly gang to pieces, but it didn't occur to the storekeeper that what was happening now might have its roots in that holdup eight years ago.

Neal stepped into the Mercantile, and going to the post office that was located in a rear corner, opened his box. He took out a handful of mail: two papers, a bill, a catalogue, and one letter. He stared at the address. NEAL CLARK, CASCADE CITY, OREGON, written with a blunt pencil just as all the warning notes had been. He glanced at the postmark. The letter had been mailed here late yesterday.

"Harvey," Neal shouted. "Harvey, where the hell are you?"

Quinn poked his head up from the counter on the other side of the room. "What's biting you?"

Neal crossed to the other side of the room and held out the envelope. "Got any idea when this was mailed, Harvey?"

Quinn was painting some empty shelves. Carefully he squeezed the brush against one side of the can and stood up. "How do you expect me to know when a letter's mailed?"

"I thought you might have noticed."

"Well I didn't. Chances are it was mailed late yesterday afternoon. But hell, you can't expect me to stand around and see who mails every letter. . . ."

"All right, Harvey, all right. Maybe you can remember whether Tuck Shelton or Ben Darley came in yesterday."

"Yeah. Shelton did. I sold him a box of .45 shells."

"Did he mail anything?"

"I don't know, damn it." Quinn ran a hand through his hair. "What are you up to?"

"I've had some notes threatening my family. This looks like another one. I've got a hunch it's Shelton. Or maybe Darley."

"You're working damned hard to turn us against them," Quinn said. "I don't believe it. And I'll tell you something else. You keep fighting 'em like you have been, and you'll wind up on the end of a rope."

Here it was again. For a moment Neal stood staring at Quinn. He was a poor stick in many ways, the last man in town capable of intimidating anyone who had a spoonful of guts in his body. Middle-aged, thin and crotchety, he was inclined to be overcautious with his credit, but he was one of Neal's leading critics because the bank was careful with its credit.

There were several things Neal wanted to tell Quinn, but what was the use? Yesterday he had tangled with Alec Tuttle, and no good had come of that. No good would come from quarreling with Quinn, either, so he left the store and angled across the street to the bank.

As usual, Henry Abel was at his desk working on a ledger. Neal wondered how many hours he spent each day in his swivel chair, bent forward, pen in his hand, the green eye shade on his forehead. But Abel was happy. Maybe he'd be happier yet if the bank were his sole responsibility.

"Good morning, Henry," Neal said.

"Good morning." Abel looked up, smiled and went on working.

Neal walked past the cashier to his office and closed the door. He tossed the mail on his desk, then picked up the letter and tore it open. He was not suprised when he read, "I'll get your wife as well as your kid. It's too late now to save their lives. You should have thought of that eight years ago. Ed Shelly."

Neal threw it down and paced the length of the room and back. A feeling of unreality gripped him, as if this were a part of that old horrible nightmare he'd had so many times. Funny, he thought, how it struck him. It seemed to him he was a spectator, watching a series of plays, so many of them that the sharp edge of his feelings had been blunted.

He sat down at his desk, staring at the papers Abel had left here for him. He had letters to write, but he wouldn't do anything today. Maybe he never would again. Maybe he'd just go off and let Abel handle all of it. He was still sitting there when he heard a knock on the door and called, "Come in."

Joe Rolfe stepped into the office. "How are you, Neal?" the old man asked, his wrinkled face shadowed by concern.

"You ought to know." Neal handed him the note. "Another one in the mail this morning. They're fools, Joe. You can make a man go crazy, but that's as far as you can make him go. What are they trying to do?"

Rolfe looked at the note and threw it on the desk. "You ain't quite crazy yet, Neal, and you ain't dead. They'll settle for either one. If you blow up when the stage gets in, there'll be a mob after you with a rope. That's why I'm here. You've got to stay in the bank or go home."

"I won't do either," Neal said.

Rolfe sighed. "You're making a mistake, son. Jane and Laurie are more important to you than anything that can happen when the stage gets in."

Neal shook his head. "Jane's home. She can handle a gun, and she knows what's been going on. Now suppose you tell me what's so important about the stage getting in."

"Darley's spread the word about this fellow Stacey. If he invests ten thousand dollars in the deal, Darley says they'll start work in the morning. Even if you get a report from your survey crew, it'll be too late if Stacey is the sucker Darley thinks he is."

"Stacey may be a ringer," Neal said. "Playing Darley's game. Thought of that?"

"Sure I've thought of it," Rolfe said, "but it don't make sense. They ain't got anything to gain by playing it that way because they've already milked this country for all it's worth unless you make the loans they want. What I'm saying is that if you jump in and tell Stacey what you think of the project, they'll lynch you. Tuttle and O'Hara and that bunch are like a wolf pack with Darley and Shelton running in the lead. This time I won't be able to stop 'em."

Neal got up and walked to the window. No one was in sight, but there was a long line of horses tied in front of O'Hara's bar. The farmers and townsmen were inside, drinking and listening to Darley. Rolfe was right. Anything could happen if Neal met the stage and tried to talk to Stacey. Rolfe was right, too, in saying the crowd would not believe the report of Neal's surveying crew if he had it. Too late, he thought bitterly, too late to do any good. Any good at all.

But he couldn't go home, and he couldn't just sit here in

the bank when the stage wheeled in. Jane had said he had some of the flint that had been in his father. Maybe he had too much. Maybe he was just mule-headed, but he had to stay here and try, and he had to depend on Jane to look after herself and Laurie. She could, he thought. She had the revolver and she'd keep the doors locked.

"I'm going to be on the street when the stage gets in," Neal said. "It's the only thing I can do and you know it."

Rolfe spread his hands. "Yeah, I reckon, seeing as you're Sam Clark's boy. There's another thing. This fellow Ruggles is in O'Hara's bar, but he ain't drinking much. He's talking about getting you."

"I sure won't stay off the street on his account." Neal wheeled from the window to face Rolfe. "Have you found out what the hookup is between him and Darley and Shelton? I told you that when Mrs. Darley saw him yesterday, she got on her horse and took out of there like she had a bee under her tail."

"I don't know," Rolfe said. "I was in Shelton's office this morning. I gave him hell for shooting through the door, and he said just what Doc said he'd say, that he had to protect the money in their safe and he didn't know who was in the hall. I showed him them notes, but he didn't bat an eye. Claimed he'd never seen 'em. I mentioned Ruggles and he said he'd never heard of him."

"You didn't expect him to admit anything, did you?"

"No," Rolfe conceded, "but I figured I might be able to tell something from his face. Most men give themselves away when you get 'em in a tight corner, but not Shelton. You know, Neal, I have never seen that man show feeling of any kind since he came to town. Now I'm thinking he is about half-cracked."

As Rolfe turned toward the door, Neal said, "It would take that kind of man to threaten a child."

"It sure would. Sometimes he acts like he's all frozen up inside." Rolfe opened the door and stood there, his hand on the knob, eyes pinned on Neal's face. "You won't change your mind?"

"No."

Rolfe sighed. "Well, I'll be on the street. So will Doc Santee. Maybe you'd better get Abel out there, too."

Neal shook his head. "Not Henry, Joe. He stopped a bullet once. I won't ask him to again."

"Yeah, reckon that's right. Well, you're a brave man, Neal, or a damn fool. I ain't sure which."

Rolfe closed the door. Neal looked at his watch. Almost an hour before the stage got in if it was on time. He lifted his gun from the holster and checked it carefully, wondering how fast Ruggles was. If he was Shelton's man, he must be good or Shelton wouldn't have hired him. This was probably Shelton's plan, to have Ruggles jump him and kill him before he had a chance to talk to Stacey.

Suddenly Neal was aware of voices in the bank, of Henry Abel saying, "Wait a minute. I'll see if he's busy." And a woman screaming at him, "I don't care how busy he is. I've got to see him."

The door flew open and Mrs. Darley rushed into the office. Henry Abel was ten feet behind her, red in the face with anger. Abel shouted, "I told her to wait. . . ."

But Mrs. Darley was in no mood to wait for anybody. She took hold of the lapels of Neal's coat and twisted them in her hands, her upturned face very close to Neal's. He saw terror in her eyes, real terror. Her face was pale, her lips quivering. Suddenly he discovered she no longer held any appeal for him. She was just a frightened woman, a stranger, running to him for help.

"Neal, you've got to leave town. You've got to take me with you." Releasing her hold on his coat, she put her arms around his neck and tried to bring his lips down to hers, but she didn't succeed. She cried out. "What's the mater, darling?"

Behind her Henry Abel stood in the doorway, thoroughly shocked by this display.

Chapter Thirteen

For a horrible moment Neal looked past Fay Darley at Abel, afraid that Abel would tell his wife, and knowing what she would do with this if she heard. Then he jerked Mrs. Darley's arms away from his neck and roughly pushed her away.

Mrs. Darley whirled to face Abel, screaming at him, "This isn't any of your business." She gave him a hard push, slammed the door, and turned back to Neal.

"You'd better leave," Neal said. "If you're trying to break up my home or fix it so I can't live in this country, you're going to get fooled. I happen to be in love with my wife."

"I don't care anything about your old home or your wife,"

she cried, "and you won't live anywhere if you don't get out of here. Can't you understand? I'm trying to save your life."

This was more of the same, he thought, anything to get him out of town. He said, "I never asked you for help and I never will." He motioned toward the door. "Now get along."

"I won't go. I'm in trouble and so are you. Ruggles was brought here by Shelton and Darley. He was hiding in the brush yesterday and he heard everything we said. He told Darley all about it. Darley was so mad I thought he was going to kill me this morning. Maybe he will yet. I'm scared, Neal. I was never so scared in my life."

Neal found it hard not to believe her. She showed her fear in her voice and her face. Either it was real or she was the greatest actress in the world. He asked, "You mean Darley's jealous?"

"No, no." She gestured impatiently. "He didn't want you to know Stacey was coming this morning. Or at least that ten thousand dollars was at stake. He's afraid you'll keep Stacey from investing in the project."

Half truth and helf half lie, he thought. Just enough truth to sound good. He said, "I don't believe you. It doesn't make sense that Ben Darley's wife would come here and talk to me like this unless he had his reasons for sending you."

"You fool," she said in exasperation. "What does it take to make you understand? They're afraid of what you'll do and say, so they're going to kill you. I don't know how. Maybe a lynch mob. Or Ruggles may force you into a fight. I tell you I don't know what they'll do, but I do know they aim to kill you."

"I'll take care of myself," Neal said.

"The hell you can," she flared. "Not against them. You're stubborn and you're stupid. They're playing for ten thousand dollars. They won't let you or me or anyone else keep them from getting it. When they do get it, they'll take it and all the rest of the money that's in the safe, and run."

He looked at her flushed face, almost compelled to believe she was telling the truth. But even if she was, he thought, she was still playing Darley's game. Maybe they did intend to kill him, but on the other hand, it would be far cheaper and safer to get him to leave than to kill him.

"Go back to Darley and tell him it didn't work," Neal said.

"You crazy damned fool." Her hands knotted at her sides. "You can't get it through your head that you're up against killers. Murderers. Shelton hates you. He wants to see you dead. Darley's just greedy. He's not a killer like Shelton and Ruggles, but he could be and he would be for ten thousand dollars. Besides that, there's fifty thousand in the safe over there in the office. They planned this for months before they came here. Do you think for a minute they'd let your life or mine stand in their way of getting out of here with that money?"

"I may be stubborn and stupid," he said, "but I can't quit and run. Maybe you are in trouble because you talked too much to me, but you brought it on yourself. I can't help you." He walked to the door and put a hand on the knob. "Good day, Mrs. Darley."

"Wait, Neal," she cried. "Don't open the door yet. There's another thing I haven't told you. I didn't want to because I wanted you to think well of me, but if it will make you believe I'm trying to save your life, I'll tell you. I'm not Ben Darley's wife. He hired me to come here and pretend to be his wife."

Neal's hand dropped from the door knob. "Why?"

"I'm not much good," she said miserably. "I'd do almost anything for money and I guess I have. I've been around men like Darley and Shelton all my life. You're different, Neal. I wasn't lying to you when I said I'd had my dreams about you. I wanted a decent man, and you are, so decent that you'd throw your life away because of something you believe to be your duty." She walked to him and gripped his arms. "I'd take you on any terms. I'd do anything you wanted me to do. Just go away with me. Now. Before it's too late."

"You didn't answer my question. Why did Darley hire you to be his wife?"

"He wanted a wife to help him appear respectable. He's worked these swindles in little communities like this before. He knows how these people think and feel. He said he wanted an attractive woman who could work in his office, but who would go with him to church, too, and to people's homes when he was invited. People like Olly Earl and Harvey Quinn. So I took his money and came here and moved into the boarding house with him. I've slept with him and acted like the loving wife and all the time I've hated him. I didn't think I could ever hate anybody like I have him. He's no good, and Shelton's worse."

He saw misery in her face, and regret and shame, and he knew beyond any doubt that she was telling the truth, but the truth didn't change anything as far as he was concerned.

"I'm sorry," he said gently, "but even if I wanted to go with you, I couldn't. If they kill me, I'll be killed, but I can't run."

Tears were in her eyes when she said, "I guess I knew all the time that's what you'd say. Well, I've known one decent man in my lifetime."

She stood on tiptoes and kissed him, then he stepped away from the door. She opened it and walked out, heels striking sharply against the floor. Neal watched her until she stepped into the street, then she disappeared in the direction of Darley and Shelton's office.

She could have told the truth, he thought, and still be doing exactly what Darley wanted her to do. It seemed to him that every move Darley and Shelton had made lately was prompted by the frantic desire to get him out of town before Stacey arrived.

Neal felt Abel's eyes on him. He turned to face the cashier. He said, "Henry, I may not live very long. If they get me, I expect you to stay with the bank."

"Of course I'll stay with the bank." Abel glanced at the street door, then brought his gaze back to Neal's face. His eyes were blinking constantly, the first indication that Neal had had of the tension that had seized the little man. He said, "Neal, don't go out there."

"I don't have much choice," Neal said.

"Yes, you do," Abel said. "If they kill you, they'll come after me. They'll force me to make the loans we've been refusing." He looked at the floor, licking his dry lips. "Neal, I suppose I'm a coward, but I almost died once right here in this bank. I don't want to go through it again."

Neal could understand that. He told Abel about the notes he'd been receiving, then he said, "Maybe they don't have anything to do with Ed Shelly. If they don't, then Darley and Shelton must be the men who are responsible for me getting them. I've got to find out. Maybe I'll find out today." He nodded at the street door. "Out there."

Abel took a white handkerchief out of his pocket and wiped his face. He was afraid, almost panicky. Funny how people fooled you, Neal thought. He had always considered Henry Abel a machine, born with a pen in his hand and the green eye shade on his forehead, a machine lacking the passions and fears that ordinary people had. With one exception. He was afraid of his wife.

"Maybe I won't throw my life away, Henry," Neal said, "but whether I do or not, don't tell your wife or anyone what you saw, or what you're thinking about me and Fay Darley. In the first place, you'd be wrong. In the second place, you'd hurt Jane. And in the third place, you'd be doing exactly what they want you to do because they've been here long enough to know that your wife is the damndest gossip in the county."

"I won't tell her. I won't tell her anything."

Neal returned to his office, having no confidence Abel

could keep his word. But he had tried. It seemed to him that was all he was doing lately, just trying. He closed the door and stood at the window, staring at the crowd that was gathering on the other side of the street.

Good men, individually. He recognized most of them even at this distance. O'Hara, Sailor, Tuttle, Olly Earl, Harvey Quinn: men who had done business with Sam Clark for years. But Darley and Shelton were there, too, and they were the yeast that was making this human dough bubble.

Liquor, talk, greed, a sense of persecution slyly worked upon until it had become a savage feeling of being wronged: these were changing men from individuals into a mob. It would take only one act to bring it to fulfillment. The moment he tried to keep Stacey from investing in the irrigation project, they would be upon him, but that was the thing he must do.

Suppose he didn't say anything to Stacey? Darley and Shelton would get his ten thousand and they would probably leave the country within a matter of hours, taking the money that had been given to them by these very men who were standing in front of O'Hara's bar. Fay Darley had said that, which was exactly what Joe Rolfe had said all along they would do. For a moment he thought of asking Fay to tell publicly what she had told him, then decided against it. Even if she did, she wouldn't be believed.

The trouble was, as Joe Rolfe had said, he could do nothing until a crime had been committed. By the time this was known to be a crime, Darley and Shelton might be out of reach. If they succeeded, the county would be hurt, badly hurt, and the fine dreams Sam Clark had had would be set back a generation.

No, he couldn't let it happen. Even if he could get Stacey to postpone his decision until Neal had the report of the surveying crew, he would accomplish something. It was a matter of time. Sooner or later men like Darley and Shelton would be known for what they were.

He looked at his watch. Almost time for the stage. He checked his gun again. He thought of Laurie and Jane, of the ranch and the bank. If he died today, was Henry Abel man enough to do the job that would fall upon him? There was no way to know, but Neal thought he was.

Neal left the bank, his gun riding easily in his holster. He saw Doc Santee standing alone on the bank side of the street, and turned toward him. Neal had never seen the doctor wear a gun before, but he was wearing one today.

Santee grinned at him. "Almost time for the reception."

"I figured it was," Neal said.

Joe Rolfe was not in sight. Across the street the crowd was milling around in front of O'Hara's bar, impatient now. Shagnasty Bob, the driver, took pride in being on time. He was seldom more than a minute or two late in good weather, but he wasn't in sight yet.

Rolfe appeared, leaving the crowd to stride across the street to where Neal and Santee stood. Santee said, "There's fifty of them, looks like, and three of us. You figure it's worth dying for, Joe?"

"Nobody's gonna die," Rolfe said. "Neal, go take that gun off."

"Are you crazy?" Santee demanded. "Trying to make a sitting duck out of him?"

"No, you know damned well I ain't," the old man snapped. "I've been talking to Darley. He says he don't have no objection if Stacey talks to Neal. But it's got to be inside the bank. If Neal jumps Stacey on the street, there'll be hell to pay, the crowd feeling the way it does."

Rolfe looked at Neal, waiting for him to say he'd wait. Santee nodded as if he saw sense in what the sheriff said. "What about it, Neal?" Santee said. "You could wait inside the bank. We'll fetch Stacey."

Neal didn't answer. At that moment Ruggles shoved and elbowed his way through the crowd until he stood alone on the other side of the street, a bitter, vindictive man. He called, "Clark? You hear me, Clark?"

"I ain't gonna stand for this," Rolfe said angrily. "I told that bastard not to make trouble."

Santee caught his arm. "You've lived too long in this country to think you can butt into a deal like this. They've got to have it out, after Ruggles said what he did."

"What did he say?" Neal asked.

"That he saw you and Mrs. Darley in the brush . . ."

Neal stepped off the walk, not waiting for the rest. He called, "I hear you, Ruggles, and I want everybody else to hear. You're a liar, a goddamn liar."

The crowd parted behind Ruggles, leaving him alone as Neal was alone, in the morning sun, sharp and bright on the gray dust of the street.

Chapter Fourteen

Neal had seen men face each other with guns on their hips right here on this very street, never dreaming that someday he would be playing a part in the same grim drama. Cascade City was an island around which the current of civilization had flowed. It would change when the railroad came, but it had not changed yet. Here men still decided their personal differences with guns. Doc Santee understood this. So did Joe Rolfe.

This was not like the time Neal had shot the Shelly gang to pieces. That had been spontaneous, but this was deliberate, and Ruggles let it play out, hoping to break Neal's nerve. Suddenly—and he was surprised by it—Neal discovered he was not afraid. He didn't look around for Shelton or Darley; he kept his attention riveted on Ruggles, his right hand close to gun butt.

There was this moment which seemed to drag on and on. A wind raised a faint haze of dust, and from somewhere behind the Mercantile a dog barked, a sudden, disturbing sound in the silence. In the end it was Ruggles who broke, not Neal. He threw out a curse and went for his gun.

Ruggles was fast, recklessly and unbelievably fast, and that was his undoing. He squeezed off two shots before Neal fired; one bullet kicked up dust in front of Neal and to his right, the other came close enough to his head for him to hear it snap past. Then Neal's gun sounded, powderflame a quick burst of fire, the report hammering into the silence to be thrown back between the false fronts in slowly dying echoes.

Ruggles was knocked back and partly around as his finger jerked off a wild shot that was ten feet over Neal's head. Neal's second bullet put him down; his gun fell from slack fingers, his hat came off his head to topple over so it lay with the crown in the dust.

Joe Rolfe stepped into the street, his gun in his hand. "Don't make no fast moves. Hear me, Shelton?"

"I got nothing to do with this fight, Sheriff," Shelton said indignantly.

Neal ran to the fallen man, Doc Santee a step behind him.

Neal knelt beside Ruggles, asking, "Who hired you to kill me?"

Blood bubbled on Ruggles' lips. He said, "I wasn't supposed to kill you. Just wound you so—you—couldn't—see—Stacey."

"Who hired you?" Neal demanded. "Who paid you?"

"Easy, boy," Santee said. "He's not going to answer any questions." Santee motioned to the men on the walk. "Earl. Tuttle. Give me a hand here. Let's get him off the street before the stage gets here." In a low tone, he said, "Get over there where you were. Watch it now."

Neal walked back to the other side of the street. He punched the two spent shells out of the cylinder and reloaded, then dropped the gun back into the holster. The reaction hit him and he began to tremble; sweat broke out all over him. He leaned against the front of the bank, his eyes closed. He was sick, he wanted to get back inside the bank, but he couldn't. They were watching him from the other side of the street, Darley and Shelton and the rest, hating him and now maybe fearing him a little. Joe Rolfe and Doc Santee had publicly sided him. That, too, might have a quieting effect if there was anything to this lynch talk.

He heard the stage, and someone yelled, "Here she comes."

The coach made the turn at the north end of the street, careening wildly for a moment before it settled down on all four wheels, dust piling up behind it in a stifling gray cloud. That was Shagnasty Bob's way, an old time jehu who used to make the run into Prineville from the Columbia before the railroad had been pushed south to Shaniko. He'd put on this same show as long as he was able to sit there on the high box and bring the stage roaring into Cascade City, or until the railroad came.

Neal wasn't sure which would end Shagnasty's career, old age or the railroad, but it was a good show, a relic out of the past just as the gunfight with Ruggles had been. Time would eventually put an end to both, and Cascade City would be tamed, but right now it was rough and wild and primitive. That was why men's tempers flamed high as they did, why lynch talk could be more than talk, even with Joe Rolfe wearing the star.

Ruggles' death had quieted the crowd for a time, but now the tension broke. Men ran into the street and formed two lines, yelling for Stacey and waving their hats. The stage wheeled between the lines, the silk flowed out over the horses to crack with the sharpness of a pistol shot. One moment the six horses were in motion, the stage rumbling and rattling behind them, then all motion stopped, and the street dust whirled up to almost hide horses and stage.

Shagnasty Bob, bearded and leather-faced with the front of his hat brim rolled up, yelled, "I fetched him, boys. It's up to you now. I done my part."

Darley opened the coach door and extended his hand. "This is a grand day for Cascade City, Mr. Stacey. I'm Ben Darley."

"I'm glad to be here, Mr. Darley," Stacey said as he stepped down. "When I return, if I'm still alive to return, I'm going to Shaniko by oxcart. I'll never trust my life to this wild man again."

Shagnasty Bob bellowed a great laugh and slapped a leg. Dust boiled up from the blow. "I got you here, didn't I, Stacey? What more can you ask from a man?"

Shagnasty Bob had his moment and only one, then he was forgotten. The crowd surrounded Stacey as the stage wheeled away. They all had to shake hands with Stacey, from Shelton and Harvey Quinn and Olly Earl on down to Sorrenson, the livery-stable kid. Then, studying the crowd, Neal suddenly realized that Jud Manion was not here and he wondered about it.

Aside from Manion, Henry Abel was probably the only man in the county who wasn't on hand to greet Stacey. He remained inside the bank. Joe Rolfe and Doc Santee waited with Neal in the fringe of the crowd, letting the others go ahead. Noticing this Neal wondered what was in their minds.

From where he stood, Neal had a chance to study Stacey. The man was middle-aged with gray hair and mustache. He was small, but he moved with birdlike spryness that convinced Neal he was tougher physically than his size indicated. He was no fool, either. Neal was sure of that as he watched the man's animated face. He would listen, Neal thought, if they had a chance to talk.

Suddenly the handshaking stopped, and there was a moment of awkward silence as if nobody knew what the next move should be. Then Santee and Rolfe stepped up and introduced themselves, Santee said something, and Stacey nodded. He said, "Sure, I want to meet your banker. If he wasn't here, I'd look him up."

"Hold on," Tuttle bellowed. "He ain't no man for you to talk to, Mr. Stacey."

And O'Hara, "He ain't for a fact, Mr. Stacey. Let's step into my place and we'll have drinks all around on the house."

The crowd howled its pleasure and started toward O'Hara's bar, but Stacey didn't move with it. Darley and Shelton stood beside him, Darley showing his irritation, but to Neal's surprise, Shelton was affable enough as if this didn't cut any ice with him either way.

Neal moved toward Stacey, his hand extended. "I'm Clark, the banker. I want to talk to you, but I don't think the street's the right place. Why don't we step into the bank—"

"No," Darley interrupted. "Mr. Stacey has had a long, hard ride. He's tired and he needs a drink."

"No hurry," Stacey said. "Is there some reason I shouldn't talk to Clark, Darley?"

"He thinks so," said Neal. He liked the way Stacey shook hands, the way his sharp eyes met Neal's. "You see, I'm opposed to this project. So are the sheriff and the doctor. I want to give our side of this business before you make any commitments."

Most of the men, realizing Stacey was not with them, turned in time to hear what Neal said. With Tuttle in the lead, they charged back. Rolfe stopped Tuttle by stepping in front of him, and Santee drove a shoulder into O'Hara and almost upset him.

Then Shelton, to Neal's surprise, called, "Let him talk, boys. Clark will hang himself if we give him enough rope."

"By God, we'll give him the rope," Tuttle bawled.

The forward motion stopped, the angry voices subsided. Bewildered, Stacey said, "It strikes me there's more to this than mere opposition, Clark. Is it simply that you're taking a banker's natural stand against speculation?"

"It goes deeper than that." Neal nodded at Darley. "Will you come into the bank with us? I understand you told Joe you didn't object to me talking to Stacey?"

Red-faced, Darley said, "Later, Clark. I object strenuously to your talking to him the minute he gets to town."

"All right," Stacey said. "Clark, I'll drop over to the bank as soon as I cut the dust out of my throat."

"No, I'll have my say now," Neal said. "First, I want to assure you that we welcome men with capital. Someday Cascade City will be a big place. It needs your money the same as any undeveloped town needs capital. So does the county. As far as the people are concerned, you will never find better folks, I'm asking you to do just one thing, and I've got to say it before Darley talks to you."

"Not now," Darley said. "Mr. Stacey, it's important that we don't waste any more time than—"

"This is the damnedest thing I ever ran into," Stacey interrupted. "You've been here six months, Darley. You've been writing to me almost that long. What does a few minutes mean right now, one way or the other?"

"It means a lot," Darley said. "I promised the local men

that if you invest the amount we've been discussing by mail, we'll start work in the morning on the ditch. Clark here has done nothing but delay us from the day we came to town, and for no reason."

"I've had plenty of reason," Neal said. "Stacey, right now a survey crew that I hired is checking Darley and Shelton's proposed ditch line. I'll have a report in a day or two. All I want you to do is to wait until I get that report before you make any promises."

"Wait, wait, wait," Darley screamed in a burst of infantile rage. "That's all we've done for weeks, Mr. Stacey. Well, Shelton and I are done waiting. If the people of this community will do nothing but fight progress—"

"Darley, I don't understand this need for haste," Stacey said sharply, "but in any case, I refuse to be stampeded into anything. Who's making your survey, Clark?"

"Commager," Neal said. "From Prineville. Everybody in town knows him. Boys, I've got a proposition. If Commager's report is favorable, the bank will loan every one of you the amount you've been asking for. Don't tell me the company won't need it if Stacey comes in. I never saw an irrigation project in my life that didn't need more capital than the promoters thought when they started."

"It's a trick," Tuttle said sullenly. "You won't do it when the chips are down, Clark."

"Come over to the bank, Tuttle," Neal said. "We'll make out the papers this morning, with the proviso that the money be deposited to your account if and when we get a favorable report from Commager."

"That's fair," Stacey said. "I'm tired, Clark. I'll see you after I get a drink and something to eat."

"How about it, Tuttle?" Neal asked.

"I'll take your word for it," Tuttle muttered, and turned away.

Doc Santee caught up with Stacey. "You're having dinner with me as soon as we get that free drink O'Hara promised."

"It will be a pleasure," Stacey said, and turned his head to call back, "Darley, fetch my valise."

Neal, glancing at Darley's face, saw the black fury that was in the man. Suddenly Darley stooped and picked up the valise and walked away. Neal looked at Shelton, realizing that those strange, opaque eyes had been pinned on him for some time. Shelton, he saw, showed no fury. Not even disappointment. But there was a strange attitude of eagerness about him as if he were waiting impatiently for something to happen.

It doesn't make any difference to him, Neal thought. *The money is all that matters to Darley, but Shelton's got something else on his mind.*

As Neal turned toward the bank, Rolfe caught up with him. "You stopped 'em dead, Neal. You sure did. I didn't know Commager was out there on the job."

"I figured it was a good idea to keep mum about it until I knew what his report was," Neal said, "but when Stacey got here, I had to speak my piece."

"Everybody trusts Commager," Rolfe said. "If his report is what you think it'll be, you drove a nail right into the lid of Darley's coffin. That means they'll move out tonight with the money. If they do, I'll nab 'em."

"Holler if you need me," Neal said, and Rolfe nodded as he turned away.

Now, in this moment of quiet, Neal thought of Laurie, and Jane. Wheeling, he started up the street toward home. They were all right. They had to be. Tuck Shelton and Ben Darley were here where they couldn't harm Laurie or Jane, and Ruggles was dead.

But Neal hadn't been home for several hours. He had to see Laurie and Jane again, had to know they were all right, and suddenly the dam of self-control broke and he began to run.

Chapter Fifteen

When Neal reached his house, he found the front door locked. He searched his pockets, but discovered he had left the key inside. He yanked the bell pull, momentarily irritated until he remembered that Jane was following his order. He jerked the bell pull again, the need to see Jane and Laurie a driving urgency in him.

Jane unlocked the door and opened it. Neal demanded, "Are you and Laurie all right?"

"Of course," Jane answered. "Are you?"

"Sure," he said, trying to match her matter-of-fact tone.

Laurie heard him and ran out of the parlor, screaming, "Daddy, Daddy." He scooped her up into his arms and hugged her so tight she cried, "You're hurting me, Daddy."

"I'm sorry," he said, and put her down.

She ran into the parlor, apparently thinking of something she wanted to do. She was always running, Neal thought, always in a hurry to get some place faster than she could by walking. She was usually excited about something, too, her voice made high by it. If anything happened to her so she couldn't run and couldn't squeal . . . ! He looked at Jane and saw that she was close to crying. The same fear was in his wife's mind, he thought.

He walked into the parlor, ashamed of the emotion that suddenly made him weak. There was no reason to be, he thought. It was just that he had never been one to show his feelings, not even when he'd been a boy. He often wished he weren't the way he was, that he could talk to Jane with the sweetness and tenderness he knew she needed, but it was hard for him. When he did, it was forced, lacking the spontaneity it should have had.

Laurie ran uptsairs for something. Neal got out his handkerchief and blew his nose, his back to Jane. He couldn't remember feeling this way before, a dull ache in his chest and an all-gone emptiness in his belly. Reaction from killing Ruggles, he thought. Or from relief, knowing now that Laurie and Jane were all right.

Well, they were going to stay all right. He wouldn't leave the house until Darley and Shelton were in jail. They were whipped. He was sure of that. They'd make their run tonight and Rolfe would arrest them, and the greedy hard heads like Tuttle and Sailor and O'Hara would find out what Darley and Shelton had intended to do all the time.

"Neal."

He turned. Jane stood just inside the hall doorway. He saw that she had been crying, and he asked, "What's the matter?"

"You don't know?" she asked. "Neal, don't you know?"

She put her arms around him and he held her close. He touched her hair, saying as lightly as he could, "I don't have the foggiest notion. I'm the one who's been worrying."

She was angry then and stepped back, her face showing her resentment. "Don't you give me any credit for feelings? I heard those shots a while ago. I thought that Shelton and Darley were trying to kill you. Or that O'Hara and Quinn and Olly Earl . . ."

"So you've heard that talk. Some of our gossipy neighbors . . ." He stopped. No use to vent his anger on Jane. He moved to her and took her hands. "I'm sorry. I just haven't been thinking very straight lately. But it wasn't anything like that. It was this fellow Ruggles who's been hanging around. Shelton was behind it, I suppose. Anyhow, it didn't work. I got him."

Resentment fled from her face. "You mean he tried to kill you?"

"Yeah, he tried. It was just before the stage got in. I was standing in front of the bank waiting like everybody else, and he comes out of O'Hara's bar and jumps me."

"Where was Joe Rolfe?"

"He was there."

"Couldn't he stop it?"

She should have known better than to ask a question like that. Short-tempered again, he said. "Joe didn't try."

She whirled, her skirt billowing out from her slim ankles. She said, "Oh, you men!" and started toward the kitchen.

"Dinner ready?" he asked.

"No, it isn't," she flung over her shoulder, and disappeared into the dining room.

Neal rolled and lighted a cigarette, realizing he shouldn't be irritated, that he shouldn't have spoken so brusquely to Jane. It was only natural that her nerves should be frayed, just as his were.

He couldn't relax, even now that he was here in his own parlor, knowing that no harm had come to Laurie and Jane. He took a long pull on his cigarette and let the smoke out slowly, then dropped into a rocking chair, his legs stretched in front of him.

Laurie came downstairs and wandered aimlessly into the kitchen. Neal smoked another cigarette, restlessness gathering in him again. He wasn't sure he could stay here all afternoon. Maybe he didn't need to. Darley or Shelton wouldn't try anything during the day. Maybe they hadn't been sending the notes. It might have been Ruggles, and if that was true, the danger to Jane and Laurie was past.

He heard Laurie's shrill voice begging her mother to let her go outside to play, and he heard Jane say in a cranky tone to quit asking. She had to stay inside. This trouble was costing all of them, he thought, and he had been stupid in not realizing that Jane was paying the same price he was.

He tossed his cigarette stub into the fireplace and walked into the kitchen. Laurie was sitting on a chair sulking, her feet kicking the legs. Neal said, "That's not a pretty face you've got today."

Laurie stuck out her tongue at him. Thoroughly exasperated, Jane went into the pantry and came back with a stick. "I haven't had to use this on you for quite a while, young lady, but—"

"Wait." Neal put an arm in front of his wife. "Laurie, you go up to your room and don't come back until you've got a pretty face." He winked at Jane. "Like your mamma's."

Laurie got up and left the kitchen. Not running this time, but trudging as if she were the most put-upon girl in town. Neither Neal nor Jane said anything until she was out of sight and they heard her on the stairs, then Jane said, "A pretty face like mamma's! Now isn't that a great thing to tell your daughter?"

Neal laughed, a sudden breaking of the tension that had kept his nerves tied up for hours. He kissed Jane on the tip of her nose. "It's the prettiest face I ever saw. Now what about dinner?"

She laughed, too, a shaky laugh but still a laugh. "Thank you for the grand compliment. I'll get dinner started right away. I forgot you didn't have any breakfast." She went into the pantry, calling back, "Now I want to know what happened this morning. Everything. I'm getting tired of being treated like I was Laurie's age."

He told her, leaving out Fay Darley's visit and what Ruggles had said in O'Hara's bar. She'd hear someday, but maybe not until this was over. When he was done, she said, "Then we still don't know who sent the notes or shot at you or whether there really is an Ed Shelly."

"No, but it was probably Ruggles who shot at me. Maybe the whole thing was just to make me run, or stay here in the house. Anyhow, Joe will pick them up tonight."

She stood in front of the stove looking at him. "You really think it's over?"

"It will be as soon as Darley and Shelton clean out their safe and leave town."

She shook her head. "I don't think so. We don't know who sent the notes or what the purpose behind them was. We can't draw a good breath until we know the answers to both questions."

He rose, the good feeling of relief gone that had been in him a short time. Jane was right. He walked back into the parlor, remembering how Shelton had acted this morning. A killer, Fay Darley had called him. A half-crazy one, too, if Neal's judgement of the man was correct. No, Jane was right. Nothing would be settled until Shelton and Darley were locked up in jail.

The doorbell startled him. He walked into the hall, drawing his gun before he opened the door. He was surprised to see Henry Abel standing there because it was two hours until closing time, and Abel wasn't a man to go off and leave the bank.

"Come in, Henry," Neal said. "I didn't expect—"

"No, of course you wouldn't." Abel slipped in quickly as if afraid to remain outside. "I locked the bank up and put a sign outside that it would be closed until morning. Have you got a gun? Another one, I mean?"

Puzzled, Neal said, "You're not much of a hand with a gun . . ."

"No, but I can try. I can't stay in the bank. Ed Shelly saw his father and brother shot in front of the bank, and if he really is around here somewhere, he'll try again. I've got a hunch." He swallowed. "Now don't go off half-cocked. I'm saving you and me both a lot of trouble by locking the bank up in case O'Hara and Quinn and the rest of them get a notion they can force you to make the loans they want. The proposition is Darley doesn't want to wait for Commager's report."

Neal motioned for Abel to go into the parlor. "What do you want with a gun?"

"One gun isn't as good as two," Abel said as he walked into the parlor. "Three's still better. Jane shoots pretty well, doesn't she?"

"Yes, she's a good shot." Neal walked to the fireplace and leaned against the mantel, looking at Abel. The man was pale and trembling, thoroughly frightened, and Neal had no idea what had brought it on. "Henry, what's the matter?"

"Maybe nothing," Abel said, "but Stacey has talked to Joe Rolfe and Doc Santee, and he told Darley he wouldn't make any decision until he had that report you told him about this morning." Abel swallowed. "Darley almost went crazy. He told O'Hara and Quinn and that whole bunch that you'd killed the project. They'll try to lynch you, Neal. They're blaming you for everything."

"You think they'll come up here?"

"Sure they will. I came here to help you fight."

Neal thought about it a minute, knowing that what Abel said was a definite possibility. Stacey's decision would bring this to a head, and with O'Hara setting up the drinks . . . Neal rubbed his face, wondering how he could ever have felt they were out of the woods.

"There's a .38 upstairs on the bureau," Neal said, "and a .22 pistol in the pantry. It's on the top shelf to keep it out of Laurie's reach. If they want a fight, Henry, they'll get it."

"Good," Abel said.

Jane came into the parlor. "Hello, Henry," she said. "I didn't know you were here. Dinner's ready. I'll put another plate on the table."

"I'm not hungry, Jane," Abel said. "I'll just have a cup of coffee."

"Whatever you say, but there's plenty." She called Laurie

who came down the stairs slowly, still sulking. "You hungry?"

"No," the child said, then she saw Abel and ran to him. "Henry, they won't let me go outside and play. You tell them it isn't too cold."

He picked her up and carried her into the dining room. "It's pretty cold, Laurie. I just came in. My teeth are chattering." He snapped his teeth together. "See?"

She giggled. "You're fooling."

"No, it's cold," Abel said.

He put her down and she crawled into her chair. "I'll eat," she said, "but I'm not hungry."

"All right," Jane said. "We don't care if you're hungry or not as long as you eat."

No one talked while they ate except Laurie who was over her sulks and chattered incessantly. They had barely finished when the doorbell rang.

Neal glanced at Abel as he rose. "I'll see who it is," he said, and left the kitchen, wondering if Abel's fears had been realized.

His gun was in his hand when he opened the door. Joe Rolfe stood there. Doc Santee was in the street forking his black gelding, his Winchester in the boot. The sheriff's horse stood beside the gelding.

Neal replaced his gun, relieved again, and he thought how often this had happened. Every time he had thought their trouble was over, he had soon found it wasn't.

"I didn't expect you," Neal said. "Henry came a while ago and said Darley was trying to work up a mob."

Rolfe's lined face was bitter. "He tried, and for about an hour I thought he'd make it, but there's a little horse sense left in people. Saddle Redman up, Neal. We ain't got much time. After Darley seen he'd lost out all around, he and Shelton cleaned the safe out and pulled out with the money."

"Then everybody knows?"

"Some of 'em do, and the rest will hear soon enough."

Abel had followed Neal and had heard. He said, "Neal, let me ride Jane's mare. I'll go with you."

"No, you stay here with Jane and Laurie," Rolfe said. "I ain't real sure what happened, not sure enough to leave Neal's women folks alone in the house. I'm glad you're here, Henry."

"If there's any chance those bastards are still in town," Neal said, "I'm not going."

Rolfe jerked his head at Neal. "Come on, I'll help you saddle up."

They walked around the house to the barn, Neal saying

stubbornly, "Joe, I've been through hell worrying about what was going to happen to my family. I tell you—"

"They ain't around," Rolfe broke in. "I didn't want Henry going with us. I found out years ago that a small posse of men I can count on is a hell of a lot better'n a big one of men I ain't sure about. I ain't sure about Henry. Sometimes I think he ain't got no guts at all."

"He doesn't have as far as his wife's concerned," Neal said, "but I think he'd be all right on something like this."

"Well, he's not used to riding," Rolfe said. "He's better off here. Go ahead and saddle your horse and I'll tell you what happened. It's like I said this morning. I figured they'd make their run tonight, so I wasn't paying no attention to 'em. Fact is, I didn't even know they'd left town until Jud Manion rode in a while ago. He'd been over to Prineville trying to borrow some money and he seen Darley and Shelton riding toward the desert hell for leather. Jud started toward 'em, and one of 'em took a shot at him. He got sore, as any man would, so he told me soon as he got to town."

Embarrassed, Rolfe cleared his throat. "I should have been watching, but I wasn't. I hiked up to their office, and by God, that safe was open and clean as a hound's tooth. Nobody there. When I started asking questions, nobody had even seen 'em lately."

"Stacey?"

"Stacey hadn't, neither. I went to the livery stable. Shelton had taken their horses, saying they was heading out to Barney Lakes to see your survey crew. It would have made sense if I hadn't seen the empty safe."

"We'll find the money on them, won't we?" Neal asked, leading Redman out of the barn. "They wouldn't be likely to cache it, and come later?"

"No sir," Rolfe said. "This is a place they won't ever want to come back to. Better put your sheepskin on. It's gonna get mighty cold if we don't catch up with 'em before sundown."

Rolfe took the reins and led the horse around the house. Neal went inside, told Jane what had happened, and kissed her and Laurie. He came out a moment later wearing his sheepskin and carrying his rifle. Henry Abel was waiting with Rolfe and Doc Santee.

"Stay here, will you, Henry?" Neal asked. "I don't think there's any trick to this, but I'd feel better if I know you're in the house."

"Sure, I'll stay," Abel said, nodding gravely.

Neal mounted and rode east, Rolfe on one side of him, Doc Santee on the other. Once he looked back to wave. Jane and Laurie were on the front porch with Abel. All three waved, then Neal turned and did not look back again.

Jud Manion understood at last, Neal thought. So would the others, but Manion was the one whose friendship he had hated most to lose. But as he thought about it, it struck him there was something which wasn't quite in place, some little part that didn't fit.

Then it came to him. He asked, "Joe, where's Mrs. Darley?"

"Hell, I don't know. She wasn't in their office. I suppose she's at the boarding house."

She could be, Neal thought, but he remembered how close to panic she had been that morning, certain that her life was in danger. Then the terrifying thought came to him that Darley or Shelton might have killed her to keep her from talking. They were capable of it, and he didn't doubt that they would if they knew what she had told him this morning.

He was having his nightmare again, he thought. No, this was real. He could not shake the feeling that Fay Darley had been honest with him and somehow he was responsible for what had happened to her. He tried to put it out of his mind, but the doubt grew until it became a torturing sense of guilt.

Chapter Sixteen

Watching Neal ride away, Henry Abel wondered if it was over at last. He had seen the worry and tension grow steadily in Neal, and now if he could relax . . . ! But he couldn't because it wasn't over and it wouldn't be over until Darley and Shelton were in jail or dead, and Neal knew for sure who had written the notes and what the intention was behind them.

I should have gone and let Neal stay here, Abel thought. He started to say that, then held his tongue as Laurie went skipping past him and through the door, calling something to her mother.

"We've still got to be careful," he said. "I'm going to stay here till Neal gets back."

But worry had rolled off Jane's shoulders. She laughed and

shook her head at him. "There's no need to, Henry. You go on home."

"To what?" he asked somberly.

Jane understood. "I'll be glad to have you if you want to stay. I just don't think it's necessary."

She went into the house, but he stood outside for several minutes, unable to feel the confidence Jane did. He was haunted by a vague worry he could not identify except that it seemed to him danger had disappeared too quickly to be real. But maybe he had overestimated the danger, maybe he listened too much to the idle talk of men like O'Hara and Quinn and Olly Earl when the only real danger had been from Darley and Shelton, and perhaps from Darley's wife. She was a bitch if he'd ever seen one.

The uneasiness lingered in him even after he went back into the house. He stood in the parlor, listening to Jane and Laurie's chatter from the kitchen. They were too far away for him to hear what they said, but it wasn't important. He thought about Neal and Jane and Laurie, and about his own wife, whom he was sure he hated. He shook his head. He wasn't going to think about her now. This was important. He could think about his wife any time.

A moment later Jane went upstairs with Laurie, and when she came down, she said, "Laurie's taking her nap. I'm going downtown if you're going to stay here. I haven't been out of the house all day."

"I'm staying," Abel said stubbornly, sensing that Jane didn't really want him to stay. She didn't have any confidence in him for a thing like this. Joe Rolfe didn't, either. Well, by God, he'd show them. He said roughly, "Jane, Neal said he left a .38 revolver on the bureau upstairs. Will you get it for me?"

She hesitated, then said, "All right," and went upstairs to her bedroom, returning a moment later with the gun. She handed it to him and went on to the hall door. "I won't be gone long." Then she turned and looked at him. "Henry, you don't think Neal will get hurt?"

"No, there's three of them. Shelton's the one they've got to look out for. Darley's just got a slick tongue."

"I guess they won't be back for a long time."

"May be quite a while," he said, "but Joe Rolfe knows the high desert like you know your front yard. So does Neal."

She laughed shakily. "Funny how I felt a while ago. Like I'd been all bound up. Tied so I couldn't move or even breathe. Then when I heard that Darley and Shelton had left town, it seemed like we were free. Like it was all over. But it isn't for Neal. I guess I'm just selfish, thinking of myself that way."

"No, you aren't selfish," Abel said gently. "Neal's a very lucky man."

"Oh, I'm the lucky one, Henry. Well, I'll be right back."

He stood at the window watching while she went down the street, walking fast the way she liked to when Laurie wasn't with her. He'd seen her walking that way along Main Street, or stopping to talk with some other woman in town, her face animated. Neal was lucky, all right. He didn't know what a bad marriage was, or what it did to a man.

A knock on the back door broke into his thoughts. He crossed the dining room and went into the kitchen, his mind still on Jane. He opened the back door and froze, shocked into immobility. Tuck Shelton stood a step away, a gun in his hand. Ordinarily Shelton's face was devoid of expression, but now it was filled with a kind of wolfish eagerness.

So it had been a trick! Somehow Shelton and Darley had circled back to town.

Darley must be around here, too. Maybe in front of the house. Abel knew he had to do something. Shelton was alone now. If Abel had any chance, it would be before Darley and Shelton got together.

Abel had been a coward from the day big Buck Shelly had shot him, but he wasn't a coward now. He thought of Laurie upstairs, and of the notes Neal had received. He stood there staring at Shelton for a matter of seconds, his thoughts racing. The man wouldn't shoot because he'd alarm the town.

Encouraged by that thought, Abel jumped back and grabbed for the .38 he had slipped under his waistband. But he was slow. Far too slow. Shelton took one quick step forward and slashed him across the head with the barrel of his gun. Abel went down in a loose-jointed fall, knocked cold.

Shelton holstered his gun. Picking up the .38 that Abel had dropped, he looked at it, then stuck it under his waistband. He stood motionless for a time, his head canted to one side, listening, but he heard nothing. He shut the back door and quickly searched every room on the first floor. Finding no one there, he picked Abel up and carried him into the parlor and slammed him down on the couch.

He scratched his jaw thoughtfully, then swung around and ran up the stairs. He looked into the bathroom. Empty. So were the first two bedrooms, but the third wasn't. Laurie was asleep on the bed.

He retreated into the hall and shut the door. He grinned as he went down the stairs. Abel was beginning to stir. Shelton rolled him onto the floor and dug his toe into his ribs. He sat down on the couch, his revolver in his hand, and waited until Abel sat up, holding his head.

"Got a headache, banker?" Shelton asked.

Abel pulled himself into a chair and sat there holding his head. Shelton said, "Better answer me."

"Yeah, I got a headache."

"Where's Clark?"

"Out in the desert with Rolfe and Santee. They're chasing you."

"Not me," Shelton said. "This didn't work quite the way I planned, but it's all right. I hid in a closet in the office and left the safe open. Rolfe took one look and when he saw the safe was empty, he lit out of there like his tail was on fire."

"Jud Manion told Rolfe he saw you and Darley."

"He saw Darley, all right, but not me. The other one was Fay, riding astraddle. Manion must have seen 'em off a piece and mistook her for me." He scratched his jaw, his opaque eyes narrowed. Finally he said, "Where I missed out was thinking Clark would stay home."

"I wish he had," Abel said. "You wouldn't be sitting there. . . ."

"Where's Mrs. Clark?"

"She went downtown."

"When will she be back?"

"I don't know."

Shelton was silent for several minutes, then he said, "You kind of like the Clarks, don't you, banker? You like 'em extra well, seeing as Clark's your boss."

"Sure I like them."

"Now that little girl sleeping upstairs. Be a shame if anything happened to her, wouldn't it?"

"If you touch her—"

"Shut up, banker. You won't do anything if I touch her. He jabbed a forefinger in Abel's direction. "I don't like squalling brats. If she starts yelling, you'd better get upstairs and see she shuts up. If she don't, she gets hurt. And if you try leaving the house, or try anything when Mrs. Clark comes in, you'll get hurt. Savvy that?"

Abel nodded, his head hurting so much he couldn't think straight. He only knew that being shot eight years ago was nothing compared to the trouble he was in now. And there wasn't anything he could do about it. Not a damned thing.

Shelton sat on the couch ten feet in front of him, his gun on his lap, a grin on his wild, wolfish face. *He's just waiting for me to make a wrong move,* Abel thought, *but I won't do it. I won't do it.*

Chapter Seventeen

Neal rode in silence when they left town. He had no desire to talk. Apparently Joe Rolfe and Doc Santee didn't either. They probably felt as he did, a little limp now that it was practically over. It was simply a matter of staying on the trail of the two men until they were found. After all the uncertainty he had been through lately, Neal was sure of one thing. This would prove to everyone in the county that he had been right. The money would be on Ben Darley and Tuck Shelton.

Well, Rolfe would bring the two men in. They'd be jailed and tried and convicted and sent to the state prison at Salem, and that would be the end of the whole business. The money would be returned. No one, unless it was Fay Darley, would be badly hurt except for the broken dreams of greedy men. There would be no quick profits. O'Hara and Quinn and Tuttle and the rest of them would learn again that hard work and patience marked the slow passage to prosperity.

As Neal's father had said repeatedly, the exceptions are few indeed. But there were other dreams, the solid kind that his father had had which were far more practical than this will-o'-the-wisp thing Darley and Shelton had come up with. Holding back more water on the upper river so there would never be a shortage, a railroad giving downgrade passage to the Columbia, modern sawmills to harvest the pine crop that was ready for the harvesting: these were dreams worth working for and could be attained, with sweat and outside capital. Maybe he could get Stacey interested before he went back to Portland.

Now, with the town well behind them, the narrow road cut eastward through solid walls of juniper; hoofs stirred the deep lava dust. Above them the sun dropped steadily toward the towering peaks of the Cascades, then the junipers began to thin until there was only a scattering of them in the sagebrush and lava ridges that were scabs in the shifting, sandy soil. They reached Horse Ridge and began to climb the road that was hardly more than a trail looping up the slope in long, sharp-turning switchbacks.

Neal had tried not to think about Fay Darley; he tried to keep his mind on the one important fact that the two men who had come close to bringing disaster to Cascade County were ahead. But now, with the sun almost down, he began to worry again. The uneasiness that had been in him when he'd left town had never completely deserted him.

He began thinking of the things that could go wrong. They might not be able to pick up the fugitives' trail. Both men knew the high desert. At least they had spent a good deal of time at the lakes in the Barney Mountain area. So, knowing the country, they could have taken any of a dozen routes.

If Darley and Shelton did escape with the money, the county's progress would be retarded for years. With typical human forgetfulness, the men who had invested in the project would blame Joe Rolfe and Neal for letting it happen.

"You figured it would go like this," Quinn or O'Hara or Tuttle would say, "anl you let 'em get clean away. What kind of a lawman are you, Joe?" Or, "You wanted 'em to pull this off, Clark. You had to prove you were right."

Or it might have been a trick to get Neal and the sheriff out of town. Jud Manion would not have willingly had any part in such a maneuver, but he might have been used. Possibly they had shot at him so he'd do the very thing he had done. Darley and Shelton might have disappeared into the junipers and be headed back to town right now.

Neal could not stand it any longer. When they reined their horses to a stop halfway up Horse Ridge, he demanded, "How are you going to know which way to go, Joe? This is a hell of a big country."

Doc Santee was looking at Rolfe, too. The same question was in his mind, Neal thought. He had been called out here more than once to tend to a buckaroo with a broken leg or bullet hole in his belly. Invariably he'd ridden back to town alone, guided only by the stars. Like Neal, he knew how it was out here: dry washes, miles of rimrock that looked alike, alkali flats, and a juniper forest that ran for miles and miles, the trees so close together in some places that the only direction a man could see was up, a country where fifty men could lose themselves as easily as two.

Rolfe knew all of this as well as Neal or Santee did, and the doubts showed on his weather-burned face. He said testily, "I can guess what you're thinking. We're too far behind 'em to catch up. We didn't fetch any grub, and there's no place out here to stock up until we get to Commager's camp on the lakes."

"That's part of it," Neal said, "but there is a chance they might have circled back. We haven't been watching for any sign. Chances are we wouldn't have caught it anyway, with as many tracks out here on the road as there are."

Rolfe snorted his contempt. "They're ahead of us. You can count on it. Besides, why would they circle and head back, now that they've got the dinero?"

"Those notes I got were plenty of reason," Neal said, "You forget them?"

"No, I ain't forgot 'em," Rolfe snapped. "I thought about leaving you in town, and I would have if there was anybody else I could have brought, but I didn't figure you'd got boogery like this."

"You still haven't explained those notes," Santee said.

Rolfe's frayed temper suddenly snapped. "Why, goddamn both of you for a pair of chuckle-headed idiots. You know as much about this business as I do and most of the time you ain't stupid. They wanted Neal out of town and they had good reason. If he hadn't talked to Stacey this morning, everything would have been different."

Neal was silent. Whatever he said would be the wrong thing, with Rolfe as sour-tempered as he was. If Jud Manion had said he'd seen three riders, Neal would have been convinced that everything was just as it appeared to be. He didn't want to think they had killed her, but they wouldn't have gone off and left her, knowing she would talk. Darley might have dreamed up some excuse for being out here, but he wouldn't have any chance to make it stick with Fay testifying against him. Neal didn't know what to think, so the uneasiness continued to plague him.

Santee, too, said nothing. Presently Rolfe, a little ashamed of his outburst, said mildly, "If we'd hung around town long enough to get rigged out proper like, it would've been dark afore we got started. This way there's a chance we might catch 'em. Darley ain't no horsebacker." He cocked his head, glancing at the sun that was resting atop the peaks. "Gonna be dark purty soon. Maybe they'll stop and cook supper and we'll see the fire."

"Not Shelton," Doc said. "He's too old a hand at this game, if I've got him figured right."

Rolfe shrugged and started toward the top, with Neal riding beside him. Presently the sheriff said, "I've been digging at this in my head ever since we left town. Before that, too. Only one thing you can be sure of. Them notes you got was just a bluff to get you out of town so they could suck Stacey into the deal. I kept thinking Shelton had something else in his noggin, but I reckon he didn't."

Neal, remembering the fury he had seen so plainly in Darley when Stacey had arrived that morning, and the unexplainable lack of anger in Shelton, was not convinced Shelton didn't have something else in mind. Suddenly he knew he had to go back. But he hesitated, not knowing how he could tell Rolfe about the crazy, twisting fear that was in him.

Santee said, "You ducked Neal's question, Joe. You're an old hand at this game, but being an old hand doesn't cut down the size of the country."

"I thought you'd forget the question if I got you side-tracked," Rolfe said. "All right, I'll tell you the way I've got it figured. Darley's a weak sister. He'll break. The desert will do that every time to a man who ain't used to it. You both know that."

"Sure," Santee agreed, "but meanwhile we're riding—"

"We'll head for the lakes if we don't pick 'em up between here and there," Rolfe cut in. "It's my guess we'll be hunting one man, not two. Shelton will plug Darley and go on with the dinero. I thought we'd get Commager and his men to help. Chances are we'll have to keep right on going. . . ."

A rifle cracked ahead of them; the bullet sounded to Neal as if it had barely missed him. He dug his spurs into Redman, swinging off the trail to the left; Rolfe and Santee went to the right. Again the rifle sounded, the bullet clipping a branch off a juniper tree just above Neal's head. Then he was behind a tall lava upthrust and pulled his horse to a stop. Jerking the Winchester from the boot, he swung down.

They had almost reached the top. Probably Shelton and Darley were forted up in a nest of boulders right on the rim. To go on straight up the ridge was sheer suicide. Again the Winchester cracked, the bullet striking the lava and screaming as it fled into space. Just one rifle. Neal puzzled over that. If Shelton and Darley were both here, there would be two. Darley might be a weak sister just as Rolfe thought, but he'd fight, cornered as he was.

One thing was sure. Neal couldn't go back now. Maybe Rolfe had been right in thinking Shelton would kill Darley and go on with the money. That could explain why only one rifle was working. But it didn't seem right. Shelton wasn't the kind to hole up. He'd be riding and riding fast. He was too smart to stop and fight unless he had to, with the odds three to one.

Neal took off his hat, and breaking a branch from a dead-fall juniper, poked his hat above the rock. The rifle shot came the instant the hat appeared. Neal pulled it down. No hole. It wasn't Shelton. He wouldn't have fallen for an old trick like that, or if he had, he'd have hit the hat right through the band.

Neal's first reaction was one of relief. Darley must have

shot Shelton. That meant Darley was outnumbered three to one. They should have no great difficulty getting him into a squeeze of some kind.

Neal looked across the road, but neither Santee nor the sheriff was in sight. The junipers were small and scattered here, but the lava which had spewed out of some ancient nearby crater was a tumbled mass clear to the top of the ridge. Darley had Neal pinned down, but there was a good chance Rolfe and Santee were working their way toward the rim, their horses hidden among the rocks.

The relief was short lived in Neal. Shelton might have gone back. It was inconceivable that Darley could have got the drop on a man like Shelton and killed him. Neal remembered how he had quit fighting and crawled under the desk. No, Ben Darley was not a fighting man, and it would take a good fighting man to get the best of Shelton.

The need to find out what had happened to Shelton became a necessity to Neal. He shouted, "Darley! Can you hear me Darley?"

"Sure, I can hear you," Darley called back. "You coming up to get me?"

"Where's Shelton?"

Darley laughed. "What will you give me to tell you?"

"Your life," Neal said, "if you'll throw out your gun."

Silence then. After what seemed minutes, Darley said, "He didn't leave town with me. He was going to call on your family. You know what he said in those notes."

It could be true. Or it could be a trick to get him into the open. Neal pulled his Colt, leaving the rifle leaning against the lava. He had to know.

Santee called from the other side of the road, "Stay where you are, Neal." But he couldn't stay. Time had run out for him. He lunged from the rock and started up the slope, slipping and sliding in the loose sand. Darley opened up the instant Neal came into view, bullets kicking up the dirt at his feet. At that moment, with lead striking all around him, the nearest rock that was big enough to give protection seemed a mile away.

Chapter Eighteen

For a long time Henry Abel sat staring at Shelton, the throbbing in his head a constant ache. He had been afraid of many things in his life, but he had never experienced the hopeless fear he felt now. He knew that Neal was not immune to fear, but Neal was different. Abel respected him as he had never respected another man, and that was probably the reason. Neal conquered his fear, he did what he thought was right, and in that regard, Abel knew, Neal was a better man than his father had ever been.

Now, right now, Henry Abel knew he was up against something that would test him as he had never been tested. But what could he do? Jane would come in through the front door any minute. Laurie might wake up and start to cry. And Neal might not be home any time tonight. Maybe not even tomorrow.

Finally, because Abel could no longer stand the silence, he asked, "What do you want with Neal?"

"I'm going to kill him."

Abel shut his eyes. Shelton had said it as calmly as if it were something he did every day. A conversation like this couldn't be real. Abel was having a nightmare. But when he opened his eyes, he knew it was no nightmare. Tuck Shelton hadn't moved. He might have been a figure carved of granite if it hadn't been for the blinking of his eyes, and that crazy, eager expression on his face.

Bitter self-condemnation was in Abel. He remembered his feeling that the trouble was over too quickly, too easily. He should have known, should have been more careful when he'd heard the knock on the back door. Now he and all the Clarks might die because of that one moment of carelessness.

He leaned forward, his hands pressed palm down against the couch on both sides of him. He asked, "Why do you want to kill Neal?"

"You can call it an old debt," Shelton said. "But maybe I won't kill him after all. Maybe I'll kill his wife or his kid and let him watch. I'm in no hurry to get it finished. But whatever I decide to do, he's going to watch."

Still no change in his expression. Abel forgot his headache. He even forgot how afraid he was. There was something strange about Shelton, something weird and unreal as if he had only one strong feeling of any kind that was driving him to murder. But why?

Perhaps he would never know, Abel thought. He could read nothing in Shelton's face except that crazy eagerness, an eagernes that, oddly enough, was balanced by the ability to wait. Watching Shelton, the thought occured to Abel that the man actually enjoyed the waiting.

Neal might find out what was prompting Shelton to do this, after it was too late. There was no way Abel could warn him unless he was willing to sacrifice his own life. Abel wasn't sure what he could do when the time came. It all depended on what happened when Neal got here. He might walk into the house and be under Shelton's gun before Abel had a chance to do anything.

On impulse Abel rose, wondering what Shelton would do. He had to test himself, too, as well as Shelton's reaction. He hadn't moved for so long that he wondered if he were paralyzed. Fear could do that, he'd heard Doc Santee say.

Abel discovered he could move all right, up slowly and down rapidly. Shelton simply tilted the gun up so it was lined on his chest.

"You start getting boogery and I'll blow your heart right out through your backbone," Shelton said. "Don't expect me to tell you again."

Abel licked his lips. He said, "Shelton, Laurie's alone. When she wakes up, she might be scared and start crying."

"I've already told you," Shelton said. "I can't stand bawling kids, so she'd better not start."

"Be reasonable," Abel cried. "You can't keep a child of that age quiet."

"I can," Shelton said. "I can fix it so she'll be quiet for a long time."

He could and would, Abel thought. It was all right to tell yourself that a grown man would not harm a child like Laurie, but you'd be wrong because what an ordinary man would do had no relationship with what Tuck Shelton would do. So Abel sat staring at the man, his head hammering, his mind reaching for something he could do, and finding nothing.

The front door opened. Abel started to get up again, and stopped when Shelton said, "Hold it, banker. Let's see who it is."

Jane, Abel thought. It had to be her. Again he had the terrifying thought that it might be days before Neal got back. What would they do? Jane? Laurie? What would he do?

What could anyone do living in the house with a maniac. Abel would be driven out of his mind with fear and anxiety and the sheer tension of waiting. So would Jane. He didn't know much about children, but he did know that Laurie, used to running and singing and banging around the way she always did, could not be expected to remain quiet for any length of time.

But this was now, right now, with Jane coming in and not knowing what she was going to find. Instinctively Abel sensed that the one thing they must do was to keep from shocking Shelton, to refrain from doing anything violent or sudden that would precipitate action. So, in spite of Shelton's warning to "hold it," Abel said in a low tone, "Easy, Jane. Don't scream."

She stood in the hall doorway, head tilted back, mouth open, staring at Shelton, who had moved to one side of Abel so that he could shoot either Jane or Abel if he had an excuse. Jane might have screamed if Abel hadn't spoken the warning. As it was, she controlled herself, standing motionless, a basket of groceries in her right hand, a package of meat in the other. Her face turned pale, but she made no sound, and Abel felt a quick burst of admiration for her. Under these circumstances, his wife would have been hysterical.

"Good," Shelton said. "I was afraid you were going to start yelling. I can't stand yelling women. Crying ones, either. Fact is, I can't stand women unless they're good cooks. Can you cook?"

Jane nodded. Abel said, "I've eaten here. She's a fine cook. It's time for supper. Why don't you let her show you?"

"I was thinking it was a good idea," Shelton said. "You cook a good meal." He nodded at Abel. "She'll need some wood, chances are. Fetch in enough for breakfast while you're at it."

Abel had not expected this. He got up and started toward the kitchen, fighting the temptation to run. Jane moved after him, stiffly as if she had lost control of her joints. Just as they reached the dining room door, Shelton said, "Wait."

They turned, Abel groaning in spite of his effort not to. Shelton had almost made a mistake. Once Abel was through the back door, he'd have headed for the alley and run for help. He'd have been back with someone in a matter of minutes.

But Shelton had not come as close to making a mistake as Abel had thought. He said, "Mrs. Clark, your daughter is upstairs asleep. I don't want to harm her. Not yet, anyhow. I don't want to do anything until your husband gets back. No sense in doing what I'm going to do unless he's here to see it.

I've waited eight years. I can wait a few more hours."

He grinned at them. Not really a grin, Abel thought. More of a grimace, but it was meant for a grin. Shelton said, "I sent them notes to worry him. I did, didn't I?"

Jane was unable to say anything, so Abel said, "You worried him plenty."

"A small payment on what he owes me," Shelton said. "I'll collect the rest when he gets here. Trouble is, we don't know when that will be, do we?"

"No," Abel said.

"We may have to live together for quite a spell," Shelton went on. "Too bad you got caught here. Your wife's going to miss you, ain't she, banker?"

"She may start out looking for me," Abel said.

"But maybe she won't think of coming here," Shelton said. "I don't want anybody else in the house. If she does, get rid of her. And if you have any visitors, Mrs. Clark, get rid of them. Tell 'em Laurie's sick or something. She's got to stay in her room."

Shelton glanced at the stairs thoughtfully. "When she wakes up, you go tell her she's got to stay in her room and keep still. I was telling the banker I can't stand bawling brats. Now I'll tell you how it's going to be. My plan worked out perfectly except for one thing. I didn't figure on Clark leaving the house like he done. Well, nothing I can do now but wait for him. Until he gets back, you'll feed me. I'll sleep upstairs across the hall from your kid. I'm a light sleeper. If I hear anything wrong, I'll be into her room mighty damned quick. You know what I'll do to her?"

Jane nodded.

"What?" Shelton said. "You tell me, Mrs. Clark."

Jane moistened her lips with the tip of her tongue. She opened her mouth and shut it without saying a word, then swallowed. "Well?" Shelton said. "Can't you talk?"

"You'll kill her," Jane whispered.

"That's right," Shelton said. "I don't want to yet, but I will if either one of you don't toe the line. I won't kill her quick, Mrs. Clark. Remember that, too."

Jane nodded again. Abel simply stared at Shelton, knowing what was in his mind. Here was an animal-like cunning and cruelty that prompts a cat to promise freedom to a captive bird without having the slightest intention of keeping that promise. Still he had to ask the question, "Suppose I bring help?"

The grimace was on Shelton's face again. "You do that, banker. You do that." His eyes were on Abel's face. "I'll tell you what'll happen. The first time you try to get the kid out of a window or bring help or to kill me, she'll die and so will Mrs. Clark." He nodded toward the kitchen door. "All right, get some supper."

Jane crossed the dining room to the kitchen, Abel following. In spite of Shelton's warnings, Abel had a feeling that this was their only chance, even though it meant a gamble with Laurie's life. There must be another gun in the house. Neal had taken his revolver and rifle. Shelton had the .38. Then Abel remembered Neal saying there was a .22 in the pantry.

The instant Abel reached the kitchen, he shut the door. "Where's the .22, Jane? Neal said you had one. I'll kill him. I've got to. We can't take any chances on waiting."

Jane's self control broke. She dropped the grocery basket and meat, and grabbing Abel by the shoulders, shook him. "No, no, no." She began to cry, and Abel took her into his arms and held her until the moment of hysteria passed. Presently she stepped back and dried her eyes.

"I'm sorry, Henry." She swallowed. "You're brave to even think about it, but we can't gamble with Laurie's life. It's what Shelton wants us to do. We can't risk it."

So she thought he was brave. Nobody else did. Nobody else had ever said it to him. Well, he'd show her that he was. He walked past her into the pantry. She didn't understand. If they waited, they'd die. In some terrible way that only Tuck Shelton would think of. Better take a gamble now than wait until it was too late.

He examined one shelf after another, but the gun wasn't in sight. He heard Jane crying from where she stood beside the kitchen table. He stepped back, wondering if he'd better get a chair and examine the top shelf that was above his head. If the gun was in the pantry, it must be up there on that shelf.

He raised a hand and felt along the shelf, knowing that if it was close to the edge, he'd find it and wouldn't have to get a chair. Then he felt it and drew it off the shelf. It was loaded. He swung around, then stopped dead still, the gun in his hand. Shelton was standing in the dining room doorway, his revolver lined on Jane, his gaze on Abel.

"Lay it on the table, banker," Shelton said.

Abel obeyed, his head starting to hammer again. Jane had been right when she'd said this was exactly what Shelton wanted them to do. He'd given them a minute or two, then he'd come into the kitchen and had caught Abel in the act of doing what Shelton had guessed he'd do.

Now, with the gun on the table, Shelton motioned Abel toward the back door. He said, "You're a God-damned fool, banker. I warned you, but no, you wouldn't listen." He backed toward the dining room door. "Go for help, mister. Run like hell. I'm going upstairs. By the time you get back, it'll be too late and you'll see something you'll wish—"

"No, Shelton," Jane cried. "No. He won't do anything again. I promise. We'll do exactly like you tell us to."

Shelton hesitated as if weighing her words against the promise he'd made. "I don't know, Mrs. Clark," he said. "I gave you my proposition, but this fool didn't want to take it."

"I promise," Jane cried. "I promise."

Shelton seemed pleased. "I want your husband to be here before I do anything. All right, we'll see. Now go get that wood, banker. We'll find out if you've got enough sense to learn anything."

Shelton wheeled and returned to the parlor. Jane said, "Henry, are you going to do what I asked this time?"

He looked at her, utterly miserable. "I don't know. I thought I was right. What can we do?"

"Wait," she said. "We won't do anything until Neal gets back. It would be a poor bargain for him if he got here and killed Shelton and then found out Laurie was dead."

"So we live with a crazy man," Abel said. "Stay here and wait on him and not know whether we'll be dead or alive the next minute. Is that what you want to do?"

"Yes," Jane said. "It's what we've got to do."

Abel didn't say anything more. He built a fire and walked slowly across the back porch and on to the woodshed. He sat down on the chopping block and rolled and lighted a cigarette. He thought of a dozen possibilities and realized that none would work, but he knew he was right and Jane was wrong. If Neal had to go on clear to Barney Lakes with Rolfe and Doc Santee, he'd be gone for two or three days. Abel knew he could not stand it that long. Neither could Jane nor Laurie.

If he could think of anything that promised success, he'd do it no matter what Jane thought. He could carry a ladder that leaned against the woodshed around the side of the house and get Laurie out through the window. No, Shelton would hear him.

He looked around the woodshed. He saw a rusty knife on a shelf inside the door. He could slip that inside his shirt and use it on Shelton when he was asleep. There was a hatchet lying in the chips in a corner. He could slip that under his belt and when he had a chance, split Shelton's head open like a cabbage.

On and on, one idea after another running through his

mind, and then the first returned and he went through the list again. They were like petitions to Heaven on an Oriental prayer wheel. Every one promised failure because Abel knew he wasn't man enough to try any of them with the slightest chance of success. If he were Neal, he could try and maybe succeed, but he wasn't Neal. He was Henry Abel, scared of his own wife.

He got up and began splitting wood with slow, methodical strokes, but his mind wasn't on his work. He kept thinking of Laurie, alone in her bed. She'd be waking up soon and Jane would have to go to her. So, sick with a baffling sense of futility, he told himself he would do nothing. Like Jane, he would wait.

Chapter Nineteen

Neal realized he had made a mistake the instant he was in the open, with bullets kicking up geysers of dirt all around him. A slug sliced through his pants just above the knee and raised a painful welt along his thigh. Another cut through his left boot above his ankle. Then, halfway to the top, he dived headlong to one side, gaining the protection of a low ridge of rock.

He lay on his belly, sucking in great gulps of air. Both Joe Rolfe and Doc Santee had opened up from the other side of the road, Rolfe nearly to the top of the ridge, Santee about halfway up. Now the firing stopped.

The sun was almost down; the light was thinning rapidly. Neal wondered if that was the reason he was alive. Darley had been shooting against the setting sun. Perhaps the slanting rays had blinded him. Or he may have been worried by the burst of fire from Rolfe's and Santee's guns. Or he might be a bad shot who just couldn't do any better.

The minutes dragged by, with Neal hugging the downhill side of the rock. He was so close to where Darley had forted up that the promoter was bound to score a hit if Neal made a standing target. He couldn't raise his head to see exactly where Darley was hiding, or if there was a weakness in his position.

All Neal could do was to lie here with his nose in the dirt and curse himself for an impulsive action that had put him into this jam. He was not going to be of any help to either Jane or Laurie if he got himself killed out here on Horse Ridge. But that line of thinking did not bring him any comfort. He had to know about Shelton. He had got this far with nothing more than a scratch. Maybe he could go all the way next time.

One moment he'd been telling himself he was damned lucky to be alive and he'd been a fool, the next moment he knew he couldn't go on lying here. Fool or not, he had to do something. He tried to hold himself back, tried to assure himself that Rolfe and Santee were working around on the other side of Darley and they'd have the man boxed. Logic was one thing, but lying here and thinking about what might be happening to Jane and Laurie was another.

Carefully he wormed his way to the end of the ledge, and pulling his gun, eared back the hammer. He eased his gun around the rock and threw a quick shot in Darley's general direction, then jerked his hand back.

Darley answered the shot immediately, his bullet kicking up dust a few inches from where Neal's hand had been. Rolfe and Santee cut loose again. Neal couldn't pinpoint their positions, but judging from the sound of the firing, he was convinced they had not moved up.

Neal cursed, a closed fist pounding the dirt. They were stuck. One man had them pinned down. Neal called, "Throw out your rifle, Darley. I'm coming up after you."

"Come ahead," Darley said, "but I'm not throwing out my rifle."

Neal glanced at the sun. Time he was moving in. It would be dark soon, and Darley would make a break for it then. That was a chance Neal refused to take. If he lunged into the open again, he'd get it. Darley would expect him to show up from the side he'd just fired from. If he went the other way, he'd have a better chance, with Darley a poor shot and having slow reactions.

Slow reactions! Neal considered that a moment, thinking of the way the man had fought the day before in his office. He wasn't a driver. He'd landed one good punch, but he hadn't followed up.

This was the only angle he could think of, the best bet for escape from what was an untenable position. Quickly Neal slid his hand back to the end of the ledge, pulled himself up on one hand and his knees as high as he could without exposing the hump of his back, and fired.

He came upright like a jack-in-the-box, whirled, and dived toward another ledge farther up the hill and closer to the road. Darley fired as Neal had been sure he would, and fired again just as Neal gained his new position, the bullet striking a corner of the rock and screaming through space.

"Joe," Neal called. "Can you hear me?"

"Yeah, I can hear you," Rolfe answered.

"Doc?"

"Over here," Santee answered. "I just picked up another ten feet. We've got him hipped."

"Hold on," Rolfe cut in. "No use getting shot up. I think the bastard's hit."

"I can't wait any longer," Neal shouted. "I'm the closest. I'm going after him."

"We'll all move when you do," Santee said. "Can you see where he is?"

"No," Neal said, "but we've got him from three sides. One of us ought to be able to see him."

"He's down in a hole," Santee said. "Rocks all around him, but I don't have far to go before I can look down at him."

"Come ahead," Darley screamed. "I'll get Clark, you god-damned sons of—"

Darley never finished his sentence. Rolfe came running in along the lip of the rim. Darley, his attention on Neal, didn't see him until he fired, and in that same instant Neal and Santee charged Darley's position, Neal angling slightly to the right and Santee crossing the road coming in from the opposite direction.

Rolfe had the longest way to come. He was zigzagging, bending low, shooting steadily as he ran. Darley fired at him, and that gave Neal the small advanatge of time he needed. He was the closest. Before Darley could turn his gun on him, Neal took a long jump to the top of one of the rocks that hid Darley. He fired and missed, and Darley threw a shot just as Santee cut loose; the doctor's bullet raked Darley along the side. It was enough to throw him off.

Darley had the one chance at Neal and missed, but this time Neal didn't miss. He caught Darley in the chest, knocking him against the rock behind him. His feet slid out from under him and he sat down, his gun dropping from his hand.

"Got him," Neal called.

He saw Fay Darley, lying on her back in the bottom of the hole, her hands and feet tied, a dark streak of dried blood on her forehead and down one side of her face.

"Cut me loose, Neal," Fay said. "He slugged me with a gun barrel and tied me up."

Neal holstered his gun, and jerking out his pocket knife, cut the ropes that held the woman. Darley wasn't dead, but he was going fast. Neal whirled on him demanding, "Where is Shelton?"

"Go to hell," Darley said.

Santee jumped down into the hole beside Neal and squatting beside the wounded man, opened his shirt and shook his head. "You're finished, Darley. You better talk."

Darley, who had never been a brave man, died like one. He said again, "Go to hell," and fell sideways, blood trickling down his chin.

Neal helped Fay to her feet. She leaned against a rock, her eyes shut. She put a hand to her forehead, muttering, "My God, my head feels like he's still hitting me."

Rolfe holstered his gun, and climbing to the top of the rock, held down his hand to her. She opened her eyes, and took his hand. Neal gave her a boost out of the hole with Rolfe pulling on her hand, then she stood beside Rolfe, swaying uncertainly until Neal scrambled up beside her and put an arm around her. Rolfe slid off the other side of the rock and helped her down.

"What happened?" Neal said. "Where's Shelton?"

"In town." Fay's knees gave and she sat down, her back against the rock. "We've got the money. It's in the saddle bags." She motioned toward a clump of junipers where their horses were tied. "We were headed for the lakes. Shelton was going to meet us there. I didn't know why he stayed in town until after we left."

Neal glanced at Santee, who had climbed out of the hole and was watching, then at Rolfe who was holding a wadded-up bandanna against a bullet gash in his left arm. Rolfe said impatiently, "All right, tell us about it."

"Are you going to arrest me?" Fay asked.

"You're damned right," Rolfe said.

"On what charge?"

"I don't know, but I'll throw you in the cooler for something. Go on now, tell us what happened."

"I tried to help," she said. "I wanted you to catch us. I couldn't let Shelton go ahead with what he'd planned. After we left town, I saw Manion and I shot at him. He went after you, didn't he?"

"That's right," Rolfe said.

Fay Darley was not the woman Neal had seen in town that morning, or beside the river the day before. She was dirty, her hair disheveled, her face contorted with pain, but for the first time he sensed a quality in her that had been missing before. Compassion. Or mercy. He wasn't sure. Perhaps humility.

"Jud took you for Shelton," Neal said.

"I was riding Shelton's horse," she said. "That was why. He was a long ways off. I don't think Shelton intended to meet us at the lakes. He wanted us out of town, thinking Rolfe would chase us. This whole swindle was Shelton's idea in the beginning, but I don't think the money was what he wanted any of the time."

"What did he want?" Neal asked.

"Those notes," she went on as if she hadn't heard the question. "He wanted to hurt you. I thought they were a bluff. It's like I said yesterday. They were trying to get you out of town so they wouldn't have any trouble with Stacey. They even put Ruggles on you. He was supposed to wound you. That way you'd be home in bed. Shelton wanted you there so he could kill you. He's a crazy man, Neal. I knew it all the time. Or I should have. He's the only man I ever met who didn't care anything about me. I was like another man to him."

"Who is he?"

"I don't know," Fay said. "Darley met him in Arizona. Darley's always been a promoter of some kind. Or a con man working the mining camps. Shelton told him about this country, the lakes and the high desert, and convinced him he could make a fortune here. That's why he came. At least that's what Darley and I thought, but Shelton had something else in his head. I didn't know what it was, and I don't believe Darley did until the other day. He told me on the way out. I couldn't stand it. When we got here, we stopped to rest our horses. We were on the ground and I shot him in the leg. He slugged me and tied me up. He said he was going to fight it out. He said you men would kill him if you could and he'd bled too much to make a hard ride."

"Fay." Neal knelt beside her. "What did he tell you?"

She looked at him, trying to smile. "Funny, isn't it?" she said in a low voice. "Most of the things I said to you weren't lies. I didn't think you'd believe them, but I knew they planned to kill you and I wanted to keep them from doing it." She looked up at Rolfe. "Will it help any? What I did? Darley might have gone clear to the lakes. You might have lost him."

"Sure, it'll help," Rolfe said.

Neal took her hands. "Fay, what did Darley tell you?"

She put her head against the rock and closed her eyes. "Shelton's nursing a grudge against you. He had been for eight years. He planned this to get revenge. Turn everybody against you. Hang you maybe. Injure your family. Anything to make you suffer. Even take it out on your little girl. When I heard that, I knew I had to stop Darley. I thought I could ride back and warn you, but he wasn't going to take any chances. . . ."

She opened her eyes. Neal was gone, running down the slope toward Redman. Rolfe called, "Wait, Neal. You'll need help."

Santee said, "Let him go, Joe. This is a job he'll want to do himself."

Chapter Twenty

As Neal ran down the slope to his horse, he remembered how it had been that time, stepping out of Olly Earl's hardware store and shooting the Shelly gang to pieces, with only Ed Shelly escaping. *But Tuck Shelton could not be Ed Shelly.* Joe Rolfe had proved that to Neal's satisfaction. Now Fay said Shelton had nursed a grudge against him for eight years, so Shelton must, in some way, be tied up with the Shelly outfit.

Neal swung into the saddle and cracked steel to Redman. Fay said Shelton was a crazy man. She was right. No one but a crazy man would want to injure Laurie. Neal had told himself that repeatedly from the moment he'd received the second note saying Neal's wife and girl would pay for the murder of Ed Shelly's father and brother.

Only Henry Abel stood between Laurie and Shelton. He would be no match for a maniac. Then Neal realized he had spurred Redman until the horse was in a hard run. He pulled the gelding down to a slower pace. If he killed the animal between here and town, he'd be on foot, at least until Rolfe and Santee caught up with him, and they would be slowed by having to take care of a sick woman and leading a horse with a dead man tied across the saddle.

Dusk settled down, then darkness, the last scarlet trace of the sunset dying above the Cascades. To Neal Clark, with this driving sense of urgency in him, the town seemed as far away as ever. As he rode, the fear grew in him that no matter how long it took him or what he did, he would be too late.

Neal nearly killed Redman that night. He would rein the horse down, then, before he realized it, he'd have him running again. During the long ride to town, he was vaguely aware of the beat of hoofs against the sandy soil of the road, of the slack shapes of the junipers as they flashed by, of the stars overhead, of the wind rushing down from the high peaks of the Cascades that penetrated into the vary marrow of his bones.

He was aware of these things, but they did not form a conscious pattern. Only time mattered. Redman's life was not important as long as the horse stayed on his feet long enough to get to town. Neal's own life was nothing unless he could barter it for Laurie's. And Jane's. But he had no idea how he could manage it. He couldn't even guess what he would find when he got home.

So he rode, the hours and miles falling behind, and hope that had been in him when he'd left Horse Ridge began to fade until it was no hope at all. When at last he reined his lathered, heaving horse to a stop in front of his house, he saw that there were lights in Laurie's room and in the parlor.

Cold logic told Neal that a sensible man would have done whatever he intended to do and been on his way hours ago, but now he saw the lights and hope blazed high in him again. There would be no light in Laurie's room unless she was all right, he thought.

Neal dismounted and crossed the yard to the porch, moving as silently as he could. He turned the knob, opened the front door and stepped inside. Closing the door, he drew his gun and eased along the hall to the parlor, the floor squeaking under his feet. He had forgotten about the squeaky boards.

He should have gone around to the back. Too late. The parlor door was open and the light fell through it into the hall; he could not go past the door without being seen, if Shelton was in the parlor. But Shelton might be anywhere in the house, even up in Laurie's room with a gun pointed at her head.

So Neal waited, hearing no sound except the ticking of the clock on the mantel, waited while sweat dripped down his face. After his wild ride, plagued by a thousand fears, impelled by his compulsive urge to find out what had happened, he was caught here in his hall.

Then he heard Shelton's even-toned, monotonous voice, "Come in, Mr. Clark, with your hands up unless you want your banker killed."

For a moment Neal couldn't move. This was not what he

had expected. Shelton was in the parlor, so he must have known Neal was in the house and he had let him stand there, finding pleasure in the torment of uncertainty which he knew was plaguing Neal. The paralysis passed. He had no way of knowing whether Henry Abel was under the man's gun or not, but he couldn't take any chances. He slipped the gun under his waistband and walked through the door, his hands high.

Abel sat on the couch, his hands folded on his lap, and in the lamplight his face was shiny with beads of sweat. Shelton stood in the fringe of light, his gun lined on Abel. He did not indicate by even a slight movement of his head that he had seen Neal come in.

"That's fine, Mr. Clark," Shelton said, emphasizing the *mister*. "I expected obedience from an intelligent man like you. Now lay your gun on the table. Draw up a chair and sit down. If you try to shoot me, I'll kill you and your banker, and everyone else in the house."

"Laurie?" Neal asked.

"She's all right," Abel said.

"So far," Shelton added significantly. "She's in her room. Her mother's with her. As a matter of fact, Mr. Clark, we've had a real good evening. I was sorry to hear you ride up."

So he'd known the instant Neal had dismounted in front of the house. It wouldn't have made any difference if he had come in through the back door. Probably it was locked anyhow. He hesitated, wondering if he had any chance to get his gun into action before Shelton killed him. A slim one, he thought, but it meant throwing Abel's life away, and he couldn't do that. Not yet, so he obeyed Shelton's orders, slowly drawing his gun from holster and laying it on the table. Then he sat down.

"I rode my horse harder than I should have," Neal said. "I'd like for Henry to go out and take care of him."

"A cowman first, a banker second," Shelton said. "All right, Abel, you do that. Rub the horse down. He's a good animal. We've got to take care of him. I'll need him before morning."

Slowly Shelton turned so his gun covered Neal. Abel rose, glancing at Neal as if trying to read his mind. Here was their chance, Neal thought, and Abel would take advantage of it. He could move the ladder that leaned against the back of the house and put it to Laurie's window. They could escape, Laurie and Jane. Neal was a hostage, but that didn't make any difference. He was a dead man anyway.

Neal nodded and Abel started toward the dining room. He

reached it just as Shelton said, "Go out through the front door, banker, and lead the horse around the house. Leave the back door locked."

Shelton was silent until Abel reached the hall door, then he laughed. It was the first time, Neal thought, that he had ever heard the man laugh, an odd sound that broke out of him suddenly and was gone as quickly as it came, leaving no lingering trace of humor on the man's cruel mouth.

"You're a pair of fools, Clark," Shelton said. "I know what you're thinking. He'll ride that horse down town and get help. Or find a gun. Or get back into the house through a window and surprise me. All right, banker, you try it. If you do, there's a woman and a kid upstairs who'll die, but if you do what I tell you, they won't get hurt." He nodded at Neal. "This is the bastard I want, not the woman or the kid or you, banker. Savy that?"

"I savvy," Abel said.

"I'll give you fifteen minutes," Shelton said. "You'd better be damned sure you're back here by that time."

Abel left the room. When the door closed, Shelton said, "I reckon you caught up with Darley and his woman."

"On Horse Ridge," Neal said. "Darley's dead."

"Shoot himself?" Shelton asked.

"No," Neal said, and told him what had happened.

Shelton shrugged. "Darley was the kind of man I needed in most ways, but he lacked guts. I'm surprised he forted up that way. He wouldn't have if she hadn't shot him and he figured you'd never fetch him back alive." Shelton turned his head and spit in contempt at the fireplace. "Women! What damned good are they? It was Darley's idea fetching her here. Now she shoots him 'cause she's worried about you and your kid. I figured she was too smart to do a trick like that."

"Maybe she's human," Neal said.

"Meaning I'm not? You're right, but you made me what I am. You're to blame, Clark. If your wife and kid get hurt, you're to blame. For eight years I haven't wanted to do anything but squeeze the hell out of your soul. I have, haven't I?"

"You know you have," Neal said.

Shelton sat down, the gun dangling between his legs. "This is just a beginning. Now you're gonna know why. That's important, Clark. I've lived tonight a million times in my mind, dreaming about how I'd be sitting here just like I am now and telling you what you done eight years ago. Listen to me, Clark. Listen damned good because you haven't got long to listen to anything. If you're thinking of that .22 in the pantry, you can quit. Or your .38 that Abel had. I've got both of 'em."

Shelton was sitting so he could watch the stairs and Neal, but the hall at the head of the stairs was dark. Neal had been hoping Jane would get the .38 and shoot at Shelton. She wasn't a very good shot, but it would give Neal a chance to try for his gun on the table. Now even that slender thread of hope was broken.

"I'm listening," Neal said.

"You've been wondering if Ed Shelly was around here, haven't you?" Shelton asked. "And you've wondered what I had to do with him. You and Rolfe scratched around trying to figure it out, the notes and Ruggles being here and who I was. The name Shelton's purty close to Shelly, ain't it?"

Neal nodded. "I'm still listening."

"Well, when you shot the Shelly outfit, you made the biggest mistake a man ever made. My name is Tuck Shelly. When I came here, I called myself Shelton because it was close enough to Shelly to make you wonder, but you couldn't prove nothing. I took the shot at you last night and missed on purpose. I hired Ruggles to come here and shoot you. Not bad. Just enough to lay you up so you'd be here when I wanted you. I missed on that. Ruggles wasn't as good with his gun as he was supposed to be."

Neal sat with his hands fisted on his lap, knowing Shelton was purposely stringing this out to make him suffer, but not knowing how long he could stand it. "All right, all right," He said. "Let's have the story." Funny, now that he thought back. Neither he nor Rolfe had seen the real significance in the names Shelly and Shelton.

"I've dreamed about this for eight years," Shelton said. "I don't aim to hurry now. I've got to make a few hours do to you what all them years done to me. I'm Ed Shelly's uncle. I was out there in the desert with my brother and his two boys. I was supposed to help on the holdup, and if I had, you wouldn't be alive today, but just before they hit the bank, I sprained my ankle, so Ed took my place."

He waggled a forefinger at Neal, his voice suddenly becoming high and shrill. "I didn't have any kids of my own. I guess I never loved anybody in my life except Ed Shelly. He looked like me and acted like me. When he was little, I took care of him a hell of a lot more'n his dad ever done. Ed's mother died when he was a baby.

"He was just a kid when you killed him. He had no business coming to town, but they had to have someone to hold the horses. You hit him. By the time he got to camp, he'd bled bad. I helped him off his horse and watched him die. From your bullet, Clark."

He got up and walked to Neal. He slapped him with his left hand, the gun gripped in his right, then struck him on the other side of the face, rocking Neal's head. He backed off, saliva running down his chin from his lips. He wiped a shirt sleeve across his mouth, and began to curse.

"I can't hurt you enough, Clark. Not half enough. I watched him die and I couldn't even go for a doctor. I couldn't do anything but watch him die, I tell you. He did, and I buried him. I sent that note from Salt Lake City so you'd know that sooner or later you'd get it. I spent my time since then thinking about what I'd do to you and who I'd get to help me. Darley was the best I could find.

"Ever since I came here I've watched you. You lost your friends. We seen to that. I thought they'd hang you. They came purty close to stringing you up, too, but they didn't, so I figured this was the next best. Get Rolfe chasing after Darley who had the money. Manion seeing 'em and telling Rolfe was luck. I hadn't counted on that, but I figured somebody would come up and see the safe was cleaned out, and guess that Darley had the money."

Neal didn't move, his hands clutched so tightly the knuckles were white. As he watched Shelton, he saw spit run down the man's chin again. His eyes were wide and wild, and Neal knew that there was nothing he could say or do that would touch him.

"Get up," Shelton shouted. "By God, you're gonna get on your feet and go upstairs with me. You'll watch what I'm gonna do to your wife and kid."

"It's me you want," Neal reminded him. "You said it wasn't Jane or Laurie."

Again Shelton wiped his mouth with his sleeve. "Did I say that?" He laughed just as he had before, a laugh that was no real laugh at all. "What are words? Nothing, Clark. Nothing! Now get on your feet and start up them stairs."

Chapter Twenty-One

Neal rose, knowing that Shelton had only one purpose, to torture him in every way he could. That had been his purpose in sending the threatening notes about Jane and Laurie; it was his reason for making them suffer now.

"I'm not going," Neal said. "Go ahead and shoot me. That's what you want to do, isn't it?"

"No," Shelton shouted angrily. "I want to twist your guts around your heart till you're dead. I won't tell you again. Get up them stairs."

"I won't go," Neal said.

This was something Shelton could not comprehend. He stood motionless, breathing hard. He cocked his gun, aiming it at Neal's chest, then he lowered it and shook his head. "I ain't letting you off that easy. We'll wait till you banker gets back."

Shelton motioned for Neal to sit down again. For a time he eyed Neal, then he began to pace around the room. Watching him, Neal thought he understood. Shelton had spent eight years planning this, relishing in anticipation his revenge upon the man he hated. Now, having reached the end of the game, he didn't know how to extract the greatest pleasure from his vengeance. Anticipation, Neal knew, gave more satisfaction than realization, and in that regard Shelton was perfectly normal.

Neal's gun was still on the table where he had placed it when he'd first come into the room, not more than ten feet from where he sat. He could make a dive for it, maybe reach the table, then Shelton would cut him down. Probably not kill him. Maybe shoot him in the leg and let him bleed to death. It was a price Neal would pay if he could save Jane and Laurie, but what possible good would it do?

No, Neal had to wait until he saw at least a slim chance of success. Henry Abel was outside. Suddenly Neal remembered the gun he had taken from Ruggles and tossed into a manger in the barn. But Abel wouldn't know about it. If Neal had thought to tell him . . . had given him some kind of signal before he left the house . . . !

No good, Neal told himself. Henry Abel was not a man to get a gun and come back into the house and shoot Tuck Shelton. He wasn't a man to run, either. He had too much loyalty for that. But for the moment he was outside and he might think of something. So Neal sat there, sweat pouring down his face, his belly muscles as tight as a drum.

Shelton sat down, leaning forward a little, his gun still in his right hand. He remained motionless for several minutes, the clock on the mantel ticking off the seconds with slow monotony. The man's eyes were riveted on him, but Neal wondered if Shelton was actually seeing him. A strange expression had taken the place of the wolfish eagerness on Shelton's face. It seemed to Neal that Shelton was so lost in the past that the present had ceased to exist for him.

Neal thought he had a chance now. He rose slowly, for a moment thinking that Shelton was in a sort of self-imposed hypnotic trance. But it was only wishful thinking. Shelton motioned with the gun, and Neal dropped back.

"Sit down, Clark," Shelton said. "I ain't ready to kill you yet, but I will if you make me. I was thinking how it's been with you, a big ranch and a bank. A purty wife and a kid you love and a fine house, everything I didn't have."

He licked his lips, and leaned forward again in his chair. He began to talk, fast, as if words could relieve the pent-up hatred that had festered in him so many years.

"My brother Buck never thought much of me. I was a back one by his lights. I was younger'n he was, and smarter. He didn't know anything except to take what he wanted by force. His wife died when Ed was little. That's why I raised him. Buck was so damned ornery he wouldn't take care of his own kid, so Ed didn't like him, but he did like me.

"I tried to keep Ed from ever riding the owlhoot. We kept him straight for a long time. Had him in school in Eugene. He didn't even know what we were till he was about thirteen. Finally Buck said he was gonna make a man out of him or kill him trying. That's what he done, with your bullet. I don't care anything about you killing Buck. Or the other boy. They had it coming. Sooner or later I'd have done it if you hadn't, but you made a mistake when you shot Ed."

Shelton got up and, walking to the table, picked up Neal's gun and slipped it under his waistband, then came back and sat down. Neal didn't understand why Shelton felt this need to talk, to explain to the man he was determined to kill, but he did realize something he hadn't before. Much of Shelton's brooding hatred had been fastened upon his brother, but Buck Shelly was dead, so he could not take his revenge on him. Only Neal.

"I told you Ed was a lot like me," Shelton went on. "I loved him. I never loved nobody else before or afterwards. I told you I watched him die, by inches out there in a dirty dry camp in the desert, and I couldn't do a damned thing. I couldn't move him. I couldn't leave him to go after a doctor. I didn't have any decent grub for him. When he died, I died, too. You killed him. When you done that, you killed me, but you didn't kill me dead. That was another mistake. You should have put a bullet into me."

The front door opened and closed. Abel was coming back! For a moment a wild hope was in Neal that Abel might have found Ruggles' gun, that he'd come out of the hall with the gun blazing. Even if Abel died, Neal would hve a chance to rush Shelton. That was all he could do, with his own gun now under Shelton's waistband.

But he knew at once he was like any drowning man reaching for a straw. Abel appeared in the doorway, pale and shivering from the cold or from fear. He said, "You rode that horse pretty hard, Neal, but I rubbed him down and I think he'll be all right."

Shelton was on his feet, his gun on Neal. He motioned for Abel to sit down. When Abel had obeyed, Shelton said, "Now Mr. Clark, we'll go upstairs. Ed was like my own son to me so I'm going to kill your girl. I've got to, you see, to be fair."

Neal leaned back, hands gripping the arms of his chair. He said, "You'll have to kill me here, Shelton. I told you I wouldn't do it."

"I think you will. If you don't, your banker gets it. First in the knees. Then both elbows. I won't kill him. He'll live, but he won't be worth a damn for anything. How about it?"

Neal looked at Abel, knowing he would have to do what Shelton wanted. He might have a chance while they were going up the stairs, or after they reached the hall. But he couldn't sit here and see Henry Abel shot to pieces, and Shelton knew he couldn't.

"Tell him to go to hell, Neal," Abel said. "He won't touch Laurie if he can't get you up there to watch it."

Shelton whirled on Abel, cursing him. Neal, looking at Abel, felt a rush of admiration for the little man who had called himself a coward, who had many times admitted he was thoroughly cowed by his wife, and who must have been through hell during these hours since Shelton had been in the house. Yet he had made this gesture, and Neal sensed he was right. Shelton probably wouldn't harm Laurie unless Neal was there to watch.

"Wait, Shelton," Neal said. "You need some advice."

Shelton turned his gaze on Neal, his eyes wild again. He said, "By God, I don't need any advice from you."

"Will you listen to me?" When Shelton was silent, Neal rushed on, "Darley had the money. If he'd got away, he'd have waited somewhere for you, wouldn't he? You'd have split and then gone on, after you finished with me. That right?"

Diverted for the moment, Shelton nodded. Neal hurried on, "This way, with Darley dead, and Santee and the sheriff bringing the money in, you'll leave here broke. Well, it just occured to me that you're stupid to ride out that way as long as the bank's safe is filled with cash."

Again Henry Abel did a surprising thing. He laughed, a good, deep laugh as if he actually saw some humor in this situation. He said, "Shelton, that would put the frosting on the cake for you, leaving here with your pockets full of Neal's money. He'd die knowing you were going to have it easy the rest of your life and he was paying for it."

"That would be smart, wouldn't it?" Shelton snarled. "Me walking down through town just as old man Rolfe showed up. Or some of these town bastards seeing me go into the bank with you."

"Rolfe and Santee won't be back till sunup," Neal said. "They've got Fay who won't be able to ride fast, and they're fetching in a dead man to boot. As for the town bastards, I guess you've fixed it so they wouldn't believe anything good of me. If they caught us cleaning out the bank safe, they'd think it was my doing."

"They sure would," Abel said. "They'd hang you and pat Shelton on the back probably figuring he was trying to protect the bank's money."

This plainly appealed to Shelton. He scratched an ear thoughtfully, looking at Neal and then Abel, and Neal again. It wasn't the money so much, Neal thought, but rather the fact that his revenge would be lengthened and sweetened. He didn't want this to end or he'd have finished it before now. He was like a child with a piece of hard candy in his mouth, sucking it, trying to make it last as long as he could.

"Got another horse in the barn?" Shelton asked finally.

"Jane's mare," Neal answered. "She's a good animal."

"A side saddle?"

"Jane rides one, but there's another saddle in the barn we can use."

"How come you're giving me advice?" Shelton asked. "Pretty good advice, too, seems to me."

"If you kill me now, it's over with," Neal said, "but if we clean the bank safe out and start across the desert, I'll get you. I don't know how, but I'll find a way."

Shelton shook his head, a tight smile on his lips. "A man in your shape naturally looks for a miracle. You won't find it, Clark. I've lived this too many time. I won't let anything happen. The fact is, I'm way ahead of you. Now I'll tell you what we will do."

Shelton paused, letting the seconds ribbon out. For a little while hope had been high in Neal. Once he got Shelton into the barn, he'd do something. He'd get hold of Ruggles' gun. Or a pitchfork. Throw a lantern into Shelton's face. Anything, he thought wildly. At least he'd have Shelton out of the house and Jane might escape with Laurie through the front door. But now, seeing the satisfaction in Shelton's face, he felt the hope die.

"We'll go out to the barn and saddle the horses." Shelton said. "Then we'll go to the bank and you'll open the safe. We'll take the money and be out of town before sunup. I hid my tracks once from Joe Rolfe and I can do it again."

He nodded at Abel. "While Clark's saddling up, you have Mrs. Clark dress the kid. She's going with us. I'll give you five minutes to get her to the barn. It'll take Clark that long to saddle the horses. I'm toting the kid. If anything goes wrong, she gets it. Understand, both of you?"

Abel nodded. Neal stood up, thinking dully that he should have forseen this. Shelton had known all along that the best way to hurt Neal was through Laurie. Whatever Neal did, he must do before Abel reached the barn with Laurie. After that he would be helpless.

"Funny I didn't think of this before," Shelton said. "There's been a lot of talk about the Barney Mountain lakes. Well, that's where we're going. I'm going to throw your kid into one of them lakes, Clark, and you're going to watch."

Neal didn't look at Abel as he walked toward the dining room. He couldn't. He couldn't even think, but he knew Shelton would do exactly what he had threatened. If Abel had sense enough to take Laurie and make a run for it through the front door . . .

"Wait, Clark," Shelton said. "Where's the key to the front door?"

"It's in the lock," Abel said. "I locked it when I came in."

"Maybe you're lying," Shelton said. "Don't make any difference, I guess. If you try taking the kid through that door, or through a window, I'll kill Clark. Understand? You've got five minutes. No more. All right, Clark. Find a lantern and light it. Let's get started."

Chapter Twenty-Two

Neal walked through the dining room into the kitchen, Shelton called back to Abel, "Damn it, get that kid dressed. Five minutes. No more. Can't you get that through your head?"

Then Shelton was only a few feet behind Neal, with the cocked gun lined on his back. He said. "There's a lantern on the back porch."

"Light it," Shelton said.

Neal unlocked the back door and opened it. "Too much wind to keep a match going," he said.

"Then get it inside," Shelton snapped. "You trying to use your five minutes up before we even get to the barn?"

He was jumpy now and nervous. It was in his voice, and when Neal took the lantern off the nail beside the door and stepped back into the kitchen, he saw it in Shelton's face. Once more hope flared up in Neal. A jumpy man makes mistakes. Up until now Shelton had been supremely confident, as if he was positive in his mind that he had the situation under control.

Neal jacked up the chimney, lighted the lantern, and lowered the chimney. He went out through the back door carrying the lantern; Shelton followed closely. They crossed the yard to the barn, and Neal could hear Shelton's hard breathing behind him.

He wondered about the nervousness in the man, and what had brought it on. Perhaps the desire for money had taken hold of him. No, that wasn't it. He had been motivated by revenge, not money, and it was unlikely he would change now. It must be that he was afraid Jane and Henry Abel would sacrifice Neal for Laurie and that would take the real flavor from his vengeance. His perverted mind had brooded so long upon the loss of his nephew that he had to have Laurie's life to satisfy him.

Neal opened the barn door as Shelton said, "Put the lantern down. I'll hold it. Get those saddles on."

Very deliberately Neal placed the lantern on the straw-littered floor of the barn. He said, "You'll never see Laurie, Shelton. Abel will tell Jane what your plan is and they'll take Laurie out through the front and get help."

"There won't be any help for you if they do," Shelton said. "Anyhow, your wife won't do that. She loves you and when a woman loves a man, she never thinks straight. She'll try to save both of you and that means she'll lose both of you."

Neal saddled Redman while Shelton stood directly back of the stall. Neal said, "This horse won't go very far tonight. I rode him too hard getting to town."

"Then you'll be walking," Shelton said. "I'll take the mare."

Neal stepped out of the stall, certain that more than five minutes had elapsed, but Shelton wasn't checking by his watch. He'd wait until Laurie got there, Neal thought. But with Laurie in the barn, and Shelton as jumpy as he was . . . ! Neal knew he couldn't wait, he couldn't risk it.

Neal glanced at the wall with its clutter of bridles and halters and harness. He said, "What the hell did I do with his bridle?"

"You've got a dozen of 'em hanging in front of your nose," Shelton said angrily. "You're stalling, Clark, and I'm out of patience. To hell with the money. We're leaving town as soon as Abel gets here with the kid."

Neal was not surprised at that. The money in the bank had been only a temporary temptation to Shelton, but now fear had worked into him, the fear of failure, of not getting the revenge he had brooded on for so long. Rather than risk having anything go wrong during the time they were getting the money, Shelton would head for the desert and put as many miles between him and town as possible before sunup.

"I remember," Neal said, and walked back along the runway. "I tossed that bridle over here."

"Damn it, you want me to plug you now?" Shelton raged. "What's the matter with these bridles?"

Neal stopped back of the empty stall. "Most of them were brought in from the ranch when Dad was alive. I don't need them any more because I just keep two horses in town. I'm going to get Redman's bridle, so hold on a minute."

The kitchen screen slammed shut. *Abel was coming with*

Laurie. Neal started toward the manger where he had dropped Ruggles' gun. This was the first time in his life he had ever been called upon to do a job of acting, and he wasn't sure he had put it across. Shelton, holding the lantern in one hand and the gun in the other, was looking at him one instant, then at the door to see if Abel and Laurie were in sight.

Neal reached the manger and leaned forward, right hand feeling for the gun. In that moment he had no doubt he was a dead man. Shelton, as jittery as he was now, would shoot the instant he saw the gun in Neal's hand.

For some strange reason Neal wasn't scared. He felt perfectly calm for the first time since he'd walked into the parlor tonight. He'd die with Shelton's bullet in him, but he had to live long enough to get Shelton. He could turn so his body would hide the gun. . . .

"Hurry up," Shelton shouted. "They're coming and you've only got one horse saddled."

"What's the hurry?" Neal asked, his hand running through the hay in the bottom of the manager. "I guess I'm not going anywhere without you."

"You're damned right you're not," Shelton snapped.

There was hay in the manger. Neal couldn't find the gun. He knew this was the right manger. Or was it? Had he tossed it . . . ?

Outside Laurie called, "Daddy, are you there?"

"Come in here, Abel," Shelton shouted. "It took you long enough to get here."

The sickness of final failure was in Neal. This was his only chance and Laurie was just outside. Then he found it. The gun had slipped down into the corner, Neal's searching fingers having missed it as they had stirred the hay.

He had the gun by the butt, saying, "I've got it, Shelton," and cocked the gun and whirled. Shelton must have heard the sound of the hammer being pulled back. He must have seen the gun, too, but when he fired, it wasn't at Neal. He threw his shot at the door. He was trying to kill Laurie!

Neal's shot slammed into the echoes of Shelton's, the blasts ear-shattering inside the confines of the barn. Shelton was knocked back against the wall, falling into a tangle of harness. He tried to swing his gun to Neal. Neal shot him again. When Shelton's finger pulled the trigger, it was a paroxysm of death, the bullet kicking up a geyser of barn litter. His legs gave under him, and he sat down, his back against the barn wall, his mouth springing open as blood began to drool from the corners.

Shelton was dead. Neal didn't even stop to look at him. He threw the gun down and ran outside. Jane was crossing the yard, crying, "Neal, Neal, are you all right?"

"Yes, I'm all right," he called.

Henry Abel was on the ground. Laurie was huddled against the wall, crying. A bundle of bed clothes had fallen from Abel's hands. Neal gathered the child into his arms, not knowing what had happened or whether Abel was hard hit. Now his mind was numb from relief. It was as if he could not think beyond two facts which blotted out everything else in his mind. Shelton was dead and Laurie was still alive.

Jane knelt beside Abel. She said, "He's been hit. Carry him into the house. I'll get the lantern. You're all right, Laurie. You can walk."

Jane got the lantern, saying nothing about Shelton. She didn't faint from the sight of a man who had just been shot. She didn't even cry out. She was made of solid stuff, Neal thought, as he slipped a hand under Abel's neck and another under his knees and lifted him from the ground.

They crossed the yard to the house, leaving terror behind them. Jane led the way with the lantern in one hand, and holding Laurie's little hand in her other one. Neal followed with Abel in his arms. Laurie was sniffling as she padded along in her bare feet. It would be a long time before she recovered entirely from the shock of this, but she would eventually, and she was alive, and for that Neal would be thankful as long as he lived.

Neal put Abel down on the couch in the parlor. "I'm not hurt," Abel said. "Just shock, I guess. Thought I was hit worse than I am."

Neal opened Abel's shirt and undershirt. It was only a flesh wound, and except for the soreness, it would give him little trouble. "Better put a bandage on it," Neal told Jane. "Just something to cover it until Doc gets a chance at it."

Neal picked Laurie up and held her. He leaned back in his chair, eyes closed, Laurie cuddling against him. He felt tired, so tired he couldn't move, but there was a sense of satisfaction in him. There would be no more nightmares for him. He could go back to the Circle C. He'd let Henry Abel run the bank, maybe coming in once a week to talk things over with him. He thought briefly that it wasn't what his father had wanted, but he immediately put it out of his mind. It didn't seem important.

He'd see Stacey in the morning. There was so much to be done here, things that took capital. If Stacey had money to invest, this was the right place for him. Suddenly he remembered the bundle of bed clothes Abel had dropped and his eyes snapped open. Jane was still kneeling at the couch.

"What kind of sandy were you pulling, Henry?" Neal asked. "That bundle . . ."

"It was Henry's way of repaying you for what you'd done for him," Jane said. "That was what he told me. I couldn't argue with him. There wasn't time."

"Hell, I never did anything for you to repay me for," Neal said.

"You're wrong, Neal," Abel said. "I've never had any illusions about myself. I've been afraid of almost everything since the day I was shot, but you kept me in the bank. I guess I just had to prove I was some good to somebody. I knew Shelton would think that bundle was Laurie all wrapped up. I had her keep out of the light so she wouldn't get hurt and told her to call to you so Shelton would know she was there."

"I don't get it," Neal said. "What were you figuring on doing?"

"I didn't know for sure myself," Abel said. "I didn't know you had a gun out there, but I knew you were going to jump him, so I thought I'd hand the bundle to him and say this was Laurie. He'd be so mad he'd go crazy and you'd have your chance, but I didn't think of him shooting at me when I came in."

Neal was silent, thinking about how Shelton hadn't cared about his own life, or Neal's, really, but he knew that if he killed Laurie and let Neal live, it would be a living death. Brutal, ruthless, maybe half mad, but he had understood perfectly how Neal felt about Laurie. Unconsciously his arms tightened around her.

Jane came to him and knelt beside him. She said. "For a long time tonight I thought I'd lose you."

"I wondered myself," he said, and put an arm around her. He looked at Abel, shocked by the thought that here was a man he had known for a long tine, and yet he had not understood him at all. Tonight Henry Abel had been willing to give up his life. He blurted, "Henry, you've got more guts than any man I know. I'm going to turn the bank over to you. We're moving out to the Circle C."

"I'd—I'd like that," Abel said simply.

Laurie had gone to sleep in Neal's arms. Jane was smiling at him, trying to hold back the tears that threatened to run over. He was lucky, luckier than he had ever realized. There was time to work on Sam Clark's big dreams. Time to help

Jud Manion out and repay an old debt. Time to let O'Hara and Olly Earl and the rest of them know he didn't hate them. Why, there was time to live, now that the shadow of Ed Shelly was no longer upon him.

The Gunfighters

1

Clay Roland saw the horse and rider when they were so far out on the desert that they were cut down by distance to the size of a slowly moving dot. He stood in front of the Piute City jail, the fall sun glinting on the silver-plated star on his vest, his gaze on the approaching horseman as he speculated about him. He might be a cowhand from a nearby ranch or he might be a stranger; he might be a friend or an enemy.

Six years' service as a law man had taught Clay many things. The one that caused him the most concern was the fact that when he pinned on the star, he made himself a target. Dead men had friends who were bound to catch up with him sooner or later, so, as a matter of habit, he gave every new man a careful appraisal.

When this one reached town, Clay saw that he was a complete stranger. At the moment he had no way of knowing whether the man was an enemy or a friend, so he remained on the street, wanting the rider to see his star. Often that was enough to determine whether a newcomer was hunting him or not.

When the stranger was opposite the jail, Clay saw that he was young, probably eighteen and certainly no more than twenty. He sat evenly balanced in the saddle as a good rider does who knows how to spare himself and his mount. Judging from the coat of dust on both the horse and the rider, they had come a long ways since dawn.

Their eyes met briefly, then the stranger looked away and rode on as if to say his business in Piute City had nothing to do with the law. Suddenly he seemed to realize he had come to the end of the trail. Probably he was anticipating a drink and supper, Clay thought, and perhaps a shave and bath and a good night's sleep as well.

The boy straightened in the saddle, alert now, his gaze swinging from one side of the street to the other. He was looking for somebody, Clay decided. It might mean trouble, it might not, but if it did, he would be involved whether the kid was looking for him or not.

Clay watched the boy turn into the livery stable. Presently he appeared in the archway and stopped, glancing up and down the street. Even at this distance Clay saw that the kid carried himself with a sort of arrogant certainty, his revolver holstered low on his right thigh and tied tightly in place as it would be with a man who realized that his life depended on the speed of his draw.

The boy stood there a full minute as if wanting to make sure he was seen, the afternoon sun throwing his long shadow against the boardwalk. Then, slowly and deliberately, he turned toward Kelly's Bar and went in.

The kid's brand seemed easy enough to read. He had come to make trouble. If Clay was guessing right, he had the choice of going directly to the boy and facing him, or waiting it out until the kid made his move.

In a case like this, Clay was never sure which was the right choice. If he picked the first alternative and the kid was proddy, he might cause trouble which was unnecessary. On the other hand, if he waited, he might permit a killing which could be avoided.

Better play it slow, he decided. There was always a possibility he had misjudged the kid. There was also the chance the boy had said something to the liveryman about his reason for stopping in Piute City. The next town was twenty miles away, long miles across a red rock desert that was never a pleasant ride. Maybe the boy knew that, or had been told, and so was stopping for the night.

Clay strode past the saloon and went on into the livery stable, his thoughts turning sour. He should be thankful for trouble. It created a job for him. If there wasn't any, a town would have no need of a marshal. Still, it was a hell of a situation when he got jumpy every time a strange, gun-packing kid rode into town.

He thought about law officers he knew who had served twenty or thirty years and had stayed alive to save enough to buy a ranch and retire. He knew of others who had been killed the first year they had worn a star.

He turned into the gloom of the stable, thinking how often he had considered doing something else. He had a few hundred dollars saved, but not enough to buy a ranch or a business. And he didn't have a home to go to. His father wanted no part of a son who was a gunman, whether he was on the right side of the law or not.

"Pop," Clay called.

The liveryman stepped out of a stall halfway back along the runway. "I was going after you if you didn't show up purty soon," the old man said. "The kid who just rode in was asking for you."

Clay drew his gun and checked it and slipped it back into leather, thinking he had known all the time that this was the way it would be. He knew something else which was even more disturbing, that regardless of how this particular affair came out, sooner or later he would meet a stranger who was faster than he was or who would wait for a chance to shoot him in the back.

Clay raised his gaze to the liveryman's face. "Did he say what he wanted me for?"

The old man shrugged. "No, but he's sure got the looks of a tough one. You see the way he carried his gun?"

"I saw it, all right," Clay said, "but it didn't prove anything. You can wear a gun the right way and still be slow."

"I wouldn't count on it." The liveryman shrugged. "Hell, it's your business. I didn't tell him you was the marshal. I said if he waited in Kelly's Bar, you'd show up sooner or later. I got the notion he knowed your name and nothing else."

"Thanks, Pop," Clay said. "I'll see what he wants."

He turned toward the archway. Before he reached the boardwalk, two shots slammed into the afternoon quiet from Kelly's Bar, coming so close together that the second might have been an echo of the first. He ran toward the saloon, wondering how there could be trouble before the kid even found him.

He drew his gun as he rammed through the batwings. The boy lay on his face near the bar, his gun on the floor within inches of an outstretched hand. Except for the bartender, the big room was empty.

"Blacky Doane done it," the bartender yelled. "Gunned him down, by God. The kid pulled his iron, but he wasn't fast enough."

Clay knelt beside the boy and, lifting a wrist, felt for the pulse. There was none. He had been shot through the heart. Clay rose, asking, "How did it happen?"

"Nobody but me and Blacky Doane was here," the bartender said. "He was sitting at a table playing solitaire like he's been doing ever since he rode into town. You know how he was. Never said a word. Tight-mouthed, Doane was."

Clay nodded, knowing exactly how it was with Doane. Ten days ago the man had ridden into town as much of a stranger as the dead boy. He had put his horse in the stable and had taken a room in the hotel, and since then had spent nearly every waking hour playing solitaire in Kelly's Bar. Not once had he indicated where he had come from or why he was here. Now it was plain enough he had been waiting for the boy, but how did Clay fit into the picture?

"Go on," Clay said.

"Well, this kid walks in like he was tougher'n a boot heel," the bartender continued. "Swaggering as if he wanted everybody to know he was the proddy kind. He comes up to the bar and asks for a beer. I give it to him and he bitches about it being warm. All the time Doane was watching. Purty soon the kid slams a letter down on the bar and says he's looking for you. He's supposed to deliver the letter to you personal. Says he'd been looking for you for a couple of weeks."

"What happened to the letter?" Clay asked.

"I'm getting to that," the bartender said. "When Doane hears that the kid has this letter for you, he gets up and says he'll take it. I guess the boy thought Doane was you till I told him different. Then he says for Doane to go to hell and puts the letter in his pocket. Doane starts toward him, saying he'll take that letter if he has to blow the kid's head off to get it. Right then the kid goes for his gun, but Doane beats him to the draw. That's all there is to it. You've got nothing to hold Doane on. The boy drew first and that's a fact."

"The letter, damn it," Clay shouted. "What happened to the letter?"

"Oh, the letter. Well, Doane kept his gun on me and told me to stand pat, then he kneels down beside the boy, takes the letter out of his pocket and goes out through the back door in a hurry."

Swearing, Clay wheeled toward the door. Pushing through the crowd that had been attracted by the shooting, he left the saloon on the run. Doane must have been sent here to keep the boy from delivering the letter. Now that Doane had the letter, he'd try to get out of town fast.

Clay guessed right. Doane was in the livery stable saddling his horse when Clay got there. He said, "I want the letter, Doane."

The man stepped out of the stall into the runway. He faced Clay, his legs spread, right hand close to the butt of his gun. He said, "I didn't aim to make you no trouble, marshal. I was paid to keep you from getting this letter. The kid would of been all right if he'd given it to me like I told him."

"You're making the trouble," Clay said. "For yourself if you don't give me that letter."

"I wasn't paid to kill you, marshal," Doane said, as if trying to reason with a stubborn child. "They don't care whether you're dead or alive. They just don't want you coming back. Now I always do what I'm hired to do and I was hired to keep you from getting the letter, so don't push me."

"Who hired you?"

Doane hesitated, then said, "I don't know, marshal, and that's the truth. Abe Lavine contracted me, but I don't know who got him to do it. I never asked. Fact is, I didn't want to know. Abe told me where you were. A man like him always has ways of knowing them things. The kid didn't. He had to hunt for you and that's why it took him longer to find you. Now I'm climbing into the saddle and I'm leaving town, so get out of my way and keep on living."

"You'll leave town when I get my letter," Clay said.

"Now look, marshal," Doane said. "The letter ain't worth dying for. You sure ain't got no cause to hold me. Killing the boy was self-defense. He pulled first. If you make me kill you, I'll do it, but it ain't smart. It just ain't smart."

Doane might be the man who was faster than he was, Clay thought. There was no way of knowing until it was tested. Doane was right, too, about having no cause to hold him. Clay didn't even know how important the letter was, or what Doane had meant about someone not wanting him to go back. That could refer to any of a dozen places, to any of a dozen people. He knew nothing about Abe Lavine, either, except that the man was a notorious gunfighter.

The point was it had become a personal thing now. A boy had died trying to deliver a letter to him. If Clay had stopped him as he'd ridden past the jail and told him who he was, this wouldn't have happened. But what was past was past; all he could do was to play it out from here.

Clay let the seconds pile up, smiling a little at Doane. This was one of the tricks he had learned. He didn't feel like smiling, but it was a mark of confidence. Let the other fellow see you were dead sure, let his nerves tighten until he broke. Maybe Doane would, maybe not. You never knew.

"All right, Doane," Clay said softly. "I've given you plenty of time to think it over. You're the one who'll decide whether you'll die or not. If you don't want to, give me my letter."

He paced slowly along the runway toward Doane. Now uncertainty had its way with him and he broke as Clay hoped he would. He threw the letter into the litter on the barn floor. "To hell with it," he snarled, and wheeling toward his horse, led him out of the stall and stepped into the saddle. He dug in the steel and went out of the stable on the run, scattering the men who had gathered in the archway.

In one of the back stalls the liveryman let out a long sigh. He asked, "How'd you know he'd cave?"

"I didn't," Clay said curtly, and picking up the letter, left the stable.

He returned to the jail, ignoring the curious stares of the townsmen who stood on the boardwalk.

2

Clay sat down in his office and threw the letter on the desk in front of him. The envelope was worn and dirty from being carried in the boy's pocket. Two words were written on it: Clay Roland. That was all. The handwriting seemed vaguely familiar, but Clay could not identify it.

He rolled and lighted a cigarette, thinking that the letter had caused the death of the boy and had very nearly caused his or Doanc's. He'd do well to throw it away and never look at it. The chances were it was an offer of a job from some other town where he had worked. Leadville. Trinidad. Santa Fe. Tucson. Hell, it could be any of a dozen places.

He picked up the envelope and started to tear it in two, then stopped. Some friend might be in trouble and was sending for him. Friend? He laughed silently. In six years of drifting from one tough town to another, he had formed no friendships. He had none here in Piute City.

His life was as empty as a man's could be. That was one of the penalties he paid for being a law man. You were always caught in a squeeze between the law-abiding and the lawless. If you killed a man, you were censured by one side; if you didn't, you were criticized by the other. If you were offered a bribe by the lawless ones, you were condemned by the righteous; if you turned it down, you were doubling the chances of being killed.

The worst of it was that when the chips were down, you could seldom count on the good people backing you. As far as friendships were concerned, it never paid to form any.

Friends only added to a law man's troubles. If they broke the law, they expected their friendship to get them out of trouble. So one thing was sure. The letter had not come from a friend.

He tore off the end of the envelope and drew out the single sheet of paper. If someone thought the letter was important enough to hire Blacky Doane to keep him from getting it, the least he could do was to read it. He unfolded the letter and sat up, suddenly alert. It was dated October 3, a little over two weeks ago, and was signed by Anton Cryder, a lawyer who was his father's best friend.

Quickly he read:

> Dear Clay:
>
> The last anyone in Painted Rock heard from you, you were in Santa Fe. I have no idea where you are now, so I cannot mail this letter to you. That's why I'm hiring Ernie Layton to find you and deliver the letter personally. He's just a boy and sometimes he's a little smart alecky, but he's about the only person on Skull Mesa I can trust. If he stays out of trouble, he'll find you and see that you get the letter.
>
> It is my sad duty to inform you that your father was killed three days ago. Apparently he was kicked in the head by a horse. He was living alone and was found in front of his house probably a day or more after he was killed. His will leaves the Bar C to you. I also have a letter for you from him.
>
> Conditions are very bad on Skull Mesa these days, with Queen Bess becoming more arrogant as time passes. She does not want a man of your reputation returning to Painted Rock, so she will go to extreme lengths to keep Ernie from finding you, and if she fails in that regard, she will go still farther to keep you from coming back. For that reason I suggest that you arrive in Painted Rock at night and come directly to my house.
>
> Sincerely yours,
> Anton Cryder

Clay read the letter through twice, then laid it on the desk. His father's death was not anything for him to grieve over. His mother had died when he was twelve and his father had raised him with considerable help from a leather strap that hung from a nail on the kitchen wall. Now, thinking back, he wondered why he had stayed home those last nine years.

John Roland had been a strong man, strong enough to do

two men's work. He had demanded a day's work from Clay even when he had been a small boy. Whatever brightness had been in Clay's life as a child had come from his mother. After her death there had been none.

Clay leaned back in his chair, thinking how it had been before he'd left home. He was twenty-one, old enough to be in love with Linda Stevens. She had been in love with him, too, but he had killed a man on Painted Rock's Main Street and his father had told him he no longer had a home. Not that it made much difference. He would have left anyway, for the situation had become intolerable.

The trouble was he asked Linda to go with him. He had no money and no job, so he couldn't blame Linda for saying no. Not the way he looked at it now, but at the time he had blamed her. He'd got roaring drunk and left town the next morning with a head as big as a barrel.

If he had any friends, they were back there on Skull Mesa. Bill Land in particular, big and handsome and ambitious. Clay had written to him a few times and it was probably from Land that Cryder had learned he'd been living in Sante Fe. Rusty Mattson, too, who never gave a damn about anything except his freedom. A strange trio, not alike in anything but still held together by the mysterious bonds of friendship. They had gone to school together, they had hunted together and fought and drunk together. More than once they had taken on six of Queen Bess's riders in the Belle Union and whipped them, making a shambles of the saloon.

Clay's friendship with Land and Mattson had added to his troubles with his father, who considered both boys worthless. To John Roland all moral values were black and white with no gray whatever. Strangely enough, Linda Stevens had been on the white side. If Clay had married her before the breakup with his father, he could have brought her to the Bar C and she would have been welcome.

Clay rose, and wadding up the paper, shoved it into his pocket. The decision was not a hard one to make. He was going back. The Bar C was his. He'd run it regardless of Queen Bess. She had always been one to lord it over her neighbors. It probably would be no different now.

If he needed help operating the ranch, he'd get it from Bill Land and Rusty Mattson. Maybe he could hire them to ride for him, and the three of them would be together again. Linda? She had been nineteen when he'd left. She'd be twenty-five now. If she was still single . . . No, that wasn't likely, but at least he could dream.

He went to the bank and withdrew his money, then he

turned in his star to the mayor, who objected because he wasn't giving the usual notice. "I've got to go home," Clay said. "I just had word that my father died." With that the mayor shook his hand and wished Clay well.

Home! Clay thought about the word on his way back to the jail. It had seldom been in his thinking for years; the idea that he would ever go back had not been there at all. But it was there now. With his father gone, the Bar C was home. It would never be a big outfit. The range was limited because the Flagg outfit had expanded until the Bar C was surrounded, but it was big enough for Clay, big enough to make a living for him and Linda if she was still single and would marry him. Foolish thinking, he told himself, but it was the way he would think until he learned she was married.

He picked up the few personal things in the marshal's office that belonged to him, then left the building and strode rapidly to the one-room cabin he rented. A place to sleep and to cook his meals. No more, but it had been all he needed. Now he hurriedly packed the things he wanted. Not much to show for six years, he thought. The next six would have to be better.

He rolled up his blankets, filled a flour sack with bacon and coffee and bread, and picking up his Winchester, started toward the door. He stopped, swearing softly. Blacky Doane was coming toward him across the vacant lot in front of the cabin.

This was a hell of a piece of bad timing, he thought angrily. In five more minutes he'd have saddled his bay gelding and been on his way out of town, heading east across the desert. He had no more official business here; he had nothing against Blacky Doane except that the man had killed Ernie Layton. Maybe the killing couldn't have been helped, but Doane had got down and crawled in the livery stable and it probably had been gnawing at him ever since. Clay knew how it was with a man like that. Once the sand began to run out, there was nothing left unless it was stopped. Doane had to make his try or he was finished.

Clay turned back into his cabin, laid the things that were in his hands on the table, and stepped outside. Doane was thirty feet away. Clay said, "The letter told me my father was dead. I'm going home. I've turned in my star. I don't want any trouble with you, so let it stand." Doane stopped, his legs spread, the sun almost down behind him. The corners of his mouth were twitching; his right hand, splayed over his gun butt, was trembling.

"Let it stand, you say? You know I can't do that, Roland. I was paid to keep you from getting that letter. Lavine said they didn't want you to come back. Well, you got the letter, so I've got to keep you from going home."

"We both know the letter's not the reason you came back," Clay said. "Likewise we both know what the reason is. It's not worth your dying for."

"I ain't the one who's going to die," Doane shouted. "God damn you, I've got to make you stay. The only way to do that is to kill you."

"You aren't fast enough to take me," Clay said. "You knew that in the stable or you wouldn't have caved. I tell you it's not worth it, Doane."

The man shook his head, his face hard set and stubborn. He said, "Make your play, Roland."

No, it wasn't worth Doane's dying for, Clay told himself, yet he had seen men die for less. For pride. Or shame. Or the fear of going on living with their reputation gone.

Clay took one long step forward, pulling his hat brim lower over his eyes. "You need all the edge you can get, Doane. You've got the sun to your back. You need that, too, so go ahead and pull."

This was adding insult to injury. Doane cursed him, and then, because he had come too far to back down, he made his draw. Clay's hand swept down, lifted the gun from leather and leveled it. He fired, his bullet hitting Doane in the chest.

Clay felt the hard buck of the walnut handle of the .45 in his hand, saw the powdersmoke roll out into the thinning light, heard the roar of the gun. This time it was Blacky Doane who was a split second too slow, his bullet kicking up dust at Clay's feet. He went down in a curling fall, his gun dropping from his hand. He lay quite still in the dust, the harsh sunlight upon him.

Clay stared at Doane's motionless body, sick with regret. He had done all he could to avoid a fight, but it hadn't been enough. According to Anton Cryder's letter, this was only the beginning if he returned to Skull Mesa. But he could not turn back. In that way he was like Blacky Doane. His course was set for him.

Wheeling into the cabin, he picked up the things he had laid on the table, and walking rapidly to the shed in the rear, saddled his horse. A few minutes later the town was behind him. He would never go back to wearing a star. That part of his life was closed out. Six years of it. Too long. Whatever lay ahead would be what he made it.

3

Clay rode steadily for three days. He crossed a desert, an empty land covered by tangy sage with hummocks of sand built up around each stalk, the dry branches rattling in the ceaseless wind. He crossed a mountain range covered by cedars and piñons; he camped near the summit in the aspens beside a small stream of clear, sweet water. He smelled the mountain smells, he heard the mountain sounds, and he breathed deeply of the thin, pure air. This was the world of the high country in which he had grown up, and he had missed it more than he had realized.

Late in the afternoon of the third day he started down a long ridge covered by cedars. Other spiny crests tipped up on both sides of him with deep canyons between them. Here and there streaks of red sandstone broke through the black-green of the cedars. These were the Smoky Hills just over the Colorado line from Utah, an outlaw country carefully avoided by men who carried stars.

A few greasy sack spreads were scattered through the hills. Men settled where they could find water, usually single men, for few women could stand the monotony and the loneliness that this harsh country forced upon them. Most of the men were wanted by the law somewhere. Tired of running, they had settled down to live their lives out in peace.

This was Rusty Mattson's kind of country. Clay had often come here hunting with him, but never with Bill Land, who was afraid of it and its people. Clay had often thought about that because it told him something about the two men. Land had no friends here, but the latchstring was always out for Mattson. Clay was accepted because he was Mattson's friend. It would have been the same for Land if he'd had the courage to come with Mattson and Clay, but he never had.

Ahead of Clay the rim of Skull Mesa was a sharp black line, as straight as if it were a ruler laid against the sky. Beyond that line on the lush grass of the mesa were the Bar C and the Flagg outfit and other ranches and the town of Painted Rock. They were two worlds, Skull Mesa and the

Smoky Hills, separated by that rim, and only a few men like Rusty Mattson and Long Sam Kline claimed citizenship in both.

Clay intended to spend the night at Kline's place at the foot of the rim where Storm River cut a gash through the cliff that was nearly a thousand feet high. A road of sorts followed the river to the top, a road barely wide enough for a wagon. It took a good man like Long Sam to bring a loaded wagon down off the mesa. On one side the hubs almost scraped the bank while on the other side they hung over fifty feet of nothing, the boiling water of Storm River directly below them.

Kline ran a combination store, saloon, and roadhouse where the Smoky Hills men bought their supplies and occasionally spent the night if the weather was bad or if they consumed too much of Long Sam's whisky, which was potent if it wasn't good. The mesa ranchers viewed the Kline establishment with distrust and talked vaguely of raiding the place and destroying it because it was a hangout for rustlers and outlaws.

On the other hand, the Smoky Hill men hated the mesa people with the deep and passionate hatred that those outside the pale often have for the wealthy and righteous who sit in the seats of the mighty. They said that if Kline's place was destroyed, they'd burn every ranch on the mesa. Clay was convinced that it was this threat more than anything else which had saved Kline's business.

Six years was long enough to dim a man's memory of a country. Somewhere Clay took a wrong trail that brought him off the ridge and down to the river below the Kline place, wasting at least an hour for him. It was dark before he heard the pound of the river in the gorge and saw the lights in the windows of the Kline house ahead of him.

A man stepped out of the shadows as Clay pulled up and dismounted. He asked, "Looking for a place to stay?"

"That's right," Clay said, wondering who the man was. "Got an empty room?"

"You bet." The man leaned forward, peering into the darkness. "You can get a drink and grub inside if you're running low."

"I'll settle for supper and breakfast in the morning," Clay said. "Where'll I put my horse?"

"I'll take him," the man said. "Which way did you come in?"

"From Utah, if it's any of your business," Clay said.

Something wasn't right here, Clay thought. As he remembered the place, Long Sam never hired any help. He had a daughter named Ardis who took care of the rooms and the kitchen and served the meals. Kline did everything else.

Caution took hold of Clay. He backed away, asking, "This the Kline place?"

"That's right." The man hesitated, then asked, "You wouldn't be Clay Roland?"

"Long Sam never used to ask questions," Clay said.

"Long Sam's dead," the man said. "Ardis is running the outfit. I'm working for her. Name's Monroe."

"Ardis particular about who she does business with?"

"No, it ain't that." Monroe hesitated again, then prodded, "You ain't said whether you're Clay Roland."

"I'm Roland," Clay said. "What the hell difference does it make?"

"Difference, he says," Monroe said softly, as if the question made Clay a fool for asking it. "I'll tell you and I'll make it quick. You're close to being a dead man. I don't know you, so I don't give a damn one way or the other, but I'd like to keep Ardis out of trouble. Now I'll tell you what you do. You go into the dining room and stay out of the store side. There's two front doors. I guess you've been here before, so you know which is which."

Monroe would have led the horse away into the darkness if Clay had not grabbed his arm. "This takes a little explaining. Why do you want me to go into the dining room?"

"I'm trying to save your life," Monroe said. "We've been watching for you and now you're here. Do what I tell you."

Anger began building in Clay. "This takes a little more explaining, mister."

"I've told you all I'm supposed to." Monroe jerked free of Clay's grip. "From what I hear, you've got two friends in the whole damned country and you'd better do what you can to keep 'em. Ardis is one. She wants you to come in through the dining room. If she ain't there, go on back to the kitchen."

This time Clay let him go. So Long Sam was dead and Ardis was Clay's friend. He remembered her as a redheaded tomboy who kept the place clean and cooked good meals and could ride as well as most men. She'd been about sixteen or seventeen, he thought. She'd be a woman now, but he didn't know why she was his friend. And who was the other one? Anton Cryder maybe.

Clay hesitated, staring at the windows, then he shrugged. Just as well do as he was told. He stepped up on the porch and opened the door into the dining room. It was empty and the door into the store and bar was closed. He heard pans rattle in the kitchen. He looked at the door into the store and wondered what was on the other side of it that he wasn't supposed to see.

He walked between the tables to the kitchen. A woman was standing at the stove washing dishes, her back to him. She was small, not over five feet tall, the size Ardis had been the last time he had seen her. He remembered her hair as being fiery red, but it was darker now, more auburn than red. She had filled out, too, but that was to be expected, for she had been as slim-bodied as a boy six years ago.

He said, "Ardis."

She whirled, holding her dripping hands in front of her, and stared at him for a moment, her eyes wide. Pretty, he thought, much prettier than he had expected her to be, with the saucy, lively face of a woman who enjoys every moment of life.

"Clay," she said. "Clay, I didn't think you'd ever really come."

She ran to him, wiping her hands on her apron. When she reached him, she threw her arms around him and kissed him on the mouth, then she drew her head back to look at him, her strong young arms still around him.

"It's a funny thing how you keep hoping for something to happen," she said, "and you count the minutes and keep on hoping, and all the time you don't think it ever will." She dropped her arms, and motioned toward the table in the middle of the room. "I'll fix your supper right away. You don't mind eating in here, do you?"

"Of course not, but I want to know something. Your man told me not to go into the store. Why?"

She hesitated, her eyes searching his face as if not quite sure what he would do, then she said, "Abe Lavine's waiting for you in there. I don't want him to know you're here."

"Why?"

"Because . . ." She swallowed, her gaze still fixed on his face, then she forced herself to go on. "Because he'll kill you."

4

For a long moment he stared at her, questions pushing at him. Why had she greeted him the way she had? Why was she so anxious to keep him alive? Why was Abe Lavine waiting to kill him? He could guess the answer to that one. Lavine had not been sure Blacky Doane would do the job for which he had been hired. Lavine's presence here was simply insurance that Clay never reached the mesa. He could not think of answers to the other two questions.

He said, "Ardis, did it ever occur to you that I might kill Lavine?"

"Do you know him?"

"No."

"If you knew him, you wouldn't ask that question. About a year ago Queen Bess hired him and a punk kid named Pete Reno. In the year they've been on the mesa, they've killed five men in gunfights in Painted Rock. Pa saw the last one. He said he'd never seen a man as fast as Lavine, and Pa knew a lot of gunmen. Some of the best have stayed here in this house."

Clay nodded, knowing that was right. Long Sam Kline might have been right about Lavine's gun speed, too, but right or wrong, Clay was not a man to duck a fight. If he was going to live on Skull Mesa, this was a situation that had to be met sooner or later.

"I'd better let Lavine know I'm here," Clay said.

He turned toward the dining room. She cried out, "You can't do this, Clay. You just can't."

He swung back to face her. "Would you think any more of me if I hid here in the kitchen and ate supper, then sneaked upstairs to a bedroom and sneaked out in the morning without him knowing it?" He shook his head at her. "I don't think you would, Ardis, and I know I'd think a lot less of myself."

This time she let him go. She stood motionless beside the kitchen table, her hands clenched at her sides, her face very white. Clay paused before he opened the door into the store and bar, checked his gun, and eased it back into the holster. Turning the knob, he opened the door and stepped into the other room.

Nothing had changed here. He remembered the room well. The store counter was on the side next to the dining room, the shelves behind it filled with staples. A pine bar was on the other side, a bracket lamp on the wall above it. One man stood in the fringe of light at the far end of the bar. Clay moved slowly toward him, feeling the man's probing gaze on him.

"You serve yourself if you want a drink," the man said, "and you lay your money on the bar. The girl who runs this layout thinks everybody is honest."

"I don't want a drink," Clay said. "You're Abe Lavine?"

"I'm Lavine," the man said.

Clay was ten feet from him when he stopped. Lavine was as tall as Clay, and more slender, a barren-faced man with a black mustache, whose feelings and thoughts were secrets known only to himself. His eyes were pale blue, his hair dark brown and thatched with gray at the temples.

Lavine was older than Clay had supposed he was, his sun-blackened skin deeply cut by lines around his eyes and down his cheeks. Forty at least, Clay decided, and possibly even older, a veteran at the gunfighting game. His expressionless eyes, his long, supple fingers, the black-butted gun holstered low on his hip: all this was evidence that he knew his business.

"I'm Clay Roland," Clay said. "They told me you've been waiting for me."

Lavine gave a half-inch nod of agreement. "It ain't been so bad, waiting here. The whisky is worse than you would believe if I told you, but the girl is a good cook and the bed's all right." He picked up his hat from the bar and put it on his head. "I'll go tell Queen Bess you're here. She'll want to know."

Lavine moved toward the door, passing within three feet of Clay but not looking at him. His back would have been an inviting target for some men. Clay said, "Lavine, you've lived a long time to be this careless."

Lavine turned, a faint smile touching his lips. "I know quite a bit about you, Roland, so it isn't carelessness."

"Maybe not," Clay said. "I didn't suppose you knew that much about me. Maybe you know something else. Why does Queen Bess want to keep me off the mesa?"

"You'll have to ask her. I just work for her."

"Then take a message to her. I'm going to live on the Bar C."

"I'll tell her. Anything else?"

A cold one, Clay thought, this Lavine, and probably as dangerous as Ardis thought. He said, "One more thing. Blacky Doane is dead."

"I'm not surprised," Lavine said. "He never was as fast as he thought he was."

"A kid named Ernie Layton had a letter for me and Doane killed him to keep me from getting it. Why?"

"I wasn't there, so I don't know. I told Doane to keep you from getting the letter, but I didn't tell him to kill the Layton boy. I avoid trouble if I can. The way I figured, it would save a hell of a lot of trouble if you never heard from Cryder. Trouble is it didn't work. Two men are dead. You're going to run the Bar C, and that means more dead men, so I was wrong."

He gave Clay that short nod again, and turning to the door, opened it and went out. Clay cuffed his hat back and scratched his head. He had been geared for a showdown that hadn't come. He didn't understand it. He returned to the kitchen to find Ardis standing exactly where he had left her. When she saw him, she pulled a chair back from the table and sat down quickly as if her wobbly knees would no longer hold her.

"I didn't think it would be you," she whispered. "I thought it would be Lavine."

"And I'd make a run for it." He shook his head at her, frowning. "Never run from anything, Ardis. If you run once, everybody hears about it and they'll figure you'll run again. Chances are you will, too."

She rose. "I'll fix your supper."

He hung his hat on a nail and sat down at the table. "Did he tell you he was going to kill me?"

"No, but everybody around here knew that Anton Cryder had sent for you, and everybody knows Queen Bess won't let you run the Bar C. She's said it often enough and I guess nobody ever heard of her going back on her word. Pete Reno was here for a while watching for you, then he left and Lavine came. If they didn't aim to kill you, why were they here?"

"I sure don't know," he said. "Lavine was real polite. Just told me he'd let Queen Bess know I was here. Said she'd want to know, but I don't savvy why she's so bound to keep me from coming back."

"I don't know." She dropped slices of ham into a frying pan and returned to the table. "There's something else, Clay, something I want you to help me with. Will you?"

"Sure. I'll try anyhow."

She stared down at her hands that were folded on her lap. "Funny how well I remember you, Clay. It seems a long time ago and we were both young. I guess I was just a kid to you, but you weren't a kid to me. Rusty was. He still is in some ways. I don't think he ever will grow up, but it was different with you. I don't know why, but you always gave me the feeling that you were going to do something big and good some day."

He grinned at her. "I never had any such notion in my head."

"Maybe not, but it was what I thought. Rusty says you never had sense enough to be afraid. I guess you're still that way, or you wouldn't have gone after Lavine the way you did." She paused, biting her lower lip, then added, "Clay, I think my father was murdered. I want his killer punished."

"How did he die?"

"His wagon went off the road in the gorge last June. The river was terribly high. We didn't find his body for two days. When we did, it was all chewed up the way it would be in the river. He'd gone to Painted Rock for a load of supplies. He might have been a little drunk. He was sometimes when he came back from town, but drunk or sober, he could bring a wagon down that gorge blindfolded. I just don't believe it could have been an accident."

"Why would anyone kill him?"

She rose and going back to the range, turned the ham. "For the same reason that mesa bunch has always talked about," she said. "Things have changed since you were here, Clay. For the worse. Did you know that Queen Bess was paralyzed from the waist down and spends her time in a wheel chair?"

He shook his head, shocked by what she had said. He remembered Queen Bess as an active woman who had run her ranch with great skill, an excellent rider who knew as much about the cattle business as any man Clay had ever met. It was impossible to think of her bound to a wheel chair and delegating the responsibility for running the outfit to her foreman, Riley Quinn.

"What happened?" he asked.

"Apparently she was thrown from a horse," Ardis answered. "At least her horse came in and her men found her several hours later between her place and the Bar C. She was unconscious. They got Doc Spears and he brought her around, all right, but she was paralyzed. Not long after that she hired Lavine and Pete Reno. A lot of bad things have happened since then, including the death of your father.

Mine, too. I think both of them were murders. Maybe she's gone crazy, sitting there in that chair the way she does."

"Now hold on," Clay said. "What makes you think Dad was murdered?"

"A hunch," she said. "He knew horses as well as Pa knew that gorge road. I don't think he'd let a horse kick him to death any more than Pa would drive off the road."

"But who would do it?" he demanded. "And why?"

"Riley Quinn maybe. Or Lavine or Reno. I believe Queen Bess ordered it done, but I don't know why. Not your dad. It's easy enough to guess why they killed Pa. They were talking about rustling before you left. There's been a lot more talk lately. Pa got the blame for it."

She forked the ham from the frying pan into a plate and took it to him, then brought bread and a dish of beans from the pantry and coffee from the stove. He watched her quick, graceful movements, thinking about what she had said.

Ardis was right in saying there had always been talk of rustling and the Smoky Hills men had always been suspected, but Clay doubted that it had ever amounted to much. When there was more winter loss than was expected, a rancher naturally thought of rustling. This was one of the reasons Clay's father had objected to him running with Rusty Mattson, who had been linked with the Hills men since he'd been a kid. No one had ever proved anything against him, but Rusty's rootless life naturally brought him under suspicion.

"Where's Rusty?" Clay asked.

She smiled. "Hard to tell. You can find his campfires all through the hills, winter or summer. He comes here often, so I'll see him one of these days. When I do, I'll tell him you're back, and he'll come to the Bar C to see you."

She turned quickly from him and walked to the stove. "Then I suppose they'll kill him. They've posted him off the mesa. They've put posters up all along the rim that say he's got to stay off the mesa. If he doesn't, anyone will be paid five hundred dollars who shoots him or brings him to Painted Rock a prisoner."

"They can't do that. There's no law that says . . ."

"Oh, Clay," she cried. "Don't you know there's no law on the mesa except Flagg law? Queen Bess was the one who got Ed Parker appointed marshal in Painted Rock. He never arrests a Flagg hand, but he'll arrest anyone else. He'll arrest you if she says to whether you've done anything or not."

Clay shook his head, unable to believe that Anton Cryder had meant all of this when he had written that conditions were bad on Skull Mesa. He'd see Cryder tomorrow and ask him.

Ardis came to him and put a hand on his shoulder. "Maybe you don't believe me, Clay, but after you've been here a while you will. I loved my father. He never hurt anyone. In his way he did a lot of good. It just isn't right that his murderer should go unpunished. Will you do something about it?"

He looked at her and nodded. "I'll try," he said, and wondered if he, like Rusty Mattson, would be posted off the mesa.

5

Abe Lavine reached the Flagg ranch sometime after midnight, put his horse away, and slipped into the bunkhouse so quietly that even Pete Reno, who slept across from him, did not wake up. He stared at the dark ceiling, only half hearing the snores of the men, although he was always aware when the foreman, Riley Quinn, rolled over on his back. Quinn was a powerful snorer, but no one complained. Flagg men soon learned that it didn't pay to complain about anything to Quinn.

Lavine's thoughts fastened on Clay Roland. He had wanted to meet Roland for a long time. By Lavine's standards, everything he had heard about Roland had been good. In many ways they were similar. He had been pleased to observe that physically they were somewhat alike. Both had pale blue eyes and brown hair, both were about six feet tall and slender, with Roland having heavier shoulders and arms. Roland was younger, too, maybe twenty-six or twenty-seven.

Lavine was forty-two, old enough to worry about age slowing him up. He had been bothered about this for the last two years, realizing that the years had subtracted just a little from the fine physical co-ordination which had given him the fast draw that had earned him his reputation. Even more important than anything age was doing to him was the fact that he had begun to worry. That was fatal, he knew. This would have to be his last job. That was something else which had worried him. He didn't know what else he could do. Guns had been his life for twenty years or more.

Clay Roland was young enough to have many good years ahead of him, but he was smart to come back to a ranch that belonged to him. Even considering the odds he was bucking, he was still smart. He didn't scare, and that was a big mark on his side of the ledger. It was hard to whip a man who didn't scare. But the main thing was that Clay Roland had something of his own to fight for. That was the big difference between Roland on one side, and Abe Lavine and Pete Reno on the other.

Gunfighters came in all sizes and shapes, each with his own individual code of ethics. It made no real difference that some carried stars and some didn't. Lavine had known law men who liked to kill and used their badges to make the killings legal. There were others, like himself, who had never carried a star but lived by a strict code that kept them from killing unless they were forced into a fight.

The star was immaterial. The standard by which a man lived was the important thing. If you knew a little of a man's history, you could make a fair guess as to what his standard was. That was why Lavine had felt perfectly safe in turning his back on Roland at the Kline place; he knew Roland's history for the last six years.

Lavine thought about Pete Reno, who had ridden with him for a couple of years. Reno was only twenty now. He seemed to get worse instead of better. He was somewhat like the Layton kid who had gone down before Blacky Doane's gun, brash and arrogant and too eager. If Reno had been staying at the Kline place when Roland rode in, he'd have forced a fight and probably been killed. Lavine wished it had happened. He never should have let the boy throw in with him, but he had, and now it was hard to get rid of him.

Lavine's thoughts returned to Roland again, and he realized with keen regret that fate had put them on opposite sides, that sooner or later he'd be facing Roland with a gun in his hand if he continued to work for Bess Flagg. The smart thing to do would be to quit now, but he liked it here. The pay was good. And he liked Linda Stevens, who worked for Queen Bess. Not that he had any chance with her. She was engaged to marry Bill Land and that was too bad.

The gossip was that Linda had been Clay's girl before he'd left the country and that Land had been Roland's friend. An interesting situation that was loaded with dynamite, he thought, as he dropped off to sleep.

He woke with the crew at dawn. He dressed and shook Pete Reno awake. The boy would sleep through breakfast if Lavine didn't wake him. The cook wasn't one to put himself out cooking an extra breakfast for a kid like Reno. Lavine sat down on his bunk and rolled and smoked a cigarette as Reno rubbed his eyes and yawned. Quinn and the crew had left the bunkhouse.

Reno dressed, still yawning and shaking the cobwebs out of his head. He asked, "Roland show up?"

"He's here," Lavine said.

"Kill him?"

"No."

Reno shot him a quick glance. "Why not?"

"You know our orders," Lavine said. "Come on or we'll go hungry."

They stepped out into the cold dawn light, both men buckling their gun belts about their waists. They found seats at the end of the long table, Riley Quinn and the crew ignoring them. This was the way it always went, for the two of them were set apart from the others. All of them, Riley Quinn in particular, resented their presence.

Lavine drowned his flapjacks with syrup as he considered Quinn. He guessed he wasn't as happy here as he kept telling himself. He certainly had no reason to like Quinn. The foreman was a squat man, five feet six or so, and almost as wide as he was tall, with a neck that reminded Lavine of an oak anchor post and a temper that resembled a buzz saw.

Glancing at him, Lavine noticed that a stubborn lock of hair had fallen across his forehead. Impatiently Quinn swept it back with a big hand and went on eating. He wasn't a good foreman in Lavine's opinion. He was too hard on his men, too unyielding on any question on which he had made up his mind.

Quinn was fanatically loyal to the Flagg outfit and to Queen Bess personally, a characteristic which did nothing to improve Lavine's opinion of him. Loyalty alone wouldn't keep him from making a mistake. Being the kind of man he was, any mistake he made would be a whopper.

The crew drifted out, spurs jingling. Reno looked at Lavine when the last man had left. He said, "Sometimes I wonder how long it would take him to break the neck of a man like you or me."

"Or Clay Roland," Lavine added.

Reno nodded, grinning. "There's a neck he'd enjoy breaking."

"No more than yours or mine," Lavine said. "He was

sore the day Queen Bess hired us and he's been sore ever since. He'll keep on being sore until she fires us, figuring that there's nothing we can do he can't."

"Maybe there ain't," Reno said. "I sure don't savvy why you didn't plug Roland when you had a chance."

Lavine finished his coffee. He glanced at the boy's pimply face, the pouting lower lip, the green eyes, and shook his head as he rose. "I never learned you nothing," he said. "I'm not sure whether I'm a bad teacher or you're stupid."

He went out into the early morning sunshine, glancing southward at the sandstone cliffs on the other side of town from which Painted Rock got its name. At midday they were maroon, but at this hour when the sun rose into a clear sky, they changed to a fiery red. To Lavine they were beautiful, even a source of strength at times. He never quite understood how that was, but it was true, although he never mentioned it to anyone.

He drifted across the dusty yard to the corrals where Quinn was giving the orders for the day. Reno caught up with him, saying petulantly, "I ain't going to be called stupid."

"Can I help it if you act stupid?"

"You're scared of him," Reno said.

"Don't tell anyone," Lavine said. "I sure don't want it to get out."

The men began riding off. Quinn wheeled his horse toward Lavine and reined up, his big head tipped forward so that his eyes raked Lavine. He said, "I guess Roland showed up or you wouldn't be here."

"That's right," Lavine said.

"You tell him to stay off the mesa?"

Lavine shook his head. "My orders were to tell Mrs. Flagg if he showed up. That's what I'll do."

Even after working out of doors for years, Quinn's face was not tanned by the high country sun. Instead it burned, with the result that his skin was red and constantly peeling. Now it turned scarlet as quick anger boiled up in him. "By God, I wish I could give you an order once in a while. I'd work your tail off."

"I guess you would." Lavine grinned as the foreman whirled his horse and raked him cruelly with his spurs. He nodded at Reno. "We're about done here, Pete. Either we go or Quinn goes."

"We ain't going," Reno said. "This is too good a job."

"Maybe," Lavine said. "Maybe not. Well, I'd better go see the boss."

He turned toward the big ranch house, wondering whatever had possessed old Hank Flagg to make him build a sprawling, two-story house like this. It had happened years ago, but Lavine had heard the gossip in Painted Rock often enough. Twenty years or more ago Hank Flagg had married Bess and brought her here. He had built the house over her objections, telling her brusquely it was her wedding present. Hank had lived three years and died, leaving Bess the ranch with a house she didn't want. Now the outfit was twice what it had been in Hank's day, and according to the talk in Painted Rock, Bess was twice the man Hank had been.

Lavine went around to the back of the house where he knew Queen Bess would be having breakfast, and knocked. She called, "Come in." He opened the door and stepped inside, nodding at Ellie, a Negro woman who kept house for Bess, and went on to the table where Linda Stevens sat beside Bess.

"Have a cup of coffee, Lavine," Queen Bess said in her big voice. "Ellie, fetch him a cup."

"Yes, ma'am," Ellie said, and brought a cup and the coffeepot to the table.

"Thank you, I will," Lavine said, and dropped into a chair across from Linda as Ellie filled his cup.

"Good morning, Mr. Lavine," Linda said.

"I hadn't noticed if it was a good morning or not," Lavine said. "I guess it is, though."

"What's the matter?" Bess asked. "Have trouble with Roland?"

Lavine shook his head. "A short night. That's all. He got in after dark, so I was late getting here."

He glanced at Bess, who had rolled her wheel chair back from the table and was studying him intently. Even at forty she was a handsome woman. In spite of her big voice and large, capable hands, she was very much a woman, and he thought he would have liked to have seen her before her accident.

He said slowly, "This Roland seemed to be all right. Why don't you let him . . ."

"Lavine, I'm surprised at you," she broke in. "Clay Roland will never work the Bar C. It doesn't even exist. It's part of Flagg range. Did you tell him that?"

"No. He gave me a message for you. He said he was going to work the Bar C."

"You're a fool, Lavine. That's when you should have killed him."

He was always shocked at the change that came over Bess when she talked about Clay Roland. Ordinarily she seemed a pleasant woman who was easy to get along with as long as she wasn't crossed. She seldom was. In the year he had been here, he had watched her hatred for John Roland grow until it had become a poison in her. After his death she had fastened that hatred on Clay.

He shook his head at her, not liking the darkness that flowed across her face, the ugly way her mouth tightened against her teeth. He said, "No, I'm not a fool. Two weeks ago we decided how to play this. It was the right way. Don't change it now."

She tapped her fingers on the arms of her wheel chair, staring at him in the strange, blank way she always did when they talked about Clay Roland. It was as if she was seeing Roland in her mind and not Abe Lavine.

"We will change it," she said. "We'll post him off the mesa the way we did Mattson. Somebody else will kill him. If they don't, we will. I want you to go to town and have the posters printed today. Tomorrow you and Reno see they're put up."

"You have no grounds for that," he said.

"Suspicion of rustling is all the grounds I need," she snapped. "Everybody knows he used to run with Mattson. If Mattson steals cattle, so will Roland."

"No, it's different with Roland," Lavine said. "Folks know about him. He has a reputation as a law man. I heard about him a long time before I came here. It's easy enough to pin a rustling charge on a drifter like Mattson, but you can't do it with Roland."

She leaned forward, her hands gripping the arms of her chair so hard the knuckles turned white. "Lavine, are you telling me my business?"

"No ma'am," Lavine said. "This is my business. You're paying for my experience as well as my gun. I wouldn't be earning my pay unless I gave you some suggestions."

She leaned back in her chair. "All right, Lavine. Let's hear your suggestions."

This irritated him, for they had covered the ground carefully two weeks ago before he had hired Blacky Doane to see that Cryder's letter never reached Clay Roland. Now there was nothing to do but go over it again.

"You've got to figure out how to deal with each case," he said. "Nobody cares whether Rusty Mattson is posted off the mesa or not except his friends out there in the hills. He's smart enough to stay off. It's different with Clay Roland. The sheriff may live a hundred miles from here, but he's heard about Roland. So has the governor. If this isn't handled just right, somebody, Anton Cryder maybe, will send for the sheriff. Or write to the governor. You don't want either one to happen."

"Why not?"

He picked up his cup of coffee and drank it, wondering why she would ask a question she could answer as well as he could. He put the cup down. "You know why."

"I want to hear you say it."

"Mrs. Flagg, I've seen operations like this before. In the long run the pattern is the same. People stand for it for a while. They grumble but they stand for it. Then something happens that's a little too much for 'em to stomach. They'll holler for help from anybody who'll give it. Maybe the sheriff comes and rolls back the rug. He starts at the corner and keeps rolling and pretty soon the whole thing comes out into the open."

"Nobody can prove anything," she said harshly.

"It's not always a matter of proof," he said. "It's more a proposition of somebody fitting the parts together."

"I see. So we've got to wait until we see the right method of handling Roland. That it?"

"That's the size of it. Maybe it'll take a month. Six months. A year. You've got plenty of time."

"That's where you're wrong. I'm not waiting any six months. Or even one month. You're going to town this morning and get those posters printed. We'll hold them till it's time to put them up or something else comes along that looks better." She nodded at Linda. "Hitch up the buggy and take Linda with you. She hasn't been to town for a long time."

Lavine glanced at Linda as he rose. She nodded and said, "I'd like to go with you if you don't mind."

"My pleasure," he said, and left the kitchen.

Linda was ready by the time he brought the buggy to the front of the house. She stepped into the seat, smiling at him. She was a tall, willowy woman, with black hair and dark brown eyes that were expressive. She was pretty enough, but not too pretty. That was one of the things he liked about her. He had known too many women who were in love with their own beauty.

"I didn't particularly want to go to town," she said, "but I did want to talk to you. How did Clay look?"

"Fine. He's a good man. He deserves a chance to live here in peace."

"You liked him, didn't you?"

He nodded. "Funny thing. I don't usually cotton to a man the first time I see him."

"It's too bad," she said bitterly. "Sooner or later you'll kill him, won't you? Or he'll kill you."

"Maybe not. I don't know how much longer I'll keep this job. Quinn's getting pretty ringy."

"Quit it now, Mr. Lavine," she cried. "Right now."

"Why?"

She looked toward the mountains to the east, their slopes still dark with morning shadows. She said slowly, "Did she have you kill Long Sam Kline and John Roland?"

"No. That's not my style."

"But she did have them killed, didn't she?"

"I think so. I couldn't swear to it."

"Don't you see what will happen? You'll be the sacrificial lamb if Queen Bess has to offer one. Riley Quinn is her man. He'd do anything for her, and she'll save him regardless of how many others she throws to the wolves."

"It could work that way," he said. "People around here naturally think the worst of me." He glanced at her, wondering why she kept on working for Queen Bess and why she had ever accepted Bill Land's proposal of marriage. He said, "I guess you want to see Roland."

"I'd like to," she said.

He thought about that all the way into Painted Rock, finally deciding that Linda would never have accepted Land if she had known Roland was coming back. Seeing him today would be a mistake, but he couldn't think of any way to stop it. All he could see ahead was trouble, and both he and Linda were caught right in the big middle of it. He wished he could tell her how he felt about her, but that would be stupid, telling a woman seventeen years younger than he was that he loved her.

Then the bitterness took hold of him. It wasn't the years; it was the life he had lived. He would not make any woman a fit husband. Even if he had a chance with her, he couldn't tell her. He wanted to put his arms around her, to feel her young body against his, but he looked straight ahead, holding himself under tight discipline. She might as well have been a mile away.

6

Clay left the Kline place after breakfast, telling Ardis he would be back as soon as he could and for her to keep Rusty Mattson off the mesa. Rusty couldn't do any good now. He'd just get himself killed. Ardis agreed, although she wasn't sure that wild horses could keep Rusty off the mesa once he'd heard that Clay was back.

Halfway up the gorge Clay dismounted and looked over the edge of the shelf road at the rumbling river below him. This was where Long Sam Kline had gone over. The river was low now, but during the spring runoff it was a swollen monster, overflowing its banks on the mesa and then roaring down this narrow canyon as it ate at its imprisoning walls and sent boulders as big as houses thundering down the full length of the gorge.

There was nothing to see now, of course, not even a trace of the wagon or the horses in the canyon below Clay. He wished he had been here when Kline was first missed. He might have found something then. From experience he knew that the best-disguised plan for murder always leaves traces behind it if a man searches carefully enough. But the chances were that no one had looked.

He mounted and rode on, thinking about it and about his father's death. He could not see a good motive for the murder of either one. But there was much he didn't know. He wondered if Bill Land or Anton Cryder would talk freely to him. Or Linda Stevens. He had not asked Ardis about her and Ardis had failed to mention her. That was the first thing he would ask Cryder.

He reached the mesa a few minutes later and went on up the river toward the Bar C. The road to Painted Rock ran parallel to the stream, the ridges on both sides of the small valley cutting off the view except for the San Juan Mountains that lifted above the horizon far to the east, a sawtooth line of granite peaks that raked the sky.

An hour later he reached the Bar C. He rode slowly now, old memories crowding his mind. His gaze swung from one building to another and then to the long, narrow hay fields that lay on both sides of the river.

Nothing had changed, he thought, except that there had always been Bar C cattle around, grazing on the ridges or the fields among the haystacks. None were in sight now. No horses in the corral. No dog to bark a welcome. Not even an old hen scratching around the barn and sheds. His father had always kept a few Plymouth Rocks because he liked fresh eggs.

He dismounted in front of the house, leaving the reins dragging. He felt a strange, unfamiliar ache in his chest. This was home, but it wasn't home. Just a deserted ranch house, the front door open. No smoke rising above the chimney, no sign of life anywhere.

He drew his gun and strode up the path to the door, suddenly realizing that if Queen Bess wanted him killed, she might have stationed one of her men inside to shoot him when he stepped through the door. Instead of going in, he wheeled sharply, and ducking under the windows, ran around to the back and went into the kitchen. No one was there.

He crossed to the front room, his boot heels making sharp echoing sounds on the floor. He searched the bedrooms, glanced into the closets, and then, returning to the kitchen, looked into the pantry. The house was empty.

He holstered his gun, feeling foolish although he knew that his suspicion of an ambush had not been caused by a sudden jangling of nerves. It had been a very real possibility. He prowled through the house again, going first into the bedroom that had been his. As far as he could tell, it had not been touched in the six years he had been gone. The bed was made up, and that raised the thought that perhaps his father had expected him to come back sometime. His clothes were still in the bureau drawers. A pile of toys and other boyhood possessions were in the closet. He remembered his father had asked him several times to go through it and throw away the things he didn't want, but he never had.

Back in the kitchen he saw that the woodbox was full, a pile of kindling on the floor beside it. His father had been methodical that way, seeing to it that there was always enough kindling to start another fire if the one in the big range went out.

The table was clean except for the coating of dust upon the red-and-white oilcloth. The pantry shelves were stacked with cans and sacks of food. Here again his father had been methodical, always laying in a month's supply of food in case a bad storm made the trip to town impossible.

His father hadn't changed and never would if he had lived another twenty years. Clay felt this even more strongly in the front room with its leather couch and potbellied heater, the claw-footed table with the chessmen set alongside the board, the whites on one side, the blacks on the other.

Anton Cryder had likely been here not long before the accident and they'd played a few games, maybe spending a full Sunday afternoon at the chessboard. It was the one relaxation his father had had, and the games were usually nip and tuck between him and Cryder.

Clay remembered that Queen Bess used to visit with them, although he seldom stayed home when she was here. His father had laughed when he'd told Clay how he had taught Bess to play chess, but after a few games, she refused to play. She hadn't won any. She couldn't stand losing, even something as unimportant as a game of chess.

Suddenly the echoing emptiness of the house got to him. He couldn't stay here, not even long enough to cook a meal. He couldn't stand it, living by himself the way his father had for six years. He would have welcomed Rusty Mattson's company, even knowing the danger it meant to Rusty.

He closed the window and the doors, and mounting, rode on up the river toward Painted Rock. He'd find out about Linda. Maybe he could get Bill Land to come out and stay with him for a while. He had forgotten to ask Ardis about Land. He had no idea what his friend was doing, but he remembered that Land had never been much on hard work if there was any other way to make a living. He'd be company even if he didn't work. Or maybe Anton Cryder could find a good man who needed a job.

Clay tried to make plans as he rode. The cattle were gone, probably driven out of the country as soon as his father's death had become known. The horses were gone, too. Well, he'd have to buy a small herd and a few horses.

Then he shook his head. Foolish thinking, he told himself. The first thing was to prove he could live on the Bar C with someone or alone if he had to. He had no idea what Queen Bess would do, but he had no doubt she would make her move soon.

He climbed steadily. Gradually the slopes on both sides of the valley flattened out and he could see for miles across the rolling mesa, the Flagg buildings making a lump on the horizon north of town. The red cliffs that gave Painted Rock its name lifted sharply above the mesa to his right. Farther to the south were the Snow Mountains, and on his left to the north was the long, aspen-covered ridge known as the Divide. This was Flagg summer range, the best in the country, and he could be reasonably sure that Queen Bess hadn't given up an acre of it.

He reached Painted Rock at noon, seeing a little, piddling town with no more than two dozen buildings spilled out here on the mesa. It was Queen Bess's town as surely as the Flagg ranch was hers.

As a boy it had seemed a city, but to Clay Roland, the man, coming back after six years, it was nothing, yet he sensed that it was filled with all the evil that would be spawned from hate and greed and arrogance. He still didn't know the reason why so much of it should be aimed at him, but maybe Queen Bess had reached the place where whim instead of reason dictated her actions.

He passed the stable, the tar-papered shack that housed the Painted Rock *Weekly Courier* across the street from it. Some vacant, weed-covered lots, then the Belle Union, the hotel, the bank, and Doc Spears's drugstore. He glanced at the upstairs window of the drugstore and shock hit him like a hard fist in his stomach. Letters painted on the glass read William Land, Attorney at Law.

He reined up in front of Walters' Mercantile and dismounted and tied, his gaze still on the sign. So Bill Land was a lawyer. Clay knew he shouldn't have been surprised. Land would be a good lawyer by some standards—big, handsome, glib-tongued, and not too particular about how he made a dollar.

When Clay had been a kid running around with Land and Rusty Mattson, these things hadn't been important, but they were now, and the truth jolted Clay. Six years had done this, three boys who had gone three separate ways and had become men. Looking back, Clay could see why his father had felt the way he had about the other two.

Anton Cryder's office was over the Mercantile. Clay turned toward the outside stairway that led to the second floor of the building. Funny how Bill Land's sign, the one thing on Painted Rock's Main Street which was different, had given Clay's thoughts a new turn.

Lawyers were the same as other men. Some were honest and some were crooks. Cryder was one of the honest ones. Nothing would ever change him. Clay was ashamed of his thoughts about Land, yet he could not escape the conviction that the man who had been his friend was the exact opposite of Anton Cryder.

He was halfway up the stairs when he heard heels pound on the boardwalk in front of the Mercantile, then a woman's voice called, "Clay."

He glanced back. Linda Stevens stood there, her head

tipped back, her dark eyes shining as she said, "Clay, I was hoping I would see you."

For a moment he didn't move. His heart suddenly began doing crazy things in his chest so he couldn't breathe. This was Linda in the flesh, an older and mature Linda, but still the girl he had loved when he'd left, and now he told himself he had never quit loving her.

"Clay, what's the matter with you?" she asked. "Aren't you glad to see me?"

He moved then, rushing down the stairs to her. "Glad?" he shouted. "I was never gladder to see anyone in my life than I am you."

She started to back away as if frightened by something she saw in his face, but he would not be put off. He grabbed her in both arms and picked her up and whirled her around. "Clay, put me down," she cried. "Put me down. You're a madman."

"Sure I am," he said.

He put her down and kissed her, never thinking he should ask if she was married. For a moment she resisted him, her lips stiff and cool, then resistance fled and it was the way it used to be, her mouth sweet and eager, her long, willowy body melting against his.

The street had been deserted a moment before, but it wasn't now. A big hand caught Clay's shoulder and whirled him around, another hand slapped Linda across the face, slamming her against the store wall.

Bill Land said, "By God, I'll kill you for that. She doesn't belong to you now."

A fist caught Clay flush on the jaw, a hard blow that jolted him and sent a flow of stars dancing before his eyes. His feet went out from under him and he sat down hard, his head ringing. He looked up into Land's fury-filled face, and he saw murder written there as clearly as he had ever seen it on the face of any man.

7

Clay was momentarily dazed. He could see and hear, but he couldn't move. Bill Land was reaching into a coat pocket for a gun, deliberately as if he had all the time in the world. Watching him, Clay had the nightmarish feeling that he could do nothing but sit here and take Land's bullet.

He heard the pound of a man's boots on the boardwalk, then Lavine's voice, "Land, I'll kill you if you pull that gun." Linda flung herself at Land and tried to grab his right arm, but he struck her on the side of the head, a hard blow that spun her away from him and almost knocked her down.

Clay came unstuck then. Lavine was still twenty feet away when Clay got to his feet and lunged at Land just as a small gun appeared in his right hand. He dropped it and swung his left as he backed up, a futile blow that missed by a foot, then Clay was on him. He had never been as crazy angry before in his life and he had never hit a man harder. His right was a looping uppercut that caught Land flush on the jaw and swiveled his head half around. He followed with a left that smashed Land's nose and brought a spurt of blood.

"Use your gun on him, Roland," Lavine yelled. "He was going to kill you."

Clay heard the words, but their meaning didn't get through to him. He couldn't think of anything except beating Bill Land into a helpless mass of flesh. The unfairness of the attack, the totally irrational and stupid attempt at murder from a man he had once called his friend, a man he had looked forward to seeing again: all this combined to turn Clay into a fighting maniac.

Land dropped the gun into the dust and kept backing into the street, unable to defend himself against Clay's furious attack. He pawed at Clay; he tried to keep his hands up in front of his face, and when he did, Clay lowered his blows to the man's heart and stomach. Land was never able to regain his balance; he was on the defensive and Clay kept him there, the sound of his blows meaty thuds that could be heard the length of the block.

Unable to stand Clay's punishing blows to his body, Land lowered his forearms to protect his stomach, then Clay caught him with a swinging right to the chin and Land went down. Standing over him, Clay said, "Get up, Bill. Or have the law books made you so soft you're whipped already?"

Land got to his hands and knees. One eye was almost shut, his lower lip was split and bleeding, and his nose was a mass of jellied meat and blood. He tried to get to his feet, but the strength wasn't in him. His arms broke at the elbows and he fell flat on his face into the dust.

Land rolled over on his side, saying thickly, "I'll kill you for this, Clay. By God, I'll kill you."

Clay backed off, panting and sweaty and sick at his stomach. It was more than Bill Land's battered body lying in the dust in front of him that made him sick; it was the end of a dream he had cherished through all the long miles from Piute City to Painted Rock.

Clay whirled and walked away as Linda's voice came to him, "I'm sorry, Clay. I'm engaged to marry Bill."

Men had rushed out of their places of business to watch the fight, men Clay had once known well. Bud Walters who owned the Mercantile, Doc Spears, Link Melton from the Belle Union; men who should be welcoming him home and shaking his hand, but they only stared at him in sullen silence. He could not mistake what he saw in their faces. They might as well have said in words that they wished he'd stayed away.

Clay reached the foot of the stairs when Lavine caught up with him. He said, "You're good with your fists, Roland. Real good for a man who has a reputation as a gunfighter."

Clay stopped and turned to face Lavine. The man was friendly, if expressionless neutrality could be called friendly. Clay said, "Maybe that reputation is something I won't need around here."

"You'll need it," Lavine said grimly. "What shape are your hands in?"

Clay held them up and closed them into fists and opened them and closed them again. "Knuckles skinned up a little. That's all."

"You were foolish," Lavine said. "You're too good a man to go under because you've bunged up your hands on a bonehead like Bill Land."

"My hands are all right," Clay murmured, staring at his closed fists. "I'm going to be working cattle. There's plenty of things that can happen to a man's hands when he's on a ranch." He lifted his gaze to Lavine's thin, saturnine face. "Which side are you on?"

"An interesting question," Lavine said as if not quite sure himself. "I think I'm on the wrong side."

Lavine wheeled away to where Doc Spears and Linda were kneeling in the dust beside Land. When Land saw him, he said bitterly, "You threatened to kill me."

"You know why?" Lavine asked. "I guess you wouldn't, so I'll tell you. If you'd shot Roland when he was lying there half knocked out, nobody could have saved you from a hanging, not even Bess Flagg."

Clay turned and climbed the stairs. So Bill Land, attorney, belonged to Queen Bess. Well, he should have guessed that, too. Was there anything on Skull Mesa she didn't own?

He opened the door to Anton Cryder's office and went in. The lawyer had been standing by the window watching the street. Now he turned, and Clay, seeing his face, deeply lined and as gray as ancient parchment, realized that these six years had been long ones for Anton Cryder.

The old man was very thin and apparently he had a catch in his back that kept him from standing erect. One of the things Clay remembered about him was the ramrod-like posture that had seemed remarkable for a man in his late sixties.

"You're a fool, Clay," Cryder said as he crossed the room and offered his hand.

Clay shook hands with him. "A lot of people seem to think that," he admitted.

"I wrote to you to come to my house at night," Cryder said, "but no, you couldn't do anything that was intelligent and safe. You show up at noon as bold as brass, riding down Main Street so everybody'll see you, you kiss another man's girl, and then you beat hell out of him. If you could have done anything to make your score worse with Queen Bess, I guess you'd have done it."

"Could it be any worse?"

Cryder's liver-brown lips curled in a smile. "Now that you mention it, I guess it couldn't." He motioned to a chair. "Sit down. You're looking well. I'd say Land never laid a fist on you." He chuckled softly, and added, "I've been waiting for quite a while to see somebody make hash out of Bill Land. I enjoyed watching it."

Clay sat down and rolled a smoke, thinking that Cryder was right in calling him a fool. But playing the safe, sly game was not his style. In the long run, the direct way of meeting trouble was the best for him. He wouldn't have done anything differently if he could have gone back and lived the last hour over.

"So Linda's going to marry Bill," Clay said.

"That's what Bill says," Cryder agreed, "but there's a funny thing about it. She works for Queen Bess, you know. Sort of a companion as I get it. Land is Bess's fair-haired boy about like Riley Quinn. I guess Linda is engaged to him, all right, but he can't seem to get her to the altar even with Bess's help."

"You're saying she don't love him?" Clay demanded.

"Hell, how would I know who she loves?" Cryder grunted. "All I'm saying is that Land hasn't been able to get the knot tied, which doesn't mean you can move in and take her away from him. A lot of folks on the mesa like being on the winning side. It's safer. Maybe Linda's like that. Anyhow, it would be a hell of a thing to marry her just so she could be a widow the next day."

"You talk like I was whipped already," Clay said irritably. "Well, I'm not."

"No, but you will be," Cryder said. "You're a good man, Clay. We've heard a lot about you since you left." He opened a drawer and took out a long envelope. "Here is your dad's will and a letter he wrote a month or so ago. I haven't read the letter. Maybe he's told you he was proud of you, but he was a hard-headed man. Backing up on anything he ever said was a tough thing for him to do, so maybe he didn't. But he was proud of you. You can take my word for that."

Cryder laid the envelope on his desk, and picking up his pipe, filled it and fished in his vest for a match. "I'm sure you're a brave man, Clay. Likewise you're a fighting man, but any way I count you, you're still only one man. The odds are too long against you. What you don't know is that there isn't anyone on the mesa you can count on to help you. I would if I could, but you need fighting help, and I'm too sick and old for that."

Clay nodded and flipped his cigarette stub into the spittoon, then reached for tobacco and paper and rolled another one. After what had happened just now, he believed what Cryder told him. It wasn't just Bill Land. It was all the others, Ed Parker and Link Melton and the rest, men he had liked and who had liked him in the old days for all of his wildness; but a few minutes ago they had looked at him as if he were a carrier of typhoid fever.

"Queen Bess came to see me the other day," Cryder went on. "You knew she's paralyzed?"

Clay nodded. "I stopped at Kline's place last night. Ardis told me."

"She couldn't get her wheel chair up my stairs, so she sent that gunslick Lavine to tell me to come down. I thought she had some legal business for me, but I should have known better. She gives all of it to Land and passes the word for everybody else to do the same."

Cryder scowled at the filled bowl of his pipe. "That's a hell of a thing, Clay. I've been here ever since they laid the chunk. For years I was the only lawyer within fifty miles. Whatever legal business there was, I had it. Well, Bill Land went to Montrose, read law in Judge Zale's office, and came back here and put out his shingle. Now I don't get any work. If I didn't have some savings, I'd starve to death."

Anton Cryder had never been a bitter man, but Clay saw the bitterness that was in his face now, the bitterness of an old man who has been made useless through no fault of his own.

"Well, she told me to tell you if you showed up that she would pay you one thousand dollars for the Bar C, lock, stock, and barrel, and you were to keep on riding. I thought I'd tell you before you read your dad's letter. Now she didn't say what she'd do if you turned her offer down, but you can guess. She's always been a strong-willed, driving kind of woman, but after she got hurt and Doc Spears told her she'd never get any better, she got mean. Crazy mean. If you stay, she'll get you killed, one way or the other."

Cryder handed the envelope to Clay. "The will is short and simple. Everything goes to you. A quarter section of deeded land where the buildings are, the cattle and horses, and the cash in the bank. Not much. Less than a thousand dollars."

"I've known men to die for less," Clay said.

He read the will which was as short and simple as Cryder had said, then he tore the envelope open which was marked, "Clay." He glanced at the smooth, flowing handwriting that he remembered so well, handwriting that was as easily read as printing. Clay rose, and walking to the window, stood with his back to Cryder as he read the letter.

> Dear Clay,
>
> You will not be reading this letter unless I am dead. Right now my health is perfect, but violence has a way of taking lives in this country and I have a feeling that I will not live very long. Everything I have goes to you, of course. I hope you will live on the Bar C and keep it up as I have, but do not consider

this the binding request of a dead man. Do whatever your best judgment dictates.

I am writing this letter for only one reason. I want to tell you that after all these years I realize I was wrong when I sent you away. I am proud of the record you have made as a law man. A wild country like the West needs men like you. I will not try to explain why I sent you away. At the time the reasons seemed good. The truth was I thought you would go away and get the wildness out of your system, but you didn't. Perhaps it is better this way. I don't know. I do know I'm lonely and I would like to see you. If you decide to make the Bar C your home, I hope you will be as happy as I was when your mother was alive.

Your father,
John Roland.

Clay folded the paper and slipped it back into the envelope. For the first time in his life he had a feeling of sympathy for his father he'd never had when John Roland was alive. As he turned to face Cryder, he said gravely, "I would have come back if he had written this to me when he was alive."

"He couldn't bring himself to do it," Cryder said. "He was my best friend, but I knew his good qualities as well as his faults. He was a hard man in many ways and maybe a foolish one for not surrendering and writing to you, but I don't think he could."

"I'm not any more anxious to die than the next man," Clay said, "but you tell Bess Flagg I don't want her one thousand dollars. I'm staying."

"I thought you would," Cryder said, "being John's son. I'll do anything I can for you, Clay. Don't forget that. It's just a question of whether you can use what I have to offer."

"Ernie Layton is dead," Clay said, and told him what had happened in Piute City.

Cryder puffed hard on his pipe, hiding his face behind a cloud of tobacco smoke. A long minute passed before he could control his emotions enough to say, "I sent the boy to his death."

"It wasn't your fault," Clay said. "He played it like a fool. He saw me standing in front of the jail. He must have known I'd be the marshal because from the time he started tracing me he would have heard I was a law man, but he didn't stop. He just wanted to make a show of finding me, I guess."

"I still sent him to his death," Cryder said.

He would torture himself over this as long as he lived, Clay thought, whether it was his fault or not. Clay changed the subject with, "Ardis Kline told me she thought her father was murdered."

Cryder nodded. "I wouldn't be surprised. You know the talk about the Smoky Hills boys rustling mesa cattle. Later on it got worse and Kline was blamed for it because they hung around his place. Riley Quinn is a brutal son of a bitch. It's a good bet that he talked Queen Bess into getting rid of Kline. Not that it would have been hard."

Clay sat down again. He had laid the last cigarette he'd rolled on the corner of the desk. Now he picked it up and lit it, then he said, "Ardis told me she thinks Dad was murdered, too."

Cryder nodded again. "I wouldn't be surprised at that, either. A couple of Flagg men found him and brought his body to town. I drove out there and looked around, but I was at least twenty-four hours too late to find anything. Some horse tracks were in front of the house, but they didn't prove anything. I asked Doc Spears about it, but I didn't get any satisfaction out of him. He wouldn't tell me if he knew. The side of John's head was caved in, but I couldn't tell from looking at it whether the injury was from a beating with a club or the kick of a horse."

Clay leaned back in his chair, frowning, the cigarette dangling from one corner of his mouth. "Why did Queen Bess do it? And why is she so set on keeping me from living here?"

"I'll tell you, but I don't think you'll believe me," Cryder said. "She was in love with John, but he wouldn't marry her."

Clay jerked the cigarette out of his mouth. He shouted, "By God, Anton, that's the craziest thing I ever heard."

"It's the truth," Cryder said, "crazy or not. It's not so hard to understand, either. John was a handsome man, the kind that would appeal to a woman like Bess. She's been a widow for a long time. She had no interest in men who ran after her. John didn't, and that challenged her, so she ran after him. It's public knowledge, though I doubt anyone else would tell you. After you left, she just about hounded John to death. He could have had a good life with her if he could have let himself be bossed, but he couldn't. Besides, he loved your mother. After she died, there was never another woman for him.

"Well, Bess would go over there and cook for him. She stayed late at night and he couldn't get her to leave. Finally she got to coming during the night. She tried her damnedest to seduce him. Once she undressed in front of him. I don't know whether she ever made the grade or not, but she might have. She was a fine-looking woman before she got hurt and John was a lonely man. Anyhow, he wouldn't marry her.

"About a year ago they had a fight. Bess couldn't stand being put off any longer. She lost her temper and hit him and he pushed her out of the house and locked the door. Being Bess Flagg, she went clean crazy, I guess. She got on her horse and rode out of the yard like a rocket. Somewhere between there and her place she got thrown. She still went to see him, making Lavine lift her into the wagon seat, then he'd put the chair in the bed of the wagon. She kept telling John he was to blame. Somewhere along the line she got to hating him. Maybe she decided that if she couldn't have him, nobody else would."

Clay got up and dropped the cigarette that had gone cold into the spittoon. "What about me?"

"Your name's Roland," Cryder answered. "She hates anyone who has that name. Being John's son, you're all that's left of him." Cryder shook his head. "Maybe it's more than that, though. A lot of people hereabouts hate her. You won't hear any of them talking about it, but they hate her, all right. Those two gunslicks she hired make it worse. Riley Quinn doesn't help, either. It might be that a man with your reputation could be a leader who would make big trouble for her. She's not going to take that risk."

Clay slipped his father's letter into his pocket and turned toward the door. Cryder asked, "What are you going to do?"

"I'm going to live on the Bar C," Clay answered.

"You can't go out there now," Cryder said. "They'll raid the Bar C and kill you. Stay here in town with me for a few days."

"Would tomorrow be any better to move out there?" Clay asked. "Or the day after tomorrow? I don't think so, Anton."

He nodded at Cryder and left the lawyer's office.

8

Clay ate dinner in the hotel dining room, ignoring the curious stares that were fixed on him. After he finished eating, he stepped into Doc Spears's drugstore in the vague hope that he could persuade the medico to tell him more than he had told Cryder about his father's death, but the doctor wasn't in.

"He's upstairs fixing Bill Land's nose," Mrs. Spears said. "You don't look sick to me. Don't bother Doc unless you are."

"Thank you kindly, ma'am," Clay said, and going outside, climbed the stairs to Land's office.

He found Land sitting at his desk, Doc Spears across from him. The lawyer's battered nose was bandaged, one eye was shut, and his mouth was so bruised and swollen that it was an effort to talk. When he saw Clay, he shouted, "Get to hell out of here."

The words were slurred so that they were hard to understand. "You don't talk very plain." Clay closed the door behind him and nodded at Spears. "You're the one I want to see. If I was looking for a lawyer, I wouldn't hire one who was inexperienced like Bill, especially with his face marked up like that."

Land muttered a curse and yanked his top drawer open. Spears said sharply, "Don't be a fool, Bill."

"That's right," Clay said. "You try using that gun on me again and I'll kill you. I'm not sitting on the walk knocked silly by a sneak punch like I was a while ago."

Land hesitated, his good eye glittering with virulent hatred, then he slammed the drawer shut and sat back. He said thickly, "Get out."

"What's the matter with you, Bill?" Clay asked. "The whole mesa has gone crazy, and I'd say you're the craziest one on the mesa unless it's Queen Bess. All the time I was riding back I was thinking you were the one man I could count on. Well, I sure counted wrong."

"I represent Mrs. Flagg," Land said. "It is my duty to inform you that the Bar C has been absorbed by the Flagg ranch and you will be treated as an outlaw if you attempt to operate it as a ranch."

Clay cuffed his hat back, staring at Land and shaking his head. "Sounds like you've been reading Queen Bess's special set of law books. Maybe she can steal my range, but she sure as hell can't take a quarter section of deeded land. Even a stupid lawyer knows better than that."

"You're forgetting you're on Skull Mesa," Doc Spears said. "You're right when you talk about Queen Bess's special set of law books. They're the ones we go by here."

Land motioned to the door, a quick, violent gesture. "Get out. By God, I won't tell you again."

Clay didn't move. He kept his gaze on the lawyer, wondering if this was the same Bill Land he used to ride with. He asked, "How's Rusty?"

"I don't know," Land answered. "He never comes to town any more."

"He has to keep off the mesa, doesn't he?" Clay pressed. "That's more of Queen Bess's law, isn't it?"

Land got up, his fists clenched in front of him. "It's not like it was six years ago, Clay. Can't you understand that? Can't you savvy that if you stay here, you're committing suicide?"

"No, it isn't the same for a fact," Clay said. "We used to have a lot of fun, you and me and Rusty, but it looks like we never will again."

"We were boys then," Land said. "Just kids helling around. You think you can ride off and come back six years later and find that life has stood still all the time you were gone? You think you can pick up with Linda just like those six years were six days?"

"No, I couldn't expect that," Clay admitted, and yet he knew that was just about what he had expected. "But I sure didn't think I'd find you bought and paid for by Queen Bess." Clay turned to Spears. "He's no different than everyone else on the mesa, is he, Doc?"

"No one except old man Cryder," Spears said, "and he's starving to death. Anybody who bucks Queen Bess will starve to death." He grinned mockingly. "What did you expect to gain, coming up here and talking tough as hell to us?"

Spears was a small, weasel-faced man in his middle thirties. He had not been considered a good doctor six years ago, but he was the only one within fifty miles. It was probably the same now. Like Bill Land, he wanted to be on the winning side. Maybe what he had said was true, that you starved to death if you weren't on that side.

"I came here to ask a question," Clay said. "Was my father kicked to death by a horse or was he murdered?"

"No question about it," Spears said blandly. "He was kicked to death by a horse."

"I think you're lying," Clay said. "I expect to see you again one of these days, and when I do, I'll get a different answer out of you."

"I'll see you, but you won't see me," Spears said. "I'm an undertaker, too, you know."

Clay wheeled and left Land's office. He would get the same answer everywhere he went, but now that he had gone this far, he'd go a little farther, for the record if nothing else.

Crossing the street to the barber shop, he found Ed Parker alone. Clay said, "I want to ask you a question, Ed."

Parker wasn't wearing a gun, but the marshal's star was on his vest. He glanced at the star as if he thought it held some magic that would give him strength. Finding none, he backed up so he stood behind his chair. "I'm not wearing a gun, Clay."

"Do you need one?"

"I don't know. I don't know why you're here."

"Funny thing, Ed. I used to have a lot of friends in this town. I've sat in that chair a hundred times and we talked about a lot of things. It was the same when I'd go into the Belle Union. Or just stand on the street. Hunting talk. Fishing talk. Cow talk. The kind that goes on between friends, but do you know that in the hour or so I've been in town only one man has offered to shake hands with me?"

"You know the reason." Parker shook his head sadly. "Every day I think about moving with my wife and children, but I stay. We've been here a long time and I keep thinking that something will happen to change the situation, but it never does and I guess it never will."

He was honest, Clay thought, more honest than Bill Land or Doc Spears. He was big and strong, with unusually supple fingers for a man of his size. Clay had never seen him draw a gun, but he might be reasonably fast. It wouldn't help if he was, for there was no real courage in him. Most of the townsmen were like Parker, Clay told himself. Probably the mesa ranchers were, too. The only man on the mesa who had any sand in his craw was Anton Cryder and, as he said, he was too old and sick to fight.

"I feel sorry for you, Ed," Clay said. "You don't sleep very well, do you?"

"No, I haven't slept very well since Queen Bess hired Abe Lavine and Pete Reno." Parker motioned toward the Belle Union. "Five men have been shot to death over there in less'n a year. I saw it happen twice. The other three times I was sent for after it was over. All five times I had to call it justifiable homicide. Self-defense. They weren't even held for trial."

"Were all these killings in fair fights?"

"Sure, if you want to call 'em that, but Lavine and Reno are gunslicks. They were brought here to put the fear of the Lord into the rest of us and they have. I wouldn't have any chance against either one of 'em. No more'n I would against you. Neither would Bill Land or Doc Spears or Bud Walters." He hesitated, then added in a belittling tone, "Somebody's got to wear the star. Once in a while I lock up a drunk. That's all I'm good for."

"How would it work if I wore that star for a while," Clay said. "I wouldn't want the job permanent. I'd see you got it back."

"The town wouldn't hire you," Parker said.

"Because Queen Bess wants me to move on, I suppose," Clay said. "Anton Cryder gave me two or three reasons. One was that a lot of people hate her. If I stayed, I might turn out to be a leader for those people. You won't admit it, but for the sake of your family you'd like to see things different. For the right to sleep at night, too, I guess. Could be that there are a lot of other people like you."

Parker shook his head. "It's no use, Clay. Get off the mesa while you can. They'll kill you if you stay. I've heard it said too many times after your pa was killed."

"I've handled men like Lavine and Reno," Clay said. "I can do it here."

"They're just symptoms, boy," Parker said wearily. "They're not the cause. Suppose you did kill 'em? She'd hire others."

Clay nodded, knowing it was true. "All right, Ed. I came in to ask you if you knew anything about Dad's killing. Or Long Sam Kline's. I heard both men were murdered."

"I don't know nothing about 'em," Parker said. "I don't have any authority outside of town. You know that."

"And if you knew, you wouldn't tell me, would you?" Clay said bitterly.

He walked out of the barber shop, not waiting for Parker's answer. As he strode along the walk toward his horse tied in front of the Mercantile, he thought about going in and asking Bud Walters if he could have credit to buy supplies to last the winter. But it wouldn't do any good. Walters would be like the rest. He'd tell Clay he wasn't a good risk. Queen Bess knew all the ways to squeeze a man, and credit or lack of it was one of the best. She had the town treed and no mistake.

He untied his horse, and mounting, rode out of Painted Rock. Everyone would be relieved when they saw him go, he thought. They'd be more relieved if he left the mesa, but that was something they'd never see.

Now that Clay had read his father's letter, he knew he could live on the Bar C alone. Maybe it wouldn't make any sense to anyone else, but it did to him. For the first time in six years he was at peace with the memory of his father. The letter had done that for him.

Suddenly the thought struck him that Ed Parker had been right about symptoms. On an impulse he turned off the road and angled north toward the Flagg ranch. He had always believed that the way to head off trouble was to meet it before it got to him. Trouble with the Flagg outfit was too certain and too big to head off, but at least he'd show Bess he wasn't running. He might be foolish to take the risk, but he had little to lose and he might gain something. At least it made more sense than arguing with men like Bill Land and Doc Spears.

Linda was kneeling on one side of Bill Land, Doc Spears on the other, when Abe Lavine took her firmly by the arm and pulled her to her feet. He half led and half dragged her down the street to the buggy.

"I'm going to take you home," Lavine said. "You can't do him any good."

She knew he was right. He gave her a hand into the buggy seat, then untied the horse and stepped up beside her. Taking the lines, he drove out of town.

She sat huddled there, her hands folded on her lip, shoulders hunched forward, not feeling the chill wind that blew across the mesa. She hated Bill Land. Still, she knew she had been wrong. She shouldn't have come to town. She shouldn't have called to Clay. She shouldn't have let him kiss her.

Linda was not always honest with other people, but she was with herself. She had come to town in hopes of seeing Clay, she would have been miserable if she hadn't called to him, and she had enjoyed his kiss. In that one sweet moment she had been stirred in a way that no man had stirred her since Clay had left.

Staring at the dusty ribbon of road stretching ahead of the buggy like a taut, gray ribbon, she asked herself why she had ever promised to marry Bill Land. She didn't love him. She never had, she never would, and she had never told him she did. He said he loved her, but she didn't believe it. It would be a marriage of convenience for both of them: security for her, and for him a capable wife who would be a credit to him and his career.

After Clay had left, she'd turned down several men who would have made acceptable husbands. She should have left the country with Clay when he asked her, but her mother had been alive then and her mother had needed her. Besides, the desire for security had always been strong in her mind, and security was one thing Clay could not give her. Still, the hope that some day Clay would come back for her had been the reason she had turned down the men who had courted her. She was well on the road toward becoming an old maid when her mother died and Queen Bess gave her a job.

Linda had been reasonably happy with Queen Bess and that was a strange thing. Bess had no friends unless you call men like Riley Quinn and Bill Land friends. She had been terribly lonely, so she had hired Linda, a paid-for companion who would sit with her and sew or read or talk if Bess felt like talking. No real work was required except helping Bess dress or take a bath or get into bed.

The strangest part of the arrangement was that Bess had made it plain from the beginning that she wanted Linda to marry Bill Land. He began courting her from the time she had moved out to the Flagg ranch and Bess had said repeatedly that Bill had a great future ahead of him, in politics as well as law. She was going to have him run for the legislature next year.

As Mrs. William Land, Linda would have all the security in the world, so she had finally surrendered and accepted his ring, but that had been a year ago. Somehow she had succeeded in putting off the wedding date, much to Land's disappointment. She couldn't do it much longer. Both Bess and Land were getting impatient.

After what had happened today . . . She was sick with fear as she thought about it. She'd lose her job. Bess would have a tantrum if she found out Clay had kissed her and then beaten Bill Land into the dust the way he had. She could not stand defeat and Bill Land's defeat was hers.

They were a mile from town when Lavine's words broke into her thoughts, "Damn a man who hits a woman. You can't marry him. You're too good for him."

She looked at him in surprise. He was not one to let his feelings show in either his voice or his face, but now he spoke in hot anger. She saw it in the somber cast of his strong-featured face, heard it in the harsh tone of his voice.

Impulsively she laid a hand on his arm. "Thank you," she said, "but I'm not good. It's the wrong word to use about me."

"No it isn't," he said quickly. "You're a woman a man should be proud to call his wife. You're not a woman to be batted around on the street in front of everybody."

"I don't know," she said miserably. "I was wrong, but he was more wrong. It was just that I hadn't seen Clay for so long . . ." She stopped, unable to tell him how wrong she had been, how much she had wanted to see Clay and what his kiss had done to her. She added, "Bess will have a fit when she hears."

"You don't have to stay out there," he said. "Quit your job and give Land's ring back to him. You're not a slave to be sold or bought." When she remained silent, he demanded, "You're not in love with Land, are you?"

"No, I'm not," she said, and wondered why she was admitting it to Lavine. She tried to change the subject with, "Did you get the posters?"

"No, they won't be ready till evening." He gave her a searching look, then he said bluntly, "You can't love Clay Roland, either. You can't love a man who went off and left you for six years, a man who will be dead in a matter of hours."

That shocked her. She knew it, but still it was shocking to hear it said so bluntly. Her hand tightened on his arm. "Abe," she said, and stopped, realizing it was the first time she had ever called him by his first name. She hurried on, "Can't you help him? It isn't fair for him to come back and have his home taken away from him and get killed because Bess wants his land or just hates him because she hated his father."

"No, it isn't fair," Lavine admitted, "but there isn't much that goes on around here that is fair. There won't be as long as Queen Bess runs things. I've known a lot of cattle barons. Men, I mean. They all run to about the same pattern. The bigger they get, the bigger they want to be, squeezing and strangling everybody who's in their way.

"Most of my jobs have been helping men like that. I've always hated them because they didn't have enough courage to do the job they hired me to do. Bess is the worst I ever ran into, her and Riley Quinn. Now seems like I can't stand myself any more. I guess it's partly because I like the cut of Clay Roland's jib. Like you say, it isn't fair, though I never thought much about fairness before. But there's nothing I can do for him."

He pulled the horse to a stop and turned to her. "Linda, I said to myself a while ago when we were going to town that I wouldn't tell you how I felt about you. I'm too old for you and I've got too many men on my back trail who will try to kill me if they ever catch up with me, but after what happened in town, I've got to tell you. I love you. I want you to marry me. Today. Tomorrow. As soon as you can. Then I'll take you away from here."

She stared at him, wide-eyed. She had never been more surprised in her life. She had talked to Lavine so few times; she had never dreamed he had any decent human emotions. He was a cold-blooded killing machine, or so she had thought, but now she sensed a softness in him she hadn't known he possessed.

"Oh Abe, you never . . . I mean . . ."

She could not say what was in her mind. She could not find the right words, but he seemed to understand. "I know how people look at me and think about me. Most of them hate me. If you hate me for what I've been and what I've done and what I'll probably have to do in the future, say so and that will be the end of it. I'll never speak to you about it again."

"I don't hate you," she said. "It's just that I never thought of you that way, but I know I've got to leave here and maybe you're the one to take me. I need to think about it. I've got to think about Clay, too. It was a shock, seeing him today."

"I'll wait," he said. "You think about it."

She leaned forward, her face close to his. Slowly she raised her hands to the sides of his face and kissed him, then she sat back, smiling at him. "I don't understand this. I never knew you before, but all of a sudden it seems that I do."

Embarrassed, he spoke to the horse and they went on. Presently he said, "No one knows me, Linda. I've never let anyone know me, but I want you to. Maybe in time you will love me. I've loved you ever since I've been here. I like to watch you, the way you move, the way your face changes expression with your feelings."

He had been staring straight ahead, but now he looked at her again. "You don't belong here, Linda. Not with Bess Flagg. If you stay long enough, you'll be warped and twisted into something different than what you are now. I've got to get you out of here before that happens."

She nodded, knowing what he meant. At times the feeling of evil about the Flagg place was so great that it stifled her. This had been more noticeable since Bess's accident. Yet, surprisingly enough, Bess was usually a pleasant person to work for. She would sit at her desk for hours, working on her books, sometimes humming a tune that was running through her mind, or she'd sit on the front porch, her binoculars to her eyes as she studied the movements on the grass. She demanded very little of Linda except her company.

Linda could remember only one occasion when Bess had been angry with her. That was after Linda had heard about John Roland's death and she had said she hoped Clay returned to live on the Bar C. Bess had lit into her as if she'd said something treasonable, then she'd looked straight at Linda and said, "He'll never live on the Bar C or anywhere else on this mesa if I have to kill him."

There had been times when she had seen Bess furious with her housekeeper Ellie or some of the crew, so furious she had seemed almost crazy. Linda wasn't sure why, with that one exception, she had been spared the bite of the woman's anger unless it was that Bess felt the need for company, and she knew Linda would be hard to replace.

Lavine spoke only once more before they reached the Flagg house. "I guess I've known all the time that the day would come when I'd hang up my guns. It's here. Or will be when you make up your mind. There is one thing you should know before you decide. I have a little over ten thousand dollars in a Denver bank. If you go with me, we'll take it and buy a business somewhere a long ways from here. California. Oregon. Anywhere you say."

She smiled at him, thinking that ten thousand dollars was a fortune and that she would not have many more opportunities to marry a man with that much money. Probably none. This was heady wine, the knowledge that a man like Lavine loved her, that he was thinking of her future as well as his.

The need for security was always in her mind, some insurance against having to marry a poverty-stricken rancher or keeping house for one. At this moment, tormented as she was with the knowledge that she had to break with Bill Land and that Clay could promise her nothing, the thought of marrying a man who was worth ten thousand dollars was dazzling.

"I think I'd like California," she murmured. "I've heard so much about the nice climate."

She hooked her arm through his and sat close to him so that he would feel the pressure of her breast. Her mind was made up now, but she wouldn't tell him yet. It was better to let a man dangle for a while. A woman who came too easily was a cheap thing. She could not afford to have Lavine think of her that way.

He did not stop in front of the house, but drove on past it to the corral. Bess was sitting on the porch watching them, and suddenly Linda was uneasy as she wondered how she was going to tell Bess about what had happened in town.

Pete Reno had been lounging in the bunkhouse doorway. Now he strolled across the yard, a cigarette dangling from his mouth. Lavine swung down from the seat and wrapped the lines around the brake handle, then gave Linda a hand as she stepped to the ground.

"Any excitement in town?" Reno asked.

"A little," Lavine said. "Clay Roland showed up."

"You kill him?"

"No. Put this horse away."

"What the hell!" Reno said, backing up. "I ain't no hostler."

Lavine stepped away from Linda. He said quietly, "Put the horse up, Pete."

Reno swallowed and turned his gaze away. "Sure, Abe."

Linda had started toward the house. Lavine caught up with her, saying, "Let me do the talking."

Linda said in a low tone, "How can you stand him, Abe? I feel dirty just having him look at me."

"I'm not going to stand him much longer," Lavine said. "I saved his life two years ago. I thought I could do something for him, but I can't." He paused, the small smile touching the corners of his lips again. "Once in a while I get a sentimental notion that surprises me. I thought I was responsible for Pete because I saved his life, but that's crazy thinking. When I ride out of here, he's not riding with me."

"He'll get himself killed in a year," Linda said.

"In a month," Lavine corrected her. "If I couldn't learn him anything in two years, I couldn't do any better in ten."

When they reached the porch, Bess asked, "Get the posters?"

"No," Lavine said. "They won't be ready till evening. Clay Roland was in town. He saw Linda and kissed her and Bill Land hit him. Then Roland beat hell out of him. I didn't want to leave her in town after that. I'll pick up the posters in the morning."

"Why didn't you shoot him?" Bess demanded. "You know I want that bastard dead."

"It was Bill Land's fight," Lavine said. "Mrs. Flagg, there are times when you think like a man, but there are other times when you just don't understand. If Bill Land is going to be anything more than your legal puppy, he's got to finish anything he starts."

Bess flushed with the criticism, and for a moment Linda thought that the woman's temper was going to boil up again, but there was too much truth in what Lavine said for her to ignore it. Besides, Lavine had a way of saying things like that to Bess and making her take it, a quality that Linda had not seen in any other man.

"All right." Bess jerked her hand at the bunkhouse. "I'll send for you if I want you."

"Yes ma'am," Lavine said.

He touched the brim of his hat and strode away. Linda watched him go, wanting to cry out for him to take her away now, that to go on the way they had been was a dangerous thing for both of them, but she couldn't bring herself to say it. Then she heard Bess's harsh voice, "Will you explain to me why you let a man like Clay Roland kiss you?"

Linda looked at Bess; she saw the way the older woman's face had turned ugly, the way her lips were pulled tightly against her teeth. These were familiar storm signals Linda had seen too many times.

"I was in the store when I saw him walk by," Linda said slowly, knowing that the choosing of each word was important. "I called to him. When he saw me, he grabbed me and lifted me off my feet and whirled me around. Then he kissed me."

"And just what were you doing all that time?"

"What could I do?" Linda demanded. "I was in his arms. He's a big man."

"Yes, I suppose he is." Bess eased back in her chair, her anger fading. "Bill saw it and didn't like it? That it?"

"No, he sure didn't," Linda admitted.

"I don't blame him," Bess said. "I don't blame him one bit. Well, go get your fancy work and sit a while."

Linda fled into the house, glad to get out of it that easily. She hadn't told Bess the whole story. There would be trouble later when Bess heard it, and sooner or later Bill Land would ride out here and tell it. She ran upstairs to her room. She didn't go back for a time, but she couldn't dawdle all afternoon. When she had taken as much time as she dared, she picked up her sewing basket and went back down the stairs.

When she reached the porch, Bess said, "Get my shawl. It's a little chilly."

Linda went back into Bess's room and returned with a red shawl. She wrapped it around Bess's shoulders and sat down in a rocking chair. She was embroidering a table runner, busy work which she enjoyed. For a time she sat in silence, her mind on Lavine. She would make him a good wife, she told herself. It seemed a miracle, a man like that telling her he loved her, a miracle lifting her out of a situation that had become more difficult with each passing day. She couldn't keep on postponing her wedding and she had not been able to think of any way out of her bargain.

Bess had been watching the road through her glasses. Linda saw a rider coming in across the grass, but she didn't recognize him. Bess put the binoculars on her lap, swearing softly. She always kept a small revolver in her chair beside her. Now she laid it across her lap and, pulling the shawl from her shoulders, dropped it over the revolver.

"Get Lavine," Bess said. "Have him keep Reno in the bunkhouse in case we need him."

Alarmed, Linda put her sewing on the floor beside her chair. "What's the matter?"

"Matter?" Bess said angrily. "There's plenty of matter. That's Clay Roland coming. He's either a fool or a brave man. Now get a move on."

Linda did. As she raced across the yard to the bunkhouse, she thought dismally that this was the worst thing that could happen.

After Clay left the road and turned toward the Flagg ranch, he thought about Queen Bess and what he would say to her. He had never been well acquainted with her, although he used to see her in town on Saturdays and on a few occasions had been in her house.

He had worked roundup with her crew along with the other small ranchers on the mesa. He had seen her a few times when she visited the roundup camp, although he doubted that she had been aware of his presence. Usually she talked to the foreman, Riley Quinn, and ignored everyone else. When she visited the Bar C, it was on Sunday afternoon when Clay had a date with Linda or a ride rigged with Rusty Mattson and Bill Land.

The more he thought about it, the more the present situation seemed incredible. But the most incredible part was Anton Cryder's statement that she had been in love with Clay's father and that her hatred for Clay stemmed from that frustrated love. Still, he could not overlook a few facts. Cryder wouldn't lie. His father would have confided in Cryder as he would in no other man because Cryder had been his only close friend. What the lawyer had said, then, must be true.

The Flagg buildings loomed ahead of Clay: the sprawling house, the barns and corrals and bunkhouse and various outbuildings. No change here at all. In fact, there had been few if any changes since Hank Flagg had died. He had built big and he had built well, utility his only object except with the house which had been built for show.

The point that used to strike Clay and still did was the complete absence of feminine touches: no trees around the house, no flowers, no curtains at the windows. A stranger riding in would have thought this was a bachelor's ranch.

Clay approached the house slowly, not at all sure he had been smart in obeying the impulse that had brought him here. Bess Flagg was in her wheel chair on the front porch, Linda sitting on one side of her, Abe Lavine standing on the other.

Clay's gaze swept the yard. A man stood in the bunkhouse door. He was a stranger. He must, Clay thought, be the Pete Reno that Ardis Kline had mentioned. He wouldn't be here in the middle of the afternoon if he were a member of the crew.

Reining up in front of the porch, Clay touched the brim of his hat as he said, "Howdy, Mrs. Flagg. Howdy, Linda." He nodded at Lavine who nodded back, his lean, strong-featured face expressionless. Linda was plainly frightened, but Clay couldn't tell what was in Bess Flagg's mind. She looked older than he remembered her, older than the additional six years should have made her. Aside from that, she had changed very little and that surprised Clay. For an active woman to be imprisoned in a wheel chair must be little short of hell.

"I was sorry to hear about your accident, Mrs. Flagg," Clay said.

"You didn't come here to tell me that, Roland," Bess said. "State your business."

She made no effort to keep the hostility out of her voice, but that, Clay told himself, was exactly what he had expected. He looked at Lavine. "There's a man standing in the bunkhouse door. If he's been put there to shoot me, I want to know it."

"That's up to you," Lavine said. "He won't throw any lead if you don't start the ball."

"I didn't come for that." Clay brought his gaze back to Bess Flagg. He wished Linda wasn't here. He didn't want to see her, to even think about her and Bill Land. "Mrs. Flagg, I was told by Anton Cryder today that you had made an offer for the Bar C. I rode out here to tell you I'm not selling. I plan to live there."

"No, you won't live there," she snapped. "When your father was alive, I let the Bar C alone because he was an old friend, but I owe you nothing. If you think I'm going to let a two-bit outfit like the Bar C exist in the middle of my range, you're crazy. You'd better take what you can get for it and move on."

Clay sat quite still, watching the man in the bunkhouse without appearing to do so. He could take him, or he could take Lavine, but he couldn't take both if they went for their guns at the same time. After what Lavine had said, Clay didn't think they would, but if Reno was the jumpy kind, he might start it. If he did, Lavine wouldn't stand still.

"This is downright peculiar, Mrs. Flagg," Clay said. "You don't need the Bar C, but ever since I've got back, people have been telling me you're going to drive me out of the country."

"That's right," she said, "so don't be a fool and try to hang on."

"I would be a worse fool if I walked off and left it," he said. "I never like to believe gossip, but I've heard quite a bit since I got back. That's the real reason I rode out here. I know where you stand. Now you know where I stand, but there is one thing I still don't savvy. That's the why of it."

"I told you," she said in her harsh voice. "If you have a pimple on your face, you pop it out. You don't let it get bigger and bigger. The Bar C is a pimple on the face of Flagg range."

"I have no intention of making the Bar C bigger," he said. "It's no threat to you. Neither am I. All I'm asking is the right to live on my property. Is that too much to ask?"

"Way too much," she said. "This is the time to close the Bar C out and that's exactly what I aim to do. Now get to hell out of here before I lose my temper."

"Not yet," he said. "Cryder told me you were in love with

my father, but he wouldn't have you, so you hated me. Is that why you hate me?"

"It's a God-damned lie," she screamed. "Shoot him, Lavine. Cut him out of the saddle. I won't be insulted . . ."

"Is that the reason you had Dad murdered?" Clay broke in.

Her face went dead white. For a brief moment she sat motionless, her lips parted, then she cried out, an incoherent sound, and throwing the shawl to one side, snatched the gun from her lap.

"No, Bess," Linda screamed, and grabbed her arm.

Clay sat motionless, knowing that the slightest move would bring the man out of the bunkhouse, his gun smoking. He heard Bess Flagg curse him as if she were a crazy woman while she struggled with Linda, then Lavine reached down and took the gun from her.

"You've said enough, Roland," Lavine said. "You'd better ride."

"I hoped it wouldn't be like this," Clay said. "I wasn't sure before that Dad was murdered, but I am now. That's more than enough reason for me to stay on this range."

He rode away, turning his head to watch the man in the bunkhouse doorway until he was out of revolver range. If Riley Quinn and the crew had been here, he wouldn't have left without a fight. He would probably have been shot out of his saddle. Lavine, for reasons of his own, had not made a fight of it, and he had probably called the turn for Pete Reno. Tomorrow would be another day. Even tonight. . . . He shook his head. There was simply no way of telling what Bess Flagg would do.

Clay had often been successful in putting himself in another man's place and figuring out what he would do, but he could not put himself in Bess Flagg's place. Six years ago he had considered her a rational woman, running her spread in a businesslike way as a man would have done. When he had first seen her, he thought she hadn't changed except for the lines that time had carved in her face, but now he knew he had been wrong.

Bess Flagg was nothing like the woman he had known six years before. She was crazy. When he had told her what Cryder had said, Clay had seen her face change. The only way he could describe it was that she had suddenly lost her reason. Then he realized that maybe she hadn't changed at all, that he had never seen her goaded into the wild fury that he had brought on. Now he knew exactly where he stood.

Perhaps he would never know the whole truth about her

and his father; he might never know how his father had died, but he hadn't wasted his time riding to the Flagg ranch. He had brought the trouble to a head. If a fight was inevitable, he wanted it to come soon. He had no capacity for waiting.

When he reached the Bar C, he watered and fed his horse. He went into the house and walked through the empty rooms again as he had early that morning, pausing at the chessboard and thinking how it was with Anton Cryder.

Cryder was a lonely old man, his legal business destroyed, his one good friend killed. Now he might feel the knife of Bess Flagg's anger. Clay regretted that. He thought about riding back to town and asking Cryder to move out here, but that would be foolish, for the Bar C was the most dangerous place on the mesa.

On more than one occasion Clay had arrested men for murder. He had attended the trials, he had seen their faces when the judge sentenced them to death, and he had watched them slowly wither and die while they waited for their date with the rope. In a way he was in the same position. Bess Flagg had decreed his execution. There was nothing for him to do but wait.

To Linda each passing second was an eternity while Clay rode away. She wasn't sure what Lavine would do and she was even less sure about Pete Reno. She dropped a hand on Bess's shoulder. She had the disturbing feeling that the woman had been turned to stone. Suddenly Bess began to tremble. She raised her right hand and, gripping Linda's wrist, flung her arm away. She glanced at Linda, the corners of her mouth working, then she looked at Lavine.

"I sure hired me a pair of dandies," she said bitterly. "By God, I did."

Clay was out of range of her gun now. Lavine laid it in her lap. He said, "You're mixed up, Mrs. Flagg. You don't recognize loyalty when you see it."

"Loyalty?" She glared at him. "Now that's a damned funny

word for you to use. You knew I wanted that bastard dead, but you didn't have the guts to do the job. I would have, but you wouldn't let me. You call that loyalty?"

"Yes ma'am," Lavine said.

"Oh hell." Bess glared at Linda who had sat down in her chair. "You used to be sweet on him. Maybe you still are. That the reason you grabbed my arm?"

Linda picked up the embroidery she had dropped. "No, Bess," she said. "He came out here in good faith to talk to you. If you had shot him, it would have been murder. He wouldn't shoot at a woman. I think you knew that."

"Sure I did." Bess turned her head to glare at Lavine. "You aren't in love with him. What's your excuse?"

"I don't have any excuse," he said. "I kept you from making a serious mistake."

She threw up her arms in disgust. "You heard him say what he was going to do and you know I'm taking the Bar C. He's not like the sheep we've been dealing with. What else is there to do but kill him?"

"In the right place and time," he said. "I can't seem to make you understand that, Mrs. Flagg. I've been here long enough to know how some of these people feel that you call sheep. You've got them buffaloed now, all right, but I've seen sheep become wolves. It could happen on this mesa if you kill Clay Roland under circumstances like you were going to."

"Lavine, I don't know how in hell you could have got the reputation you have," Bess said hotly. "You talk like a cautious old woman."

"I'm cautious," he admitted. "A man in my profession has to be or he doesn't live long. In time I'll get the job done without any risk to you. In the year Pete and me have worked for you, we've rubbed out five men. Men you wanted out of the way. I got two because they accused me of cheating in a poker game. The other one was because I overheard him making a remark about you. Pete got his because he heard 'em cussing the Flagg outfit and some of Riley Quinn's deals. People don't like us because of those killings, but they were fair fights and Ed Parker had nothing to hold us on. You didn't get any blame except for hiring us."

"And I suppose you think you'll get into a poker game with Roland? Or you'll hear him making an insulting remark about me?"

"Something of the kind," Lavine said. "But when you let Quinn do a job like he did on Long Sam Kline and John Roland, you're taking a chance on turning every man on the mesa against you."

"How do you know Quinn killed them?" she demanded.
"I added it up," he said. "It's a simple matter of two and two making four. If I can add it up and get the answer, so can other men. It didn't take Clay Roland long. I've learned one thing in this business, Mrs. Flagg. If you've got to kill a man, do it in the open where men can see it done and know why. Both of those killings were mistakes and I'd have told you so if I'd had a chance."

"I believe you would have," she said slowly. "You tell me more things I don't want to hear than anyone else on the mesa. Some day I'm going to fire you because of it."

"But not until my usefulness to you is gone," he said. "I'm not sure I'll stay here that long."

She leaned back, her eyes closed. "I'm tired. Go on back to the bunkhouse. Linda, wheel me inside and call Ellie. I think I'll lie down for a while."

Lavine stepped away from her chair, his gaze meeting Linda's briefly. He said, "Yes ma'am," and left the porch.

Linda pushed Bess into her bedroom, then called Ellie from the kitchen and together they lifted Bess from her chair to the bed. She said, "I won't need you till evening, Linda."

"Thank you," Linda said, and fled to her room.

She tried to read but she found her mind wandering so that the words made no sense to her. She returned to the porch and, sitting down, picked up her embroidery, but she was too restless to work on it. She had to see Clay once more. Bess would be furious if she knew, but maybe she'd never find out.

She ran upstairs and changed to a dark-green riding skirt and a leather jacket. She slipped out of the house, hoping Bess wouldn't hear her. Lavine and Reno were talking at the corral gate. Lavine said something to Reno and the younger man walked across the yard toward the bunkhouse.

Linda was aware that Lavine watched every move she made as she approached him. She had been used to his barren expression so long that she had supposed it was a natural part of him, but now she realized that it was a mask to keep people from reading his thoughts. The knowledge came as a surprise to her. She was pleased. She knew a side of him no one else did. Now his lips held a smile which thawed his face. Even his pale blue eyes lost their chill.

When she reached him, he said, "Seems to me you get prettier every day, Linda."

She was pleased by that, too, for complimentary words coming from him were unexpected. She would have a good life with him, she thought, and she would be a foolish woman to turn him down.

"Thank you," she said softly. "It's funny, Abe. I feel that I have made a discovery that no one else has ever made."

"What discovery?"

"There are two Abe Lavines," she answered, smiling. "I'm the only person in the world who knows the real one."

"I hope you do," he said.

He took her into his arms and pulled her to him. He kissed her, tentatively at first, then he did a thorough job. When he released her, she stood close to him, her eyes wide. "Abe, Abe," she breathed. "What are you trying to do to me?"

"Tell you I love you," he said. "I've waited too long. I've got to get you away from here. I saw that this afternoon when Clay Roland was here."

"What do you mean by that?"

"Bess is going to raise hell and prop it up with a stick," he said. "I haven't told Bess this, but the boys out in the Smoky Hills are the ones she'd better watch out for. They're a tough lot and they've been sore ever since Kline died. If she kills Roland, and she's bound to do it, Rusty Mattson will get that bunch together and she'll have the fight of her life."

Linda nodded, thinking about Rusty. She had not seen him for a long time, but before Clay had left the country, she had known Rusty well and she had liked him. He was a redheaded banty of a man, a natural maverick who set himself against all authority. He didn't know what fear was, and he had a fierce loyalty to Clay that was almost unreasonable. At least that was the way he used to be. She didn't think that he had changed.

"Rusty would help Clay if he knew he was back," she said.

"Trouble is he's hard to get hold of. He's on the move all the time." Lavine took her by the shoulders. "Have you decided yet? About me?"

She wanted to tell him that she had, but she must not forget the feminine principle of playing hard to get. "I like you," she said. "I like you more than I ever thought possible, but I've got to get used to the idea."

"I should have told you before," he said with regret, "but you were wearing Land's ring and I never thought you could see anything in a man like me."

"Well I do," she said, "and I like what I see, but I want

my marriage to last as long as I live. You want me to be sure, Abe. I know you do."

"Yes," he said. "I sure do. I wouldn't be hurrying you if all this crazy business wasn't working the way it is. I've got a hunch that neither one of us has much time."

"I know," she said, thinking how Bess had tried to kill Clay. "I want to take a ride, Abe. Maybe I can get my thinking straight if I can get away from here and be alone for a while."

"I'll saddle your mare for you," he said.

She waited beside the gate until he led her mare out of the corral. She rode often, the one relaxation that she'd had since coming here, and she was sure no one would think anything about it today. Lavine gave her a hand into the saddle, then she said, "I never knew how bad Bess was until she tried to shoot Clay. I'd never seen that side of her."

"She's bad enough, and she'll get worse." Lavine stepped back, adding, "Don't stay too long. Too much can happen, the way things are stacking up."

"I'll be all right," she said, and smiled at him before she reined her mare around and left the yard at a gallop.

She took the road to town, pulling the mare down to a slower pace. As soon as she was out of sight of the ranch, she angled westward toward the Bar C. Even Lavine would not understand why she had to see Clay, she thought. She wasn't sure herself, actually, except that she wanted to see him again, to talk to him, perhaps to bury an old love that had never really died.

As she rode, her thoughts turned to Lavine. She didn't love him. She never would, but she would tell him she did. He would never regret his bargain with her. She did not doubt his statement that he had more than ten thousand dollars in the bank. She could afford to lie a little to a man who had that much money. Perhaps, with his record, he would never be able to put his guns up. She might be a widow within weeks or months, but that wouldn't be so bad. She'd have the ten thousand.

She found Clay building a fire in his kitchen range when she reached the Bar C. He hadn't seen her ride up, so when she appeared in the kitchen doorway, he stared at her as if he thought he was dreaming and she wasn't real.

"Clay," she said. "I thought you'd be glad to see me."

"I'm glad to see you," he said, "but I've dreamed about you too many times in the years I've been gone to believe it's really you. You're just another dream."

"I'm real," she said. "I'll prove it."

She crossed the room to him and kissed him, confident

that he still loved her. She stepped back, disappointed and hurt, for he had not returned her kiss. He hadn't even put his arms around her.

"What's the matter, Clay?" she demanded. "You didn't act like this in town."

"I didn't know you were going to marry Bill," he said. "I should have asked if you were married or engaged. I have no claim on you. I couldn't expect you to wait for me when I didn't even write to you."

He swallowed, busying himself with the fire for a moment, then he added, "I guess I can't even blame Bill for being sore. From the way you kissed me, I sure didn't figure any other man had his loop on you." He motioned toward the door. "I guess you'd better go."

"Not yet," she cried angrily. "I won't let you treat me this way. I'm not going to marry Bill. I don't know why I ever said I would. I don't love him and I never did."

"All right," he said, "you've loved me all the time, but you won't marry me because I'm not any better risk than when I left six years ago. I may be dead by morning." He motioned toward the door again. "You're still wearing Bill's ring. I don't want you here. He tried to kill me in town. If he finds out you came here to see me, he'll have a real excuse to kill me."

She had intended to tell him she was going to marry Lavine, that she would get Lavine to help him and he ought to try to find Rusty Mattson, but she was too furious to tell him anything.

"I think you will be dead by morning," she cried, "and I hope you are."

She whirled and ran out of the house. She stepped into the saddle and quirted her mare into a run. She didn't mean what she had said, but she wasn't going back and apologize. He didn't want her help. Well, that was all right because he sure wasn't going to get it. He'd find out how far he'd get bucking Queen Bess by himself.

12

Dusk was moving in across the mesa by the time Clay finished supper and cleaned up the kitchen. It had been a struggle to force the food down, but he knew he had to. He might be on the run by morning and not have another chance to eat for a long time.

After he finished eating, the food lay like a rock in his stomach. He'd cooked and eaten too many meals by himself, he thought. It was no way to live. He had expected a different life here on the Bar C. In spite of all logic about the matter, he had hoped to find Linda waiting for him; he had hoped to tell her he could support her now that he owned a ranch. He had expected to marry her and bring her here and have the kind of life any normal man wanted.

It was fine and dandy to tell himself that this was the idle dreaming of a lonely man, that it was only natural for a woman of Linda's age to marry or become engaged. As he had told her, he had no hold upon her, no reason to think she would wait for a man who had not bothered to write to her during the time he had been gone. But the cold fact was he could not be logical about it.

He wouldn't have been hit as hard as he was if she hadn't called to him there in front of the Mercantile, if she had told him she was engaged, if she hadn't returned his kiss with the passion of a woman who still loved him and had been waiting for him to come back to her.

She must have known Bill Land would see them kissing and that he'd be furious. Clay would have felt the same way if the situation had been reversed. Then to find her out there on the Flagg porch beside Queen Bess. . . . And her coming here and kissing him and telling him she wasn't going to marry Bill Land after all! It was too much, far too much. Either she had changed or he had never really known her.

No, that was wrong. She hadn't changed and he had known her. He began remembering things about her he had wanted to forget. Time and distance and loneliness had made him idealize her in a foolish, adolescent way. She had been a flirt even when she had been his girl and everyone on the mesa had known she belonged to him.

When he had taken her to dances, he had never been sure how many times he would be able to dance with her. When he had taken her to basket and pie socials, she had often told other boys what her pies and baskets looked like and he had been forced to outbid his rivals and pay twice as much as he should for the privilege of eating with her.

He could think of plenty of things to hold against her, but the worst was her refusal to go away with him. Sure, her mother was an excuse, but the truth was she was afraid to risk the security she had here in Painted Rock, living in her own home among people she knew. But if a woman really loved a man, she would go with him wherever he went and not give the flimsy excuses he had heard six years ago.

He had to quit thinking about her, he told himself. It was time he started figuring out how to survive. That was exactly the problem, survival or death. After his visit to the Flagg ranch, he had no illusions about the next few days. He'd be hunted as if he were an outlaw.

He filled a flour sack with food, thinking that if he did have to make a run for it, at least he wouldn't starve. In the end the Flagg outfit might get him, but they'd know they'd been in a fight before they did.

He stepped out through the back door and stood motionless for a moment, his gaze sweeping the narrow valley and the crest of the ridge to the north. The sun was down now, the sky afire with its passing, the gold and scarlet banners reaching out to the far rim of the earth.

A terrifying prickle ran down his spine as he considered the impossible odds he was facing. Riley Quinn could bring a dozen men if he thought it would take that many, but there was no one Clay Roland could call on for help, no law man he could go to.

He would accomplish nothing by riding to the county seat and demanding protection from the sheriff. He could guess what had happened. Queen Bess had probably told the sheriff that she would deliver the mesa votes if he let the mesa alone after he was elected. No, Clay Roland stood strictly alone.

He stepped into the kitchen, leaving the back door open. He lit a bracket lamp on the wall, and going into the front room, lit another lamp on the claw-footed table. He went out through the front, leaving that door open, too, so that a long finger of light fell across the trodden dirt of the yard. Again his gaze swept the road and the river and the ridge to the south. No sign of life anywhere. Once more the pressure of the terrible loneliness settled down upon him. He had a crazy feeling he would welcome Abe Lavine or even Riley Quinn.

Carrying the sack of grub, he walked quickly to the corral, saddled his bay gelding and led him around to the west side of the barn. He tied the sack behind the saddle and returned to the east wall of the building, his Winchester in his hands.

The barn was constructed of logs, solid enough to hole up in and fight off the Flagg bunch when it came. He considered bringing his horse inside the barn, shutting the doors from the inside, and waiting until Quinn came. But that would be suicide. He'd be pinned down. Sooner or later they'd set fire to the barn and they'd shoot him when he fled from it.

No, he'd fight as long as he could here on the outside where he could change position. If the odds against him were so big he didn't have a chance, he'd run and keep running until he could turn and fight with the possibility of winning. If he could get into the Smoky Hills and find Rusty Mattson, they'd lead Quinn and his bunch all over hell's back pasture. Rusty knew the Hills as well as most men know their front yard. Sooner or later the Flagg bunch would break up into small bands to hunt for him and then he'd see to it that they found him.

He squatted along the side of the barn close to the southeast corner and waited. Night closed in, the last dull glow of the sunset dying above the Smoky Hills, the only light that from the windows in the house and the open doors. He wanted to smoke, but decided against it. He had no way of knowing when they would come. If they did, he hoped they would think he was inside the house. That would give him a chance to smash them before they located him.

So he waited, the minutes piling up into an hour, and then another, slow minutes that tightened his nerves until the waiting was intolerable, but it was his kind of game. As a law man he had faced situations much like this many times. Necessity had taught him patience he had not possessed six years ago.

He dozed off and woke almost at once, sensing that some vagrant sound had stirred him back to consciousness. Suddenly uneasy, he slipped back along the wall of the barn and stood there, seeing only the vague shape of his horse. He listened for a long moment until he was convinced that no one was there, then he returned to the corner where he had been waiting.

He stood motionless, still listening and now hearing sounds from the river to the south. He wasn't sure what they were, maybe only innocent noises of the night: a prowling animal slipping through the brush, a breeze rattling the windows, the whirring of a bird's wings. But again they might have been caused by some of Quinn's men. Maybe the whole crew was out there in the darkness, surrounding him to make sure he could not escape when they moved in on him.

The sound did not come again, but still Clay stood there, finding it hard to breathe, the stony fist of fear driving his stomach against his backbone. As he remembered Riley Quinn, the man did not possess the slightest talent for being sly or sneaky or subtle. He was the kind who met an enemy head on, overpowering him by sheer animal strength. That was why Clay expected him to ride in with his men, boldly and directly without making any effort to disguise their coming.

Suddenly Clay realized there was one possible error in his thinking. Bess Flagg might send Abe Lavine and Pete Reno to do the job. Lavine was smart. Whatever he did would not be with the overriding strength and possible stupidity that would characterize Riley Quinn's action.

The more Clay thought about it, the more he was inlined to reject this possibility. It simply wasn't Lavine's way, judging from what Clay had heard and seen of him. Lavine would wait for him in town and somehow maneuver him into a gunfight for everyone to see. If Lavine was the faster man, Clay would die, and because Lavine was Queen Bess's man, Ed Parker would say it was a fair fight and he had no grounds on which to hold the killer.

Just as Clay had done many times when he'd carried the star, Lavine would gamble on his gun speed saving his life. It was the only way he could operate, but with Queen Bess in the temper she was, Lavine's method would be too slow. No, Riley Quinn would be the one. Clay was as sure of it as he could be sure of anything which depended upon the imponderables of human nature.

Then he heard them, the faint drum of hoofs off to the north. Clay grinned, his nerves relaxing. This was the way he had thought it would be. He did not feel the fist of fear in his stomach, for now he was sure of the action his enemies were taking. It had been the uncertainty that had bothered him.

They came in fast, swinging to the east so they made a wide half-circle of the house before they rode in close. Clay could not see them. The moon wasn't up and an overcast covered the sky so that the starshine was blotted out, but from the sound, Clay judged there weren't many of them, three or maybe four at the most.

They rode toward the front door from the south, having gone almost to the river before they turned toward the house. They reined up in the fringe of lamplight, Quinn bawling, "Roland, we want to see you."

Clay eared back the hammer of his Winchester, hoping he would not have to fire until they were in the finger of light that fell through the doorway. Apparently there were only three of them. He identified Quinn by his voice, but the other two were only vague shapes in the thin light.

"Roland, if you don't come out, we'll drag you out with a rope around your neck," Quinn shouted.

"He ain't a fool," one of the men said. "We'll have to go in after him."

"All right, Ives," Quinn said. "Root him out."

"Not by myself," the cowboy snapped. "I hear he's handy with his iron. You get him, Riley."

"Bellew, ride around to the back door," Quinn ordered, ignoring what Ives had said. "We'll give you one minute, then we'll go in the front. Unless he sneaks out through a window, we've got his hide nailed to the front door."

Clay had hoped to get all three massed in the lamplight in front of the house, but now he knew he couldn't afford to wait. He probably wouldn't have a better chance than he had right now.

Bellew was arguing, then Quinn said loudly, "By God, if you want to work for the Flagg outfit, you'll take my orders."

Clay opened up then, pulling the trigger and levering another shell into the chamber and firing again. He couldn't aim in the darkness, so it was almost blind shooting, but he spread his shots from one side of the riders to the other, laying them in about shoulder high on a horse. He was bound to hit something.

His first shot was a miss, but the second brought a yelp of pain from one of the men. They scattered immediately, taking off toward the river. Clay kept shooting, having nothing to go by except the sound of their movements. Quinn gave out one great bawling curse, then he yelled, "He's yonder by the barn. We'll run him down. He can't see no better'n we can."

One of them fired at Clay, the slug ripping into a log above his head. He slipped back along the wall, dropping his empty Winchester and drawing his revolver. He held his fire, not wanting to give them anything to shoot at. They had scattered out and were coming at him on the run, then the completely unexpected happened. Someone cut loose from the river, flashes of powderflame dancing from the willow thicket.

"There's another one out there," Ives yelled.

"They've got us in a crossfire," Bellew shouted. "I'm getting out of here. He hit me once. He ain't gonna get a chance to do it again."

"Come on, damn it," Quinn raged. "It don't make no difference who's in the willows. He's too far away to do any damage."

But Ives and Bellew had whirled their mounts and were digging in the steel, heading east. Quinn hesitated a moment, then he rode after them, apparently having no desire to do the job alone. Clay emptied his revolver, knowing he was wasting lead, but they were on the run and he hoped he would hurry their flight. He reloaded, still hugging the barn wall as he wondered who had sided him in a fight that had been strictly his own affair.

The fading hoofbeats were far to the east now. Quinn and his men wouldn't come back. Clay was certain of that. The wounded man would probably go into town and see Doc Spears. Quinn and Ives would return to the Flagg ranch and the next time Quinn came, he'd have enough men to do the job. Fighting off three cowboys was one thing, but tackling a dozen or more was quite another. Staying would be suicide.

"Who's out there?" Clay called.

"You all right?"

A woman's voice! For one quick, crazy moment Clay thought it was Linda who had returned to help him fight, but the voice wasn't Linda's. It had to be Ardis Kline. There wasn't anyone else it could be.

"I'm all right," he answered, and ran toward the river.

She met him halfway, throwing her arms around him and hugging him with anxious strength. "Clay, Clay. I knew they'd come tonight, but I didn't know where you'd be or what you'd do. I was afraid you were in the house."

"I knew better than that," he said. "Now will you tell me what you're doing here?"

"I came to help you," she said simply. "You needed someone's help, didn't you?"

He wanted to say no, that he had always taken care of himself and he always could, but that would have been his male pride talking. If Ardis hadn't started firing, Quinn and his men would have kept coming and in the darkness anything could have happened. He might have got one, or two if he was lucky, but the chances were that in the end the three to one odds would have been too long against him.

"I guess I did," he admitted, "but I sure never aimed for you to risk your hide for me."

"I know you didn't," she said, "but I've been crazy with worry ever since you left my place. I sent Monroe after Rusty. He thought he could find him, but it may take all night. Rusty couldn't get here till morning and I was afraid it would be too late then."

"Might have been," Clay said. "Where's your horse?"

"By the river. You aren't going to stay here now, are you, Clay? They'll come back. You know that."

"Sure, I know it. I guess I'd better go somewhere." He turned toward the house, calling back, "I'll blow the lamps out."

She caught his arm. "Clay, where will you go?"

"Off the mesa," he said. "That's all I'm sure of. If Monroe finds Rusty, I'll stay in the Smoky Hills because he knows all the trails and the places to hide."

"I know the trails and the places to hide as well as Rusty does," she said. "I'll guide you, Clay. I can't let you go like you did before."

He didn't understand this. He stared at her in the darkness, seeing only the pale oval of her face. Her hand still clutched his arm, gripping it hard as if she were afraid he'd leave her if she let go.

"Look, Ardis," he said. "They want to kill me. They'll keep after me until they do or I bust them up so bad that the Flagg crew rides out of the country." He paused, realizing there was no way out for him, no chance to ever live here on the mesa and not be hunted. He added bitterly, "Even if they do pull out, she'll hire more men and she'll keep after me till she gets me."

"I know that," Ardis cried. "I've thought about this ever since Pa was killed. I could have got Rusty and Monroe and the rest of the Smoky Hills bunch and we could have made Bess a lot of trouble, but none of them would have killed her. She's got to be killed, Clay. You'd shoot a mad dog, wouldn't you?"

"Yes, but I couldn't shoot Bess Flagg. No man could."

"Then I'll do it if I get a chance," she said. "Right now we've got to get to my place. Maybe Rusty will be there, but whether he is or not, I'm going with you."

"You can't. It's my fight, not yours."

"If it's your fight, it's mine," she said impulsively, then paused as if regretting she had said it. She dropped her hand to her side and stepped back. "I mean, it's my fight until the men who killed Pa are punished. Bess too. She's just as guilty as the men who did it."

He saw no sense in arguing with her now. He said, "Get your horse. I'll be back in a couple of minutes."

He strode toward the house, thinking that her presence here didn't make any sense. Her insistence that she was going with him made even less. He walked through the house to the kitchen and stood looking around the familiar room, almost unchanged from the time he had been a boy. Probably he would never see it again. He did not doubt that if he left the Bar C, Bess would burn him out. Suddenly he rebelled against leaving, but the rebellion died almost at once. If he was going to make a fight out of it, he had to stay alive.

Lifting the lamp from the bracket, he stepped into the room that had been his bedroom and for a moment stood looking at the picture of his mother that was on his bureau. It had been taken less than a year before her death. In many ways he favored her, but for the first time in his life, he realized how much he favored his father, not in looks so much as in disposition. The stubborn streak that kept him from taking Bess's offer and leaving the mesa had certainly come from his father. Bess had probably threatened him, too, but John Roland had stayed.

Returning to the kitchen, Clay blew out the lamp and set it back in the bracket. He went into the front room and, blowing out the lamp on the claw-footed table, left the house. When he reached the barn, he found Ardis waiting for him.

"Ready to go?" she asked.

"I'm ready," he said, and stepping into the saddle, rode west toward the gorge, Ardis beside him.

13

Bess Flagg lay in bed, the lamp on the stand beside her turned low. She couldn't sleep and she probably wouldn't until Riley Quinn returned. Actually she didn't want to sleep. She told herself it was better to stay awake so she could feel her hate for Clay Roland.

She didn't feel anything when she was asleep. That made sleeping a waste of time. She didn't even dream any more. She was glad of that. In her last dream John Roland had been alive.

The only emotion that gave any meaning to her life was hate, but it was hard to hate a dead man, and John Roland was dead. Riley Quinn and a cowhand named Ives had taken care of that, but she wondered if it had been a mistake.

If John Roland were alive, she could have kept on punishing him. Now that he was dead, he was out of her reach. But mistake or not, she had no regrets. He had rejected her and rejection was one of several things she could not bear. He had paid for it by dying, and soon his son would pay, too.

She glanced at the clock on the wall. Almost midnight. Quinn should be back soon. She folded her hands over her breasts. They were as round and firm as ever, but she hated her helpless, atrophied legs and kept her hands away from them as much as possible.

She worried about being so helpless that she had to depend upon Ellie and Linda for the most animal-like functions of life. She was half alive and half dead, and she hated the part that was dead. She had reason for hating John Roland. He was responsible for the killing of the part of her that was dead.

She hated Linda Stevens, too, hated her for her youth and beauty and her graceful way of moving. She hated her because a man like Bill Land was willing to marry her, because Clay Roland had once loved her and maybe still did. Lately she had noticed the way Lavine was looking at Linda. He loved her, too. It was incredible and for some reason shocking, the idea that a man of Lavine's age, a man who killed for hire, could love Linda Stevens.

She closed her eyes, weary with life and the few pleasures it had given her. She could put her finger on what was wrong. She had never loved anyone, and as far as she knew she had never been loved by anyone. Oh, years ago Hank Flagg had said he loved her, but what merit was there in being loved by a tobacco-chewing old man who drank too much and shaved once a week and stunk like a wolfer?

John Roland could have given some meaning to her life. That was why she hated him so much. There had been a time when she thought she had loved him, but now she was convinced that it had been an illusion, that she had no capacity for love. Probably she never had. She had been able to control everyone else, everyone except John Roland, and he had stayed out of her reach in spite of anything she could do.

She dropped off into a light sleep for a few minutes. When she woke, she heard Riley Quinn putting his horse away. Ives and Bellew should be with him, but she didn't hear them talking. That made her uneasy. Maybe Clay Roland had killed both of them. If he had, she had little hope that Quinn had done the job by himself.

Presently she heard Quinn's heavy steps as he came through the back of the house and crossed the kitchen to her room. A moment later he stood beside her bed looking down at her, an ugly expression on his sun-reddened face. She knew before he opened his mouth that he had failed.

"So you let him slip between your fingers?" she said.

"How'd you know?"

"I could read it in your face," she said. "You have an easy face to read, Riley."

"Don't give me any of your smart talk," he said sullenly. "We tried. By God, we tried the best we could. He had the house all lighted up and we figured he was inside. We was going in both doors so we'd have him bottled up, but he opened up on us from the barn. Bellew got hit, but he didn't quit. We was going after him when somebody else started shooting at us from the river. They had us in a crossfire, so we pulled out."

"Was it Mattson?"

"Hell, how would I know? I figured it was, though. I can't think of nobody else who would side Roland."

"How bad's Bellew hurt?"

"Got a slug in his thigh. He was bleeding some when I left him, so I sent Ives to town with him to see that he made it to the doc."

She shook her head, thinking that she had to depend on someone else's legs and in the past Riley Quinn's had served her well. But he was stupid or he wouldn't have gone at this job the way he had. He was like a bull. The only way he knew how to do anything was to lower his head and charge.

"All right," he said irritably. "Don't tell me I don't have a brain in my head. I'm the best you've got and don't you forget it."

"I won't, Riley," she said.

"I'll get him tomorrow," he said. "I'll take the crew. If I'd done it this time we'd have had him."

"So it's my fault because I told you to take two men," she said. "Maybe so, but three men ought to be able to handle even a hard case like Clay Roland. The fewer men who know what's going on, the better for us. You know that."

"Yea, I reckon I do," he grumbled, "but now he'll run and we'll have to chase him, and it'll be a hell of a tough job if he heads for the Smoky Hills, which same I figure he'll do."

She nodded. "He will if he's got Mattson with him."

"We'll get him if it takes a week." He turned toward the door, then thought of something and swung back. "How much longer are you gonna keep them two gunslinging bastards on your payroll?"

"I'll fire them the day Clay Roland dies," she said. "We won't need them any longer."

"We don't need 'em now," he said. "We never did."

"They've been useful," she said. "I thought we could lay Clay Roland's death on them, but we can't now."

He took a hitch on his belt, licked his lips, then blurted, "Bess, I've asked you before to marry me. I ain't gonna keep on asking you any more'n I'm gonna keep on risking my neck and working my tail off just being your hired man. You put me off once more and I'm riding out of here and to hell with Mr. Clay Roland."

"Afraid, Riley?" she asked softly.

"You know damned well I ain't."

"Marrying me would make you a rich man," she said, "but I couldn't be a real wife, so I don't see why you want me."

"Reason enough," he said.

She smiled mockingly. "I suppose that with all the money you'd have, you could find plenty of women. You'd bring one right out here under my nose probably. But maybe you wouldn't have to. Linda would do, wouldn't she?"

"By God, Bess," he said in a tone of utter frustration, "I ought to twist your neck. You can be a real bitch when you set your mind to it. I've talked to Doc Spears about you. He said there's nothing wrong with you that would keep you from being all the wife a man would want. I'd never bring a woman here, and if I did, I wouldn't settle for a skinny one like Linda."

She masked her face against the worry that his words had aroused in her. Riley Quinn and Ellie were two people she could not do without. In a way she liked Riley. Usually he succeeded in his bumbling way in doing what she asked him to do, and he seldom questioned her decisions. Being married to him wouldn't be so bad. She could handle him.

"I'm glad to hear that, Riley," she said. "Linda wouldn't be a good woman for you. I don't think she's good for any man."

"You hate her like you hate everybody else," he said bitterly. "What's the matter with you, Bess? Sometimes I think you live on hate. It's what keeps you alive."

"I suppose it is," she admitted, "but I don't hate you, Riley. I guess we belong together. We're a lot alike. At least we're not hypocrites. I'm glad you didn't give me any of the hogwash about loving me the way most men would. I know you don't and you know I don't love you, so we can start out being honest with each other. If you understand that, I'll marry you."

"When?"

"The day Clay Roland dies."

He shook his head in disgust. "I knew you'd get around to something like that. You're no good, Bess. Neither am I."

"That's funny, Riley," she murmured. "I didn't think you had any more notion about being good than I do."

He cursed and, wheeling, ponderously walked to the door, his spurs jingling. He turned back, scowling. "You better send for the preacher 'cause it won't take me long to cut Roland's ears off and fetch 'em back to you."

He left the room. A moment later she heard the back door slam shut. She lay on her back, her hands still folded over her breasts, smiling a little as if she enjoyed a private joke. Doc Spears was right. She could be a wife to a man, and she would if it meant keeping Riley Quinn.

She could keep Riley in line, she told herself. By using him and Bill Land, she could handle anyone else on the mesa. This was the one pleasure of a life that had become a burden, controlling able-bodied men who didn't need to use someone else's legs, controlling them and breaking them and yes, even killing them.

She dropped off to sleep, the small smile still on her lips.

14

The overcast had cleared away and a moon was showing above the rim to the east when Clay and Ardis rode out of the gorge into her yard, the dark bulk of the buildings looming ahead of them. No lights showed in the house, so apparently Monroe had not returned with Rusty Mattson.

Ardis found a lantern in the barn and lighted it. She stayed with Clay while he took care of the horses, and then, lifting the lantern off the peg where she had hung it, she walked beside him to the house.

"If you're hungry, I'll fix something to eat before we go to bed," she said.

"No, I'm not hungry."

"Want a drink?"

"No thanks. I'm ready to roll in."

They went into the dining room. Ardis lighted a lamp and handed it to Clay. "The same room you had." She hesitated, her eyes searching his face, then said, "How much time do you think we have?"

"Not more'n a few hours after daylight," he said, "if I'm figuring Quinn right."

"They'll go to the Bar C, then come here," she said. "Is that the way you're guessing?"

"That's it. Riley Quinn isn't very smart, but Bess is."

"Then we'll have an early breakfast and ride out whether Rusty's here or not," she said.

He nodded. "Looks like we'd better." He thought of urging her to stay here, but he didn't think she would. Besides, this would be a more dangerous place for her to stay than on the trail with him. He still thought of her as a tomboy, saucy and impetuous as she had been six years ago, but now, his gaze on her face, it struck him that she wasn't the same girl he remembered. This startled him. Linda hadn't really changed, but Ardis had. Her piquant face was shadowed by worry. Fear, too, perhaps.

Impulsively he put out both hands and gripped her shoulders. "Ardis, why don't you give up this business of punishing your father's killers?"

She swayed toward him, her lips parted, then checked herself. "Will you give up the Bar C?"

"No. I can't."

"Then you know the answer to your question." She turned away, calling back, "Good night, Clay."

He went upstairs, placed the lamp on the pine bureau, and sat down on the bed. He tugged off his boots, then laid his gun belt on a chair beside the head of the bed. He blew the lamp out and lay down, tired and sour-tempered. Tomorrow he would start running and ducking and hiding. Nothing went against his grain as much as that.

He had to find a place where Ardis would be safe. He might have to cross the Utah line to find such a place. He certainly couldn't keep her with him indefinitely. She would slow him down, and if the Flagg bunch cornered him and there was a finish fight, he couldn't expose her to danger.

She was obsessed by revenge, he thought, and that again

wasn't like the girl he remembered. When he used to come here, he had talked with her very little. Rusty was the one she had been interested in, with a good deal of joshing going on back and forth between them, while Clay laughed and Long Sam Kline listened with concern because he didn't want Rusty for a son-in-law.

Now it was different, with Long Sam dead. If she was in love with Rusty, they should be married. Rusty had certainly been fond enough of her. It was one reason he used to come here.

He dropped off to sleep, still wondering what kept them apart. He was aroused by the tap of Ardis' knuckles on the door. She called, "Breakfast will be ready in a little while. I thought you'd want to feed the horses before we eat."

"I just got to sleep," he complained.

"It's after five," she said.

"All right." He sat up and yawned. "I'll get dressed."

When he returned from the barn a few minutes later, she had two bowls of oatmeal mush and a platter of ham and eggs on the kitchen table. She poured the coffee as Clay sat down. This morning she was wearing a man's shirt and pants; her auburn hair was brushed back and pinned in a bun behind her head. The worry that had been so noticeable in her last night was gone. She looked fresh and slim and young, and it struck him that she was an uncommonly pretty girl.

"You look mighty pert not to have slept much last night," he said. "How do you do it?"

She laughed. "Just being with you, I guess."

"I thought you and Rusty would be married before now," he said.

She looked up from her plate, startled. "Not Rusty. He'd never be tied down by a woman. He's the most restless man I ever knew. He's on the go all the time. Nothing seems important to him."

They ate in silence after that, Clay thinking that Rusty must have lost his common sense in the last six years. A man would have to be crazy to become a drifter when he could settle down with Ardis Kline.

They were finishing when someone shouted from in front of the house. "They're here," Ardis said, and jumped up.

Clay followed her outside. Monroe was watering the horses and Rusty was walking toward the house. When he saw Clay he let out a war whoop. "You old horse thief," he yelled, and strode toward Clay, his hand extended. "Damned if it ain't been a long time." He shook Clay's hand and pounded him on the back. "Yes sir, a long time. You've made yourself a big man from what I hear."

Clay shook his head. "Not on this range."

"Then we'll change it." Rusty whacked him on the back again. "You look just like you used to, son. I sure have been wondering about that. You've been away and you seen the elephant, and now you're back, but you still look just the same. Hell, I thought maybe you'd growed a set of horns and a tail by now."

"They're there," Clay said. "You just don't see them, Rusty. You're the same, too. Maybe a little thinner. That's all."

He was lying and he was sure Rusty knew he was. He couldn't tell Rusty how much he had changed. Clay was stunned by it. Rusty had the look of the wild bunch on him. Clay had seen it in too many men to be mistaken. It was typical of the men who lived in the Smoky Hills, but still it shocked Clay to see it so plainly in Rusty.

Actually this was not a thing Clay could describe except in the way Rusty's thin lips set hard against his teeth. The furtive darting about of his eyes, too. But mostly it was a feeling Clay had of wildness in the man as if he cared nothing about anyone or anything.

There was this moment of uneasy silence, then Ardis said, "I'll cook breakfast for you, Rusty. Clay thinks we'd better get started."

"I'm hungry enough to eat," Rusty said. "A whole cow if you've got one."

"I'll call you when it's ready," she said, and ran into the house.

For a moment Clay and Rusty looked at each other, Rusty's thin, stubble-covered face grave. Finally he said, "All right, son. Tell me what you see."

"A man on the run," Clay said. "I'll look the same in a few days. I'm on the run, too. But what are you running from?"

"From myself," Rusty said. "From all the things I might have been and the things we used to dream about being. You went out and done 'em, but me, I just went to pot." He grinned and shrugged his skinny shoulders. "Well, it's a little more'n that. I'm running from Queen Bess same as you are. Maybe you heard she posted me off the mesa."

"I heard," Clay said, "but there's other places in the world than the mesa and Painted Rock and the Smoky Hills."

"I've been to a few of 'em, but none of 'em would do," Rusty said. "You seen the great man since you got back?"

"Who's that?"

"Honest Bill Land, the legal voice of Bess Flagg."

"I've seen him." Clay hesitated, then told him what had happened in town.

Rusty slapped his leg and guffawed. "I wish I could of watched that. He's had a licking coming for a long time. He's sold out, Clay. Sold his soul to that bitch of a Bess Flagg."

"Is he in love with Linda?"

"Love?" Rusty snorted in derision. "Son, he don't know the meaning of the word. Neither does Linda. She wants a husband who's important like a lawyer, and Bill, bless his shriveled little heart, wants to sleep warm in the winter, and if his woman's got Bess Flagg's blessing, that's all the better."

Ardis called from the porch, "It's ready, Rusty."

They went into the dining room. Rusty tossed his dusty hat on a table and followed Ardis into the kitchen. He sat down and wolfed his food as if he hadn't eaten for twenty-four hours. Perhaps he hadn't, Clay thought. From his appearance Clay judged Rusty hadn't eaten well for a long time.

"I'm in trouble," Clay said. "I guess you know about Dad's death and Bess saying she's taken the Bar C over."

"Sure, we've all heard it."

"Well, it wasn't my idea to send for you. I mean, if you side me, you'll be in trouble, too."

"You're trying to say you don't want me?"

"No, I'm not saying that at all. I'd be proud to have your help, but I'll have Riley Quinn on my tail. Before long, I think. Ardis says she's going with me, so I've got to get her to someplace that'll be safe."

"She'll stick with you." Rusty looked around. "Where'd she go?"

"Outside to tell Monroe to saddle up for us, I guess. She helped me out of a hole last night when Quinn came after me." He told what happened at the Bar C, then added, "Damn it, Rusty, I don't want either one of you killed or hurt on account of me."

Rusty sat back chewing on a mouthful of ham. He swallowed it, then said, "We're in trouble already, Clay, Ardis and me both. It's always been a question of time until they burn this place and hunt down every one of us who live in the hills. We do some rustling. Enough to keep us eating. That's about all. So what happens? They treat us like dirt. Posting me off the mesa, for instance. They don't want us coming into Painted Rock. Not any of us."

He waggled a finger at Clay. "It's more'n your hide or mine, son. There's plenty of people on the mesa who would like to see Bess cut down to size. They've needed somebody like you for a long time."

"Well then," Clay said, "I guess the main thing is to stay alive."

"That's right," Rusty agreed. "Monroe will stay here. I don't like it much, but that's what he says he's gonna do. But Ardis now, you've got to keep them sons of bitches from getting their hands on her. They ain't forgot she's Long Sam's girl and they figure she's doing all that they used to accuse him of doing."

"Is she?"

"Hell no. Sam never done 'em, neither."

Rusty gave him an angry glance and Clay wished he hadn't asked the question. Ardis came in a moment later and, going into the pantry, filled a flour sack with food. When she came to the table, she said, "The horses are ready."

Rusty picked up the last piece of ham from the platter and shoved it into his mouth as he rose. "We're ready."

Ardis took a Mackinaw off the wall by the back door, put on her hat, and left the house. Rusty glanced at Clay. He said softly, "She's real, son. She ain't like Linda who used to lead you around by the nose."

Clay followed Rusty outside. A moment later they mounted. Ardis lingered to say something to Monroe, then they started climbing the ridge to the west, the buildings soon lost to sight as the cedars and piñons closed in around them.

15

Bess Flagg slept fitfully until dawn, awaking in time to hear the crew going to breakfast. She stared at the ceiling as the first gray light crept through the window and slowly became brighter until she could see across the room. This was the hour when she usually called Ellie in from the kitchen and Ellie would help her dress and lift her into the wheel chair and push her to the table for breakfast, but today it was different. She wanted to watch the crew leave and she couldn't see the yard from the kitchen.

She turned her head toward the window in time to see Lavine and Reno leave the bunkhouse and go to breakfast. A moment later Riley Quinn and the crew left the cook shack and drifted across the yard to the corral where they gathered to listen to Quinn. She could see what was happening, for now the sun had tipped up above the peaks of the San Juans and was laying its first sharp rays upon the dust of the yard.

Bess wished she could hear what was being said. She could see there was an argument and she could guess what it was about. Every cowboy out there resented Lavine's and Reno's presence. Quinn had told her that more than once. The way they saw it, Lavine and Reno didn't work, but they drew fighting wages while the cowhands received the regular forty a month and found. Now they were probably saying that if there was fighting to be done, let Lavine and Reno do it.

They had a sound argument, Bess admitted to herself. She wished that she had never hired Lavine and Reno, but that was water over the dam. She'd let them go in a day or two. Right now Quinn would have to make his orders stick or he was finished. He knew that. He had absolutely no finesse, but he had brute strength. So far that had been enough.

By the time Lavine and Reno left the cook shack, the crew had saddled up. Quinn said something to Lavine and Lavine said something back, then Reno got into the argument. Lavine wheeled and slapped him across the face, spinning the younger man half around. Reno backed off, right hand poised above his gun. Lavine watched contemptuously until he turned and went into the bunkhouse, his head down.

Quinn and his men mounted and struck off in a southwesterly direction, some of the horses bucking until they were pulled down by the steady hands of their riders. She didn't have a poor cowboy in the crew. She could thank Quinn for that. The poor ones didn't last.

At times she wondered why any of the men stayed, with Quinn working them as hard as he did. It wasn't the wages she paid. Maybe it was pride in working for the Flagg outfit. They had a status on the mesa that lifted them above the cowhands who worked for the run-of-the-mill neighboring ranches. Bess liked to think that was important to them.

She reached for the bell that was on her night stand and rang it. A moment later Ellie came in with a towel, a washcloth, and a basin of hot water. "Mornin', Miz Flagg," Ellie said. "You slept later'n usual."

"I haven't been asleep," Bess said. "Linda up?"

"No ma'am."

Ellie helped Bess sit up and braced her back with pillows, then placed the basin of water on her lap. Bess said, "Get Linda up. There's no room on this ranch for sleepy heads."

"Yes ma'am," Ellie said. "I'll get her up right away."

Bess washed, set the basin on the bed beside her, and taking her brush and comb from the night stand, began brushing her hair. She hated Linda so much that it was hard at times to be pleasant, but she always had maintained the fiction of being fond of Linda, or nearly always, often enough that Linda was not likely to leave.

Now it was time to force the situation with Bill Land. She laughed as she thought about it. Neither Linda nor Bill wanted to get married, but they would because she told them to. They'd have a hell of a married life, she told herself, once they started living together.

Bess laughed again, thinking how much she would enjoy having the wedding in her parlor. Everyone was a puppet in her hands if she could find the string, and she always could if she had time. John Roland was the one exception. She swore and slammed the brush down on the night stand. John was the one great failure even though she had tried harder with him than she had ever tried with anyone else.

Ellie came in, saying, "Linda's dressin'. She'll be down in a minute."

"Help me dress," Bess ordered, "and then get me into that damned chair. The morning's half gone."

"Yes ma'am," Ellie said.

Bess was almost finished with her breakfast when Linda came down the stairs from her room. She said, "I'm sorry, Bess. I guess I overslept."

"I guess you did." Bess leaned back in the wheel chair, her coffee cup in her hand. "Linda, you've been shilly-shallying around with Bill long enough. I've got my heart set on having your wedding right here in this house. Don't put it off any longer. I'll send for Bill and we'll set the date." She smiled. "Maybe for this afternoon."

Linda sat down at the table and dipped her spoon into the sugar. Without looking up, she said, "All right, Bess. You go ahead and send for him."

"Good," Bess said, and motioned for Ellie to fill her cup.

Bess drank her coffee slowly, assuming an expression of bland interest as she watched Linda eat her breakfast, but all the time her mind was working in another direction. She would have to get along without Riley Quinn for two or three days and she didn't trust Abe Lavine. Pete Reno was just a punk kid who had no brains, so she couldn't depend on him. She should have got rid of them a long time ago, and she would have if she hadn't thought she'd need them to cut Clay Roland down.

As it turned out, Lavine was too cute with his planning and talking about the right time to do a job like that. Maybe he was afraid of Roland. In any case she had been forced to send Quinn after Roland, but she didn't want to be left without a man on the ranch, so she'd keep Lavine and Reno until Quinn got back. That left no one she could trust but Slim Ives, and he'd probably be back early this morning.

"Wheel me out to the front porch," she said to Ellie. "Fetch my sweater and my binoculars. You go ahead and finish breakfast, Linda. I've got some thinking to do and I can do it better if I'm alone."

She thought Linda looked relieved. She wondered why, and then put it out of her mind. When Ellie rolled her out through the front door to the porch, she found the morning air chillier than she had expected and told Ellie to bring a blanket. She raised the binoculars to her eyes and studied the road to town. A rider was coming in and a moment later she saw it was Slim Ives.

Ellie returned with a blanket and tucked it around Bess's shoulders. "Go back and clean up the kitchen," Bess said. "I'll be all right now."

"Yes ma'am," Ellie said, and retreated to the back of the house.

Bess waited with impatience until Ives came within hailing distance. At times like this when she was eager to do something, her helplessness made her physically sick. For years she had prided herself on being as capable as any man, going where she wanted and doing what she wanted without asking for help from anyone. Now she was dependent upon an ordinary cowhand just to go to town.

When she called to him, Ives reined over to the porch and touched the brim of his hat to her. He said, "Mornin', Mrs. Flagg. Riley gone yet?"

"He took the crew and went after Roland," she said. "How's Bellew?"

"Weak," Ives said. "He lost a lot of blood before I got him to town, but Doc Spears says he'll make it. Well, I guess I better see if I can catch up with Riley."

"No hurry about that," she said. "I want you to harness up the wagon and take me to town."

He hesitated, letting his face show his distaste for the job, then he said reluctantly, "Yes ma'am," and rode on to the corral.

A few minutes later he was back with the wagon. Bess called Ellie from the house and Ellie rolled the chair down the ramp that had been built for her alongside the steps.

"Lift me up to the seat," she ordered Ives, "then tie the chair down in the wagon bed so it won't roll."

He obeyed, and when he stepped into the seat beside her, she was holding the lines. "I'll drive," she said. "Been quite a while since I drove a team. Ellie, you tell Linda I won't be back for a spell. I have some errands to run."

"Yes ma'am, I'll tell her," Ellie said, and turning, trudged into the house.

Ives was normally a silent man and now he seemed embarrassed by having to sit beside Bess. She looked at him, amused. He was tall and slim, with a knobby, scarred face that gave him a tough look. She was a good judge of men, and she had a feeling he was just as tough as he appeared to be. She knew Quinn trusted him completely, that he had been taken along every time she had given Quinn a dirty job to do.

Ives received the same wages the rest of the men did. He must have something in mind or he wouldn't stay. Maybe Quinn had told him that sooner or later he'd marry the boss and Ives would be foreman. Well, it didn't make any difference. She would use him as long as she could. She'd use Quinn, too. She could play hard to get with him as well as Linda could play it with Bill Land.

When they reached town, Bess stopped in front of the drugstore and told Ives to ask Land to come down. When the lawyer appeared a moment later, she was shocked by the bruised and battered condition of his face.

"Good morning, Bess," Land said, and stood waiting for her to tell him what she wanted.

"My God, Bill," she whispered. "Did Roland do that to you?"

"He sure as hell did," Land said. "If I ever see him again, I'll kill him."

"That's a chore you won't have to do," she said. "Riley has taken the crew and gone after him. He tried last night and missed. Bellew got shot in the fracas."

"So I heard," Land said.

Bess glanced at Ives who discreetly remained at the foot of the stairs. She said, "Tell me exactly what happened between you and Roland."

Land obeyed, not sparing himself, then he said, "Clay was always better'n me with his hands. I should have plugged him." He paused, running the tip of his tongue over his swollen lips, then he said, "I won't marry Linda, Bess. She's a bitch. You should have seen the way she kissed him. She's been in love with him all the time. And then that damned Lavine comes running up saying he'll kill me if I plug Clay."

Bess nodded, a slow fury beginning to burn in her as she compared Land's story with what Lavine and Linda had told her when they had got back from town. Well, she'd attend to them later when she got home.

"I don't like to be made a fool of any more than you do, Bill," she said, "but you're marrying Linda and you're going to tame her. Chances are she's had her mind on Clay Roland all these years, but she'll forget him when he's dead and she's your wife."

Land said nothing. He stood staring at his feet. Sensing his silent resistance, she said sharply, "Don't back down on me, Bill. I'll double the monthly retaining fee I pay you and I'll get you into the legislature, but you've got to get one thing through your head. If you want my help, you'll do what I tell you."

"But why have I got to marry Linda?" he demanded.

"Because I'm fond of her," Bess said blandly, "and because I want you to have a woman who is attractive and will help advance your career. I've got big plans for you, Bill, and they include Linda."

"All right," he muttered, his gaze still on the ground.

"Fine," she said brightly. "I think we'd better get this knot tied pronto. Get the preacher and fetch him out right after dinner."

"The preacher's out of town," Land said uneasily. "He won't be back until evening."

"All right, bring him out first thing in the morning," she said brusquely, then called, "Ives, I'm ready to go."

The cowboy stepped into the seat. Turning the team, she drove west down the river, not taking the turn north to her ranch. Ives asked, "Where are we going?"

"To the Bar C," she said. "It's mine. I want to look at it."

He scowled, and she added quickly, "Roland won't be there. If Riley found him, he's dead long before now, but it's my guess he's lit out for the hills."

"I ain't afraid of him, Mrs. Flagg," Ives said sharply, "if that's what you're thinking. No use cussing Riley, but he didn't play it smart last night or we'd have nailed Roland then."

"I agree with you," she said. "Riley is a good man in a lot of ways, but like you say, he isn't always smart. I've wondered about John Roland and Sam Kline. Was it yours or Riley's idea to take care of them the way you did?"

"Mine," he said. "Maybe you don't know it, but rubbing Kline out was a mistake. He wasn't doing us no hurt."

"His place was a hangout for thieves and rustlers," she said sharply. "I'm glad he's gone." She gave Ives a long, speculative glance, then she said, "I might have known you were the one who figured how to handle them. I guess I've been overlooking a good man, so I'll see that the situation is remedied."

"It's about time," he said, glancing at her as if not sure how to take what she had said.

"Yes, it is," she agreed amiably. "I've left too many things in Riley's hands."

"Lavine's and Reno's, too," he said angrily.

"I'm getting rid of them in a day or two," she said. "Just as soon as Riley gets back."

He was silent until they reached the Bar C. She pulled the team to a stop, her gaze sweeping this place where she had come so often when she had been pursuing John Roland. Bitterness clouded her mind as she thought about the foolish things she had done, the only time in her life when she had been foolish that way.

She had loved him, all right. That was the only reason she would ever have done what she had. The truth was she had never been completely honest with herself before. Now she was here again to torture herself with painful memories, but it was the last time.

"Take the chair down and put me in it," she said "I want to go inside."

He hesitated, not understanding what was in her mind, but he obeyed. He wheeled her into the house. For a moment she sat looking around. Nothing was changed. The room was as familiar as her own parlor. Even the chessmen and the board on the claw-footed table in the middle of the room had been there the last time she was here.

She considered how it might have been between her and John Roland, how she thought it was going to be for a long time. Then she remembered their quarrel. She had not been able to stand being put off any longer and she had asked him to marry her. He had gone into his bedroom and come out with his wife's picture.

"I married her forever," John Roland had said. "I'll never marry you or anyone else."

He had never said that to her before. She had been so sure she could wear him down sooner or later, but she had failed. There had been a furious argument, and finally she'd lost her temper and slapped him, then he'd pushed her out through the front door and locked it.

The frustrating memory of her broken dreams crowded into her mind, hurting her with an agony she had never thought she would feel again. "Damn him," she cried out. "God damn him." Her hand came out in a violent gesture and swept the chessmen off the board and sent them banging against the wall. She grabbed up the board and ripped it down the middle and slammed the pieces down. She snatched up the lamp and threw it against the floor, the glass breaking. She watched the coal oil flow across the boards, she caught the smell of it and she began to cry.

"Light it," she screamed and swiped a sleeve across her eyes. "Damn it, burn the house down."

He obeyed, still puzzled by her behavior. For a moment she watched the flames creep along the floor. She thought about loving John Roland and then killing him. Now she would burn all that was left of him. Riley Quinn would destroy his son. Then she thought of Linda. Maybe the girl still loved Clay Roland. She must, from what Bill Land had said. Then Bess would destroy her, too, just as she was destroying this house.

"Wheel me outside and put me in the wagon," she said. "You drive."

She did not look back at the burning house as the wagon climbed out of the valley. All of this was behind her. It was gone, wiped out. That was the way it would stay. In the end she would destroy John Roland, root and branch. Even the memory of him would be gone. It would be as if he had never lived.

16

Near midmorning Clay, Ardis and Mattson reached a high point on the ridge west of Storm River. They pulled up to blow their horses and dismounted, Mattson stretching and yawning as he looked down at the buildings of the Kline place, reduced to toy size by the distance.

"I've got a hunch we didn't get away none too soon," Mattson said. "By dark we'll have Flagg riders all through these hills."

"Sooner than that," Ardis said, and walking up the trail, disappeared into a thicket of cedars.

Clay's gaze followed her until she was out of sight, thinking that in the men's clothes and heavy Mackinaw she was wearing, she was still completely feminine. He said, "Funny thing, Rusty. Before I left, I thought she was just a hare-brained kid, more boy than girl. When I first got back, I kept seeing her the same way, but I was wrong. She's a woman."

"A hell of a lot of woman," Mattson said. "What are you fixing to do with her?"

"I don't know," Clay said. "The only reason I let her come was because I figured she wouldn't be safe at home when Quinn got there. I was hoping I could talk her into going on into Utah and staying till this is over."

"She won't do it," Mattson said. "She's as good as any man when it comes to riding through these hills, and she can shoot as straight, too. She figures you need her, so she'll stick with you."

Clay nodded, thinking that Rusty was right. He said, "I remember how you used to josh her and she'd come right back at you. I thought you two would be married before now."

Rusty had started to roll a cigarette. Now he stopped, the paper curling in his fingers as he stared at Clay. "My God, man, have you gone daft? It's always been you from the time we first started coming to her place. She's had a dozen men after her to marry them, some pretty good men that Long Sam liked and figured would make good husbands for her. She never told her pa how she felt about you, but she's told me plenty of times. Whenever I showed up she always asked if I'd heard from you or heard anything about you. Then she'd ask me if I figured you'd be coming back some day, but hell, I couldn't answer her. How would I know what a man like you was going to do?"

Clay turned away. His first thought was that Rusty was mistaken, but he knew almost immediately that his friend was right. If he hadn't been blind, he would have known. A woman wouldn't be doing what Ardis was if she didn't love him. He would have known before this, if Linda hadn't filled his thoughts the way she had.

Rusty sealed the cigarette and lighted it. He said, "I reckon this ain't anything you want to hear, but you're going to hear it. Linda wouldn't have been good for you. She was flirting on the side with every man she could. The only reason she had any time for you was because she figured you could take her to the Bar C and support her. After your pa kicked you out, she was done with you."

Clay whirled on Rusty, wanting to tell him he was wrong. A woman couldn't kiss a man the way Linda had kissed him in town if she didn't love him. But loving him and marrying him were two different things. Rusty was right.

Linda had probably never had a serious thought about anyone except herself. Well, it didn't make any difference. He had put her out of his life forever.

Ardis was coming toward them down the trail, walking rapidly and gracefully. Clay, watching her, was struck by a great wave of feeling for her. She had asked nothing of him, but she was willing to give anything. Rusty was right. He had been blind.

When she joined them, Rusty was staring at the river far below them. He asked, "Where are you taking Clay?"

"To the stone cabin," she said. "It's the safest place I know. I thought about trying to get a bunch of the Hills men together to fight Quinn, but it's not their fight."

"I figured we'd keep going across the line and find a place where you'd be safe," Clay said. "Moab, maybe."

She shook her head defiantly, her lips tightly pressed against her teeth. "I don't want to be safe. If you're going to Utah, I'll go with you. If you come back, I'll be with you. I won't let you fight the whole Flagg crew by yourself."

One look at her face told him there was no use to argue with her. They'd probably be safe enough in the stone cabin, wherever that was. He said, "All right, we'll go to the stone cabin."

"We'd better ride," she said, irritated by his suggestion that they go on into Utah.

"Take a look down there," Mattson said. "They ain't far behind us."

Clay saw the riders pouring out of the gorge. They were too far away to be recognized, but Clay did not doubt that it was the Flagg crew, Riley Quinn riding in front.

"They've made good time," Clay said.

"They sure have," Rusty agreed. "That's Quinn for you. He's been pushing those boys since breakfast and no mistake."

"How far is it to the stone cabin?" Clay asked.

"We'll be there by noon," Ardis said, "or a little after."

"You tell Monroe where you're headed?" Mattson asked.

She nodded. "He won't tell them."

"No, reckon he won't," Rusty conceded, "but chances are they'll beat hell out of him trying to make him tell. Don't make no difference if he does. Quinn will have that breed, Pete Blackdog, with him, and Pete can track a fly across the top of a table."

Ardis pinned her gaze on Clay's face. "I expect them to find us. We can keep running and I think we could stay ahead of them, but it seems to me it's better to let them find us. If we hole up in the stone cabin, we can cut them up. I don't think it will take much of a loss to pull them off."

"How do you figure that?" Clay asked.

"What makes men fight?" she countered. "I mean, want to fight enough to die?"

"A lot of reasons," Clay answered. "Duty. Loyalty. Money, maybe. All depends on the man."

"Sure it does," she said, "but do the men who are following Riley Quinn have a sense of duty that makes them want to fight you? Are they loyal to Queen Bess or to Quinn? Are they getting big pay to run you down and risk their lives?"

"I don't know about the pay . . ." Clay began.

"I do," Rusty said. "Bess pays Lavine and Reno fighting wages, but not to the crew. What she don't know is that she hurt herself with every man on her crew when she hired them gunslicks."

"You know more about these things than I do, Clay," Ardis said, "so you can tell me if I'm wrong, but it seems to me that if we could knock a couple of them out of their saddles, and we were holed up in the stone cabin where they couldn't get at us, they wouldn't have much stomach for fighting."

"You never know for sure how men are going to perform in a fight," Clay said, "but the chances are you're right."

"We're wasting time," Rusty said impatiently. "Won't take 'em long to find us once they start up the ridge."

They mounted and rode west, the trail dipping and turning around tall upthrusts of red rock. At times they crossed open areas fifty acres or more in size, the grass brown and dry. Twice they spooked big bucks that went bounding off into the cedars, and occasionally they rode past small bands of cattle. Some of the brands had unquestionably been worked over, but if Rusty noticed, he said nothing. Clay wondered if the Bar C herd was somewhere here in the Smoky Hills.

They reached a fork in the trail and reined up. This was where Clay had taken the wrong trail on his way in and had wound up down on the river below the Kline place. If he had turned right instead of left, he would have stayed on top of the ridge as they had just done and so saved himself at least an hour of time and several miles of riding.

"The stone cabin's three, four miles ahead and off to the south," Rusty said. "We ain't gonna hide our tracks less'n we put wings on these horses. Now the way I figure, it's gonna be tough fighting the whole outfit, but if you were bucking just half of 'em, you could discourage 'em like Ardis said."

"If you're driving at what I think you are," Clay said, "I'm against it."

"So am I," Ardis said. "If we separate, we'll make the same mistake Custer did. Ever hear what happened to him, Rusty?"

"Seems like I did." Rusty grinned and winked at her. "But this is different. I wouldn't think of busting up if we was on the mesa, but I'm supposed to be safe around here. Now they're gonna be some puzzled when our tracks split. Monroe will tell 'em Ardis is with us. They may think she went that way," he nodded at the left fork, "figuring she'll circle back home. But Quinn won't be sure. He might just as easy think it's you, Clay, wanting to duck around 'em and double back to the mesa. But whatever they think, they're gonna divide up. Sooner or later they'll get together, but meantime you won't be fighting more'n half the crew. I reckon you can handle that many if you're the man I think you are, Clay."

"Sure," Clay said, "but what about you?"

"They won't hurt me if they do find me," Rusty said. "Not when they're chasing you. I'll ride down the trail a piece, then take off through the cedars. I'll make camp somewhere down yonder and go to sleep. I'm about all in."

Clay still didn't like it. He doubted that Rusty was as all in as he claimed. Six years ago Rusty could have ridden two days and one night without being worn out and Clay didn't think the years had changed him that much.

"I'm still against it," Clay said. "I say to stick together."

Ardis scratched the back of her neck, frowning as her gaze turned from one man to the other. Finally she said, "Clay's right. Sometimes Quinn goes as crazy mad as Queen Bess does. You know that as well as I do."

"I'm going this way." Rusty jerked his hand to the north. "You can do what you want to, but I ain't sitting here all day arguing about it."

"I guess we can't stop you," Ardis said. "Looks like you want out of it."

"Sure I do." Rusty grinned at her again. "You two can do the fighting. Me, I don't cotton to the notion of stopping any Flagg lead."

He whirled his horse around and rode off, following the north fork of the trail. He looked back once to wave, then disappeared down the slope among the cedars.

"He's lying," Clay said. "He wants to get Quinn off our tail, and he's going to get himself killed doing it."

"I'm sorry I said what I did, but I've known Rusty most of my life and I get mad at him every time he has one of his stubborn spells." Ardis paused, biting her lip then said, "We'd better mosey along."

They went on, Clay knowing exactly what Ardis had meant. Rusty had always been bullheaded on things like this. Clay remembered he used to be able to talk Bill Land out of almost anything, but he'd never changed Rusty's mind once he had decided on something he considered important.

Half an hour later they turned off the ridge and followed a narrow trail to the south that showed little recent use. It led to the bottom of a canyon that held a small, clear stream running over a red-rock bottom. They turned up the canyon, the walls steep and so close together in places that they cut off the noon-high sun. Another mile brought them into a grass-covered bowl. At the upper side to the west was the stone cabin, built on a ledge ten feet above the floor of the valley.

They rode across the bowl and dismounted below the cabin. Ardis untied the sacks of food as he pulled their rifles from the scabbards, then motioned upstream. "There's a corral above the narrows," she said. "Take care of the horses while I get dinner."

"Any way out of here?" he asked. "Except the way we came in."

She smiled. "Up. That's all."

Picking up the sacks of food and the rifles, she climbed the rough steps that had been chipped out of the sandstone. Clay pulled gear from her horse, then mounted his bay and led the other animal upstream. There was nothing to do but wait, he thought, wait for Riley Quinn and the Flagg crew.

17

Riley Quinn set a hard pace from the time he left the Flagg ranch, the crew strung out behind him. He was not a perceptive man on matters that had to do with human relationships, but even anyone as insensitive as he was could not help feeling that something was wrong between him and the crew. They had been close to rebellion back there at the corral, mostly because they had been hired to work. They said Lavine and Reno were paid to fight, so let them go after Roland and do the fighting.

Well, he'd curried them down, all right. He'd told them Queen Bess had given them the job of running Roland down, so it was up to them to show her they could do any job she gave them.

The rebellion hadn't amounted to anything, he told himself. There wasn't a man in the crew who could stand up to him in a fist fight. He'd demonstrated that on more than one occasion. The men who didn't like his methods left, the others knuckled under. Still, he was plagued by the feeling that something was different this morning. The men had turned sullen when he'd told them what they were going to do, and they remained sullen. He didn't hear a word back along the line all the way to the Bar C.

They'd get over it, he told himself. The thing to do was to keep them busy. They knew who gave the orders. Ease up on a bunch of men and some loudmouth starts to talk, then you've got trouble. His job was to see it never got to that place.

They made a quick check of the Bar C, found it deserted, and went on down the gorge to the Kline roadhouse, Quinn confident they would find Roland there. They moved in fast and searched the buildings, but turned up no one except Monroe.

Quinn motioned to Pete Blackdog. "See if you can pick up any fresh tracks. Roland might have gone down the river, or he might have taken the trail up the ridge if he aims to get out of the state. It's my guess he ain't got more'n two, three hours start on us, so you oughtta be able to cut sign all right."

Blackdog nodded and, mounting, rode downstream. Quinn turned to Monroe. He had never seen the man before. He hadn't heard what Ardis Kline had done after her father was killed, so when Monroe said he was the girl's hired man, it was reasonable to think he was telling the truth.

"All right, Monroe, if that's your name," Quinn said, "you're going to talk. I ain't real sure Monroe is your name. You're all rustlers and horse thieves down here, and the chances are you've been riding the owl hoot ever since you were big enough to fork a horse. It's my guess you've got to look at your hat band to see what handle you're using now."

Monroe stood in front of Quinn, a stolid, dark-faced man

who was a full six inches taller than Quinn and therefore looked down at him. Quinn was always conscious of his lack of height, and to have Monroe tip his head so that he gave the appearance of looking down his nose made Quinn furious.

"It's my name," Monroe said.

"All right, all right," Quinn said harshly. "Where did Roland go when he left here?"

"I don't know," Monroe said.

Quinn hit him on the side of the head with an open palm, the sound of the blow a meaty thud like that of a butcher's cleaver on a side of beef. Monroe was spun half around, and when he turned back to look at Quinn, the side of his face that had been struck was a dull red.

"That's just a beginning," Quinn said. "I can slap you silly, and when I get tired, there's ten other men here who can work on you. If that don't do the job, we'll take your boots off and we'll fry your feet. If you stay stubborn, I'll take a knife to you. I'm the gent who taught the Apaches all they know and I ain't forgot any of it. Now talk up 'cause we're in a hell of a hurry."

"I'll tell you anything I know," Monroe said, "but all your beating and burning and knifing can't get something out of me I don't know, and I don't know where Roland went."

"Then let's hear what you do know. Roland was here last night?"

"Yeah, he was here," Monroe said. "He rode in late with Ardis. I don't know where they'd been or what they'd been doing, but Roland was here this morning. I just work for Ardis. She don't tell me all she knows or all she does."

So it had been the Kline girl who had opened up on him and Ives and Bellew from the river last night, Quinn thought, and all the time he had been so sure it was Rusty Mattson. He cursed, then caught himself. He'd be the laughingstock of the mesa if it got out that three of them had been run off the Bar C by Roland and a girl.

"Did the Kline girl go with him when he left this morning?" Quinn asked.

Monroe nodded. "Rusty Mattson was with 'em, too. He showed up this morning, ate breakfast, then lit out with the other two. Ardis, she said for me to look after things till she got back. She didn't say when that would be."

So Mattson was in the picture now! Quinn considered that fact a moment, realizing it put a different face on the whole picture. The three of them would be hard to take if they forted up somewhere. If they had enough time, there was a chance they could drum up some help from the Smoky Hills bunch, and Quinn and the whole Flagg crew could be wiped out in an ambush.

Quinn glanced around the circle of faces, still sullen and tight-lipped, and it occurred to him that Ardis Kline could shoot as straight as Roland or Mattson, and fighting her wasn't going to appeal to his men. If it came to that, he wasn't sure he could even keep them in line.

"One more question, Monroe," Quinn said. "Which way did they go?"

Monroe jerked a thumb toward the ridge to the west. "That way. They was going up the trail the last I seen of 'em."

"They went that way, all right, boss," Pete Blackdog said. He had just ridden up. Now he jerked a thumb behind him toward the ridge. "Three of 'em. Didn't look like they've been gone very long. Mebbe less'n two, three hours."

"All right, Monroe," Quinn said. "You stay here. I may have use for you before the day's over. If you do what I tell you, you won't get hurt."

"I'll be here," Monroe said.

"Mount up," Quinn ordered, and stepping into the saddle, started up the ridge.

The slant was not steep, for the trail followed the crest of the ridge which lifted slowly, but Quinn had pushed the horses too hard to keep the pace up. Presently he signaled a stop and motioned for Blackdog to get down and study the trail. He chafed at the delay, hating to lose even a minute. The way he saw it, his one chance of catching Roland was to close the gap and get him before the three of them recruited help.

Blackdog rose. "They're still ahead of us, but we ain't far behind 'em."

"Then we'll keep on their tail," Quinn said.

"You trying to kill our horses and put us afoot?" Stub Moon asked.

Moon was a loudmouth and Quinn had no intentions of letting him get started. "We've got a job to do," Quinn said. "Let's do it."

He went on, Blackdog behind him, the rest strung out behind him. He didn't stop again until they reached the fork in the trail. Again he motioned for Blackdog to get down. He watched the cowboy walk slowly along the main trail, then come back and follow the north fork for twenty yards or more.

When he returned, Blackdog said, "Two of 'em stayed on top. One of 'em took the north trail."

"Where does it lead to?" Quinn asked.

"Circles down off the ridge," Blackdog said, "then curls around till it comes to the river several miles below the Kline place."

"Got any notion which one went that way?" Quinn asked.

Blackdog shook his head. Quinn sat hunched forward in the saddle, his muscles aching with the tension that gripped him. They had separated to fool him, he knew, but he was a jump ahead of them. They were figuring he'd think Roland was heading for the state line and the girl was circling back to her place.

Well, he wasn't going to be fooled that easy. He saw through their trick. Roland was going back to the Bar C, so he was the one who had taken the north trail. When he reached the river, he'd swing upstream past the Kline place and follow the gorge to the mesa. The girl and Mattson were probably meeting some of the Smoky Hills men and were rigging an ambush along the trail. But Riley Quinn wasn't walking into their trap.

He hipped around in his saddle to face his men. "Looks like Roland has gone off on this north trail, but we can't be sure. Midge, you take Rance and Jones and follow the tracks on the ridge trail. If you find Roland, get him, but if you're following the girl and Mattson, let 'em alone and head back. The rest of you come with me."

He started down the north trail, watching the tracks ahead of him. He was fully aware that Roland might leave the trail and hide in a cedar thicket, hoping they'd go on by. Now he wished he'd waited for Slim Ives to get back from town. He could depend on Ives. He thought he could count on Midge, but he wasn't at all sure of Jones and Rance. At least he had the loudmouth, Stub Moon, with him. If Moon started talking again, about horses or the girl or anything else, he'd shut him up good.

Suddenly Quinn realized he had lost Roland's tracks and reined up, cursing. "He took off back there somewhere, Pete," he said. "Pick up his trail for us."

Blackdog rode back up the trail a short distance, then called, "Here."

"Lead out," Quinn said. "He ain't gonna make much speed through the cedars."

Blackdog hesitated, not liking it, but he obeyed. If they ran into Roland, he'd probably shoot the lead man, and that would be Pete Blackdog. But they'd have Roland, Quinn thought savagely. He could afford to lose his tracker if they got Roland.

For half an hour or more they followed Blackdog through

the scrub oak and serviceberry brush, sometimes dropping down a steep, boulder-strewn slope, and finally reaching a small park with a spring breaking through the ground on the upper side. There, lying beside the spring, was Rusty Mattson, asleep.

Quinn had his gun out and was covering Mattson when the sound of their approach woke him. He sat up, blinking, and reached for his gun. He stopped, his hand in mid-air when Quinn said, "You touch that hogleg, mister, and you're dead."

Mattson rose, his hand dropping to his side. He asked, "What do you gents want?"

"Clay Roland," Quinn said. "Where is he?"

"I don't know," Mattson answered. "What do you want him for?"

"I'm asking the questions, not you," Quinn snapped. "You left the Kline place with Roland and the Kline girl. Where are they?"

Mattson was the same height as the Flagg foreman, but beside Quinn's great bulk, he looked like a spindly-legged boy. He stood his ground, returning Quinn's stare. "You're off your stamping ground, Riley. You're supposed to stay on your side of the river if we stay on ours. Remember?"

Quinn took a step forward, so furious he was trembling. He had expected to find Roland instead of Mattson, and now he was angry at himself for making the wrong guess. It could easily be a fatal mistake. Now Roland had another hour's bulge at least, and Quinn had no hope that the three men he had sent on up the main trail would succeed in finding Roland. He would have been smarter if he had divided the crew equally, but it was too late now to think of what he should have done.

"Mattson, we ain't got time to fool with you," Quinn said. "Either you tell me what I want to know and do it pronto, or I'll kill you where you stand."

Mattson's leather-dark face turned bitter, his gaze swinging to the men behind Quinn, then back to Quinn. He had the look of a man who knew he was about to die and didn't really care, one way or the other. He said, "You shoot me down in cold blood, Quinn, and I'll haunt you as long as you live."

Behind Quinn Stub Moon said, "Don't do it, Riley. Murder may be your style, but it ain't ours."

Quinn heard him, but he didn't turn or say anything to Moon. The hammer of his revolver was eared back, his finger was tight on the trigger. "Mattson, I'll give you ten seconds. That's all the time you've got if you don't talk."

Mattson laughed in his face. "The brave Riley Quinn, shooting a man down in cold blood without giving him a chance for his gun. That's enough to blackball you in hell. You're just like the Flagg bitch you work for . . ."

Quinn pulled the trigger. He saw the powdersmoke drift downslope from him, he heard the roar of the shot, and felt the buck of the walnut handle against his palm, and he saw Mattson drop. He had the weird feeling that he was watching this scene but was apart from it, then he knew he wasn't and he lost all trace of self-control.

Panicky because he sensed he had just made the biggest mistake of his life, he pulled the trigger again and again until the gun was empty, every bullet slamming into the lifeless body of the man on the ground in front of him. He couldn't stop; he was a machine that had been wound up too tightly and had to run down.

The hammer dropped on an empty. He reloaded, then his right arm fell to his side. Suddenly he was limp and a little sick, and as he watched blood bubble from the dead man's mouth and run down his chin, he knew this was worse than a mistake. By one stupid, wanton act he had ruined everything.

He was not surprised when Stub Moon said, "Drop your iron, Riley. This is where we split up. We've taken a hell of a lot off of you, but we're done. We ain't riding for no outfit that murders a man like you just done."

Quinn whirled, thinking he had bulled through worse situations. He'd bull through this one. "Get down off that horse, Stub. I'm going to beat hell . . ."

He stopped, hard hit by the knowledge that he had never faced a situation like this. All the men had their guns in their hands and were pointing them at him. He had expected Moon to have his gun out, but not the others. His gaze moved along the line until it fastened on Pete Blackdog's swarthy face at the end. He dropped his gun, knowing it was no use. He had looked at plenty of men who hated him, but he had never before seen the complete revulsion that was in the faces of these men.

"Back up," Moon said. "Stand over there on the other side of the spring. You try to get that gun or make a move for your Winchester, and we'll come back and fill you fuller of lead than you filled Mattson."

He obeyed. This was a nightmare, he thought. It had to be; it was an impossible thing that couldn't be happening. Then Moon said, "I didn't think you'd do it, Riley. I'd have shot you in the back if I had." Moon's lips curled in contempt. "I reckon we're all wondering why we ever worked for you as long as we have."

Moon rode off through the brush, the rest following. A moment later they disappeared on the other side of a thicket of scrub oak. Quinn wiped his forehead. This had not been a nightmare. He was lucky to be alive.

He picked up his revolver and dropped it into his holster. He moved toward his horse in a daze, then the full impact of what he had done came to him. He couldn't go back to the ranch and tell Bess he had lost the crew; he couldn't go back and tell her he had failed to get Clay Roland.

He stood beside his horse, a hand on the horn. That was when the solution came to him. If he could flush Roland into the open and kill him, he would have accomplished what he started out to do. He could hire another crew. He had no chance alone against Roland, but if he could get him into town, he could find plenty of men to help him. Bill Land. Doc Spears. Ed Parker. Sure, he'd find enough.

The crew had ridden downslope and would take the north trail to the river. The ridge trail was the closest route back to Kline's, so he would go that way. He swung into the saddle and started climbing, satisfied with himself now that he knew exactly what to do.

18

As Clay rode up the canyon, leading Ardis' horse behind him, he wondered sourly why he had let her lead him into a box canyon like this. Sure, they could defend themselves in the stone cabin as long as their grub and water held out. The cabin had been built under an overhanging ledge so that the ledge formed part of the ceiling. Anyone standing on the rim above them could not see the cabin, so at least they wouldn't have to worry about an attack from that direction.

The trouble was Riley Quinn was a dogged kind of man. All he had to do was to sit down out there in the mouth of the bowl. It would become a question of who could hang and rattle the longest, but sooner or later Quinn, if he stayed, would starve them out. More than that, it would be easy enough to sneak past the cabin at night and steal the horses.

Looking ahead, he saw that he was riding into a cliff that was the dead end of the canyon. Apparently the stream flowed out of solid rock. But Ardis had said there was a corral up here where he could leave the horses. Maybe she had never been here before. She'd probably just heard about the place and was mistaken.

Another fifty feet showed him that Ardis knew what she was talking about. The creek made a ninety-degree turn to the left, the canyon so narrow at this point that the sky was no more than a blue slit overhead. He had to keep his horse in the water. There simply wasn't any bank.

A moment later he discovered that the creek made another sharp turn, this time in the opposite direction. The cliff he had seen ahead of him was a long narrow point around which the creek flowed. Above it the canyon widened out into another bowl similar to the one below the stone cabin.

Here was plenty of grass for the horses. Unless Quinn or some of his men had been here before, or knew about the canyon, they wouldn't know this upper bowl was here, so the horses were probably safe enough.

Clay rode through a gate in a pole fence which had been built across the opening end of the bowl. He found it solid enough and slid the bars into place, closing the gate. He pulled the bridle off Ardis' horse and stripped gear from his own, turning both animals loose.

For a moment he stood studying the sandstone cliff to the west. The creek boiled down the face of the cliff in a series of waterfalls. Beside each waterfall he saw toeholds that had been dug in the sandstone. Then he understood.

This was an outlaw hideout known only to the fraternity and the Smoky Hills people. Close as it was to the Utah line and Robber's Roost, it was perfect for a man on the dodge. Even if he was tracked as far as the stone cabin, he could hold off a posse till dark, then slip out and escape by climbing the cliff. The members of the posse wouldn't know for hours that he was gone, and by that time the outlaw would probably have stolen a horse or bought one from a nearby rancher.

Clay walked back to the cabin carrying the bridles and his saddle and blanket. A strange world here in the Smoky Hills, he reflected, a world without law, an island unexplored by sheriffs and deputies. He doubted that Quinn or any of his men were familiar with this place. Probably he could stay here with Ardis as long as he wanted and be perfectly safe.

He picked up Ardis' saddle and blanket below the cabin, and climbed the steps, thinking he had never been as tired in his life. If he had his choice, he'd be here a long time.

He dropped the saddles and blankets inside the cabin and looked around. The interior was neat and clean, so the cabin had probably been used not long before. He saw two loopholes on each side of the door which let in some light, but there were no windows.

Someone had gone to a good deal of trouble to build this cabin and furnish it, he thought. He guessed that it had been the work of Long Sam Kline who had lived on the fringe of this outlaw world for a long time. He had probably sold them supplies and horses at a great profit to himself, and had guaranteed them a hideout which would be far safer then the roadhouse on the river.

The door was a heavy, thick one which would stop almost any bullet. The cabin was furnished with a couple of rawhide-bottom chairs, a table, two bunks, and a small range. In the corner above the stove were two shelves filled with a variety of canned goods.

Amused, Ardis watched him from where she stood beside the stove. She asked, "Satisfied, Clay?"

"I sure am," he said. "I've done a lot of outlaw chasing, but I never ran into a place like this. I guess we could hold off the entire Flagg crew till we ran out of grub and water."

"They'd get tired before that," she said. "There's a seep off the cliff that never goes dry." She motioned toward the back side of the cabin. "It isn't enough water for an army, but there's plenty for the two of us. Besides the grub we brought, there's enough in those cans to last a long time. The only thing we don't have is wood, so after we eat you'd better fetch some in. There's an ax in the corner."

He sat down at the table. "This your dad's work?"

She turned to the stove to fork the bacon from the frying pan into tin plates. "That's right. I wouldn't have known about it if Pa hadn't built it. In fact, I didn't know about it for a long time, but he brought me up here last spring. He said we might find it handy sometime. He didn't do the rustling they accused him of, but he did take money from men on the dodge who were willing to pay high for a place to rest where they'd be safe. I'm not proud of him, Clay. He wasn't proud of himself, either. He aimed to sell out and leave the country this fall, but they didn't let him live long enough to do it."

"Why did they murder him? It seems more senseless than Dad's killing."

She shrugged. "How does anyone know what goes on in Bess Flagg's mind? I told you she was like a mad dog and should be killed like one."

"She may be a mad dog," Clay said, "but she's not crazy. She has a reason for everything she does."

"I guess so," Ardis admitted. "She probably believed the rustling talk. Or maybe she just didn't like anyone she couldn't run. She sure couldn't run Pa."

Ardis was silent while she brought the coffeepot to the table and filled the tin cups. Then she went on, "I think she's afraid of people she can't handle. It's safer to kill them and get them out of the way. It's probably the reason she's after you as hard as she is. The men who live in the hills are like Rusty and Monroe. They'd have done anything for Pa. Maybe Bess was afraid that some day he'd round up a bunch of his friends and raid her outfit. There's been a lot of that talk, too, you know."

Clay nodded. "I just thought of something else. We were going to stay on the trail. Keep ducking and running, but I guess you were a jump ahead of me. The Hills boys know what I've been, so they won't be likely to help or hide a man who carried a star as long as I did."

"I was afraid to trust them," she said. "I thought this was a better bet."

"You're smarter'n I was on that," he said.

She gave him a searching look. "That's hard for you to admit, isn't it?" she asked. "You've lived by yourself so long you think you don't need other people's help. That's wrong, Clay. There are times when we all need help. I was in the best position to help you. Rusty and me, I mean."

She filled the tin plates at the stove and brought them to the table. As she sat down across from him, he said, "Yes, I guess it is hard for me to admit." He looked at her a moment before he began to eat, realizing only then how tired she was. "You'd better take a nap this afternoon."

"So had you," she said. "If they track us here, we'll probably be up all night."

"None of Quinn's men know about this canyon, do they?"

"I'm sure they don't," she said. "It's a well-kept secret. Of course a good tracker like Pete Blackdog could trail us here."

"I'll fetch the wood in," he said. "If they do find us, we'll bar the door and let them sweat." He grinned. "Trouble is you may get tired of my company."

"No, Clay," she said quickly. "Not ever." Then she lowered her head, her face flushing with embarrassment.

She had not intended to say that, he thought. They finished the meal in silence, Clay's mind turning back to the lonely years he had carried the star, and because he had been lonely, he had thought about Linda. It was natural that he would, Linda being the only girl he had ever loved, but he knew Rusty had been right about her. She'd led him around by the nose, all right. He'd been blind and that was a fact.

The strangest thing that had happened to him since he'd come back was finding in Ardis the characteristics he had mentally given Linda. He hadn't thought any woman would do what Ardis had, freely because she wanted to and without even being asked.

He glanced at her across the table, feeling a love for her that was overwhelming and completely unexpected, but he could not tell her. Not until he had won his fight. The odds were still too long against him. If he died, it would be better if she didn't know how he felt.

When he finished eating, he rose. "I'd better get at the woodchopping."

"What are you going to do, Clay? When we leave here, I mean?"

"I don't know," he said. "I haven't cut the odds down any, but sometimes a man gets help from unexpected places. I've seen it happen a lot of times. But I'll win. I've got more to fight for than Queen Bess and Riley Quinn and the rest of them put together."

He picked up the ax and went outside. He found a dead piñon not far from the cabin and worked for an hour or more, piling the wood at the base of the steps. He carried an armload inside, and seeing that Ardis was asleep on one of the bunks, he eased the wood to the floor so he would not waken her. He moved to the bunk and stood over her for a moment, watching her breasts rise and fall evenly in her sleep.

The fire was out and the cabin was cold. Picking up her saddle blanket, he spread it over her, then he sprawled out full length on the other bunk and instantly fell asleep. It seemed only a moment later that Ardis was shaking him awake. He opened his eyes to look into her frightened face. He sat up, sensing what had happened before she said, "They're here, Clay."

19

Linda could not guess what motive had driven Bess to make the trip to town unless it was to see Bill Land and force the marriage. Bess had no real reason to force the marriage, Linda knew, except her hunger to control the lives of others, a hunger that had grown from the time of her accident into an obsession.

Now that Bess was gone, Linda wished she had told her straight out that she was giving Bill's ring back to him just as soon as she could, that she was marrying Abe Lavine and they were leaving the country. But it was a foolish thought. She wouldn't have the courage to tell Bess if she were here. She couldn't stand up to Bess, not on anything Bess felt as strongly about as she did this.

The more Linda thought about it, the more frightened she became. She wanted to see Lavine, to tell him they had waited too long now, that if he loved her, he would take her away today. Now! He would have taken her yesterday, but no, she'd had to play her feminine role and put him off. It was her own fault she was still here. The thought did not bring her any satisfaction.

Going upstairs, she packed everything she owned into a small trunk and two suitcases. She kept turning to the window to see if Lavine was in sight. She had to talk to him, but she didn't want to go to the bunkhouse. When, near noon, she did see him in the yard near the corral gate, Pete Reno was with him.

By noon the packing was finished. When she went downstairs, Ellie had her dinner on the table. She ate absent-mindedly, knowing that she couldn't wait any longer. She had to see Lavine soon regardless of Pete Reno. She went upstairs to her room again, trying to think what she would do if Lavine changed his mind about her. She had saved some money. She'd go away somewhere, to Montrose or Grand Junction, or maybe Denver, and get a job. Something! Anything! She had to get away from here. If she stayed, Bess would find some way to make her marry Bill Land.

For a moment she thought of Clay Roland and immediately

put him out of her mind. She would never love another man in quite the way she had loved Clay. Six years ago she could have had him. If she had been completely honest with him yesterday when he had kissed her and had broken her engagement with Bill Land then, she might still have had him. But now it was too late. To keep thinking of him was idle dreaming. She had lost him forever. Abe Lavine was her only chance and she must not lose him.

When she could stand it no longer, she carried her suitcases downstairs and left the house. Lavine and Reno were squatting in front of the corral gate whittling. They rose when they saw her coming, Reno's speculative gaze fixed on her from the moment she stepped off the porch until she reached them.

She always sensed something unclean about Pete Reno when he looked at her; it was in his eyes, in the expression on his pimply face. She shivered, a series of prickles running down her spine, but she succeeded in smiling at Lavine, refusing to speak to Reno or even look at him.

"I want to see you a minute, Abe," she said.

Lavine jerked his head at Reno. "Vamoose."

Affronted, Reno stared at him a moment, then turned on his heel and walked off. When he disappeared into the bunkhouse, Lavine said, "We're finished. If I don't kill him, he'll shoot me in the back."

"You mean because I came out here?"

Lavine shook his head. "It happened this morning. Quinn took the crew out to hunt for Roland. He threw it up to me'n Pete for not going. We're paid for fighting, he says, but we don't do nothing but sit around the bunkhouse all day while they go out and do what we're paid for.

"I told him I had my way of doing things and I wouldn't do 'em his way. Then Pete spoke up and said he'd go. When we hired on here, we agreed I was to call the turn on everything. I told him he wasn't going. He got sore then and started to cuss me, so I slapped him. I thought he was going to draw on me, but he walked off. Well, it's been eating on him ever since."

"I'm sorry if I had anything to do with breaking you up," she said.

"You didn't." He smiled at the idea. "It's been coming a long time. Should have come sooner." He looked at her, his usual barren expression giving way to one of naked hunger. "Let's talk about something pleasant. You'n me, for instance."

"Take me away, Abe," she said. "I'll marry you any time you say. I knew yesterday that would be my answer. I don't know why I waited."

"I don't, either," he said, and taking her into his arms, kissed her long and hard, not caring if Reno or the cook or Ellie saw them. Then he let her go and looked down at her, shaking his head a little as if not understanding how this had happened. "I never thought I could be this lucky."

"I'll be a good wife," she said. "I'll try as hard as I can, but right now you've got to get me away from here. I'm scared, Abe."

He pulled her close, holding her soft body against his. "I won't let anything happen to you. What are you scared of?"

"Bess. She's been good to me most of the time, but it's all on the surface. She's bad. Even after living with her for two years, I didn't know how bad she was until she tried to kill Clay. Then this morning she said I was going to marry Bill Land right away, maybe this afternoon. She'll do anything to make me do it. Anything."

"Go pack up," he said. "Won't take me long."

"I'm ready now. I've got two suitcases and a trunk. We can't carry them on a horse."

"Then we'll wait till she gets here and take the wagon. I can send it back from town. I've got some wages coming. I'd like to collect 'em before I go." He motioned toward the house. "You wait inside. I'll saddle up and be ready to go when she gets here."

She obeyed, thinking it was a mistake, that they should leave now regardless of her things or Lavine's wages, but she couldn't risk telling him. That was the way their married life would be. He was a strong-willed man whose decisions would not be changed by her or anyone. Even Bess had failed with him.

Linda waited impatiently, and finally she dragged her trunk down the stairs and left it beside the suitcases. After that she couldn't think of anything to do. A moment later she saw Lavine in front of the house with his horse and she sighed in relief. Maybe it would be all right to suggest they leave now. She could ride behind the saddle.

But she didn't make the suggestion, for when she stepped through the door to the porch, her coat and hat on, she saw Bess and Ives coming in the wagon. She walked to Lavine and stood beside him, her hand on his arm. He looked at her, frowning. He said, "We'll get married as soon as you give Land's ring back to him and we can find the preacher, but there's one thing I've got a right to know. Are you still in love with Roland?"

Her heart missed a beat, but she met his gaze, knowing this was one time when she had to be honest. "He was the first sweetheart I ever had. Can you understand that, Abe?

There's a little spot in my heart that belongs to him, but I wouldn't marry him if I could."

Lavine nodded as if he did understand how it was with her. He was silent as Ives drove the wagon to the porch. Reno was striding toward them from the bunkhouse, but Lavine ignored him. Ives pulled up, and stepping to the ground, untied the wheel chair and lifted it to the ground. Linda, looking at Bess, wondered if she had a fever. Linda had never seen her cheeks so flushed.

Reno reached them, his gaze turning to Lavine for a moment, then to Bess. He said, "Mrs. Flagg, is Ives staying here or leaving to catch up with the crew?"

"He's leaving," she answered.

"I want to go with him," Reno said eagerly. "I wanted to go this morning, but Abe wouldn't let me."

"You don't take orders from Lavine if you work for me," Bess said. "You'll go with Ives."

"Thank you," Reno said, and ran toward the corral to get his horse.

Judging from the way Ives glowered at Bess, Linda thought he didn't want Reno with him, but he shrugged and walked away, leaving the wagon in front of the house. Bess laughed, an unpleasant sound that Linda had never heard her make before.

"Well, Lavine," Bess said, "you've been high and mighty with me for a long time, but I don't need you any more. I'm going into the house to get your money, but if you want it, you'll have to put the team away."

It was a calculated insult, the final bending of Lavine to her will, but instead of obeying, he walked to her as he said, "Yes ma'am, but first I'll roll you into the house."

She didn't protest, although Linda thought she seemed puzzled by this reaction. If Bess noticed that she had her hat and coat on, she ignored it. Linda followed them inside, then Lavine stepped back.

"Now that I think about it," he said softly, "the dinero ain't real important. Let's say I'll swap it to you for the use of your team and wagon. I need it to take Linda to town. I'll see it's brought back by evening."

The flush deepened in Bess's cheeks. Then she discovered the suitcases and trunk on the floor. She screamed, "Linda, what's got into you? Bill's bringing the preacher out this afternoon or tomorrow morning and you're marrying him."

"No, I'll never marry him," Linda said. "I'm leaving. I've stayed here as long as I can."

"I've paid you well," Bess cried. "What the hell is wrong with you?"

"I'm marrying Abe," Linda said. "Not Bill Land."

"Lavine?" Bess was so shocked that her mouth sprung open and she stared at Linda as if this was too crazy to be believed, then the flush spread over her face until it was scarlet. "By God, you're not doing anything of the kind."

Lavine had started toward the trunk and suitcases, then swung around so that he stood back of Bess's chair, but her attention was fixed so intently on Linda that she didn't notice where Lavine was. She snatched her pistol from the seat beside her. Linda cried out, knowing she should have foreseen this, that Bess was out of her mind and would kill her before she would permit anything to happen which was so contrary to her plans.

Bess did not see Lavine step up behind her until his arm slid over her shoulder. He grabbed the pistol and twisted it out of her hand. As he stepped back, he said, "I never killed a woman in my life, Mrs. Flagg, but I will kill you if I have to. We're leaving. Linda is going to do what she wants to. Can you understand that?"

Bess sat there, her face turning so dark it was more purple than red, but for a moment she said nothing. Lavine handed the pistol to Linda. "She doesn't understand anything she don't want to. Keep her covered. I'll take your things out to the wagon."

As Lavine went through the door with Linda's suitcases, Bess found her voice. She screamed, "Ellie! Ellie, fetch me the shotgun. I'll blow their damned heads off."

But if Ellie heard, she ignored it. Bess began screaming obscenities at Linda. Lavine returned for the trunk. He said, "Come on." Linda backed through the door, keeping the pistol aimed at Bess. Then she realized she had no need for the pistol. Bess's torrent of words were cut off. She leaned forward, one hand over her chest, her face contorted as if she found it hard to breathe.

Lavine helped Linda into the seat, then climbed up beside her and taking the lines, spoke to the team. Lavine said gravely, "You're free now. I've watched you a lot of times when you were with her and it always seemed to me she had you hypnotized. You should have known what she was a long time before she tried to kill Roland."

"I guess I should," she agreed.

She was silent for a time, knowing why she had given the appearance of being hypnotized. She had been afraid she would do something to lose her job. She had been selfish, she told herself, putting security above everything else, even to the place of telling Bill Land she would marry him. She was doing the same with Abe Lavine, but it would be different with him. She would see to it that he never regretted his bargain.

Impulsively she slipped an arm through his. "I'm free of Bess, so I can marry you," she said. "And you're free of her, too. It was coming to the place where you would have had to do some things you didn't want to if you'd kept on working for her."

"I know," he said gravely. "I'm worse than you because I knew exactly what she was, but I liked the wages I was getting, so I stayed on."

"Abe, if Clay Roland isn't killed by Quinn and his men," Linda said, "and if he comes to town, there's no reason now to fight him, is there?"

He looked at her a long moment, his strong-featured face taking on the barren expression she had seen so many times. He asked harshly, "Is Clay Roland going to be between us all of our married lives?"

"No," she said, knowing that this, again, was a time when she must not lie to him. "It's like I told you. I was in love with him once. I would hate to know that my husband had killed him, and I would hate it worse if it went the other way and he killed you. I would like to leave here knowing you two were friends."

His face softened. "No reason we can't be. He's a good man."

They went on, her arm still through his. She felt quite satisfied with herself now. On occasion he could be as hard as tempered steel, and on those occasions she could not change him, but she could learn to live with him when he was like that. Then she smiled, her mind turning to the ten thousand dollars he had in a Denver bank. It was a pleasant subject to think about.

20

Ardis' words, "They're here," sent Clay running to the nearest loophole. Three men sat their saddles near the center of the bowl, their eyes on the cabin as if uncertain whether they should come any closer or not. He knew the man in the middle, a cowhand named Midge who had worked for the Flagg outfit before Clay had left the country. The other two were strangers.

"Only three of them," Clay said. "Looks like Rusty did what he set out to do. He's pulled Quinn and most of his men off our trail."

Ardis stood staring through the other loophole. She picked up her rifle from where it leaned against the wall. "He may be dead by now," she said bitterly. "If he is, I'm to blame."

"No you're not," Clay said sharply. "Neither one of us could have changed his mind and you know it."

"I guess so," she said. "Sometimes he acted as if he wanted to die. Several times when he was staying at our place he kept me up most of the night just talking. He hated Bill Land because he thought Land didn't believe in anything. He called Land a hypocrite for selling out to Bess Flagg. He never found a place or a job that satisfied him, so he just rode around like a tumbleweed. He said more than once that he wished he had your courage. He liked to say that dying wasn't so bad if he found something that was worth dying for."

Clay glanced at her. "What makes you think he's dead?"

She continued to stare through the loophole at the Flagg men, refusing to look at him. "I don't know. Just a feeling."

"Maybe you're wrong. You said he could play hide-and-seek with Quinn for a week."

"He could, but maybe he didn't want to." She let it drop, her face close to the loophole. After a moment's silence, she asked, "What's bothering them?"

The three men hadn't moved. Clay wasn't sure whether they were staring at the cabin or the upper end of the bowl. From their position the creek would appear to flow directly out of solid rock.

"I'm guessing they think we might be in here, but they're not real anxious to find out," Clay said. "They can't locate our horses, and the fire's out, so they don't see any smoke. I'd be wondering, too, if I was in their boots. They tracked us in here, but now it just don't add up right for them."

Ardis raised her rifle to slide it through the loophole. She said, "They're close enough to shoot."

"Not cold turkey," he said. "I'll give them something to shoot at."

He picked up his Winchester and opening the door, stepped through it, ignoring Ardis' protests. He called, "You boys looking for me?"

One rider whirled his horse and, bending low in the saddle, headed for the entrance to the bowl on a dead run. Midge had his gun in his hand. Now he threw a quick shot at Clay. The bullet struck the wall above Clay's head and screamed as it ricocheted away into space. The third man reached for his gun and had it clear of leather just as Ardis cut loose. Her first shot knocked his hat off his head, her second smashed his left arm. That took the fight out of him. He wheeled his horse and took after the first man.

Midge got off his second shot just as Clay squeezed the trigger of his Winchester. Midge's bullet went *thwack* into the heavy door beside Clay. He didn't fire again. Clay's bullet had apparently struck him in the chest. He dropped his gun and bent forward over the saddle horn. Gripping the horn with one hand, he turned his horse and rode slowly down the creek. Clay expected him to fall off his horse, but he was still in the saddle hanging tight when he disappeared through the lower end of the bowl.

When Clay stepped back into the cabin, Ardis had put her rifle down. She glared at him, her hands on her hips as she said, "Clay Roland, you're a fool. They'll fetch Quinn and he'll have us bottled up here."

He leaned his Winchester against the stone wall. "Maybe I am a fool," he admitted, "but those boys didn't want us very bad. If they'd been paid killers like Lavine and Reno, I'd have cut them all down, but they're working cowhands. They didn't want us real bad or they'd have operated different."

She looked at the floor, her quick flash of anger dying. "All right, I was wrong," she said. "I guess I was scared. I was thinking of what might happen if they killed us." Then she shook her head and walked to the stove. "No I wasn't. I just didn't see any sense of you going outside and making a target out of yourself."

"It was too far for a hand gun," he said, "so I figured they didn't have much chance of hitting me. It's my guess we put them out of the fight. Midge is a dead duck. You busted the arm of one of them, so he won't do any more fighting for a while. The way the first one took off he won't stop till he gets to the mesa."

"Clay," she said tartly, "I admitted I was wrong. Start a fire. I'll cook supper."

He obeyed, then went outside and started in on the piñon again. Maybe what he had done did look foolish to Ardis, but he had never been able to shoot a man down without giving him a chance. If he had remained inside, the situation would have continued the way it was, a sort of siege that was not to Clay's liking. This way the three men were gone and Clay and Ardis were free to leave the cabin if they wanted to.

Midge wouldn't go far, but one of the others might bring Quinn and the rest of his men. If they had killed Rusty, he hoped they did come. He'd get every one of them, he told himself, every murdering son of a bitch who worked for Bess Flagg.

Presently Ardis called him to supper. After they finished eating, he left the cabin and walked upstream through the narrows, telling Ardis he wanted to see if the horses were all right. Actually he wanted to get away by himself for a while. He could not get over Ardis' hunch that Rusty Mattson was dead.

When he returned, he carried the rest of the firewood into the cabin. He had reached a decision and he might just as well tell Ardis. It was time that he turned the tables and became the hunter instead of the hunted.

Ardis had lighted a candle when Clay shut and barred the door. She asked, "Want a cup of coffee before we go to bed?"

"No," he answered. "Ardis, I've been doing some thinking. I can't stay here because I can't get Rusty out of my mind, If Quinn killed him, I'll kill Quinn. That's a promise."

"You're leaving now?" she asked incredulously.

"Not till morning. If one of the men I let get away does fetch Quinn, I'd just as soon be inside this cabin as anywhere else, but if he isn't here by morning, I don't think he'll come. Now there's one more thing. If he doesn't show up, you're not going with me. I don't want to leave you here, either."

"Don't worry about me. I'll find a safe place." She sighed. "You're such a fool, Clay. Sometimes I think you're like one of King Arthur's knights. They had a code they lived by, too."

"I never heard of them," he said. "All I know is that I've got a job to do if Rusty's dead. He was my friend, a better friend than I knew when we separated."

"But you can't change what has happened to him," she said. "Don't you understand that what he did was to save your life? And that it's what I've been trying to do, too?"

"I know." He thought of Anton Cryder who wanted him to ride into Painted Rock after dark so he would be safe, but he hadn't done it. Now he couldn't stay here, either. He added, "Ardis, staying alive is not the most important thing in the world."

"It is with the men I've known," she said. "Most of them, anyhow, the ones who rode in looking for a place to stay, the men Pa brought to this cabin. You're not like them. You never were. I guess that's why I . . ."

She stopped suddenly and turned away from him. He

went to her and taking her by the arms, swung her around to face him. "You were going to say that was why you loved me, wasn't it. Why don't you go ahead and say it?"

She shook her head, trying to smile, but not quite succeeding. "It would be wrong for me to say it, Clay."

"It wouldn't be wrong if I told you I loved you, would it?" he asked. "I've been wanting to tell you, but it seemed to me that it wasn't right to tell you. If I didn't make it, I didn't . . ."

"Oh Clay, Clay," she whispered. "I've been wanting to hear you say it all this time. It would have been cruel for you to die without telling me."

He took her into his arms and pulling her hard against him, kissed her. She gave her lips to him, kissing him hungrily and lingeringly. Linda or no other woman had ever kissed him like that. When at last she drew her head back, he knew how much he needed her, and that now he had far more reason to stay alive than the compulsion of mere animal survival.

"It would have been a mistake not to tell you," he said. "I didn't know . . ." He checked himself, thinking of the years she had waited for him and wondering why he hadn't known, and why that Linda had been in his mind so much. "If you're not sleepy, I'd like to talk for a while."

He pulled a chair up to the stove, and dropping into it, pulled her down on his lap. He had not realized before how hungry he was for talk, how much he needed it. He told her about his plans for the Bar C, then about his father and why he had left the mesa, and finally about the six lonely years he had been gone.

Later, lying in his bunk with a saddle blanket over him, he found it hard to sleep. Old memories long dead had been brought to life when he had talked to Ardis, and now they ran through his mind one after the other, but he always returned to Bill Land who had been his friend, and Rusty Mattson who was still his friend, if he was alive. He finally dropped off to sleep, but near dawn Ardis woke him.

"I'm cold," she said. "I've been lying there with my teeth chattering."

"I'll get you warm," he said.

He moved over against the wall and she lay down beside him. He took her into his arms, holding her so that within a few minutes the warmth of his body stopped her shivering and she dropped off to sleep. Presently she stirred and whispered, "Don't go away again, Clay. Not ever." He did not say anything, and she was asleep a moment later.

There was still no sign of dawn creeping through the loopholes when a sound outside rang an alarm in him. He tensed, not sure whether it was the wind or a night animal scurrying along the ledge in front of the cabin, or a man slipping carefully toward the door. For an instant he couldn't remember where he had left his gun belt, then it came to him. It was on the table, but in the darkness it would take time to find it.

He put a hand over Ardis' mouth and shook her awake. "I think we've got visitors," he said. He slid off the bunk and felt his way across the room until he reached the table. A moment later his searching hand touched the belt. He drew the gun from the holster just as Ardis reached him.

"I heard something," she whispered. "They can't break the door down, can they?"

"No," he said.

A man called, "Ardis? Roland? You in there?"

"It's Monroe," Ardis cried. "I'll light a candle. Let him in."

"Not yet," Clay said. "He may have Quinn's gun in his back. Light the candle, then get back into the corner."

"Ardis," Monroe called again. "Roland, let me in."

Clay stepped to the door. "What are you doing here, Monroe?"

"I've got a message from Quinn for you," Monroe answered. "Damn it, let me in. I'm tired and cold and hungry."

"You alone?" Clay asked.

"Sure I'm alone."

Ardis set the lighted candle on the table and moved back to stand between the bunks. Clay lifted the heavy bar and let it fall, then yanked the door open and hugged the wall beside it, his cocked gun in his hand. In the feeble light of the candle he saw that Monroe was alone as he had said.

Clay shut and barred the door the instant the man was inside. "Why didn't you holler instead of sneaking up this way? You scared us good if that was what you aimed to do."

"It wasn't," Monroe said, "but I figured it was the only thing to do. You couldn't have seen whether I was alone or not if I'd stayed on my horse and hollered. I had a notion you'd think it was a trick of Quinn's, using me to get the door open."

Clay walked to the stove and started a fire. He said, "Well, what's the message?"

"Quinn stopped this afternoon," Monroe said. "Funny thing, too. I was in the kitchen getting something to eat when a bunch of riders went by heading upstream toward the gorge. I didn't look at 'em real close, but it was the Flagg bunch. Just after they disappeared, Quinn showed up. He looked funny, like maybe he was scared, but I reckon

I was mistaken. I guess nobody ever scared Riley Quinn. Anyhow, he told me he'd been in the barn and wanted to know if I'd seen his boys ride by. I said yes, but I hadn't paid any attention to 'em. He didn't say what he'd been doing in the barn, or why he waited while his crew rode by, and I sure didn't ask him.

"He said they'd caught Rusty Mattson and the crew was taking him to town. He said for me to find you and tell you that if you got to Painted Rock before sundown, they'd let Rusty go, but if you didn't, they'd kill him. He said this was a hell of a lot easier than hunting you down."

"Did he think Clay would do it?" Ardis demanded.

"He sure did," Monroe said. "Nothing else you can do, is there, Roland?"

"No," Clay said. "Cook some breakfast for us, Ardis. We'll pull out soon as it's daylight. You'll stay at your place with Monroe."

He held his hands out over the crackling fire, thinking this over. He had no illusions about his chances, but as Monroe said, there was nothing else he could do. At least he knew where to go.

"It's a trap, Clay," Ardis said. "The whole crew will be waiting for you. The town, too. Can't you see that?"

"Sure, I see it," Clay answered.

"You can't go," she said. "You don't even know they've got Rusty." She whirled to face Monroe. "You didn't see him, did you?"

"No, but like I said, I didn't look at 'em real close," Monroe said. "I didn't even know Quinn wasn't with 'em till he came in from the barn."

"There's something funny about that," Ardis said, "Quinn not being with his crew. You can't go just to commit suicide."

"Maybe I won't be committing suicide," he said thoughtfully. "Could be this funny business gives me a chance, though I don't know what it is. Quinn sure thinks he's got it rigged, but I never figured him much on brains, so I'll take a chance."

"All right, Clay," Ardis said sadly as she turned to the stove. "I'll get your breakfast."

Looking at her, he knew she didn't understand, but then, he thought bleakly, maybe no woman would.

21

Long-established habit woke Abe Lavine at the usual early hour. It took a moment to clear the cobwebs of sleep from his mind, to realize he was a married man and that he was in bed with his wife in a hotel room. He rubbed his eyes and yawned, and turned as gently as he could so he would not waken Linda.

He looked at her for a long time, her black hair contrasting sharply with the white pillowcase. He smiled and shook his head, thinking for what must be the millionth time that he was a lucky man. He should have told her weeks ago how he felt, but maybe she wouldn't have left with him then. Perhaps it had taken the events of the last few days to shake her free from Bess Flagg's influence.

Well, she belonged to him now and he would never give her up. The stage left late in the afternoon to connect at Placerville with the night train to Montrose. They'd be on that stage. Once he had her away from here, she would forget about Clay Roland.

He slipped out of bed and went to the window. It would be a clear, fall day filled with the warmth of Indian summer. He stared down into the empty street, thinking they would get breakfast and then he'd buy her a wedding ring at Walters' Mercantile. They'd go to Denver and he'd see she had a good time for a few days. No need to make definite plans yet.

He put on his drawers and undershirt, and going to the bureau, poured water into the bowl and began to shave. He wished the stage left early this morning. The sooner he got her out of here, the better. He was troubled by something that had happened last night, troubled because he didn't understand it and he felt that somehow it would affect Linda and him.

They had gone to their room after having had supper in the hotel dining room, then he'd had the idea that this was an occasion that called for champagne. He'd gone down the stairs, but before he'd reached the bottom, he'd heard Riley Quinn's voice.

Lavine had paused, wondering why Quinn was here. Not wanting any unpleasantness on this, of all nights, he had slipped noiselessly on down the stairs to the hall that led into the lobby. Standing in the shadows so he wouldn't be seen, he'd had a quick look at the desk. Riley Quinn, Slim Ives, and Pete Reno were standing there, Quinn saying they were going to the Belle Union, but they were staying in town and they'd be back.

They'd left the hotel, but Lavine had remained where he was for a decent interval, then he'd gone upstairs and told Linda the Belle Union didn't have any champagne. They'd have to wait until they went to Denver to celebrate.

He still couldn't make any sense out of it. He had never known Riley Quinn to stay the night in town; he didn't know where the rest of the crew was or why the men weren't with Quinn. Maybe it didn't concern him, but then maybe it did, and he didn't want trouble today any more than he had last night.

He finished shaving, thinking about the past night and how Linda had told him she'd make him a good wife. She'd made the best kind of a start, he thought. It had been a night he wouldn't forget. As he was putting his shaving gear away, he glanced into the mirror and saw that Linda was sitting up in bed.

"Good morning, Mrs. Lavine," he said.

"Good morning to you, Mr. Lavine," she said, "and will you tell me what you're doing up this time of the morning?"

"Why, I just woke up . . ."

"And I suppose you thought you were in the bunkhouse and you had to get up for breakfast," she said tartly. "Well, you're not. Now you come and get back into bed with me."

"More?" he asked.

"Yes, more."

He laughed aloud, the first time he could remember hearing his own laughter. Suddenly the barren loneliness of his past life was gone. In its place was a new and pleasant warmth, a strange feeling, but a good and welcome one. It was not too late to salvage something from his life.

"You know, honey," he said, and paused, wondering why he had called her that, then went on quickly, "I want a boy. I want a girl, too, but she'll be your responsibility. The boy will be mine and I'm going to teach him a lot of things, things that nobody ever taught me."

"You'd better start working on it," she said. "I can't do it by myself."

"It will be a pleasant duty," he said.

When he woke again, he was startled when he looked at

his watch and saw that it was after eleven. He turned over to find Linda awake and smiling at him.

"Satisfied?" he asked.

"Satisfied and hungry," she said.

"We missed breakfast," he told her. "We'll have to be satisfied with dinner."

Before they left the room, he buckled his gun belt around him. Linda pointed at the holstered gun. "Is that always going to be a part of you?"

"It will be as long as I'm in Painted Rock."

"And after we leave?"

"I don't know," he answered. "There are a lot of men who won't let me forget what I've been and what I've done. I may meet some of them again some day."

"I understand," she said, and putting her hand on his arm, left the room with him.

They had finished eating when Pete Reno entered the dining room and walked directly to them. Lavine scooted his chair back from the table, his habitual barren expression coming to his face. Reno was the last man he wanted to see.

"So you got married, Abe." Reno gripped the back of an empty chair and bent forward as if he couldn't see Linda clearly. "Is she a woman? A real honest-to-God woman?"

He was drunk. Lavine had never let him drink during the two years they had been together. Whisky and guns don't go together, he had told Reno repeatedly. This was Riley Quinn's work, Lavine thought, and wondered why.

"You're drunk, Pete," Lavine said. "Better go sleep it off before you get into trouble."

"I've been drinking a little, but I ain't drunk." Reno kept staring at Linda who had turned her head to look out of the window. "Riley, he set 'em up for me. Said I'd been missing a lot of fun." He bent closer toward Linda. "Abe, your wife fooled you. She used to be Clay Roland's girl. You know that?"

"Yes, I know." Lavine rose. "Let's go over to the store, Linda. It's time I was buying you a wedding present, a little round gold one. We'll see if Walters has one that fits."

"Now wait a minute," Reno said. "There's something I want to tell you. Clay Roland's gonna be in town today. He's coming in to get killed."

Linda's face whipped around. She stared at him, her eyes wide with terror, her lips parted. "How do you know?" she whispered.

"See?" Reno said triumphantly. "First time she's looked at me. All I had to do was to mention Clay Roland's name."

"How do you know, Pete?" Lavine asked.

"I'm gonna help kill him," Reno said. "That's how. I'm gonna be the bait. I'll be out in the street when he shows up. I'll tell him I'm gonna kill him, but he won't get no chance to plug me. I'll draw on him, all right, but Riley and Slim Ives, they'll be over yonder at the corner of the store and they'll drop him before he gets his gun out." Reno waggled a finger under his nose, his face turning ugly. "But they might miss, so Bill Land's gonna be waiting in his office and he'll plug Roland sure. He's a good shot, Land is."

"How do you know Roland will be in town today?"

"Riley says so. That's how. He got Rusty Mattson yesterday, then the crew got sore at Riley and rode out of the country. Quit, the whole kit 'n kaboodle of 'em. Riley says I'm gonna get a good job."

"Killing Rusty Mattson ain't got nothing to do with Clay Roland coming to town," Lavine said. "They're running a sandy on you."

"No they ain't," Reno snapped. "Riley, he got word to Roland he had Mattson and he'd kill him if Roland didn't show up." He waggled his finger under Lavine's nose again. "I ain't forgot you hit me yesterday. You didn't have no cause to do that, so I'm aiming to kill you just as soon as we take care of Roland. You got till then to git out of town."

"I'll sure do it," Lavine said. "You scare me."

"You'd better do it," Reno said, and straightening, turned and left the dining room, walking with exaggerated dignity.

"Was he lying?" Linda asked.

"No, he wasn't lying," Lavine said. "Let's go upstairs. We'll let that wedding present go for a while."

She walked beside him, holding back the tears that threatened her. When they were in their room with the door closed, she turned to him and put her arms around him. "Abe, I wanted to get away from here before this happened."

"So did I," he said.

"Isn't there anything you can do for him?"

"Yes," he said angrily. "I can kill Pete, then go after Quinn and Ives. Is that what you want? You're asking me to save Roland and maybe get myself killed?"

She began to cry, her face pressed against his shirt. "I've told you before and I'll tell you again," she said when she had control of herself. "I'll make you a good wife. You'll never regret that you married me, but can't you understand how I feel? If I was somewhere else when this happened, I'd be sorry about it, but I'd know I couldn't have helped him. Now maybe we can. If we just stood still and let them kill him, I'd always feel that we were partly responsible."

He pushed her away from him and went to the window. He stood staring into the street that was still empty, although now it was the middle of the day. So the word was out! Reno wasn't in sight, but Lavine saw Quinn and Ives sitting on the bench in front of Walters' Mercantile. This was the way Queen Bess would want it, a trap, but one that was sure fire, and Riley Quinn and Slim Ives were the kind who would spring it.

Linda came to him. She didn't touch him. She just stood beside him and stared down into the street. Then she said, "Abe, it isn't fair. If they were giving him a chance, I wouldn't expect you to do anything. That's all I'm asking for him, a chance for his life."

He looked at her, wishing that Clay Roland was dead. He had considered killing Roland himself. If he could erase the memory of the love she'd had for Roland, he would have done it before now, but he knew that was the one sure way of losing her. She had given all of herself to him last night. No man could expect more. He had no right to complain, no right to criticize her.

"All right, Linda," he said. "I'll do something for him because it's what you want. That's the only reason."

She put her arms around his neck and pulling his face down to hers, kissed him long and hard. "I love you, Abe. I was never really sure until now."

"Well then," he said, "it will be worth it. Don't leave this room. If you do, I won't interfere."

"I'll stay here," she promised. "Whatever you do, don't take any risks."

"I'll think of a way," he said, and left the room.

He hurried down the stairs, wondering where Reno had gone. He strode past the bank and climbed the stairs of the drugstore to Bill Land's office. He put a hand on the knob of Land's door, turning it, and pulling his gun, threw the door open and went in fast. Land had been sitting in a chair beside the open window, a rifle across his lap. When he heard the door open, he jumped up, the Winchester in his hand.

"Put it down," Lavine said. "I'll kill you if you make a move to use it."

Slowly Land leaned the Winchester against the wall. "You married my girl. Now you come barreling in here holding a gun on me. Aren't you ever satisfied?"

"There's proper ways of killing a man," Lavine said, "but your way ain't one of 'em. You're cowards, sneaking, belly-crawling cowards, you and Quinn and Ives."

"Who told you?"

"Reno."

Land cursed bitterly. "I told Riley he couldn't trust that fool kid." He paused, his eyes taking on a speculative glint. "If it's money you want, I'll give you a hundred dollars to get out of here and keep your mouth shut."

"No," Lavine said. "Sit down where you were. Don't touch the Winchester."

Someone was running up the stairs. Lavine put his back to the wall. The door opened and Doc Spears ran in, breathing hard. "She's dead, Bill," Spears shouted. "She had a heart attack yesterday. She sent the cook in to get me and I went right out, but I couldn't save her. She died this morning."

"Who?"

"Queen Bess, you fool."

"Pull up that other chair, Doc," Lavine said. "Sit down beside Land in front of the window."

Spears whirled. He looked at Lavine's face, then at the gun, and obeyed the order without a word. Lavine said, "This makes it different, don't it, Land? She propped you up for a long time, but the prop's gone now. No reason to kill Roland, is there?"

"Nothing's changed," Land said bitterly. "You think I've forgotten how he beat hell out of me the other day? He brought all this on when he came back. Now I'll see him dead. By God, I will."

"All right," Lavine said. "We'll wait."

He walked to Land's desk and sat down on it, his gun still in his hand. A moment later Spears said, "That wasn't such a long wait. Here he comes."

22

Clay lingered only briefly at the Bar C. He sat his saddle staring at the pile of ashes that had been the house where he had lived most of his life, at the blackened, twisted bedsteads and the stoves. He had expected this, yet he had not been fully prepared for what he saw.

The thing didn't make sense. If Bess succeeded in taking over the Bar C, she would have use for the buildings. Why, then, had she burned the house? Did she have a feeling she wasn't going to whip him? Or was it a case of her wanting to destroy something which was a monument to her failure with John Roland?

Clay shook his head and rode away. He could build another house, a better house than the one Bess had burned. The windows and doors had not been fitted as tightly as they should have been, and on cold days when the wind was blowing, it had been impossible to keep the house warm.

The part that hurt was the loss of little things, the keepsakes that were worthless if judged by their value in money but were priceless to Clay because they belonged to his childhood and could not be replaced: the picture of his mother, his boyhood toys, his father's chessmen, and yes, even the dishes in the cupboard which he had used as a baby.

When the buildings of Painted Rock loomed directly ahead of him, he became sharply alert, putting the loss of his house out of his mind. This was the end, one way or the other. He was convinced of that. He would die, or Riley Quinn would die, and Quinn was Bess Flagg's strength, not the Lavines or the Renos or the Bill Lands. If Quinn had caught and killed Rusty Mattson, Clay had all the more reason to kill him.

Clay reined up at the edge of town and looked along the street. He had no idea what Quinn planned, now that he had Clay where he wanted him. The Flagg foreman was not a fast man with a gun, and Clay doubted that he possessed any great amount of courage when it came to gunfighting, so he would certainly rig a trap that was geared to minimum risk for himself.

Clay could not see movement along the street, no sign of life except for a black-and-white dog dozing in the sun near the archway of the livery stable and half a dozen chickens dusting themselves near the boardwalk in front of the newspaper office. Not a single saddle horse was tied at the hitch poles, no rigs, no teams.

Casually Clay dismounted and led his horse off the street, leaving him beside the newspaper office where he would be safe from stray bullets, then he returned to the street and stood there motionless as he drew his gun from his holster, checked it, and eased it back into the leather.

He had realized from the time Monroe had brought Quinn's message that there was a chance the Flagg crew would be hidden along the street and would riddle him with bullets without giving him a chance, but he didn't think Quinn would be that stupid. In reality his scheme might be murder, but it would likely have the appearance of a fair fight so Ed Parker could say the killing was justifiable homicide.

Apparently Painted Rock was a deserted town, and this puzzled Clay as much as anything. Somebody should be in the street by now, Lavine or Reno or Quinn himself. A full minute passed with no one making an appearance.

"Quinn," Clay yelled. "You sent for me, Quinn. Are you too yellow to show up now that I'm here?"

A man came into the street from the other side of the Mercantile. He didn't walk as a man would under ordinary circumstances, but appeared to lurch as if he had been pushed. Or maybe he was drunk. For a moment Clay had trouble placing him, then he recognized him as the man he had seen in the doorway of the bunkhouse when he had gone to the Flagg ranch to talk to Queen Bess. It would be Pete Reno.

"Come on," Reno called. "I'm gonna kill you, Roland. Mrs. Flagg told you to get out of the country, but you didn't do it. Now it's too late."

Clay paced slowly toward him, thinking his words had been a little slurred. Maybe Reno had been drinking to give him courage. He stood with his legs spread, right hand splayed over the butt of his gun. He was little more than a kid. Clay realized this as the distance shortened between them.

Something was wrong. Six years of carrying a star had sharpened Clay's feelings about this kind of thing. Quinn wouldn't send a boy to do a man's job, not even if the boy had some claim to be a gunfighter. Clay's gaze swept one side of the street, then the other, but he did not see anyone. He raised his eyes to the windows of the second story of the hotel, the offices above Doc Spears's drugstore, then the windows of Anton Cryder's office over the Mercantile, but still he glimpsed nothing suspicious.

Clay stopped walking. He called, "I want Quinn. Get off the street, kid."

Insulted, Reno shouted, "I ain't a kid. I said I was gonna kill you. It's what Mrs. Flagg hired me for."

"Where's Rusty Mattson?"

"Dead, just like you're going to be. Keep walking, Roland. Are you scared of me? That why you stopped?"

So Ardis' hunch had been right! Clay guessed he had known all the time. He didn't answer Reno, but started walking again, sensing that if he dived for cover, he'd draw fire from whoever was waiting for him farther down the street.

Someone had to show soon. It would be two or three men, but not the whole outfit, he thought, or they would have opened up before now. Just ahead and to his left was a water trough that would offer some protection if he reached it. The sun pressed warmly against his back. For this moment the street was deceptively quiet and peaceful, a strange and inconsistent scene.

He was close to Reno now, so close that he could see the abject terror on the boy's face. Reno wasn't drunk enough to stand and fight. Clay said, "What makes you think you want to die for Mrs. Flagg?"

Reno caved then as Clay had been certain he would. He whirled and lunged toward the doorway of the Mercantile. A gun roared and he stumbled and fell. Before he hit the ground Quinn and another cowboy appeared around the corner of the store building, their guns talking.

Clay made his draw, right hand sweeping his gun from leather. He took the cowboy beside Quinn first, his bullet smashing into the man's chest and spinning him around and knocking him into the dust. Quinn was running toward Clay, heavily and awkwardly. He bellowed, "Shoot! Damn it, shoot."

But no other shot came. Clay swung his gun to the big man. Quinn stopped, apparently realizing he was doing a foolish thing. He fired again, the bullet kicking up dust behind Clay and to his right. Clay, motionless now, pulled the trigger a second time just as Quinn was bringing his gun down for another shot. He never got it off. Clay's bullet knocked him off his feet, but he kept his grip on his gun as he fell.

Clay walked toward him as Quinn, by sheer will power, used all the massive strength that was left in his stubby body to lift himself to his knees. He raised his head to look at Clay as he struggled to bring his gun up to fire again. Blood bubbled from the corners of his mouth and dribbled down his chin. Then his strength ran out and he toppled forward on his face.

Standing over him, Clay looked down at this man who had been Bess Flagg's strength and most effective tool. He heard Quinn's muffled voice, "Bill Land was gonna cut you down. He didn't do it."

His hands, palm down in the dust, clenched into fists. He was dead. Clay raised his head to see Anton Cryder running toward him. Other men appeared along the street now, Walters and Parker and several more.

Cryder was the first to reach him. He held out his hand.

"You've done a job no one else could do. The truth is you're the only man who had enough guts to try."

Clay shook his hand, then shook hands with the others. A strange thing, he thought, as if only now he had ridden into town after being gone for six years. They were welcoming him back, these men who had wanted nothing to do with him the day he had fought Bill Land.

"You holding me?" Clay asked Ed Parker.

"Of course not," the marshal said. "A clear case of justifiable homicide."

"Who shot the kid?"

No one answered for a moment. Doc Spears had run across the street and was kneeling beside Reno. He looked back over his shoulder to say, "He'll be all right. Just a flesh wound in his thigh."

Then Walters said, slowly as if reluctant to tell how it had been, "Quinn shot him. He was bullet bait. He was supposed to pull on you, and they were fixing to smoke you down from the side. It would have given them an excuse, you see, Reno being Quinn's man."

"It wasn't quite that way," Lavine said.

Clay hadn't seen him come up. He wheeled, hand sweeping gun from leather again, then he froze, the gun in midair. Lavine was bringing Bill Land across the street, the muzzle of his gun prodding the lawyer in the back.

"Which side are you on now?" Clay asked as he holstered his gun.

"The right side, I'd say," Lavine answered. "Reno told me what they were fixing to do, so I dropped in on your old friend here. He was sitting at the window with his Winchester all loaded and ready for you. I got it out of him just before Reno made his move. Quinn and Ives weren't supposed to show at all. Land was going to fire the same instant Reno did. They were gambling Reno would get off one shot. Nobody, including the law"—he paused to look contemptuously at Parker, then continued—"would figure out that the bullet had hit you at a downward angle. It would have been justifiable homicide."

Parker, red-faced, said nothing.

"They fooled Reno into believing they wouldn't let him get killed," Lavine went on. "They said they'd get you before you fired a shot."

"Rusty's dead?"

Lavine nodded. "Quinn killed him yesterday."

Clay turned and walked off, sick because he could not save Rusty Mattson's life. He was sick, too, of the cowardice of these Painted Rock men who considered him a hero, now that Riley Quinn was dead. In a way he was surprised, for in time Queen Bess could hire other Riley Quinns and the whole thing would have to be done over again.

"Clay, we heard your house was burned," Cryder called. "What are you going to do?"

"Rebuild it," Clay said. "It's my home. I'm going to live there and Queen Bess isn't going to run me off."

"That's right," Doc Spears said. "She's dead. She had a heart attack."

So that was it, Clay thought, the reason these men had found their courage. Again he started to turn. Lavine said, "What about your old friend, Roland? He was sure aiming to smoke you down. I think he ought to get down into the dirt and crawl out of town."

"I don't care whether he crawls, rides, or walks," Clay said, "but he better be damned sure he's out of town before I come back."

"I think he will," Lavine said. "I think he will." He holstered his gun, and catching up with Clay, strode along beside him. He said, "Roland, there's something I've got to know. Would you marry Linda if you could?"

Clay looked at him sharply. "What business of yours is that?"

"A hell of a lot. Would you?"

"No. I'm going to marry Ardis Kline."

"Why now," Lavine said, pleased, "I'm glad to hear that. She sells a poor grade of whisky, but she's a good cook." He held out his hand. "Would you shake hands with me, Roland? Linda's watching from our hotel room. You see, we were married last night and we're pulling out on today's stage. She said she'd like to leave here knowing you'n me were friends."

Clay hesitated, shocked momentarily by Lavine's statement that he and Linda were married. Then he gripped Lavine's hand. "Congratulations. Make her happy, mister, or I'll look you up."

Lavine laughed aloud, the second time that day. "I aim to try, Roland. I sure do."

Clay went on to his horse, Lavine turning back. Clay mounted, and when he was in the street, he raised his hand in a sweeping salute toward the hotel. He wondered if Linda had anything to do with Lavine interfering in a fight which was none of his affair. It wasn't like a man of Lavine's caliber. But he would probably never see Linda or Lavine again, so he would never know.

Turning his horse, Clay rode west across the mesa. Ardis would be waiting for him.